ABSOLUTION

HENRY HACK

Black Rose Writing | Texas

ISBN: 978-1-68433-843-6
PUBLISHED BY BLACK ROSE WRITING
www.blackrosewriting.com

Printed in the United States of America
Suggested Retail Price (SRP) $20.95

Absolution is printed in Baskerville

*As a planet-friendly publisher, Black Rose Writing does its best to eliminate unnecessary waste to reduce paper usage and energy costs, while never compromising the reading experience. As a result, the final word count vs. page count may not meet common expectations.

Dedicated to the life and memory of
Richard George Paul
Detective Second Grade, New York City Police Department
Proud veteran of the United States Marine Corps
(May 17, 1939 – June 21, 2021)
Semper Fi!

ABSOLUTION

PART ONE

JOEY NOONZ

(1957 – 1966)

ONE

I bolted out of the screen door into the blackness of the sweltering early morning air, tightly clutching my upper left arm with my right hand. One thought raced repeatedly through my mind – *My God, what have I done?* I momentarily stopped on the sidewalk deciding which way to turn. Pete's car was around the corner, but the keys were in his pocket back in the house. *Why did I ever get in the car with Pete Selewski?* I took off running.

I sprinted blindly for seven or eight blocks before becoming winded. I staggered to a stop, gasping for air. That was probably a good thing. A young guy running through a residential neighborhood at one o' clock in the morning could most certainly attract a few phone calls to the police, who would be most interested in how he happened to have acquired a gunshot wound.

Regaining my breath, I began to walk, followed by intermittent bouts of slow jogging in the particularly dark areas. I took a zigzag direction toward my house in Richmond Hill, about four or five miles to the north and west of Cambria Heights. I stayed on the residential avenues and cross streets, avoiding the main drags of Linden and Springfield Boulevards, where passing patrol cars could easily spot me.

By the time I reached home it was about 3:00 a.m., but tiredness had not yet set in. I unlocked the front door and crept up the stairs to my bedroom which was at the opposite end of the house from my parents' front bedroom. Their door was ajar, and I could hear my father snoring away. The two bedrooms in between were empty as my two older brothers were gone and married. The bathroom was across the narrow hall from my room, and I went inside it and softly closed the door. I took off my shirt and looked at my wound. It burned like hell, and I realized the bullet had grazed me and not entered my arm. I swabbed the wound with some witch hazel, biting my tongue to keep from screaming out. I followed that with some hydrogen peroxide, which also burned like the blazes.

I flushed the bloody tissues down the toilet and bandaged the wound, which had appeared to be no longer bleeding. I took the shirt with me into my bedroom and stuffed it in a corner of my closet. I'd figure out how to get rid of it later, but not too much later, if the cops were already on my trail. Fortunately, the wound was high enough on my upper arm that most of my short-sleeved shirts would cover it.

I needed to sleep, but I also needed to think this out. My parents arose around eight, and suddenly realizing it was Sunday morning, I knew we would all go to the ten o'clock mass at St. Mary's. I had to get a few hours of sleep. Mercifully, the mental and physical exhaustion of the past few tension-filled hours finally set in, and I closed my eyes.

.   .   .

I managed to keep my eyes open throughout the high mass as my mind raced through the events of the past several hours. I must have left some blood, and my fingerprints, in that bedroom. Jesus, what had I touched? I dreaded the walk home from church. I was sure a police car would be parked in front of my house waiting to nab me. We stopped at the bakery for rolls and buns, and at the candy store for the Sunday editions of the *Daily News* and *Daily Mirror*. As we rounded the corner to our block, I felt an immense sense of relief to see the empty parking space in front of our house and no police cars in sight.

We went inside and Mom put coffee on as Dad and I looked at the papers. He glanced over at me and said, "You look like hell, Joey. You were yawning all through the mass. What time did you-a come home last night anyway?"

Knowing my parents were usually in the sack by ten, I said, "About eleven, maybe a quarter after, but I couldn't sleep thinking about final exams and graduation, and do I go to community college or join the service. It kept me awake most of the night."

"Yeah, I understand, and-a your mother and I gonna give you something else you gotta think about. Let's go have coffee in the kitchen."

Mom and Dad, Vincenzo and Maria Mastronunzio, were first generation Italian-Americans but spoke only Italian as youngsters, learning English when they began school in Brooklyn. Every so often a bit of Italian accent came through from both of them. Now, as I took my chair at the old white-painted wooden kitchen table, I wondered what the heck the "something else" I had to think about was, when I hadn't even thought about what I really had to think about.

"Joey, you graduate in-a ten days, right?"

"Yeah, Pop."

"After that me and your mother are gonna put the house up for sale. We wanna move to Florida. You could go to community college down there."

"Aren't you both too young to retire?" I asked. "You're only in your mid-fifties."

"Who said anything about retiring?" my mother said. "Your dad can cut hair and do shaves, and I can do cuts and perms down there as easily as we can up here."

I can't say I was surprised as I had heard comments about warm, sunny Florida from them before as well as how our neighborhood was changing, and not for the better, if you get my drift. Both my parents were not great examples of religious or racial tolerance and strongly believed in sticking to your own kind.

"Good for you," I said. "I'll have a few weeks to think this over, but right now I have to go to my room and study. I have two final exams left, and the rougher one is tomorrow."

"You're a good boy, Joey," Mom said, "You come-a with us and go to college in Florida."

"We'll see," I said as I finished my coffee and headed up the stairs to my room. I put a second pillow under my head and picked up my Latin textbook and opened it up. Despite the caffeine I had ingested, I closed my eyes and felt the heavy volume slip out of my fingers.

When I awoke, I glanced at my wristwatch. I had been out for over three hours, but I still felt groggy. I went into the bathroom and splashed cold water on my face and changed the bandage on my upper arm. The one I took off was sticky, but no new blood had flowed and it looked as if it was already healing up. I guessed the hot bullet had cauterized it as it passed through my skin.

I went downstairs and grabbed a couple of crumb buns and heated up the remaining coffee from the percolator. I scarfed down the heavily crumb-laden buns hoping the sugar, cinnamon, and coffee combo would clear the cobwebs from my brain and let me come up with a plan of action. A plan, and an airtight alibi, to save my young ass from a seat in the electric chair.

The sugar and coffee worked their wonders and twenty minutes later, notepad on my desk, pencil in hand, I began from the beginning. Last night, Saturday, June 15, 1957, I went to the movies with three of my friends, Al, Bill, and Georgie. We saw *Gunfight at the O.K. Corral* starring Kirk Douglas and Burt Lancaster, two of my favorite actors. We got out about 10:30 and went to Mulligan's Bar for a couple of beers. Bill and Georgie had already turned eighteen so they were legal. Al and I would turn eighteen in a couple weeks, and if the owner, Timmy Mulligan, knew we were still seventeen, he certainly hadn't cared.

We left the bar around 11:20 and walked our separate ways home. My house was in a different direction from theirs, and I was strolling along Lefferts Boulevard near Atlantic Avenue, when I heard a horn beep twice, and a car with its radio blasting out *Little Darlin'* by the Diamonds pulled to the curb next to me. "Hey, Noonz!" a familiar voice called out. "Hop in. The top's down and it's a great night for cruising around and scouting up some chicks."

I wasn't tired, and riding around in Pete Selewski's white 1955 Ford convertible seemed like a good idea at the time. I didn't hesitate one bit, not knowing girls were the last thing on Pete's mind. What was on his mind, I was shortly to discover, were two things, heroin, and obtaining the money to buy it.

Pete had gone to Richmond Hill High School as did most of my friends. Georgie and I went the Catholic high school route, and we had to schlep into Brooklyn on the bus and subway to be taught by the kindly brothers of Bishop Loughlin. Pete had dropped out of school at age sixteen and worked full-time at the A & P supermarket, where I met him. I worked there after school three times a week and all day Saturday. We had worked together today, both getting off at six o'clock.

Pete was two years older than me and with his curly blond hair, blue eyes, good looks, and trim body, he was a natural chick magnet. The shiny white convertible with the red leather interior didn't hurt either. I guess I was thought of as a fairly good-looking guy myself because of my dark-brown curly hair, and my wide smile with a perfect set of white teeth. But my classic Roman nose could be considered on the large side, and when I was razzed about it I replied, "Just like the great singer, Tony Bennett's handsome nose, you jealous jerks."

Now, in retrospect – 20-20 hindsight is great, isn't it? – I should have paid attention to the warning signs. I knew Pete smoked pot on and off the job. He looked like he lost weight, particularly around his face. His complexion was sallow and his cheeks sunken in a bit. And he had taken to wearing long-sleeved shirts despite this early heat wave. As we pulled from the curb, it must have been 80 degrees out there, but he had on a long-sleeved black shirt and black jeans to match.

We rode around the main drags – Atlantic Avenue, Jamaica Avenue, up and down Lefferts Boulevard, listening to DJ Alan Freed play the top rock 'n roll hits of the day, but there were not many girls wandering around at this time of night. Pete took to the back streets and lowered the radio just as *Bye, Bye, Love* by the Everly Brothers came on. He turned the radio even lower as he headed east, in and out of residential areas, driving slowly, and checking out the houses. I said, "Looking for somebody you know? A house number?"

"Uh, no," he said, and I could see the sweat beading on his face. He kept cruising through these residential neighborhoods, and I wondered what the hell was going on. I mean if there were no chicks on the main drags, there certainly wouldn't be any lurking behind trees in these dark places. All of a sudden he said, "Yeah, that's it!"

I had no idea what "it" was and Pete continued driving to the next intersection, turned the corner, and parked half way down the block. "Get out," he said. "Let's go."

I opened the door saying, "Go where?" as he reached across and grabbed something out of the glove box. Holy shit! It was a gun. One of those shiny, chrome-plated revolvers the bad guys pull out in the gangster movies. "Pete, what the hell is going on?"

"Noonz, we're going to rip off a house. I gotta get money – right away."

"Don't do this, Pete. Here let me give you all I got."

"Thanks pal, but whatever it is, it ain't enough. I need a lot of dough – now."

"But, why –"

"Noonz, I'm hooked. I owe two of my suppliers over a hundred bucks each. They cut me off. I need a fix bad. I gotta pay them off and have enough left to buy more dope. Now let's go."

"Where are we going?"

"Around the corner I spotted a house with a front screen door without a solid inside door closed behind it. They probably left it that way because of the heat. Listen, this will be easy. I know people will be in there sleeping, but this way we'll be sure to find the loot. Money and jewelry are all I'm interested in."

We turned the corner, and still hoping to talk him out of this insane idea, I said, "Pete, how about detox?"

He turned the gun toward me as if I had never spoken and said, "I'll cut the screen and unlock the door. We'll go right to the master bedroom. You switch on the lights, and we'll wake them up. When they see this gun pointed at them they'll willingly tell us where their stuff is. You collect it all, and then we beat feet. Five minutes is all we need. In and out fast."

"No way, Pete. I ain't doing this," I said loudly.

"Shut up!" he screamed, bringing the gun up and pointing it right at my face. His hand was shaking, and sweat was dripping off his chin. I stared down that big hole in the barrel and felt my legs weaken. "You will do this, Joey, or so help me God I'll kill you right here."

It seemed I had no choice as he urged me forward. We had no masks and there were a lot of things that could go wrong, but I was afraid for my life. Pete had convinced me he was in such a condition that he *would* shoot me – his friend. "Okay, Pete," I said. "Calm down." I desperately hoped no one would be in that house, or if there were people in there this theft would go as easily as Pete said it would go.

"Here it is," he whispered as we climbed up the steps of the front stoop. He took out a box cutter and slit the screen next to the lock. He reached in and unlocked the latch on the door and we crept inside. No masks? No gloves, either. Pete must have been in a bad way not to have given this caper any rational planning. He took a small penlight from his front pocket, at least he thought of something, and panned it around the room.

We headed around the corner to a hallway where the bedrooms probably were. All the doors were wide open, and the first one was the master as a brief view inside with the penlight showed. The glimpse was enough to reveal two sleeping people in the bed. Pete whispered, "Feel for the light switch on the wall."

It was not on the first side I tried, but I located it on the opposite side. My fingers were wet with sweat and shaking badly. All of me was shaking badly. "Turn on the light, Noonz," he whispered, "I'll take it from here."

I switched on the light as Pete walked to the foot of the bed and yelled, "Don't move or I'll kill you both!"

As he was saying that, the guy started coming up from his side of the bed, the left side facing us, and his right arm began to rise. His hand held a small dark gun. The room came alive with deafening gunshots, the bullets whizzing back and forth in the confined space. Neither shooter could possibly miss they were so close together. I don't know who got off the first shot, but I think Pete and the guy got hit simultaneously. The woman suddenly sat up and Pete turned the gun on her – one shot. Then he turned back, shooting at the guy who let two more go, one of which hit me in the arm. Pete turned back to the woman and shot her again. Then he dropped the gun and said, "Oh, Joey," and fell to the floor.

I didn't stick around to help anybody. I assumed all three of them were dead. I mean blood was spurting out everywhere, like in the movies. Everything had gone so fast, and now I was in full panic mode. I hustled out of the bedroom trying to close the door on that horrible sight. The copper-penny smell of fresh blood mixed with a flowery smell of body powder or perfume deep in my lungs sickened me. As I turned to run for the front door I heard it – loud and piercing over the deafness and ringing in my ears caused by the loud gunshots – the sound of a baby crying coming from down the hall.

Oh, my God, what have I done?

TWO

Because of the timeframe of the murders, the story had not appeared in the Sunday morning papers, but it was all over the six o'clock radio and TV news stations. My stomach churned as they identified the victims as Andrew Simon, age twenty-five, a Nassau County Police Officer, and his wife, Veronica, also twenty-five, a school teacher in Franklin Square. "Their six-month old baby son, Michael, was uninjured, and is now in the care of relatives," the announcer on Channel Four said. "The perpetrator, who apparently acted alone, was also killed at the scene during a shoot-out with Patrolman Simon. He was a white male, but his identity will not be disclosed pending notification to his next of kin."

The perpetrator who apparently acted alone. I breathed a deep sigh of relief when I heard that, but reflected back on that terrible scene. I had fumbled with the light switch. No gloves. I got shot. Why didn't I try to grab the gun out of Pete's hand? Was some of my blood left there on the floor? Could they distinguish mine from the others? My shirt! I retrieved it from the back corner of my closet, unfolded it, and examined it carefully. The bullet had torn through the left sleeve and there was blood soaked all around the tear. I got the scissors from the bathroom and cut off the bloodied sleeve. I diced it up into small pieces and flushed them all down the toilet. Later on I put the rest of the shirt in with the kitchen garbage and took the bag, my usual chore, out to the garbage can.

On the ten o'clock news, the police identified the perpetrator as Peter Selewski from Richmond Hill. "Selewski's car was found around the corner from the house," the announcer said, "confirming this burglary-homicide was indeed a one-man job."

I breathed another sigh of relief until the announcer further said, "Detectives from the 105 Precinct and Queens Homicide will be speaking to the friends and associates of Selewski for more information, as well as thoroughly canvassing the entire neighborhood where the murders took place."

It was three agonizing days before the detectives got to me at the A & P. I tried to keep my nervousness under control as I told them the only association I had with Pete was at work, and we didn't socialize as he was a couple years older than me. I said I hadn't seen Pete that night after work and went to the movies with friends and was home, in bed, by eleven. The manager confirmed Pete was a good worker, but had slacked off recently. The detective then said, "Did you know he was a drug addict?"

He said this in front of all of us, all of Pete's fellow workers, and it was obvious they were all shocked, including me, as I feigned surprise. The manager nodded and said, "I guess that explains it. What a tragedy for everyone."

After the cops left, I went back to work in the basement of the store when, out of the blue, another fear hit me like a hot thunderbolt. Pete's car! Would they find my fingerprints on the door handle when they examined it? But I had never been fingerprinted, and unless they came back and asked for everybody's prints, I would be home free.

That night I pondered over my situation long and hard. I had to get out of this neighborhood – fast. And that was exactly what I did. One week later I graduated from Bishop Loughlin High School. The next day I was at the Marine Corps Recruiting Station in Jamaica. I would be eighteen in two weeks on July 8, so my parents had to sign the papers. They did so gladly, my father saying, "I'm-a proud of you, Joey. You serve your country like me and your two brothers did. I love-a you, son."

. . .

The date set for my entrance into the Marines was July 15. I graduated on June 25 and quit my job at the A & P the next day. I had twenty days of freedom left, and I spent them in fear and trepidation, always looking over my shoulder, always awaiting the dreaded knock on our door. The cops never came back to visit me, and I knew from my friends they checked out my story for that night. My wound had healed up cleanly, but I didn't want to explain it at a USMC physical exam. Like a lot of my buddies at that time I made the subway trip to Coney Island, and for twelve bucks, got a large tattoo to cover it up. And, deservedly, it hurt like hell.

I guess my Catholic guilt prompted me to join the Marines rather than another branch of the service. They had the reputation for being the toughest, and the tougher, the better. Self-flagellation, I figured. When the day came and the good-byes were said, I reported in and was soon on the bus to Parris Island – in July. Good, the hotter the better, and the more I could suffer and do penance for my part in that awful crime. The word penance triggered something in my mind as I rode on the rickety bus toward my destination. I had been so involved in worrying about being caught by the cops I had completely forgotten about the moral aspects of my actions. Was I guilty of a sin by my complicity in the crime? And I was harshly reminded of that crime whenever I heard *Little Darlin'* or *Bye, Bye Love* on the radio, or heard a baby cry, causing the events of that night to crash through my head like a freight train.

Over the next few hours I searched through my mind for the knowledge that twelve years of Catholic teaching and education had given me. I knew I had committed some type of sin, but couldn't nail it down. I figured I'd have to go to confession and lay it all out to the priest, but I was not ready for that confrontation right now. I hadn't intended to steal anything. I hadn't intended to kill anyone. I was forced into the situation against my will. But there were two dead people and an orphaned child left behind, and I knew they would be in my mind and dreams forever, like three bloody hundred-pound anchors, dragging me down into the abyss of hell.

.   .   .

After being screamed at and humiliated as soon as we got off the bus, we were given our uniforms, underwear, bedding, and the famous head shave. The next morning I, and 79 other sleeping recruits, were awakened at 5:00 a.m. by the sounds of shouting and the banging of spoons on a large metal garbage can. Welcome to the United States Marine Corps. We snapped to attention and met our drill instructor, Staff Sergeant Randall J. Hobbs, from somewhere in the deep South. When he came to my place in line, he looked down at his clipboard and screwed up his dark-brown face into a sneer. He leaned into my face, not more than two inches away, and shouted, "Mastronunzio? What the fuck kinda Guinea name is that?"

I didn't know if I should answer so I continued to stand at rigid attention, eyes straight forward, trembling in my new boots. He screamed, "Giuseppe Mastronunzio, what the hell do you have to say for yourself?"

"Uh, sir… Sergeant Hobbs, they call me Joey, or Noonz," realizing I probably shouldn't have said that, or anything.

But, thankfully, the D.I. smiled and said, "Joey, I like that. Short and sweet. Better than fucking Giuseppe. And I like Noonz, too, but we gotta keep it somewhat like your real moniker." He touched his hand to his chin as if in deep thought and finally said, "Joey Nunzio, that's who you're going to be in my Corps. I ain't writing no Mastronunzio on my reports, and I ain't burdening our tailor with trying to figure out how to sew that long-ass moniker on your uniforms. Are you okay with that, Nunzio?"

"Yes, sir, Sergeant!" I shouted back.

"Excellent, but let me remind you of one more thing."

"Yes, sir!"

He got his square-jaw again up close to my face and said, "You a Catholic boy, Joey?"

"Yes, Sergeant!"

"I wish to remind you, whatever your name, although your soul belongs to Jesus Christ, your ass belongs to me and my beloved Corps. Are we clear?"

"Crystal, Sergeant."

Welcome to the United States Marine Corps, Joey Nunzio.

.　　.　　.

The next day we had written aptitude tests and complete physicals and medicals including the drawing of a vial of blood. Then we had to fill out a whole bunch of paperwork, and when we were done, Sergeant

Hobbs yelled for us to line up in two columns. "We got your blood, now we're going to get your fingerprints, you maggots."

A chill went down my spine and I wanted to protest, but kept my mouth shut tight. Amazingly, so did every other member of my platoon. We had all learned never to say *anything* unless asked directly by Sergeant Hobbs. We all got up as ordered and Hobbs smiled and said, "In case you degenerates are wondering, the blood is for typing, so we can put that on your dog tags in case you need a transfusion, and the fingerprints are for identifying your bodily remains after you've been blown to bloody pieces while fighting for our wonderful country."

What a lovely picture the dear sergeant had painted on our young brains. The next day our training began in earnest, and during the course of the next twelve weeks, I pushed myself to the limit and over it, if I could. I never back-talked Sergeant Hobbs, and always paid attention to his instructions. I slept like a baby from sheer physical exhaustion, but during my waking hours, in what little down time we had, I prayed for the souls of Andrew and Veronica Simon and that their young son, Michael, would have a happy life. I also prayed for Pete Selewski, a once good guy who had succumbed to a terrible habit. Maybe he was a victim in this crummy scheme of things, too. And I always kept an eye out for a surprise visit from a couple of NYPD detectives saying, "Sergeant Hobbs, we understand you have the fingerprints and blood type of a suspect in a case we are working on…"

.

. . .

At the end of eight weeks, sixteen guys in our platoon had been sent home for various reasons. It seemed the rest of us would make it, and Hobbs began to loosen the reins a bit on us. It was obvious the purpose of our training was to make us into first-class, cold-blooded killers. "A Marine and his rifle," Hobbs quoted to us incessantly, "is the greatest fighting machine in the world, bar none." And when our recruit days came to an end we believed it. A couple of days before graduation, Hobbs pulled me aside and said, "Are your folks coming to the ceremonies?"

"Yes, Sergeant."

"How do you think they'll feel when they learn your new name?"

He was grinning broadly and I said, "I don't think we should tell them about that right now, Sergeant. But I have grown fond of it, and may make it legal some day."

"Listen, Noonz, you're a fine Marine, and the tests show you can succeed in several specialties after your six weeks of advanced infantry training up in Lejeune. Think about it. I can give you a push for whatever you want to do."

"Thank you, Sergeant. Much appreciated, and I will think about it."

My parents came down to Parris Island and one of my brothers, Leo, whose real name was Leopoldo, also showed up. Leo had been a Marine years ago, and after the ceremonies he poked me in the ribs and said, "What did your drill instructor think of your name?"

"I am now Joey Nunzio, compliments of the Corps."

"And I was Leo Mastro. Don't worry, it's not a legal change, only for USMC purposes."

I had already considered a legal name change anyway, but not to anything that resembled my real name in any manner, for obvious reasons. They now had my blood type and fingerprints on file, and I was more than a bit worried about a future knock on my door with a grim-faced detective on the other side asking to have a few words with me.

I completed my advanced infantry training at Camp Lejeune and was now a bonafide, certified killer for my country. I hoped I would never have to fire a weapon again after I left the Corps. Oh, I was a patriot through and through and wouldn't shirk my duty, but I had seen deaths by gunshot up close and personal already, and that was more than enough for one life. I was now devoted to the Corps and equally devoted to my Catholic faith. All throughout my training I attended Sunday mass, and prayed for my family and friends, but most of all I prayed for the happiness and success of the orphaned infant, Michael Simon. I couldn't, however, bring myself to enter into the dreaded confessional booth just yet.

The MOS – Military Occupational Specialty – list was detailed and offered a huge variety of choices. I had the germ of an idea as to what profession I would like to follow after my enlistment was up, but was fairly certain I needed some type of college degree to be considered. I chose aircraft repair and maintenance for two reasons – job availability and money. I knew from living in Queens, right in the middle of two busy airports, LaGuardia and Idlewild, that they were always looking for help. And with the advent of the jet age, I figured the number of jobs would only increase. I needed to make a living, a good living, to pay for tuition in night school. But did I want to go back to Queens, I wondered, as my blood type and fingerprint card flashed through my mind?

True to his word, Sergeant Hobbs pulled the right string, and I got my first choice of MOS in aviation. I had a few days off and got a lift from Camp Lejeune down to Parris Island bearing a couple of bottles of Jack Daniels. Hobbs had dismissed his newest platoon of ragged recruits minutes before and returned to his office where I found him after nearly breaking my fist knocking on the goddamned door jamb.

"Come in you maggot pussy!" he screamed.

I went in, brought myself to full attention, and saluted him. I said, "Maggot pussy Joey Noonz reporting and bearing gifts, sir!"

He laughed and said, "Get your sorry ass in here, Mastro-fucking-Nunzio. Let's see here what y'all have brought."

I handed him the package and he grinned when he saw the two half-gallon bottles of JD. "Well, I'll be," he said, "the dumb Guinea has learned well. On the rocks, okay?"

"Perfect, Sergeant," I said as he got the ice from his small refrigerator and poured us a generous splash in low-ball glasses that appeared from his bottom desk drawer.

We toasted the Corps and then Hobbs got serious. "Listen, Joey, I was happy to help a good Marine. Now listen to this old-timer. Before your hitch is up, the Corps is going to offer you a good package to re-up. Don't take it. Negotiate for a better deal."

"I'm listening, Sarge."

"I guarantee you'll be at least a corporal by that time. They'll offer you another stripe and a signing bonus, five or six hundred bucks, for a four-year hitch. Tell them no. Tell them you'll trade them the stripe, and the dough, for a shot at college and a future slot in OCS."

"You think I can be an officer?"

"I would be proud to snap off a salute to Second Lieutenant Giuseppe Mastronunzio, Marine."

I was flabbergasted. "Thank you, Sarge," I said. "Thank you for everything. I will consider, carefully, all your advice."

We knocked off half of one of the bottles, and Hobbs luckily found someone to drive my drunk ass back to Lejeune.

The three years flew by and I became a qualified aviation mechanic and proud of my new skills. As Sergeant Hobbs predicted, they offered me, Corporal Nunzio, a sergeant's stripe and $500 for re-upping for four years, but I had already made up my mind to leave the Corps. I was somewhat confident I had found my future vocation, so I politely declined. The captain I was meeting with immediately countered with, "Let me offer you another choice. A third stripe, paid college tuition, and a seat in OCS after you successfully complete your first two years of school."

Now that made me think a bit, especially since I would need a college degree anyway for what I wanted to do with my life. I thought for a whole minute. "Thank you, Captain," I said. "Both offers are more than fair, sir, but I must decline them. I'm going to leave the Corps."

"I believe you're making a huge mistake, Corporal."

"Could be, Captain. God knows, I've made them before."

One week later I was honorably discharged and left Marine Corps Aviation Station New River, NC on a Greyhound bus to Florida. After visiting my folks and my brother, Vinny, and his wife, who lived not far away from them, I asked mom and dad if I could stay with them a few weeks while I sent out job applications. "Stay as long as you want, Joey," my mother said. "We gotta fatten you up with some-a real food. Lasagne sound-a good tonight?"

Ah! Home cooking again, but it wouldn't last long. One week after I sent out the job inquiries, I got two responses and they wanted me for an interview "at my earliest convenience." The problem was the airlines who wanted me were located at Idlewild and LaGuardia. I scheduled the interviews for two weeks away hoping I'd get another offer from somewhere else, like Atlanta, Dallas or Chicago. When the two weeks passed by, and there had been no responses from the airlines in those cities, I packed up my gear, kissed my folks good-bye, and flew back to Queens. It seemed, for now, I had no other choice. Queens. The scene of the crime. The images of the bloody, murdered bodies of Andrew and Veronica Simon flashed through my mind, and I distinctly heard the sound of infant Michael Simon crying his poor, little eyes out. And I feared the cops would be waiting to arrest me as soon as I stepped one foot off the plane.

THREE

I stayed at a cheap motel in Astoria and a week later TWA offered me a job at LaGuardia Airport in northern Queens as a trainee mechanic on the four-to-twelve shift. I accepted and got a one-room apartment in a converted garage with my first paycheck.

During my stay at the motel I went to civil court and had my name legally changed to Francis Andrew Manzo. Francis for Saint Francis who I admired and studied in a high school project, Andrew for Michael Simon's father, and Manzo, using five of the twelve letters of my real last name. The judge, whose name plate read, *Silvio Notarantonio*, smiled and said, "No explanation necessary, Giuseppe. Request granted."

I registered for two courses at St. John's University for the upcoming fall semester and planned a visit to my old high school in Brooklyn. I had decided I had a desire – more a burning need – to continue my service to society. I had proudly served my country in the Marine Corps, and now I wanted to serve God in the priesthood. And I knew one of the main reasons I wanted to become a priest was to atone for the deaths of Andrew and Veronica Simon and the orphaning of their son, Michael.

Although I hadn't gone to confession, I couldn't shake the shadow of guilt that hovered over me day and night. And working my way up to a Class A mechanic at Trans World Airlines wouldn't disperse that shadow. I needed a spiritual solution, if any solution to my inner conflict existed, and I needed advice on my legal and moral status, even though I hadn't pulled the trigger. But I did run away, and I didn't turn myself in, did I? If anyone could help me with these problems I knew my old high school principal at Bishop Loughlin could, and his secretary kindly set aside an hour to meet with him two days from now.

.   .   .

Father William McClanahan welcomed me into his office with a broad smile. "How are you doing Noonz, since you left us three years ago? Have you made an impression on the big, bad world out there?"

Deciding not to mention my name change I said, "I doubt that, Father, but I have an idea how I can do that. That's why I'm here, for your advice and guidance."

"Oh, my God, Joey, don't tell me you heard the calling?"

"I think so," I said. "How do I proceed?"

"*Thinking* so is not the standard. You need a bit more conviction than that. What have you been doing these past three years?"

"Serving my country in the Marine Corps."

"Ah! The Corps scared you so badly you now want to run back into the all-loving, all-encompassing arms of Jesus?"

"No, Father," I said, as we shared a laugh. "But my drill instructor always reminded me although my soul does belong to Jesus Christ —"

"Your ass belongs to the Corps, right?"

"Right. Don't tell me —?"

"Yes, a long time ago, between the World Wars. The discipline and training have served me well my entire life."

"Then you'll help a fellow grunt?"

"Were you a good Marine? No disciplinary problems? No AWOL's?"

"I was a good Marine, Father. They wanted me to stay in and dangled a couple of good offers to do so. I came close to accepting."

He asked me about the offers and when I finished telling him, he said, "But you had the urge, the *feeling* back then, that you had a higher calling?"

"Yes, sir."

He sat back in his chair, steepled his hands together and pursed his lips. I looked into his dark brown eyes and wondered what he would say. I stared at the simple wooden crucifix on the wall behind his head, praying for his blessing. He relaxed and said, "I'll make a call. Go outside and get yourself a coke."

"A coke, Father? It's bourbon or coffee now."

He smiled and said, "I should have known, Noonz. Semper Fi."

"Oorah," I said as I left his office.

Ten minutes later he called me back inside and said, "You have an appointment with Father James Johansson at the Office of Vocations at the Seminary House in Douglaston, Queens. Ten o'clock, Thursday morning. Can you make it?"

"I certainly can."

"Good. Keep me in the loop on your progress."

"I will, Father," I said, feeling my resolve to open up to him fading fast.

The canny Priest held my hand in his as we shook prior to my departure. He said, "You're not holding back on me are you, Giuseppe?"

"Uh, I –"

"You didn't kill anybody, did you?"

He wasn't smiling, and I wondered what sixth sense this man had. I said, "Of course not, Father. Why would you say something like that?"

"Joey, I've been around a long time. Something is bothering you. I don't mind if you don't reveal it to me. But you must reveal it to Father Johansson. You cannot enter the seminary, much less the priesthood, without a clear conscience and a clean soul. Do you understand that?"

"I do, Father, and you are right, something is bothering me, and now I'm thinking I should reveal it to you before I go to that interview. Maybe you will advise me to give up my desire to enter the priesthood right here and now."

"How bad is it, Joey? Do you want this in the form of a formal confession?"

"No, Father, not yet. I am uncertain what sin I committed, and if I am legally in trouble. And when you asked if I had killed someone, you didn't know how close you were."

McClanahan reached behind him and withdrew a bottle of Jim Beam bourbon and two glasses from a wall cabinet. He poured two healthy shots into the glasses, no ice, unlike Sergeant Hobbs had preferred, and we both took a healthy swallow. "Tell me all about it," he said.

I spilled it out, every detail of it, which I remembered as if it were yesterday, and which I no doubt would remember all of my life. He interrupted twice to ask a question, and by the time I finished speaking, the bottle of bourbon was about a third gone. He said, "That's one helluva story, Joey. I remember reading about those murders, but I don't remember reading that a second suspect was involved."

"They concluded Pete was the sole killer, if what they told the press was true."

"You think they may have suspected a second guy, but withheld that fact?"

"I'm certain of it. I know I left some blood there, and I had to have left fingerprints somewhere in the bedroom, or the house, or on Pete's car."

"Why didn't you turn yourself in? I mean you were forced to participate, so I don't see how you could be guilty of a crime. And, if so, I believe you did not commit any sin that night."

"I was afraid by merely being there, I was guilty of *something.* What do you think?"

"I'm no lawyer, but I do know someone who can advise us on that. The Diocese retains a law firm to address the many issues that arise in the church and schools."

"Do they sue the parents who stiff you on tuition payments?"

"I wish that was all there was, but I'd rather not get into those other issues now. Let's get your situation addressed before you go on your interview. What's your schedule for the rest of the day?"

"I have to be at work at the airport at four."

He picked up his phone and dialed his secretary on the intercom. "Joanie, please get me Ralph Dugan from *Jackson, Rubin, Slater* on the phone."

Not two minutes later the phone rang and McClanahan said, "Ralph, I need no more than an hour of your time, if you're available now."

Evidently Ralph Dugan was available, or made himself available, to his client, because after he hung up the phone the good Priest said, "He'll be here at two. Dugan's their criminal law specialist. Their office is within walking distance. Let's go get some lunch."

.   .   .

As we were walking back from the local sandwich shop stuffed with corned beef and *latkes*, a man came striding up behind us and said, "Hello, Father."

"Hello, Ralph," he said, smiling and extending his hand. "This is Joey, and he is sorely in need of your expert advice."

I shook hands with the middle-aged lawyer whose furrowed brow, darting eyes, and moist hand gave the impression of a worried man who wished he were somewhere else. I wondered what the *other issues* he and the church routinely dealt with. "I hope I can help," he said as we entered the school and headed for the elevator.

We settled into our wooden chairs in the principal's austere office, McClanahan's secretary brought coffee in, and he got right to it. "Tell Ralph what happened from the time you got in the car with Selewski until the time you ran out the door for home."

Although the lawyer had a yellow pad on the arm of his chair and a ballpoint pen poised above it, he took not one note, but listened intently to my words and stared into my eyes until I had finished. He said, "I assume you are here because you are a former student and sought out the advice of Father McClanahan?"

"Yes, sir."

"And you want to be a priest, I also assume?"

"Yes."

"And you want to know if your actions on the night of the crime would prevent that?"

"Yes."

"My short answer is no, but –"

I saw McClanahan grin and he said, "Lawyers always have to put a *but* in their answers somewhere. Sorry, Ralph, please proceed."

"Here's the law on this situation. The *New York State Penal Code* defines what happened that night as Murder in the First Degree – an intentional act to kill someone. Maybe you could say Pete shot at the guy because he was shooting at him, but what about the wife? There is another subdivision called Felony Murder, which means if you kill someone during the course of committing a crime – and the crime here was First Degree Burglary – you are also guilty of murder. Either charge could get you a seat in the electric chair upon conviction."

So far, so good, I thought, as I stared at Dugan, knowing some other stuff was coming.

"However, by just being there, you are classified as an accomplice, and are as legally guilty as Pete Selewski."

"Wait a minute," I said. "I was not there voluntarily. I was forced to be there by Pete. He threatened to kill me after all. What the hell was I supposed to do?"

"What if Joey had turned himself in?" McClanahan asked.

"That would have been the worst decision of his life," Dugan said, "other than his present desire to become a priest."

"Screw you, Ralph," McClanahan said. "And you profess to be a fellow Catholic?"

As I was wondering what the hell was going on between the lawyer and the priest, Dugan said, "You should not be convicted of any crime committed at that scene because you acted under duress, an affirmative defense which states you are not guilty of a crime if someone forced you to do it against your will."

There you go. Duress. I was innocent!

"But there's a problem —"

"Here we go again," McClanahan said, shaking his head.

"The affirmative defense of duress must be raised at trial. In other words, you have to be arrested, indicted, and put on trial first before that can happen. Do you think the jury would believe you, Joey?"

"Would you believe me, Mr Dugan, if you were my lawyer?"

"Probably not, but that wouldn't matter."

"What if I take a lie detector test?"

"Not admissible."

"I know, but if the test says I'm truthful, at least you will believe me, right?"

"Okay, I believe you, and we go to trial, and I have to put you on the stand. You claim the defense of duress and on cross-examination the prosecutor asks if you have any corroboration for your story."

"What does that mean?"

"It means, other than your testimony, do you have a witness who could state you were telling the truth? A witness at the scene who could confirm your version of the events?"

"No, I don't."

"Then the prosecutor tells the jury you are making this whole thing up to avoid conviction for this brutal crime, and he throws in the gory details of the bloody murders once again in case they have forgotten them. Now, who do you think the jury will believe?"

"Me! I'm telling the truth!"

"A young police officer and his young wife are dead. Their six-month old child will never know them. You, young man, would be found guilty – in a hurry – and sent up the Hudson River to Sing Sing state prison to fry in the electric chair."

"Shit! This isn't right. This isn't fair."

"No, it isn't," Dugan said, "hence, my previous advice. Keep your mouth closed and never mention that night to anyone – ever. What say you, Father?"

"I agree with counsel," he said. "Keep your mouth shut to everyone but Father Johansson at the seminary. You are going to have to bare your soul to him with no holdbacks."

"And with any luck, young man," Dugan said, "you will be rejected as a candidate for the priesthood and go forth to lead a much happier and productive life."

I thought that comment would get another sharp retort from McClanahan, but he just shook his head and said, "You'd better get to your job, Joey, and keep me advised of your progress. Good luck with your interview, and I hope you get admitted."

"Thank you, Father," I said. "And thank you, Mr. Dugan, for your legal advice. If the cops ever come for me, you will be the first person I'll call."

"Good decision, young man, and if I fail you, you can then call the good Father McClanahan. I'm sure he will solemnly walk with you from your cell on Death Row, down that grim prison hallway, to your certain appointment with *Old Sparky*."

If that remark was meant to scare me into permanent silence about the night of the murders of Andy and Veronica Simon, it sure did the trick.

FOUR

Father Johansson's secretary escorted me into his spacious, expensively-furnished office. I looked around at the many framed pictures on the walls of him with various cardinals and bishops resplendent in scarlet and gold, and at least two recognizable past Popes of the Church. A huge silver crucifix, at least four times as large as the one in McClanahan's office, was on the wall directly above his polished mahogany desk. He greeted me warmly, a big smile on his ruddy face. "Father McClanahan gave you his blessing and his recommendation," he said. "I see you have a solid Catholic education, but no college training."

"I enrolled in a couple of day classes at St. John's. I work nights at TWA," I said, more intimidated now than I was by Sergeant Hobbs on my first day at boot camp. I was surrounded by the power and the majesty of the church and knew, despite his broad smile, I was shortly to be given the bum's rush out the door by the head inquisitor.

"Excellent. Now let's explore your desire to enter the priesthood, to find out if it's genuine, or as your former principal said, 'to find out what you may be running away from.'"

"I never could fool him, and I have already decided to bare my soul to you. I will not enter the seminary under false pretenses. And after I tell you everything, if you shoo me out the door, I will certainly understand, and will have to live with that."

I imagined his eyes glowing like bright-red burning coals as he said, "Go ahead, Joey. Take your time. You're my lone prospective candidate appointment today."

"For starters, Father, my name is no longer Giuseppe Mastronunzio. It's Francis Manzo. I legally changed it a couple of weeks ago."

"I can understand the apparent reason for doing so," he said with a chuckle, "but is there a more non-apparent reason you did it?"

"Yes, to continue to avoid the police for a crime I did not commit, but which I witnessed over three years ago."

"Would you like something to drink before you continue?"

"Water would be fine, Father."

The Priest got up and went to a sideboard and came back with a pitcher of ice cubes and water and two glasses. He poured us each a glass and we took a swallow. He fixed his eyes on me and said, "I am intrigued, Francis. Please begin."

I told him everything, as I had with Father McClanahan and Ralph Dugan, including the reason I didn't turn myself in. I bet I spoke for twenty minutes, maybe more, and Father Johansson did not interrupt me once. He did take a note or two on a small pad.

"That is an interesting story, young man. Tell me again about the felony murder statute and the defense of duress."

When I finished he said, "I have to agree with you, Francis. If I had heard you testify that you were present at the scene, but was forced to participate in the attempted burglary, I probably would not have believed you myself."

"Father, I have now, finally, come to the realization, despite my innocence, if I was on the jury I wouldn't believe some punk kid telling this tale to save his ass... er, butt, either. Come on, a young married couple shot to death? One of them a police officer? With a six-month old baby, who would never know his loving parents, crying his eyes out down the hall? And if I had turned myself in I would already have been electrocuted or been in prison for the rest of my life."

"Yes, I see. A life wasted. A life you now want to devote to God and mankind. And to atone for what, Francis?"

"I don't know. Maybe being there that night. Maybe not trying to grab the gun from Pete's hand. Maybe by running away without seeing if I could help them. I hope you will confirm what Father McClanahan told me, and what I now myself believe, what I was involved in that night was not a sin. I have wracked my brain, studied the bible, studied the teachings of the church and the saints, and cannot find a sin – mortal or venial – I might have committed that night."

"When was the last time you went to confession?"

"About a week before the murders, three years ago."

"You never formally confessed your actions of that dreadful night to Father McClanahan?"

"No, sir. Until two days ago I never told anyone of that night at all."

"But now you want something extremely important to you, acceptance to the seminary, and you want my blessing to allow you to proceed."

"Your blessing and your absolution, Father. If I am guilty of a sin in the eyes of the church, please tell me. I will confess it to you and ask to be absolved. And I will do penance – whatever you determine."

"Are you celibate, Francis?"

"Uh, no sir. I was a Marine."

"Yes, you were," he said, smiling at me. "I believe life-long celibacy for you, my son, will be penance enough, don't you think?"

I took in his words and said, "Are you accepting me into the seminary? Do you believe I have not sinned?"

"After I hear your formal confession right now, I'll give you my answer. Go ahead, Francis."

I hadn't committed a long list of sins since I joined the Corps, just some occasional profanity and sex out of wedlock, so my confession was a short one. Father Johansson absolved me and assigned the rosary as my penance. He said, "To answer your questions, Francis, I also believe you did not commit a sin on that night, but you did have a serious moral lapse in running away from those mortally injured people, and that is something you will have to deal with inside your soul and your heart. As far as entering the seminary, I will allow you to apply. There is a lengthy process and background investigation that must be completed before you can join us here. During that process, you and I will discover if you have the true calling to be ordained a Priest in the Roman Catholic Church."

"Thank you, Father. All I ask is the chance."

"I will give you that chance, and you can start by filling out a lot of paperwork my secretary will give you."

He showed me to his outer office and said, "Mrs. Olsen, please have Francis Manzo prepare the initial paperwork packet for admission." He shook my hand and said, "I can only imagine what it was like for you that night."

"Pure terror," I said.

Mrs. Olsen went into a supply closet and Father Johansson whispered, "Are you certain the police suspect a second person was at the murder scene?"

"No, Father, but they may be keeping that to themselves for obvious reasons."

"But you have to live with the fear they may one day come for you, right?"

"Not for a long time, I hope. Not until I prove to myself, and my church, and our society, that I am a worthy human being and worth saving."

"You have great insight for a man of your young age. You read the lives of the saints, and that's why you chose Francis, wasn't it?"

"Yes, Father."

"Good choice. You'll hear from me within a week."

While I awaited the call from Johansson, a remark he made early in our meeting re-surfaced in my mind. He mentioned I was his only prospective candidate that day, and I now wondered if there was difficulty in recruiting candidates for the priesthood. Coupled with the remarks by attorney Dugan a few days earlier, I began to suspect something was going on in the church I was unaware of. Was Johansson going to accept me because he had no choice?

. . .

True to his word, Father Johansson called me a few days later and said I had been accepted to begin the first stage of the process. I would have to meet regularly with the Office of Vocations, and then go on what he called Discernment Retreats, whereupon a final decision would be reached for entry into the seminary house. There I would study for the priesthood while also attending nearby St. John's University to obtain my degree in religious studies. If all went as scheduled, I would be ordained in six years. "Thank you, Father," I said, "but may I ask you a couple of questions?"

"Having second thoughts?"

"No sir, but are you, uh, is the church, having trouble getting students to study for the priesthood?"

"Yes, we are."

"Is it because of the celibacy issue?"

"Among other things. But that particular vow is the chief obstacle, in my opinion. There is talk of someday allowing priests to marry, but I don't believe that will happen any time soon."

"My second question is, are you accepting me because of the shortage of candidates, even though I may not be qualified?"

"Not at all, my son. You are eminently qualified and will make a fine priest. Now, put your doubts and fears behind you and pray to Jesus for support. I will pray for your success as well."

"Thank you, Father, that's all I need." I vowed I would succeed, and I vowed to never forget, and to always pray for, the souls of Veronica and Andrew Simon, Pete Selewski, and, most importantly, for Michael, the innocent crying child left behind.

Michael Simon would now be three and a half years old, and I remembered reading he had been adopted by his father's brother and wife. God bless them, too. I hope you're a happy and safe little guy but someday, a long time from now, you will have to be told what happened on that frightful night, and who you really are. And how will you react to that?

.   .   .

I continued to work nights at TWA and attend day classes at St. John's, and two years later I was accepted into full-time seminary studies. The next few years passed by, sometimes slowly, sometimes rapidly, but pass they did, and I was ordained in the summer of 1966 into the Diocese of Brooklyn at the Cathedral of St. Joseph on Pacific Street in Brooklyn. My parents, and my two brothers and their wives, all came in from out of state to attend my ordination. Father Johansson and Father McClanahan also showed up for the elaborate ceremony, the culmination of my study and devotion to God.

As I lay prostrate before the altar the Bishop placed his hands on me and said the consecratory prayer as the rich odor of incense permeated the air. I, and the others being ordained, rose and were given our vestments. The Bishop anointed our hands with holy oil and presented us with our golden chalice and paten with which we would say mass. My long journey was over. I was now a Priest in the holy Catholic Church.

I hadn't mentioned to my parents of my desire to become a priest until I had received my final acceptance into the seminary. I had flown down to Florida, on TWA naturally, and spent a few days with them explaining my choice in life. And I had to tell them my new name.

My mother said, "You know, Francis, you coulda changed Giuseppe to Joseph. He was a bigger saint than Francis. But the Mastronunzio? That I-a understand."

"Ah," Pop said. "I shoulda changed it years ago. Your brother did it. He's-a Leo Mastro now."

"Like they named him in the Marines," I said laughing.

Now, six years later, I noticed their age had started to show, to spread its lines and wrinkles on their faces and necks, to paint its brown spots on the backs of their hands. They were pushing toward seventy. How long would I have them? When would I see them again?

I put those thoughts away and hugged them after the ceremony. I was ordained. It was time to celebrate with my family. And after that, it was time to go to work – for God.

PART TWO

THE SURVIVOR

(MAY 2000)

FIVE

There is no God. The old Jew lying on the green and black tiled floor of his candy store told me that a long time ago. Thirty years? Now, as his blood seeped from the bullet wound in his almost hairless skull, his words proved true once again. Words I had been shocked to hear as a devout Catholic boy growing up in South Ozone Park, Queens, but words which I came to believe, after much soul-searching and agonizing, were absolutely true. *There is no God.* For if there were a God, he would not have allowed one of his chosen people to be brutally murdered today. Not Mordechai Stern. Not Mort, my friend, my former employer, my mentor, my philosophical adviser, my truth teller. Mort, more a father than my father, more a grandfather than my grandfather, more an uncle than my uncle.

My eyes traversed the floor looking for evidence. The floor needed sweeping, I immediately noticed, and I smiled as I remembered the hundreds, maybe thousands, of times I swept this floor for Mort and Lily Stern. As the memories flooded back, a tear started down my left cheek. I reached into my back pocket for my handkerchief – *Remember, Mikey, always carry a handkerchief, a pocket comb, and a pen knife vit you*, Mort would say. Then he would add – *And a dreidel or your rosary voudn't hoit either. Maybe both.* Odd words coming from an avowed atheist, but he knew I was a devout believer at that tender young age and didn't want to burst my bubble. That would happen a few years later when "Professor"

Stern would teach me Religion and Philosophy 101, better known as "Mort's Books of Fairy Tales."

By the time I got the handkerchief up to my face the tears were streaming down my cheeks, and I choked back a sob. I could hear the shock and disbelief in Detective John Micena's voice when he said, "Lieutenant, are... are you okay?"

"No, John, I'm not okay. Some low-life scumbag murdered one of the finest human beings I ever knew in my life. Killed him for a few lousy bucks – he never had more than twenty or thirty in the till – that's why I'm not okay."

"I'll get him, Boss, you know that."

I smiled at my top homicide detective and said, "I know you will, John. Pick your partner, and I'll get a team from the 106 Squad to assist you."

"Richie Paul. That's who I want."

"Good choice," I said as I noticed the arrival of the Crime Scene Search Unit. "Let's step outside and let them have at it."

John put his hand tenderly on my shoulder and said, "Mike, tell me all about Mr. Stern."

.   .   .

I was ten years old when I first walked into Stern's Stationery Store, a candy store, as we called it, on Rockaway Boulevard, between 126 and 127 Streets. I lived seven houses up from the boulevard on 130 Street with my parents and two older sisters. I had a craving for something sweet, and although Stern's was a block and a half farther down the boulevard than Sam's candy store, my usual place, I decided to go to Stern's. Why? Because I had heard some talk from my street buddies it was easier to snatch a candy bar there. Not that I was a regular thief, like a lot of my friends, but a dollar a week allowance only went so far. With larceny in my young heart, I nonchalantly wandered into Stern's and noticed he was behind the soda counter making egg creams for a couple of teenage girls. This was going to be easy. When Stern turned to the cash register to deposit the girls' money, I snatched a Snickers bar from the candy display, and sauntered toward the front door. Suddenly a hand – a strong hand – gripped my shoulder. How he had gotten from behind the counter to block my path in zero time was beyond my comprehension. But there he was, and there I was, terrified and humiliated.

"Forget something, sonny boy?" he said. "Like paying for the Snickers bar in your pocket?"

How the hell had he known?

"Uh, well, uh," I stammered. "I have no money, Mr. Stern."

"Mr. Stern? You know my name, and you seem to be respectful. But you are still a thief. Tell me, sonny boy, what is your name?"

I hesitated, but figured I better be truthful. "Michael Simon," I said, bursting into tears.

"Simon? Vat's a nice Jewish boy like you doing stealing candy in my store?"

"Uh, I'm not Jewish, Mr. Stern. I'm a Catholic. I go to St. Anthony's Church on Sundays, and to their school."

"Ach, maybe you do, but I know a fellow *landsman* ven I see one, and you, young man, are a Jew, whether you know it yet, or not."

I had no idea what Stern was talking about, but at least he was talking. I said, "Mr. Stern, I'd like to return this candy bar. I do not have the money to pay for it."

"Of course you don't, Mikey. How about ve make a deal?"

"Uh, deal? I don't know –"

"A deal. You're a Jew. Deals are in our blood, don't you know that?"

"Uh, Mr. Stern, I said –"

"Yah, yah, I know vat you said. Now here's the deal. Keep the Snickers bar, but sweep the floor for me. A good sweep. Sparkling clean. Can you do that?"

It sounded good, but I was worried about my parents finding this out. I said, "Yes, Mr. Stern, but suppose I agree to sweep your floor every day for the rest of the week, would you agree not to tell my parents about this…this…"

"Theft? Not tell your parents you tried to steal from an old Jew, from one of your own, Mikey?"

I had no idea how to respond, so I meekly said, "Yes, sir."

"Deal," he said laughing and extending his hand to me. "You *are* a Jew. A real little *macher.* A ten-year old deal maker. You'll go far in this life, Mikey Simon."

So I swept the floor, among other things, for the Stern's for the next eight years until I graduated from high school and joined the United States Army.

■   ■   ■

"Helluva story, Boss," Detective Micena said. "But what was Stern going on about knowing you were Jewish? I mean I know you are, but you told him you were a Catholic. What the hell was that all about?"

"That was what I was wondering, because as far as I knew I *was* a Catholic. I mean, Stern seemed to be an alright guy, but I had no idea what the hell he meant. I waited a few days and one night at the dinner table I said, 'Dad, are we Jewish?'"

"And your dad said?"

"He said nothing, but my older sister, Mary Beth, jumped up and said, 'Are you crazy? We're Catholics. Aren't you studying for your confirmation, retard?'"

"My father shifted in his seat and said, 'Why would you ask something like that, Mikey?'"

"All of a sudden I realized I should never have opened my mouth about this. I didn't dare mention Mr. Stern and open up that can of worms, so I said, 'A kid at school called me a lousy Jew because he figured our last name was Jewish.'"

'Simon is a common last name,' mom said. 'I'm sure there is every race and religion represented with our name. We happen to be Catholic.'

"Okay," I told her, digging into my potatoes and pretending to be satisfied with her answer.

"And that was the end of it?" John asked.

"Yeah, until I turned eighteen and my parents sat me down and told me the truth about myself."

"Oh, boy."

"Oh, boy, indeed, John. And it was a shocking story. My parents were not my parents at all. They formally adopted me at age eight months after my real parents were murdered in a night time home invasion. Kindly took me in and raised me as one of their own."

"Holy crap!"

"The man who raised me, who I always called my father, is my uncle – my real dad's brother. Uncle Alan Simon is Jewish. He married Elizabeth O'Toole, an Irish Catholic, and they had two daughters. Alan was not particularly religious and ceded the girls' upbringing and mine to his wife."

"Were you angry when they finally told you the truth?"

"At first, yes, but I shortly came around. They were – still are – good people, and I had a happy home growing up."

"You're half Jewish?"

"No, both my biological parents were Jewish. And my DNA results peg me as 99% Ashkenazi Jewish. And my father, Andy Simon, was a Nassau County cop."

"That's another amazing story. Did they ever solve your parents' murders?"

"Yes… and no. And that's a story for another time. Let's go back inside and see what was turned up by our forensic guys and the medical examiner."

. . .

The crime scene techs were not yet finished dusting for prints, working patiently and carefully around the cash register. "Got a couple of good ones here, Lieutenant," the senior technician said.

"Great," I said, "Let's hope they belong to our perp. Okay to come back there now?"

"Yes sir," he said.

There was something I wanted to check on. Hidden behind the register was a slot in the counter's back which led, through a short, square wooden tunnel, to a wooden money box screwed in place between two ceiling beams in the basement below. I had helped Mort construct it after he had been stuck-up at gunpoint for the third time. Anytime he got more than about thirty bucks in the register he'd slip a ten or a twenty into that slot to minimize his losses at the next robbery, which, sad to say, was certain to happen. I called over to John and said, "Let's go down into the basement. I want to check something out."

The single entrance to Mort's cellar was via the outside steel doors flush with the sidewalk. I pulled them up and went down the cement stairs, but the wooden door at the bottom of the steps was locked with a padlock. I said, "John, see if you can find Stern's keys and bring them down here."

"I took them from his pocket when the deputy medical examiner arrived. They're in a plastic bag with his other stuff. I'll go get them."

"What else did he have in his pockets?"

"An old pen knife, a handkerchief, and a wallet with six singles in it."

"No comb?"

"No, he's about as bald as a cue ball with just a few white hairs around the fringe. Didn't you notice?"

"Yeah, I noticed, but Mort used to have a thick head of hair and was a creature of habit."

"How old was he, Boss?"

I pondered over that for a moment and said, "I'm not certain. At least ninety. He survived the war – the Big War. He spent all of 1944 in Auschwitz until the Russkies liberated it in January of 1945. Did you notice the numbers tattooed on his forearm?"

"No. Jesus, Auschwitz?"

"Yeah, now I remember. He was thirty-seven, he told me, when the camp was liberated."

"That makes him ninety-two. My God, Mike, he survived the fucking Holocaust to die like this? What made him stay in this damned store all these years? Why –?"

"Because this was his life. He had other options and choices offered to him – and to his wife – but they refused to leave."

"But –"

"John, go get the keys. I'll finish the story after we wrap this scene up."

I walked back up the stairs with him and motioned over one of the uniformed cops who was keeping the on-lookers and the press at bay. I looked at her nameplate and said, "Officer Jamison, are you assigned to the sector car here?"

"Yes, sir, with my partner, Officer Ferrand."

"Don't leave here until I have a chance to chat with you both."

"Uh, I'll try Detective, but my sergeant wants us back on patrol ASAP."

"Inform your sergeant that Lieutenant Simon, Commanding Officer of Queens Homicide, will release you back on patrol at his earliest opportunity."

She snapped to attention saying, "Yes, sir, Lieutenant. Will do."

Micena came back with the keys and we went back down the cellar stairs, unlocked the door, and went inside. The dank, unfinished space was illuminated by a single hundred-watt bulb that flashed on when I flipped the switch inside the door. We both immediately noticed the wooden box lying on the floor, smashed open, the lid hanging off, and empty of all its contents. "I wonder how much the bastard got," John said.

"And I wonder how the hell he got it."

"What do you mean?"

"Did he shoot Mort, remove the keys from his pocket, come down here and unlock the door, break open this box after ripping it from the beams, go out and re-lock the door, go back upstairs, put the keys back in the old man's pocket, and then calmly leave?"

"I see what you mean. Let me check around some more."

It didn't take Detective John Micena long to discover a sizable hole in the ceiling near the rear of the basement. The old floor boards had been neatly sawn through between the beams, and the hole was big enough to slide through. Not big enough for me now, but when I was a skinny teenager it would not have been a problem. "This was no spur of the moment crime," John said. "This was planned out, and the perp knew exactly what he was looking for down here."

"I agree," I said. "Let's go back upstairs and get crime scene to check this out further."

. . .

When we went back into the store, the crime scene guys were packing up, but being the pros they were, they took their cameras and equipment, and headed to the basement at my request without a gripe. I said, "Let's take Mort's keys and go upstairs to his apartment and check it out."

"I didn't know he lived above his store," John said. "Guess he didn't travel far from here."

"No, not recently. In his younger days he and Lily would occasionally take the bus to Jamaica to see a movie. Or visit some Yiddish-speaking friends they had in the area. Maybe they'd stop for a beer at the local neighborhood joint, O'Gorman's Tavern, once-in-a-while."

"No car?"

"No car. No computer. No cell phone. One land line in the kitchen and in the store. One small TV in the living room."

"Rotary phone?" John asked with a smile.

"Nope, touchtone. And the TV is color." I said, smiling back.

I walked outside and went over to the uniformed officers. I spotted Jamison and said, "Officer, get your partner and come upstairs with me and Detective Micena."

John found the right key to the cylinder lock, and we walked up the cracked linoleum steps and into Mort Stern's sparse living quarters. A glance around the place showed no signs of disturbance. The bed was made. The dishes were drying in the rack next to the sink – a cup, a saucer, a small plate. A spoon and a fork. I motioned for everyone to take a seat in the living room. When everyone had settled in I said, "Here's what it looks like. Bad guy comes in and shoots Mort Stern. He goes to the back supply closet where he, or an accomplice, had recently cut a hole in the floor boards, goes down to the basement and breaks into the money box. He puts a wooden milk crate by the hole – it may have been under it already – climbs back up into the store and strolls out the front door. Anything to add to that, Detective Micena?"

"No, Boss, I think you got it figured out which means –"

"Which means this was done by someone with inside knowledge that Mr. Stern had a money box in the basement. Now tell me Officer Ferrand and Officer Jamison, who might have that knowledge?"

"The kid who works for Stern – the floor sweeper and box carrier," Ferrand replied.

"And his name is?"

"There have been three of them over the last few months, right Artie?"

"Right, Cindy. There was the kid from Mexico – Julio Sanchez, and the black kid, uh….Willie something…."

"I think it was Willie Turner," Jamison said. "And the white kid – the most recent employee – was Vinny DeGiglio."

"Good," I said. "Now tell us, Cindy and Artie, which one of those three killed Mordechai Stern and stole his money?"

"DeGiglio," they both said in unison.

"Explain, please."

Ferrand began, "Julio was a real good kid, and so was Willie. Julio had to go back to Mexico with his mother so she could tend to her sick father. That was about, uh –"

"Six months ago," Jamison said.

"Then Mort hired Willie who lasted about five months," Ferrand said.

"So this DeGiglio has been working here for how long?" Detective Micena asked.

"About five or six weeks." Jamison said. "Against our advice."

"Oh?" I said.

"It was obvious to us DeGiglio was a junkie, but Mort wouldn't be swayed," Ferrand said. "Told us everyone deserves a chance to earn a few bucks and straighten out."

"That was Mort," I said.

"Uh, sir, I think I noticed you on a few occasions coming out of the store. Was Mr. Stern a good friend of yours?"

"Like a father," I said. "Please continue."

"We were both certain Vinny's hard-earned dollars went right into his veins," Jamison said, "and we tried to intervene to get him some help, but he insisted he didn't have a problem."

"He's a good kid," Ferrand said. "Hard to believe he'd shoot Mort."

"Maybe he didn't. Maybe he just set it up," Micena said. "Maybe his habit demanded more money than he earned here."

"Let us go find this Vinny DeGiglio and persuade him to tell us," I said.

SIX

I had taken a liking to these two sharp, young patrol officers. They knew their assigned sector well, and it was obvious they cared about Mort Stern, which probably meant they cared about all the people on their beat, even a stone junkie named Vinny DeGiglio. I said, "Here's our initial plan of investigation. You two fine officers, assisted by four of my detectives, will find Vinny and bring him in for questioning."

Jamison and Ferrand looked at each other, appearing a bit stunned, and Jamison said, "Uh, Lieutenant, did you say four detectives will assist *us*?"

"I did. You two know what Vinny looks like, and we all don't. By the way, do you have any idea where he lives?"

"He takes the Q-10 Green Line bus to get to work, I know," Cindy said.

"I think he lives in Richmond Hill somewhere," Artie said. "I live up there, too, and saw him walking on Liberty Avenue one day. I know a lot of people around there."

"Drive back to the station house and change into your civvies. I'll call the detective squad and get you an unmarked car. My two homicide detectives, plus the two from the 106 Squad, will give us six cops to do a full-court press to scoop up DeGiglio before he leaves town, or before he overdoses from his newly-stolen wealth."

"But sir," Artie Ferrand said, "Our commanding officer, Captain McHale –"

"Don't worry, I'll clear your assignment with him. Now move out."

・　　・　　・

After they all left, Mort's death hit me again, and I plopped down hard in an armchair. I had something to do, and I had to do it sooner or later, as tough as it would be. I checked my address book and found the phone number of Mort and Lily's only child, Robert, who lived out on the West coast. I punched in the number using Mort's phone and Robert answered on the second ring saying, "Dad?"

"Hello Robert," I said. "It's Mike Simon."

"Mike? Uh, is anything wrong? Is my father all right?"

There was no easy way to do this so I said, "No, Robert, there was a robbery and Mort was shot. I'm sorry, but he's dead."

"Oh, my God! Why didn't he listen to me and Debbie? Why didn't –"

"Bobby, we both knew your parents were set deep in their ways despite what you offered them. A house in sunny California. No bills, no worries. Believe me I tried time and time again to convince them to make the move. And when Lily died I figured he'd call it quits here, but no, not Mort. 'Mikey,' he said. 'I'm an old New York Jew. Vat would I do vit all those *goyim* out there? Who vud I talk Yiddish vit?'"

"Yeah, he was beyond convincing, Mike, even though me and Debbie and his two grandkids are his only family now. I yelled at him that he was going to dry up and die in that crummy old candy store – turn into a decrepit mummy behind the counter. Do you know what he said? 'A good vay to go, no?'"

"He's at the morgue now. What do you want me to do? Do you have a funeral home in mind?"

"No, he was specific. 'Burn me up, Bobby. Take some ashes vit you to California. Throw a handful in front of the store right in front of the For Sale sign. Give some to Mikey. Put the rest by Lily's marker.'"

"I'm surprised he wanted to be cremated," I remarked. "I mean, you know, him being in Auschwitz –"

"It's sacrilegious, but as you know he was not a religious man, a non-believer as he said so many times. It's like his last act is spitting in the eye of the Lord himself."

"Yeah, I know. *Mort the Philosopher* and I had a lot of discussions about that."

"And what about you, Mike? What do you believe? Do you have any conflicts between your Catholic upbringing and your Jewish heritage?"

"No, Bobby, no conflict at all." I wanted to add there was no conflict because I now did not believe one word I had ever read, heard, or been taught in either religion. Not one. But Robert was a true believer, and this was not the time to challenge that, so we hung up and I awaited his arrival to take care of his beloved father.

Six million Jews murdered during the war.
My parents murdered when I was an infant.
Mort shot dead and lying on the floor.
There is no God.
Tell me I'm wrong.

.   .   .

While Robert was making plans to fly to New York to supervise his father's cremation, I made some plans of my own. If the effort to locate Vinny DeGiglio failed to pick him up in the next four to six hours, I'd have Ferrand and Jamison sit down with a sketch artist and draw up a composite photo of him for distribution in the metro area as a "person of interest" in the Stern homicide.

I had a bad feeling if we didn't grab DeGiglio soon we would have a hard time cracking the case. My guess was whoever killed Mort, and I didn't think it was DeGiglio himself, was savvy enough not to leave any fingerprints at the scene. Those latent prints lifted off the cash register were most likely Stern's or Vinny's, I figured, as I picked up the phone and called the Latent Print Section at the Police Lab. And, unfortunately, I was correct. Having worked fast on a homicide case, the technician, Detective Dave Metzdorf said, "Sorry, Loot, the prints we lifted off the register belong to Mr. Stern. All the other partials and smudges we lifted throughout the store were either his or unidentifiable."

"How about the money box in the basement?"

"No prints on it at all, even though the wood it was made of was smooth and varnished. The perp probably wore gloves."

Sanded and varnished by me thirty years ago.

"Any other evidence found by the crime scene guys you are aware of, Dave? Hairs? Fibers, maybe?"

"Yes on the fibers. A lot of them from the sawn edges of the hole in the floor the perp went through. And they collected some sawdust and wood samples from the floor, which was old and might be maple wood. It's all over in the lab being analyzed now. Give them a few days to figure it all out."

"Even if they identify the samples, that knowledge won't help us until we get the perp and the clothes he was wearing, right?"

"Right, Loot," Metzdorf said. "Tell Micena to go lock his ass up right now."

I knew what the technician was going to say next, with typical cynical police humor, when I responded to his comment. I played along and said what I knew he was expecting. "As soon as you tell me and Micena where the hell he is."

Metzdorf chuckled and said, "Sorry, Loot, but that's *your* job, right?"

. . .

I took one last look around Mort's apartment, but did not disturb anything, or do an unnecessary search I was certain would yield no helpful evidence. I'd let Robert and Debbie perform that sorrowful task when they arrived from the coast. I securely locked both the top and bottom doors of his apartment and went back into the store.

After Mort's body had been removed to the morgue and the crime scene truck had rolled away, the onlookers gradually drifted off, encouraged to do so by the uniformed officers stationed there. A patrol sergeant came up to me and said, "Is the scene secured, Lieutenant?"

"Yes," I said. "I'm going to take one last look around and then lock it up. You can have your guys remove the crime scene tape and resume patrol."

"Yes, sir. Uh, where's the sector car?"

"Back at the house. Jamison and Ferrand are changing into civvies. They'll be working with me for a while."

"Uh, for how long?"

"For as long as it takes, Sarge."

"They're both fairly new on the job, you know."

"Yeah, but sharp, too. Did you train them?"

"Yes, I did, sir," he said, puffing out his chest.

"You did a good job. They'll be a big help with this investigation."

The sergeant smiled, snapped off a salute, and said, "I'm sure they will, sir. Anything else we can do for you before we wrap it up?"

"Yes, station one officer at the front door until the shift changes at midnight. The sector car can keep an eye on it from time to time."

"You got it, Loot. Uh, any suspects yet?"

"We're looking at a former employee who Ferrand and Jamison know and can identify. I hope we can scoop him up and put this case to bed fast."

"So do I. I knew Mort a long time, too. Sad ending for a real good man."

"That it was, Sarge. That it was."

I walked through Stern's for the last time. The For Sale sign would no doubt be on the front door as Robert and Debbie were winging their way back to California. I gazed around looking for any evidence the crime scene guys might have missed, though I had no hopes there would be any. But my mind was not on evidence of a crime, it was awash in nostalgia as it reeled back the years to when I was a teenager. I sat on one of the round, red vinyl-covered swivel stools, spun around on it and said aloud, "I'm done sweeping, Mr. Stern. All the soda crates and candy cartons are put away and stacked neat, and all the unsold newspapers and magazines are tied and bundled for return."

"So?" he would say. "That's vat I pay you for *bubala*. Good for you. *Geh Heim.*"

Go home. But he knew what I wanted, so I didn't move off the stool. "Uh, Mr. Stern —"

"Vat? Oh, I suppose you vant an egg cream, huh?"

He was busting my chops, like he did almost every day I worked there after I finished up my chores, making me wait and beg for one of his delicious chocolate egg creams, a drink only a New York candy store owner — preferably a Jewish one — could concoct. And I always respectfully replied, "Yes, I do, Mr. Stern."

I remembered the first time he had made one for me at the end of my first week of sweeping the floor for him. He passed it across the counter and said, "You got money to pay for this, right?"

"Uh, not right now, Mr. Stern," I said. "I thought maybe if I continued to work for you, maybe when I got paid –"

"No *geld?* Maybe you vant to steal this egg cream, too? Like you stole the Snickers bar?"

I was humiliated and a tear started down my cheek. I got off the stool and turned to leave vowing to never set foot in the place again when Mort's hand on my shoulder stopped me. "Mikey," he said, "I am so sorry I said that. That was bad of me. Ach! Vat's wrong vit me? How could I say such a hurtful thing? Drink up. No charge. And from now on this is an addition to your pay. Every day, one free chocolate egg cream for my hard-working Mikey. Okay?"

"Okay," I said, taking a large gulp from the glass. And true to his word, Mort Stern never said another hurtful word to me again for the rest of his life, and I never had to pay for an egg cream again. His life. Snuffed out by some street skell who I now vowed to hunt down and arrest, and hoped he would resist that arrest so I could exact some street justice on his murdering body. Then a shadow from the past crossed my mind as I remembered I vowed to hunt down and arrest my parents' killer, the one that got away, and so far I had failed at that, hadn't I?

I went back to the cleaning closet and took the spaghetti mop and bucket and filled it halfway with water. I mopped up Mort's blood from the floor and rinsed the mop of all traces of it in the slop sink. I selected the floor broom and deliberately and carefully swept Mort's floor for the last time. When I finished, I glanced behind the empty counter and said, "All done, Mr. Stern. I'm going home. Good night."

I set the lock on the front door, closed it tightly, and locked the deadbolt with the key from Mort's keychain. I went over to speak to the patrolman assigned to guard duty. "I know this fixed post is a boring assignment, but don't be concerned about taking a little stroll once in a while for a cup of coffee. I doubt anyone will attempt to break in, but you never know."

"Anything valuable in there, sir?"

"Only my memories, son, and they're not worth anything to a burglar."

"Understood, sir. I'll take good care of Mr. Stern's property."

SEVEN

I got on the radio and asked the location of my three teams of investigators. The two teams of detectives responded that they were cruising areas of Richmond Hill and Woodhaven near the streets where the Q-10 bus stopped on its way north to the subway station on Union Turnpike. Cindy and Artie were switching between foot and car patrol on Liberty Avenue looking for Vinny and talking to people. None of them had a lead yet on Vinny's whereabouts. I said, "Keep at it. I'll be in the area. Let me know immediately if something pops."

Not twenty minutes later Unit 106-C got on the air. I recognized Cindy Jamison's voice as she said, "We got an address where our guy may be."

"Let's have it," I said.

"118-80 Liberty Avenue," Officer Ferrand responded. "It's on the second floor above a delicatessen. The el runs right by it. Uh, we got the location from a snitch I know in the neighborhood. I slipped him a twenty for the info."

"Good work," I said. "You'll get reimbursed for that. Let's all meet on the nearest side street near that address right now."

"Uh, Lieut, this is Unit 106-E. Should we get a warrant first?"

I was pissed off that this detective, Tom Catalano, from the 106 squad would broadcast that over the air. All radio transmissions are recorded and occasionally monitored. I then realized I could turn this in our favor. I said, "It's not necessary, Tom. Our guy is not a suspect at this time, merely a person of interest. We're going to knock on his door and politely request an interview. Understood?"

All three units responded with a "Ten-four" and I held my breath waiting for one of them to add, "Do we kick it in if he doesn't open up?" Thankfully, no one did.

Fifteen minutes later we convened in front of the door that led to the upstairs apartment on Liberty Avenue under the full darkness of night and I said, "Hit the bell, John."

Detective Micena's efforts at getting a response from the apartment's occupants were in vain despite pushing on the button for a good two minutes. Since we couldn't hear a buzz or chime, we had no idea if the bell was functional. I tried the doorknob, but the door was locked. It was a shaky latch, so with not much effort, I slipped it open with a credit card. After sending Catalano and his partner to the rear of the building, I led the way to the top of the stairs and motioned for Ferrand to try the bell on the door jamb. I put my ear to the door but couldn't hear a buzz. I knocked on the door a few times. I knocked louder and said, "Mr. DeGiglio, open the door! Police officers!"

When there was no response, I tried the doorknob. Locked. And this lock was no pushover like the one downstairs. Contrary to the door smashes seen on the TV police shows, any similar attempts by us to crash it in would have resulted in a broken foot or a dislocated shoulder. Damn it! I felt around on top of the door and checked under the mat. No key. I said to Detective Paul, "Richie, check the deli downstairs. It was open when we got here. Maybe he's the landlord or knows if the landlord is nearby. Please come back with this key. I don't want to call Emergency Services."

Paul nodded and went down the stairs. He was back in five minutes with a big smile on his face and a key in his outstretched hand. He said, "His brother owns the building, and he keeps a key here in case he has to get in for something."

"No problems getting him to cough it up?"

"Not at all. I spoke some German to him and we got along fine."

I had heard some wild stories about Detective Paul when he was in a South Bronx squad and I said, "I guess your German came in handy when you dressed up in that Nazi uniform you guys had in the 40 Squad?"

John Micena, who had been Richie's partner for the past five years, and who probably had heard his stories more than once, could hardly suppress a grin. He said, "Boss, Richie said that story is a nasty rumor." Then he turned to Richie and said, "Vere are your papers, you zun-of-a-bitch!"

Everyone cracked up with laughter including me – the boss – who was losing control of the situation. "Knock it off. Open the door Paul, and let's hope DeGiglio didn't escape out the back window."

"Doesn't matter," he said. "Catalano and Nitzky will catch his ass if he tries that."

"Let's find out," I said as Richie unlocked the door and the five of us rushed in, guns drawn, and went in separate directions. No one was in the apartment. No one, that is, except for the apparently dead young man slouched on the sofa, eyes half open, dried spittle on his chin. The hypodermic needle, empty of its contents, was stuck in his left arm. Several glassine bags – empty – were scattered nearby, and the foul odor of the corpse's feces permeated the air.

I broke the silence by saying, "Is that him?"

Officer Ferrand, gagging a bit, responded, "That's him, sir. That's Vinny DeGiglio."

"Shit!" said Micena.

"Shit, indeed," Detective Paul said, waving at the space in front of his face. "I wonder if this is a typical overdose or if the real perp gave him a hot shot."

Micena bent down to more closely examine the glassine envelopes. He said, "They're all stamped in red with the letters HHC." Turning to the two cops he said, "Recognize them?"

Cindy and Artie both said no, and I said, "We'll get Narco involved. Maybe they can point us in the right direction. Start making the calls, John."

So here we went again for the second time that day. Crime scene search, medical examiner, assistant district attorney on call, all of it. Two dead ones. The first one is now a goddamned whodunit, the second one is either an accident, or another goddamned whodunit. It was time to take a break and put our heads together over a beer or two. I said, "After we wrap this scene up we'll meet at *Gallagher's* and think this whole thing out."

"Uh, sir," Officer Ferrand said, "Cindy and I, too?"

"Yes. You're with this team until I say you're not. I'll clear your overtime with your commanding officer."

"Thank you, sir," they both said with big smiles on their young faces.

.   .   .

John's call to Queens Narcotics resulted in the arrival of two of their detectives at our scene. After we briefed them on the Stern shooting, Detective Lou Isnardi said, "HHC means Happy Horse Combo. We see it a lot in the north part of the boro – Corona, Jackson Heights, Astoria – and as far south as Jamaica and South Jamaica."

"What does it mean?" I asked.

"Horse, as we all know, is heroin. The combo part can be added cocaine or ground up Quaaludes. Either one makes it a powerful hit."

"How many bags would it take to kill our guy here?" John Micena asked.

"Not nearly as many as are laying empty here," the other narcotics detective, George Geyer, said.

"Could he have shot all of this at once?" I asked. "I mean, if it's so powerful, wouldn't one or two bags be enough to get him high?"

"Depends on his habit," Isnardi said, "but yeah, two should have been plenty to do the trick."

"Who's the big distributor of HHC?" Paul asked.

"Not sure," Isnardi said. "We'll kick it around with the rest of the squad and get the word out to our informants to concentrate on this for you."

"Thanks, guys," I said. "We're about ready to wrap up here and ship the body out. Care to join us at *Gallagher's* for a couple of brews?"

"Love to, Lieutenant," Geyer said, "but we got a buy/bust going down in an hour."

"Find me the guy who sold HHC to our dead guy here and next time the drinks are on me."

"You're on," Isnardi said as he and Geyer headed out the door.

After the deputy ME had examined the body, I had crime scene swab his hands for gunshot residue even though I was now convinced he was not our shooter. Vinny had nothing in his pockets except four one-dollar bills. I said to the lead crime scene tech, "Look for any weapons, but a couple of other things that may be pertinent."

"Such as, Lieutenant?"

"Tools," I said. "Our perp sawed a hole in some floorboards and went through it."

"I'm aware the team in Stern's store found fibers – blue ones – on the edge of the hole. We'll look for that shirt or jacket, and check all his clothes for sawdust as well. And any tools, saws and drills we may find."

"Great," I said as they went to work. We hung around until they finished. They found no guns or blue-colored garments, but did come up with a hand drill and a keyhole saw that had some bits of wood in its teeth. They bagged them up and took them for forwarding to the lab.

"Looks like Vinny cut the hole himself a few hours or so prior to the stick-up," John said, "and the shooter went through the hole."

"Yes, it does," I said. "Now let's go find that shooter."

We locked the place up and kept the key as the deli was now closed. I told Richie to return it tomorrow and tell the deli owner to notify his brother the apartment now needed a new tenant.

"Ja wohl, mein Leutnant," he said, snapping to attention and saluting.

We all chuckled and headed to *Gallagher's* for a much needed libation.

Gallagher's was a police hangout located on Lefferts Blvd., on the border of the 102 and 106 precincts, and it drew cops and detectives from both commands. We got a booth and ordered two pitchers of Michelob. The waitress put down a few bowls of pretzels and potato chips, and I eyed my crew as we awaited our beer.

Two young police officers, Ferrand and Jamison, their unlined happy faces bursting with enthusiasm, and obviously thrilled to be working on a murder case with us. Tom Catalano and Dan Nitzky from the 106 Detective Squad, seasoned veterans about my age – early forties – but not experienced in homicide investigations as were my two top guys on the case. Catalano, about twenty pounds overweight, mostly in his belly, rarely smiled and had a habit of running his hand through his curly, graying hair which had thinned out noticeably since I had last seen him a couple of years ago. Maybe he was feeling for new growth. Dan Nitzky was tall and thin with combed-back grayish-blond hair. He had what you would call smiling blue eyes, and he was quick with a witty remark or joke. Glancing at Richie Paul, the similarity in the color of their blue eyes – ice blue – was startling. Richie, while equally witty and funny as Dan, could turn those eyes on a suspect in such a way to make the bad guy's blood run cold. *Nazi* eyes we called them to break his chops, but it didn't seem to faze him – he seemed to relish it. He was of German and Irish descent, but down-played his Irish half saying, "The Irish are too merry for this job, that's why they study so hard and get to be top brass and off the dirty streets. Gotta submerge that good-guy tendency. Gotta be tough on these scumbags."

Denise, our waitress, poured our first round and as we raised our glasses, Detective John Micena said, "A toast to this team and to the arrest of the skell that shot Mort Stern."

We all took a long pull with shouts of "here, here" and I smiled at my senior man with the nickname *Johnny the Jack* which was hung on him years ago when he was a uniformed cop in a tough Brooklyn precinct. He claimed it was an unfair representation of him saying, "I used necessary and sufficient force on my perps in order to effect the arrest. And if my blackjack, duly authorized by the department to be utilized, was necessary, so be it."

That always got a laugh and a comment such as "Yeah, and your utilization of that jack got you four trips to Internal Affairs, right?"

John would smile that big Italian smile, his cheeks would redden a bit and his light-brown eyes would open wide as he said, *"Five* trips, and not one rap on my record from those fucking head hunters. How about that, wise guy?"

The first two pitchers of beer disappeared and Denise brought two more. I was happy with the camaraderie developing among the team and I decided to keep things light awhile longer. But things got serious in a hurry when Dan Nitzky asked Richie Paul about the rumor the 40 Detective Squad in the Bronx had a Nazi uniform to dress up in and terrify some suspects. Richie said, "In light of what happened to Mort Stern, an Auschwitz survivor, let's put that rumor on hold. I know I kid around a lot, but we can all agree that story would not be appropriate at this time. What would be appropriate is to decide how we are going to catch our perp. We should finish our beer, and get to it. Right, Boss?"

Talk about setting the stage and getting a cue. Richie went up another notch in my eyes for that little speech. I said, "We will all meet in the 106 Squad at 0800 tomorrow. First we will re-canvass along Rockaway Blvd. for a possible suspect seen going into or coming out of Stern's store. We might get lucky, as the crime was committed in broad daylight."

"Do you think Vinny was at the scene at all?" Cindy Jamison asked. "Or did he just cut the hole and leave?"

"He could have hung around as a lookout or to drive the getaway car," I said.

"He doesn't own a car," Ferrand said. "Uh, that I know of. He always took the bus."

"Then our perp may have a car," Micena said, "and maybe somebody saw it."

"Maybe," I said, "but unless we have new information to act on, I want John and Richie to follow up with Queens Narcotics and the rest of you to perform the canvass. Any questions?"

There were none so I said, "Drink up. I got the tab. You guys chip in for Denise's tip. See you tomorrow."

EIGHT

It had been a long day, a long, sad, depressing day, and I guess it showed on my face when I walked in the door at 9:30 that night. My wife, Vivian, who I had called briefly to inform her of Mort's murder before she saw it on the evening news said, "Can I get you a drink, hon?"

"I had a couple beers with the guys, but I could use a nightcap. First, I want – I need – a big hug and kiss from the love of my life."

She hugged me hard and kissed me hard all the while choking back tears and sobs. She knew Mort Stern well, as did my two teenage kids. They all had been subject to the diabolical philosophical arguments from the wise, old Yiddish sage of Ozone Park.

"You need a drink, too," I said. "What'll it be? I'll make them."

"Pour me whatever you're having – on the rocks."

I went into the kitchen and made us vodkas on ice, at least a double, and brought them back into the living room. We clinked glasses and I said, "To Mort, may he rest in peace."

We took a long sip and Vivian said, "Despite what that old *kvetcher* believed, or said he believed, I know there is a God, and that Mort is with him."

"*Kvetcher*? From a puritanical Lutheran?"

"Mort taught me well," she said smiling. "I now know a lot of Yiddish words and phrases, some not too flattering."

"Where are the kids?" I asked.

"Andrew is in his room, studying I hope, and Maddy is over at some friend's house, also studying."

"You hope."

"We hope. These two are getting a bit difficult."

"They are teenagers," I said. "They know everything, and they are a pain in the ass to their parents, same as we were. Uh, do they know about Mort?"

"Yes, I told them."

"And?"

"Tears and anger. And a surprising amount of profanity."

"Oh?"

"Andrew said, 'Don't worry, Dad will get that son-of-a-bitch.'"

"He's fourteen, and he did love Grandpa Mort."

"That's not all of it, I'm ashamed to say."

"I'm all ears."

"Our sweet, beautiful, sixteen-year old daughter said, 'I hope they cut the balls off that son-of-a-bitch!'"

"And you said?"

"I'm still in shock. She stormed out of the house. What do you think?"

"I think she'll probably be a cop someday. Drink up and let's go to bed. I have another long day tomorrow. And they will all be long days until I catch that son-of-a-bitch, as Maddy so eloquently put it."

. . .

With no new information on our plate, I dispatched my six cops after our morning coffee. They were all out the door by 8:15 a.m. I stopped in to chat with the CO of the 106 Squad, Lieutenant Bert Simmons, and thanked him for the use of Catalano and Nitzky on our murder case. "As if I could have objected," he said with a smile and reaching out to shake my hand. We had been academy classmates over twenty years ago, and we both were contenders for the position I now held. If Bert had any hard feelings about losing out, he never mentioned them, or treated me other than as a friend. Besides, his number was coming up soon on the captain's promotional list. He should get those gold railroad tracks in less than a year, I figured.

I walked down the end of the hall to chat with the precinct CO, Captain Glen McHale, again thanking him for the use of his two officers. He said, "Glad to help, Mike, but how valuable can they be to you?"

"I know they only have a couple years on the job, but they both have been of great assistance, so far." I explained how they identified and located Vinny DeGiglio and what I had them doing now.

"How long do you need them?"

"I know your manpower is squeezed, Captain, so let me say, no longer than necessary. I'd like for them to be in on the bust which I'm hopeful will be soon. Can you give me three days?"

"Three days? Not bad. I figured you were going to say three weeks."

"If we don't crack this in three days we'll be in for a long haul – probably longer than three weeks."

"Bert Simmons told me the victim was an old friend of yours."

"Yeah, that he was. He was a thick-headed survivor who wouldn't give up running his store. It shouldn't have happened."

"I hope you collar the perp soon."

"Thanks, Captain, and thanks again for Jamison and Ferrand."

I drove away and checked in with my guys on the radio, but they were all out of their vehicles, working hard knocking on doors, I figured. I called Queens Narcotics and got a hold of John and Richie who said they were waiting for information from the street snitches and were going to go out with Geyer and Isnardi to see what they could scare up. I told them I was going down to the area being canvassed and to meet me in my office in Queens Homicide at 1600 hours for a debriefing.

.　　.　　.

I spotted Tom Catalano coming out of a grocery store and waved him over. He said, "I got nothing so far, but we are going slow and thorough."

"Good. When all four of you wrap up, meet me back at my homicide office at 1600 hours."

"Will do, and I hope we have some decent info by then."

"Me, too, Tom. See you later."

I cruised around the area and as I passed Stern's, I spotted Robert and Debbie unlocking the front door. I pulled over to the curb and followed them inside. I knew Robert had a duplicate set of keys to Mort's building, and I reached into my pocket and got Mort's set, handing them to him.

We hugged each other and a few tears were shed by all. Robert said Mort would be cremated this afternoon and that Mort's ashes would be FedEx'd back to him in San Diego. "Do you still want some, Mike, like Mort wanted to give you?"

"Yes," I said. "I plan to put them around the graves of my parents."

"Ah, Mikey, the parents you never knew. Such sadness. Such unfairness."

I wanted to respond with something like, *Unfairness? Where was God?* But this was not the time to do that to these good people, so I said, "Yes, much."

Robert mentioned he had contacted a real estate agent to list the building for sale. I showed him and Debbie the hole in the closet floor and explained how it had gone down and that Vinny DeGiglio had overdosed.

"So you think his supplier had Vinny set the robbery up?"

"That's exactly what we think, and we are vigorously pursuing that right now."

"Mike, when you catch that bastard put one right between his eyes for me, will you?"

"Robert!" Debbie said. "Mike is not a vigilante. He must proceed within the criminal justice system."

"Yeah, I know. The system we now have where murderers go free on a technicality, or for some phony police procedural error."

"I'll make certain we do it correctly, Robert. Rest assured of that."

"And if you do it all correctly, and he still skates?" Robert asked.

"Then Mike will put two bullets in his head, one for you and one for me," Debbie said.

Robert opened his eyes in surprise and said, "From my wife, the bleeding heart liberal?"

"In this case, dear, my heart only bleeds for my father-in-law, and I do hope justice prevails and it won't be necessary to resort to violence, despite what I said."

"I hope so too, Debbie. I'll keep you informed of our progress. I have six good cops on this. I'll add more if necessary."

We parted ways and I headed back to my office, weighted down in sadness and the utter unfairness of things.

. . .

By four p.m. my team of six and I were assembled in my office, and I knew from the occasional contacts I had with them during the day it had been a productive one. "Let's have the canvass results first," I said.

There was silence until Tom Catalano said, "Go ahead, Cindy. You found the prize."

"That's because I started with the businesses directly across the street from Stern's candy store, and I got lucky."

"How lucky?" I asked.

"Got a description of the perp, his car, and an I.D. on DeGiglio."

"All from the same witness?"

"No, from three different witnesses. Two saw DeGiglio, two saw the perp, and all three saw the car."

"Continue," I said, getting really interested now.

"Putting their observations all together, we have a car pull up to the curb on Rockaway Blvd. with two males in it. They both get out and walk toward Stern's, looking around, 'acting suspicious' as one witness put it. DeGiglio stays outside and the other guy goes into Stern's. Not more than ten minutes later he comes out, nods to DeGiglio, and they casually walk back to the car, get in and drive away."

"Did any of those witnesses hear a gunshot?" I asked.

"No, sir. Rockaway Blvd. is wide, and a lot of traffic was whizzing by in both directions."

"Plate number?"

"No plate number, but maybe something as good."

"Oh?"

"The left front fender on the otherwise black car was painted gray prime, probably a replacement awaiting a finish coat."

"What kind of car?"

"No consensus. The three witnesses were relatively elderly and said all cars now look alike to them. They couldn't even say if it was a foreign or domestic make."

"Good job, Cindy," I said. "You got their statements, right?"

"Uh, no, but Detectives Catalano and Nitzky did when I called them to the area."

"Understood," I said, realizing this type of detailed statement taking was beyond Cindy and Artie's expertise at this stage of their career.

"Right here, Boss," Catalano said, patting a manila file folder on the desk. "We got a good description of the perp which we immediately gave to Richie and John who were in Queens Narcotics. And good on the car, as well."

"John?"

"We got the descriptions out to the rest of the narcotics squad, the anti-crime units, and the uniform force in all the local precincts."

"Great work," I said. "Now we wait for something to break. I can't see driving aimlessly around the borough without a more defined area to search for that car."

"Narco feels their informants will turn up something soon," Richie Paul said.

"We're not going home anytime soon. Let's get dinner. And no beer – coffee would be more appropriate. If something goes down tonight I want us all sharp and I don't want a detectable drop of alcohol in our blood. Agree?"

They all agreed, but I saw a perplexed look on Artie Ferrand's young face. I said, "In case we have to shoot somebody, Artie. Wouldn't go over too well with Internal Affairs if you had a high blood-alcohol level, would it?"

"Uh, right, sir. I wouldn't have thought of that. How –"

"Experience, Artie. Let's leave it at that."

NINE

After we ate at a local diner, we adjourned back to my office and we put a fresh pot of coffee on the burner. As we nervously awaited a call, we did what cops were prone to do to pass the time – tell war stories of our past exploits, cases, and situations. John Micena egged on his partner saying, "I know you don't want to talk about the SS uniform out of respect for Mort Stern, but surely you can tell this group about Harvey."

"Harvey?" Catalano asked when Richie stayed silent.

"Come on, Richie," Nitzky said. "I need a good laugh now."

"Dan's right," I said. "We'll get serious again when the phone rings. Let's hear it."

Richie Paul sighed and said, "Okay, you asked for it. There was an old movie where Jimmy Stewart had an invisible friend, a giant rabbit, named Harvey. One of my team members in the 40 Squad, I won't mention his name, decided to get his own giant rabbit. He found a rabbit costume in a shop in Manhattan. It had white fur, a pink nose, big feet, paws, and big floppy ears which were pink on the inside. He loved wearing that thing and called himself Harvey when he had it on."

"He wore it around the squad?" Cindy asked.

"Only on special occasions," Richie said, "like when a suspect was reluctant to confess to him or another detective."

"I don't get it." Ferrand said, but all of us seasoned detectives present in my office knew what was coming.

"He would put on the rabbit outfit in another room and walk, no, *hop*, into the interrogation room. He had a large carrot in his hand, uh, his *paw*, which he had made at home and inside the carrot, was his nightstick. In a squeaky rabbit voice he would say, 'You don't want to talk, tough guy?' And then he would whack the suspect a few times. Sometimes, more than a few times, and hop away."

"Did the suspect confess?" Artie Ferrand asked, obviously enthralled with the story.

"Most of the time," Richie said, "but that was a long time ago, and we don't beat suspects anymore."

John Micena chuckled and said, "And that's a damn shame. I had to retire my blackjack."

"Are you putting us rookies on?" Cindy asked with a smile creeping up on her face.

"Not at all," Richie said. "But all good things come to an end. One guy who had been knocked around by Harvey said, 'I was in Vietnam and I would have rather been captured by the Viet Cong than you guys,' and he told all about being beaten by Harvey to his lawyer and to the judge. The judge, a former assistant district attorney, told him he was crazy and disregarded his claims. But when a second defendant told a similar story a few weeks later, the wise judge called the squad commander and whispered, 'Bout time to retire the fuckin' rabbit, Lieutenant. Time to put him back on the farm, don't you think?' And that was the end of Harvey."

Other stories followed from all of us, including me, but none could top Harvey the rabbit. We were about laughed out, and Richie had started to put on another pot of coffee when the phone finally rang. I motioned for John, the lead detective, to pick it up. He listened for a moment and then pressed the button to activate the speaker phone. Detective Geyer said, "We got him spotted."

We all sucked in a breath and I said, "Give us the details, George."

"One of our snitches came through with his name and he definitely identified that his car had a primed front fender. His name is Ismael Rosario and he deals on Jamaica Avenue and Liberty Avenue in the 102, 103, and 106 precincts. Anti-Crime spotted him and phoned it in. I dispatched a couple of my undercover guys to see if they could make a buy from him. If they're successful we'll bust him right away and then he's all yours."

"Great job, George," I said. "Got an address on Rosario?"

"Yeah, a house on 146 Street between Jamaica and Hillside Avenues. He probably rents a room or apartment there."

"If all goes as planned, take him to your office in the 109 precinct and we'll interrogate him there," I said.

"You got it, Loot. Hope to call you real soon."

.　　.　　.

In my experience, narcotics cases – particularly buy-bust operations – rarely go as planned, and this one was no exception. When one of the UC's approached Rosario's car and asked to buy some smack, Rosario immediately smelled a rat and said, "Who the fuck are you to ask me that?" He peeled away and Anti-Crime, not wishing to further spook him, followed him from afar, but lost him. But we knew where he lived. And he had to go home eventually. "Ready for a stakeout?" I asked.

"Shouldn't we get some paper first?" John asked.

"Yes. You and Richie get a hold of the ADA on call and get an arrest warrant and a search warrant for his car and pad. We got more than sufficient probable cause to take him without it, but I want to do this strictly by the book. This is a murder case, and I don't want anything we find to be excluded in court by some sleazy defense attorney."

"We're on our way," Richie said, grabbing his suit jacket and heading out the door with Micena.

I told Nitzky and Catalano to split up and partner with Ferrand and Jamison. "Here's what I want you to do as we wait for the warrants. Take turns driving by the perp's house. Do it alternately, once every twenty minutes, so we don't spook him again. In between, patrol the main avenues in his distribution area to maybe spot him. But don't do anything until we have all our paper in hand. Loose and easy guys, I want to take him down when he is tucked away, fast asleep in his bed. Understood?"

They all nodded and eagerly jumped into action. This surveillance was most likely unnecessary, but I knew cops and these cops wanted to be in on the action in any manner they could. They were sick of sitting around doing nothing. So was I. After they left, I finished my fifth or sixth cup of coffee, stopped at the bathroom to eliminate the previous cups now straining my bladder, and headed for my car.

It was nearing eleven o'clock and Rosario still hadn't arrived home. I guess the drug business was going well in the Boro of Queens. My cell phone rang and it was Tom Catalano. He said he had grown up not far away in a house similar to Rosario's and there might be a problem. "Tell me," I said.

"These homes have three entrances. The front door leads into the main floor living area. A side door leads directly up to the second floor apartment, and a back door, six steps down, goes into the basement apartment. Unless there's a big family occupying the whole place, it's usually three separate apartments."

"Unless we know which door Rosario goes in, if we get lucky and spot him, we're going to need three teams to kick in three separate doors. Shit!"

"I got an idea, Boss. Put a guy in the backyard and one across the street. When Rosario comes home, we'll know precisely which one is his pad. Uh, but it can't be one of us."

"Why not?"

"We're all palefaces here. This is primarily a black and Central American neighborhood. We will be made immediately."

"Okay Tom, I'll get a couple of dark faces from Narco. I'll head over there now. Let's hope we can get them in place before Rosario shows up."

Not a minute later a plainclothes Anti-Crime unit got on the air saying they had Rosario spotted on Liberty Avenue in the 102 precinct. He was sitting in his car apparently waiting for customers. All units had been briefed that we were going to take him at his pad, but I reinforced that. I said, "Ten-four, Anti-Crime. Just observe, but let us know if he pulls away."

Rosario's location was about five miles from his home and I needed him to stay there a little bit longer. I hit the gas and ten minutes later I pulled up in the parking lot of the 109 Precinct, where Queens Narcotics had their home. I had called ahead and told them what I needed and when I arrived, the supervisor in charge, Sergeant Nellis, said, "I got your guys, Loot. Charlie Evans and Doug Monroe."

"Thanks, Jack," I said looking at the two brown-skinned detectives. I didn't know Monroe, but Evans and I had a long history together.

"Lieutenant," Charlie said, "I understand you need a couple of spooks to hide in the bushes. We's it."

Charlie Evans had been, is, and will always be, politically incorrect and racially insensitive to everyone, including his brown-skinned brothers. Having walked adjoining foot posts with him in the East New York section of Brooklyn, the notorious 75 Precinct, I can attest to that. "Hey, Jew boy" was his favorite greeting for me followed by a witticism like, "Got your yarmulke on under your uniform cap," or, "I don't want to catch you praying and bowing your head all night in front of the brick wall next to the Jewish deli." I could go on and on, but I snapped back to the present and said, "Let's go, I want you two in place ASAP."

They got in my car after we picked up three walkie-talkies, and I stepped on it. Fortunately, Rosario had not shown, and I drove by his house pointing out where I wanted them positioned. "Yassir, Massa," Evans said. "Me and Monroe be your niggers in the woodpile. We be hiding real good, boss man."

I glanced over at Monroe who was shaking his head, but he had a little smile on his lips.

"Does he ever stop, Doug?"

"Never, Lieutenant."

"I worked with him for a few years in the 75 Precinct, and he damned near drove me crazy. You know how many times I wanted to shove my nightstick down his throat?"

Monroe laughed and said, "Yeah, 'bout as many times as I wanted to go upside his head with my slapper."

"Hey, you motherfuckers," Evans said. "I am here, you know. Right here in the fucking back seat."

Ignoring his outburst Monroe said, "However, the problem we have with Charlie here is he is one helluva good cop."

"That he is," I said, "as I can attest to from our days in Brooklyn."

Evans was momentarily stunned by our comments, and when he recovered he said, in a perfect WASP tone of voice, "Thank you, gentlemen. It is about time you recognized the immense talent in my well-toned, well-educated body."

I pulled up a block and a half away and said, "Go find your hiding places. When you get a block from the car let's have a radio check. Use the talk-around frequency for the three of us."

The radios worked loud and clear and five minutes later they both radioed in they were securely hidden at their locations. "Deep in the motherfuckin' woodpile, Massa," was the way Evans put it.

"Me, too, Loot," Monroe said.

.　　.　　.

The wait was on and I pulled all vehicle surveillance well away from the house. Rosario seemed to be a street-savvy operator and who knew if he had another pad he could scurry to. Nitzky and Jamison spotted the car at 1:14 a.m. heading west on Jamaica Avenue. It turned north on 146 Street and Nitzky said, "I believe the bird is heading to his nest."

"Ten-four. Stay off the air. I'll take it from here with our two spotters." I keyed the walkie-talkie and said, "He's heading home."

Three minutes later Monroe said, "Heard a car door slam about a half block away."

Thirty seconds later he whispered, "Here he comes on my side of the street."

Another twenty seconds went by and Monroe said, "He's done looking around and he crossed the street. He's not going for the front door. Coming your way, Charlie."

"Ten-four," Charlie whispered.

One minute went by, then two. Finally, Charlie said, "He's in the basement. The door seems solid, but light is coming out of the window about five feet from it."

"Stay put until the light goes out and radio me back then."

"I hope the motherfucker be tired. I'm sick of this nigger in the woodpile shit."

"Tough it out, Leroy," I said. "I knows you can do it."

"Yassir," he whispered.

I got on the car radio and informed the team Rosario was in the basement apartment and we would wait at least a half hour after the lights went out before we broke in. Our search and arrest warrants were of the "No-Knock" type and endorsed for night service. Fifteen minutes later my walkie-talkie came to life with Evans's voice whispering, "Light's out. I have it at 1:33 a.m."

"Give it fifteen minutes Charlie, and then quietly check out that door."

"Gotcha," he said. "Want me to come out with that information?"

"If you are sure you won't be seen," I said.

"Duh, it's nighttime and so dark out I can't see my hand in front of my face. But if I could it would still be black, like the fuckin' rest of me."

"Unless you looked at the *palm* of your hand. That'd be white, right?"

"Wise-ass, Jew," he muttered.

Twenty minutes later Doug and Charlie were back in my car and Charlie said, "Not too good, Mike."

"Why?"

"The door is solid wood and the door jamb is steel and surrounded by a poured concrete foundation. And with a lotta rebar in it, no doubt."

"What about the locks?"

"A key in knob that's kinda flimsy. I tried it by the way. But there are *three* deadbolts. One about a foot from the bottom, one six inches above the door knob, and one about a foot from the top."

"Shit! Do you think ESB's door jamb spreader can do the trick?"

"I doubt it. Those deadbolts are probably an inch and a half long, and I don't think that the spreader can move that jamb more than a half inch."

"Goddamn it," I said. I picked up the radio mike and said there would be a delay. I had an ESB truck standing by for my signal. They were about a mile away, but I had to reconnoiter with them and give them the bad news. "All units sit tight until you hear from me."

"Ten-four, Loot," Micena said. "No sweat – we're on overtime."

TEN

I drove over to where the Emergency Service Truck was parked and the supervising sergeant, whose name plate read "GAJEWSKI," jumped out of the passenger seat and said, "Morning, Loot. Problem?"

"Tell him, Charlie," I said.

When Charlie finished with his assessment of the door, the sergeant nodded and said, "How about the window?"

"Three, all the same small type we're familiar with. They seemed locked tight, and there's heavy-gauge metal mesh covering the inside. I couldn't see in, but I'd bet they were padlocked at the bottom."

"Okay," Gajewski said. "No problem."

"No problem?" I said.

"Hey, Lenny," Evans said. "This here nigger's too big and muscular to go through one of them tiny windows. Maybe you got a midget cop in that truck of yours?"

"No, Charlie," he said with a smile, "but I got *this*." He opened a side panel on the truck and pulled out what looked like a chainsaw. "This, my friends, is a gas-powered hacksaw. It has a fine-toothed diamond blade. I don't even need a half-inch of spread. All I need is to see those dead bolts. Zip, zip, and zip and bingo, we're in."

"How long does each zip take?" I asked.

"Eight to ten seconds, max."

"And, uh, how loud is that saw?" I asked as I looked at the formidable piece of machinery with more than a bit of dread.

"As Charlie Evans here would say, 'Motherfuckin' loud.'"

Evidently the sergeant knew Charlie well and Charlie responded, "Motherfuckin' right, Lenny."

I considered what thirty seconds of roaring noise would do to the sleeping Rosario, but I didn't have much choice in this method of entry. "Okay," I said. "Let's do it. I need three vests, Sarge."

"Uh, Loot, don't you want my guys to go in first? That's kinda the accepted protocol now."

"I know, but it's not set in stone in the rules and procedures yet. This entry is my call. Me and my two detectives will go in as soon as you pop the door."

"You got it, Loot. We'll leave our truck here and take the equipment we need in our jeep."

"How many guys will you bring?"

"Two. I'll do the cutting after they spread the jamb. The door should swing in easily, but if not they'll ram it open."

I looked at Evans and Monroe and said, "You two want to be in on this?"

"Are you kidding?" Monroe asked. "Besides, you may need our narcotics expertise being he's a dope dealer."

"That's what I was thinking," I said.

"And you will sign our overtime slips, right? It's after midnight," Evans chimed in.

"You've already earned it. Let's move out."

.   .   .

We assembled a half mile away from the house and I laid out our battle plan. "ESB will park their jeep about ten houses down 146 Street from Rosario's place. I'll park behind the jeep. Micena and Paul will be with me. We'll walk to the house and into the backyard. When we get there I'll get on the walkie-talkie to Charlie and say, 'We're on it,' meaning ESB has begun on the door. That's your signal, Charlie, for you and all the others to move out and converge on the house for backup. Do not come into the bedroom area of the basement until we have secured Rosario, and I give you the okay. Does everyone understand that?"

They all indicated they did and ESB suited me, John, and Richie up in the top of the line body armor. Driving without lights, we reached our destination and parked our vehicles. We crept down the block on the street side of the parked cars. It seemed all the houses were buttoned down tight for the night. I checked my watch as we entered the backyard. It was 2:42 a.m., about an hour and a half after Rosario went inside. He should be sound asleep. It would help if he took some of his own dope to help him on his way.

The two ESB cops set the spreader on the jamb and began to turn the worm screw. It was well-oiled and there was nary a squeak. After four minutes of tedious work, I saw the strain in their arm muscles and determined faces, they backed off and one said, "All yours, Sarge."

I keyed my walkie-talkie and said, "We're on it."

Sergeant Gajewski pulled the start cord and the power hacksaw roared to life, and I mean roared, like wake-the-dead roared. I swear the sergeant had a murderous gleam in his eye like the nut-job in the chainsaw massacre movies. *Zip – Zip – Zip!* He went through those deadbolts like the old cliché says – *a hot knife through a stick of soft butter.*

I pushed the door open and the three of us went charging in, flashlights in one hand, double-action Glock .40s in the other. We found the light switches and raced to where the bedroom obviously was, at the far end of the apartment. The door was locked. John Micena viciously kicked it and it sprung open. He and Richie Paul went inside and I heard Micena yell, "Freeze!" Paul found the light switch and flipped it on. I was right behind the two of them when I heard the two pops. Richie's gun was smoking and Rosario was on his back with two slugs in him. His hand was reaching for a gun, an automatic, on the table next to him. I instantly assessed the situation. The gun was about three feet from Rosario's outstretched hand. Not good.

I closed the bedroom door and walked over to the gun. I grabbed my handkerchief and took it off the table and placed it under Rosario's hand. "Any problems with that?" I asked, looking at my two detectives.

"No, Mike," John said. "If you hadn't done that I would have asked you to leave the room, so I could have."

"Richie," I said, "that was a righteous shooting. Rosario was going for his gun and you popped him. No problem, but this picture will be a lot better when the headhunters arrive."

There was no need for the three of us to say another word. I had deliberately excluded everyone from being in on the takedown. The four seasoned detectives and the ESB team could most likely withstand the coming attack from Internal Affairs, but the rookies, Jamison and Ferrand, would fold like a cheap suit. No disparagement intended to these fine, young officers, just the facts of life in the NYPD. And why make it worse for any of them when they got called over to IAB? This was our homicide case, and we in homicide would deal with the situation.

■   ■   ■

Sergeant Gajewski, on the other side of the door, yelled out, "All okay in there?"

I opened the door so he could come in and take a look. He assessed the situation, nodded his head, and said, "Glad you popped him before he could get one off."

"We are too," I said. "Let me go make the calls."

I went into the living area where everyone on the team was crowded in anticipation of the news. I told them the perp was shot by Detective Paul as he reached for a weapon, an automatic I hoped was the gun used to murder Mort Stern. I said, "Search this whole place with the exception of the bedroom. We'll wait on that until Rosario's body is shipped out. As you all know I have to notify Internal Affairs and the Duty Captain of an officer involved shooting. You can speak to them now or invoke the forty-eight hour rule."

"What do you suggest?" Cindy Jamison said.

"This team has been awake twenty-four hours and running on caffeine and adrenaline. Now that Rosario is dead, I can feel myself coming down from that high, and tiredness is beginning to settle in. It's not in my best interest, or Detective Paul's or Micena's to speak with anyone now. The rest of you can, but I don't suggest it."

I knew the four detectives and the ESB guys wouldn't speak with IAB now either, but Artie Ferrand asked, "Why not, Lieutenant? I mean none of us were near the bedroom when the shooting happened."

"True," I said, "but there is a problem here with the fact Rosario was the perp who shot and killed a close personal friend of mine, and yours, too. IAB will immediately assume we inflicted street justice on him instead of effecting an arrest."

"Why would they assume that?" Cindy Jamison asked. "We had an arrest warrant."

"Despite the warrant, which they will figure was obtained to cover our tracks, they are going to come after us. And they will do so because they are fucking head hunters and measure their success by how many cops' scalps they can hang on their belts. Innocent or guilty cops, it makes no difference to them at all."

That seemed to shock the two young officers, but they said nothing. I said, "When Internal Affairs and the Duty Captain get here, they are going to ask you if you have been drinking alcohol or using drugs, and they will have all of us blow into a small tube for an alcohol reading. They have the right to do this, and the further right to have you submit to a breathalyzer test if alcohol was detected on the preliminary test. That is all they can do at this time."

Jamison and Ferrand looked at each other and nodded. Ferrand said, "Thanks for your advice, Lieutenant. We're feeling tired right now. We want to go to bed soon. Internal Affairs and the brass will have to wait to speak with us."

"Good decision," I said, allowing myself a small smile.

Smart, young cops indeed, but they were going to be in for a rude awakening in a few days.

.   .   .

The forty-eight-hour rule was loved by the rank and file and despised by the brass and politicians. It had been negotiated many years prior into all the police union contracts and the powers that be had been trying to get rid of it, without success, ever since. The rule simply stated a member of the force, from the rank of police officer up to, and including, the rank of deputy chief, was not required to speak to anyone about an incident he was involved in wherein he could himself become the target of an investigation involving criminal and/or disciplinary action. This respite gave the officer the opportunity to get his facts straight and confer with his union representative and his lawyer, if necessary.

Superior officers, assistant district attorneys and members of Internal Affairs had to cool their heels for that time period, and they did not like it one damn bit. They howled that the worst criminals arrested for heinous crimes didn't get forty-eight hours to mull things over before being required to speak. They were hauled into the station house and confronted immediately by an investigator, so why shouldn't the cops be subject to the same procedure? This was a fallacious comparison, because criminal suspects had a much better rule working in their favor – the 48-*second* rule – which was about the time it took to read him his Miranda warnings. And after his rights were read and duly noted, the suspect usually responded in one of three ways – "I want a lawyer," or "I ain't got nuttin' to say," or "Go fuck yourself, copper." Sometimes they said all three responses, just to make certain we "coppers" understood their wishes with absolutely no doubts at all.

I called the Duty Captain, the Crime Scene Unit, the ADA, the medical examiner on call, and last of all, the headhunters from Queens Internal Affairs. Before anyone arrived the search of the rest of the apartment failed to turn up any contraband drugs or additional weapons. Catalano and Nitzky went outside to notify the rest of the building's occupants what was going on. The upstairs apartment was vacant and they had to wake the first floor occupant up with repeated heavy knocking and bell ringing. He obviously hadn't heard the shots and seemed genuinely shocked to hear of his tenant's criminal behavior. And, since we hadn't come down the street with lights and sirens blazing away, there were no on-lookers at this ungodly hour of the morning.

■   ■   ■

All the troops, including two sergeants and a lieutenant from IAB, more or less converged on the apartment simultaneously. After I identified myself and the members of my team, I said, "We came here to arrest

Ismael Rosario for the murder of Mordechai Stern. We have arrest and search warrants. We broke down the bedroom door and Rosario went for a gun. Detective Paul put two into him, witnessed by me and Detective Micena."

The lieutenant from IAB identified himself as Steven Rubino and said, "Where was the gun when he went for it?"

"Lieutenant, that is all I'm going to say for now. I, and all the members of my team, wish to invoke the 48 hour rule. Call us to schedule an interview after that time has passed. None of us have been drinking alcohol or doing drugs. I suggest you have us blow in the tube so we can complete our job here."

Rubino's face reddened and he said, "Don't tell me how to do my job, Lieutenant, and I suggest you speak with us now. It certainly will not look good for a homicide squad commander to stonewall us. It could mean the loss of your command."

"Is that so? Forty-eight hours," I said. "Call me after that."

I turned my back to him and watched as the crime scene guys went to work in the bedroom. The Duty Captain winked at me, and I figured he was no fan of Internal Affairs either. The ADA, Seth Grimes, said, "Forget forty-eight hours. Nobody will talk to any officer present here until they have testified before a grand jury. I'll advise you when that will happen."

.   .   .

Crime scene bagged and tagged Rosario's gun, and after the deputy ME gave the approval, his body was removed for the trip to the morgue. I asked the ME if he could do the post in the afternoon so Micena and Paul could get some shut eye. "No problem," he said. "Will three o'clock be good?"

"Fine," Micena said. "We'll see you then."

Crime Scene technicians went into action and their search uncovered 600 decks of heroin, all stamped in red with the HHC logo and $2,445 in cash, mostly in small bills. Then they found a key piece of evidence which could definitely put Rosario at the murder scene – a dark-blue flannel hoodie with bits of sawdust in one of the pockets.

After the crime scene unit finished up I said to Evans and Monroe, "Any idea who's the big supplier of this HHC brand of dope?"

"Not yet," Monroe said, "but the information is starting to come in now."

"When you bust him, see if he can tell us more about Rosario. I'm wondering if using junkies like DeGiglio to set up robberies happened more than once."

"Will do, Mike," Charlie Evans said. "You be needin' your two favorite slaves anymore?"

I looked at my watch, 6:47 a.m., and I guessed the sun was already up outside this dingy basement pad. I said, "Go home. And thanks a lot for all the help."

Evans had to have the last word as he began to walk out backwards, bowing and scraping. He said, "Yassa, Massa, sees you around the plantation."

There were a few smiles, but we were all too tired to laugh. "It's a wrap," I said. "Sergeant Miller, will you and your guys secure the door as best as you can and cover it in crime scene tape?"

"You got it, Loot," he said, fondly cradling his power hacksaw in his arms. "Happy to have been of service."

We walked outside blinking back the bright morning sun. Micena said, "When do you want us in the office, Boss?"

"Not today. Wait, don't go to Rosario's autopsy. I'll assign Sergeant Seich to attend. That would be better, anyway."

"How so?" Richie Paul asked.

"We are going to retrieve the two bullets you put into his body. Better that they be handed to a supervisor than to you or John. Who knows which way IAB would twist it?"

"Speaking of IAB," Micena said. "You were tough on that Lieutenant Rubino. I hope it doesn't hurt you."

"Ask me if I give a shit. Meet me in my office, all of you, at nine tomorrow morning. Get as much sleep as you can. We'll plan our grand jury testimony and interview strategy with IAB then."

As the team started to drift away toward their cars I said, "Hold up a minute. You did a helluva job today. Thank you all. And I know Mordechai Stern's family will thank you as well. That's a phone call I look forward to making."

ELEVEN

The seven of us sat around a table in a small conference room loaned to us by the boro commander. There was a notepad and pens, a water pitcher and tall glasses, and mugs of steaming coffee. I looked around and was happy to see everyone looking well rested and spruced up. I said, "I have some information to tell you before we get down to business. First, Rosario's gun was the weapon used to murder Mort Stern. Ballistics said with 100% certainty the slug removed from Mort matched those test-fired from Rosario's gun."

"Too bad Ballistics won't get a chance to testify," Detective Nitzky said with a slight grin on his face. "Ismael Rosario has already been convicted – by us."

There were a few small smiles and nods of heads and I said, "Second, Mort's son, Robert, and his wife, Debbie, want me to convey their thanks and appreciation for the job this team did. They needed closure, and they got it. And, as they told me to pass on to you, 'A big thank you to all of you fine police officers and detectives who worked so hard on this case.'"

I began to applaud and they all joined in. They deserved it.

"Now for my third, and last, thing. Seth Grimes scheduled us to appear before a special grand jury at ten o'clock Tuesday morning. I'm hopeful it will be completed by day's end, and I bet IAB will be scheduling our interviews for the day after that."

"Lieutenant?" Cindy asked, "I'm sure the grand jury will find the shooting of Rosario was justified, so why do we have to be interviewed by IAB?"

Before I could answer, Detective Catalano said, "Because no cop is ever innocent in their eyes, regardless of the facts."

"Tom is right about that," I said, "but let's get through the grand jury first. John, will you go through the procedure for the benefit of our two patrol officers here?"

As we all knew, Detective Micena had been to more than a few of them and he said, "We will be asked to waive immunity, and we will comply. We will answer the ADA's questions courteously, and completely, and truthfully."

"Uh, Detective Micena?" Officer Ferrand said. "I thought you automatically receive immunity when you testify at a grand jury proceeding and all you could be charged with was perjury if you failed to tell the truth."

"In normal cases where the DA is looking for an indictment, that is correct. Not here. We're all good guys, including Seth Grimes, so that's the way we will proceed in this case."

"John's absolutely correct," I said. "Any more questions on the grand jury?"

"Should we wear our uniforms?" Cindy asked.

"Yes, our investigation is over. Also, wear them for your IAB interviews. Richie, tell them what to expect from the headhunters."

"Their chief tactic is to divide and conquer. By that I mean they will tell you lies to obtain what they are looking for—a cop to hang out to dry."

"I don't understand," Artie said.

"If we stick to our stories and tell the truth," Richie said, "they will have to exonerate us. Our case is simple. Three of us were in that small bedroom where I shot Rosario. The boss excluded the other four of you for two main reasons. One, the room wasn't big enough, and we'd be stumbling all over ourselves and probably shooting each other. Two, since you have no direct knowledge of what went on in the bedroom you can only testify to the fact you heard shots. But that will not be good enough for those rats, right John?"

Detective Micena motioned for Artie Ferrand to pull his chair out from the table and he also did, bringing it around to sit face to face with him. In a loud voice he said, "But those shots were not all you heard, was it, Officer?"

"I don't know what you mean, sir," Ferrand said, playing along.

"I mean you heard Detective Paul say, 'I shot that murdering bastard just as we planned it, Loot.' And then you heard Lieutenant Simon say, 'Great job, Richie, no trial for this scum bag.'"

"I heard no such thing, and Detective Paul did not say that, or anything like that."

I liked the way Ferrand was doing so far. Then Micena, much louder now, said, "Then why did Officer Jamison say she heard exactly those words. Why do we have that on tape? Why is she now writing out her statement explaining how your whole team, led by Lieutenant Simon, plotted and planned the execution of Ismael Rosario?"

Pulling his chair closer, so his face was only a few inches from Ferrand's, Micena screamed, "Tell me, Officer, why? Why is your partner spilling out the truth? Why are you lying? Why are you holding back? Tell me now or your career is over. Now!"

Ferrand was in shock. "I...I..."

"Enough, John," I said.

Micena pulled away and patted Artie on the shoulder. I said, "The way to answer that question is calmly and coolly. 'Sir, I have no idea why Officer Jamison would say something like that, because that did not happen.'"

"Never lose your cool," John Micena said. "Never call them liars. Never say I don't believe you."

"How long do you think they'll grill us?" Cindy asked.

"All day," I said, "and more if they think they can get away with it."

"Let me sum up the situation," Micena said. "Their prize target here is the boss. It doesn't matter who pulled the trigger. They are going to try to make the case that he planned and orchestrated the murder of Ismael Rosario and we were all in on it."

"And from their perspective, they could easily come to that conclusion," I said, "to give the devils their due. I refused to allow ESB to effect the take down, doing it myself with my two homicide detectives. Mort Stern was a personal long time friend, so I had motive, chiefly revenge. They are going to hammer me the hardest, then Richie and John. But they will also hammer you two young officers as hard, or harder, than me, because they will consider you the weakest links. Let's do some more role-playing."

.　.　.

We put the two rookies through the grinder and by the time I was satisfied they had absorbed it all it was 12:30. "Let's adjourn for lunch," I said. "My treat, then back here for a final wrap-up."

The lunch was subdued as we ate our burgers and Reuben's, mulling over what lay ahead. We were back in the office by 1:30 and I said, "Tell me Officer Jamison, what will you immediately do after IAB notifies you of the time and place of your interview?"

"Call the PBA office and have them assign a delegate to represent me at the interview."

"Correct. And then?"

"Call you with that information."

"Correct again. Got that, Artie?"

"Got it, sir."

"And without having to say it, our four detectives here will have a delegate from their union, the DEA, and I will have one from the LBA. The delegates have limited power, mostly observation and witnessing, but they can suggest the IAB interviewer give you your Miranda rights, if they feel they might be accusing you of a crime."

"My God," Cindy said. "My rights? I'm no criminal –"

"If they do that," I said, interrupting her, "do not say another word. Call a PBA attorney and be guided by his advice."

"Hey," Catalano said. "Don't look so glum. This is life in the NYPD. Get used to it."

"We didn't sign up for this crap," Ferrand said.

"None of us did," I said. "You'll get through this fine, and you'll gain good experience for your next visit with the headhunters."

"Next time?"

"You plan on quitting or doing zero police work for the rest of your career?" Catalano asked.

"Uh, no."

Catalano smiled and said, "Then there will certainly be a next time. And a next time…"

Jamison and Ferrand shook their heads and I said, "Let's wrap this up. You two can get out of here. You detectives know what you have to do so hit the typewriters. The paperwork on this case must be done."

There were no groans from them. They knew their jobs well and got right to it. We all had a long Memorial Day weekend to look forward to. On Tuesday the intensity would begin. "Oh, one more thing. Cindy, Artie?"

They stopped walking to the door and said, "Yes, Lieutenant?"

"They can question you for one hour uninterrupted, and then you're entitled to a ten- minute break. Your PBA rep will make sure they keep to that schedule and you'll have a chance to talk things over. And when you're done for the day, your interrogators will warn you – order you – not to speak with anyone concerning your statements. Feel free to disregard that order. It is illegal, and they know it. Even Internal Affairs is not above the First Amendment to the US Constitution. We will meet back here at the end of the day, and we will discuss everything."

"Thanks, Lieutenant," Ferrand said.

"Yes sir, thank you," Jamison said. "See you all Tuesday morning."

.   .   .

The first witness, me, went into the grand jury box at 9:20 a.m. By 3:30 it was all over. Twelve witnesses, my team of six, the three from ESB, and Evans and Monroe from Narcotics, all testified. At 3:40, Seth Grimes came out of the jury room and smiled. "No true bill," he said. "They were pleased with your actions and asked me to congratulate you for your excellent police work in solving this case."

Not that we didn't expect that result, but it was a relief to all of us we were not charged with a crime. Then Seth put a damper on our mood when he said, "I have to call the CO of IAB in Queens. He wanted to know the minute the grand jury gave their decision. Sorry."

"We understand, Seth," I said. "We're prepared for them – and thanks for being on our side."

"My pleasure. Keep up the good work."

By the time we got back to the squad my deputy, Sergeant Harry Megara, had already been notified of our appearances. "You all have to be over there tomorrow morning at nine sharp," he said. "Sorry to be the bearer of this shitty news."

Harry, who had been running the everyday business of the squad while I was concentrating on the Stern murder, was my right arm. I said, "It was expected, Harry. Thanks for keeping things together the last few days. One more day and I'll be back."

"Yeah, Boss," he said, "unless IAB keeps you under house arrest for an extended period."

"One day, Harry. For all of us. Period."

I noticed a few looks of surprise from my team, but Micena and Paul merely smiled. They knew I had a rabbi, a friend in a high place. They just didn't know who he was.

PART THREE

THE PRIEST

(1966 – 2000)

TWELVE

After ordination I was first assigned to a large parish in Brooklyn, Holy Family, on Flatlands Ave. I was twenty-seven years old and the youngest of the three priests assigned there. I was broken into my pastoral duties by Father Tom Reynolds who was thirty-four years old, and by the parish's Pastor, Father Edward McGrail, a stern leader, who was not easy to confide in. After a few weeks I took Tom aside after dinner and said, "Uh, Tom, did any of our female members of the congregation ever uh, you know, make advances to you?"

"You mean like, 'Hey, handsome priest, wanna get laid?'"

I felt myself blushing and he smiled and said, "It happens all the time, and I guess it's happened to you or you wouldn't have asked me that question."

"It has, Tom. More than once. I don't understand it."

"What's not to understand?"

"I am a Priest, sworn to celibacy, for God's sake."

"Oh, they know that, and they view it as a challenge. Like a young guy wanting to be the first to bang a virgin. And the priestly uniform doesn't hurt either, even though it's plain black most of the time."

"Yeah, when I was in the Marines the uniform certainly attracted the ladies," I said.

"I'm glad you're here, Francis. So young and handsome. You'll be the star with the sweet, young drooling beauties in the parish, and a lot of the heat will be taken off of me."

"This is bizarre, Tom."

"It is. Celibacy is unnatural, and Holy Mother Church knows it. We have a long history of married priests from its inception to about 1100. That's when the reigning Pope decided we must be celibate. It had more to do with property rights being passed down to priest's heirs than to the church."

"They kind of glossed over that in the seminary," I said.

"I bet they did. They are loosening up with the recent rulings coming out of the Vatican councils, but they have a long way to go. Speaking of the seminary, did you ever notice any strange goings on among your fellow classmates?"

"I'm not following you here," I said.

"Sexual liaisons?"

"I don't recall any women being smuggled in, if that's what you mean."

"That's not what I mean. I mean between your classmates *themselves?*"

I was shocked and said, "You mean homosexual acts?"

"Exactly. It's getting to be a problem throughout the church, and I don't mean sexual acts exclusively between priests. I mean between priests and young children, both girls and boys."

"That's sickening," I said. "Have you seen this first hand, because I haven't?"

"No, just a lot of rumors, and I assure you I am not a pedophile."

"That's good to hear. At least I won't have to clamp my hands over my ass when you're in the vicinity."

He laughed and said, "Marine Corps humor. I like it."

"Do you think Rome will ever change the celibacy and marriage rule?"

"They'd better. They should allow priests to marry, and they should also allow women to be ordained."

"Heresy!" I said, smiling and putting crossed index fingers toward his face.

"If they don't, the church is doomed."

"I don't think so. We've been around 2,000 years, and we'll be around thousands more."

"Don't count on it, my young idealist."

"I made my vow and I'm sticking to it," I said.

"Good for you, Francis. Yield ye not to the temptation of short skirts, and high-heels, and pretty faces, and full red lips…"

"You sound like the Devil himself."

"Make your own decision, but let me tell you not a lot of priests leave the church because of the celibacy rules. They learn to cope with them."

"You mean some priests have sex anyway? They violate the vow and remain a priest? Now, that's not heresy, that's a mortal sin, a sin as big as they come."

"I guess it is," Tom said, "but I guarantee you our dear Pastor is not one of them. Rumor has it he doesn't even have a penis, but a tiny, shriveled-up mushroom cap instead."

I burst out laughing and said, "That's certainly good to hear, but what about you, Father Tom?"

"I fall back on my vow of silence," he said.

"When did you take a vow of silence?"

"Just now, Francis."

■　　■　　■

I kept my vows, all of them, and in the autumn of 1969 I was transferred to St. Anthony's Church in South Ozone Park, Queens where Father Joseph Fusco had reigned supreme as Pastor for fifteen years. And, to my surprise, my transfer came with a promotion to Assistant Pastor. I was thirty years old, but some thirty-five year old priests were being made pastors. The attraction to the priesthood continued to evaporate at the entrance level and seasoned priests were leaving at an alarming rate. Some left to get married and others to lead a less restrictive existence. As Bob Dylan once said, *The times they were a changing*.

Father Fusco was a go-getter and a great fundraiser putting on a local Italian feast every year on the school's playground. The neighborhood was predominantly Italian with Irish and Jews making up most of the rest, although I had seen a few black faces and Spanish faces start to appear at mass. And, being of Italian heritage, I reveled in the food and pageantry of the feast.

About a year after my transfer here, I was hearing confession, and when the woman on the other side of the grate was finished, and I had given her absolution and a slight penance, she said, "Father, I'd like to meet with you about a family problem."

"Certainly," I said. "If you are free now, I'll be finished in another fifteen minutes. Or you can make an appointment with the church secretary in the rectory."

"I'll wait for you. I'll say my penance."

"Three Hail Mary's won't take you that long. You didn't confess to stealing the Crown Jewels, you know."

She laughed and said, "Then I'll pray the rosary for you, Father, and for my son, who I wish to speak to you about."

Her son. Acting up in school? Drugs? I hoped not drugs, but that was becoming more and more prevalent in these days of the Vietnam War. A vision of Pete Selewski, sweating and nervous, wearing a long-sleeved shirt in June flashed through my mind.

I finished with my last penitent and we walked over to the rectory together. I said, "I remember seeing you at mass occasionally, but we were never introduced."

"Oh, I'm Elizabeth," she said, "and I never miss mass. Please call me Betty."

We settled into chairs in my office and my secretary brought us coffee. "Please, Betty," I said, "whenever you are ready."

"Thank you, Father. It's about my son. He's always been a good boy. He attended elementary school here and is now in his first year at Bishop Loughlin High School."

"You're kidding! That's my alma mater. Good for him."

"Yes, I'm happy he's continuing his catholic education at that level. As I said, he's a good boy, but he has a history, a history he knows nothing of. But something recently happened, and I realized sooner or later we would have to let him know who he is."

"He's adopted?"

"Yes Father, and the other day he came home and asked me and my husband if he was Jewish. He said some kids from Loughlin asked why a Jew would go there. This happened once before when he was around ten years old. We lied to him then, and we lied to him again."

A vague uneasiness began to move through my body. I said, "Is he Jewish, Betty?"

"Yes. Both his parents were Jewish, but they died when he was an infant. We adopted him, and agreed to raise him in the catholic faith."

This isn't possible.

I gathered my wits and said, "And your question is when to tell him the truth?"

"Yes, Father."

I had to ask the question. "What is your son's name?"

"Michael. Michael Simon."

Although I expected it to be him, I felt the blood rush from my brain and I grabbed the edge of the desk to keep from keeling over. "Father, are you all right?" Betty asked, getting up to assist me.

"No, no," I said, "I just got a little dizzy. I haven't eaten since breakfast, and I guess the caffeine affected me badly."

I buzzed for my secretary and asked her to bring me a candy bar and some ice water. When I drank and took a bite of the chocolate bar I felt better. *Michael Simon! Here in my parish! Oh, my God!*

Now composed, I said, "My gut feeling is to wait until he's older, when he finishes high school."

She took a deep breath and said, "That's what Alan – my husband – thinks and so do all his grandparents."

"Does Michael have any siblings?"

"Two older sisters, but they were one and two and a half years old when we took Michael in. They have no idea he is not their brother."

She appeared relieved I concurred with the others' opinions. I said, "When the time comes, I think I should be there, the whole family should be there, and probably a rabbi."

"My husband is Jewish, but not observant. He goes to temple mainly on the High Holy days, and keeps his attendance a secret from Michael for obvious reasons. I'm positive Rabbi Berman will attend."

When Elizabeth Simon left she apparently seemed satisfied with her decision. Four years was a long time, but it just postponed facing the music. And what would I tell Michael Simon about the part of his history only I knew of? Nothing, or the truth? Four years to think it over. "Michael Simon, may God bless you and look over you," I said aloud as the events of that horrible night fourteen years ago came crashing full force into my brain. Not that I had ever forgotten it as I prayed for Michael every night, but that Michael was a figment, an imaginary person living out his life a thousand miles away. Now Michael was here, and he was real, and the image of the blood-drenched bodies of his parents would not go away.

. . .

A couple of days later I walked down to Stern's candy store for two reasons: I loved the philosophical discussions with the bitter survivor, and I loved his egg creams. What I didn't like was he wouldn't let me ever pay for one. "You and the cops," he would say. "Your *geld* is not good here."

On this particular day, as I sipped my egg cream, the boy who swept up the store said, "I'm finished, Mr. Stern."

"Looks good, Mikey. Want your egg cream?"

"Not today, gotta run. We have a baseball game soon."

I recognized the boy as a former student at St. Anthony's elementary school and an attendee at Sunday Mass, but I never had a reason to have any personal interaction with him. When he left, I said, "Seems like a pleasant kid. Good Catholic boy."

"So *you* say, Father."

"Oh?"

"Dat Mikey is a Jew if I ever saw one. Michael Simon? Come on, gimme a break."

Realizing immediately this boy was the subject of the discussion between me and his mother a few days ago, and connecting the dots, I said, "Mort, have you ever told him that?"

"All the time. I tease the hell out of him. He thinks I'm *meshuge* – crazy."

"Mort, I have a favor to ask. Don't tease him anymore. Don't tell him he's a Jew."

"Why not?"

"Because, he *is* a Jew –"

"I know that –"

"But *he* doesn't know it."

"I know that, too. Vere going in circles here, Francis."

"Let me explain…"

When I finished, leaving out my part in the murder of Michael's parents, of course, Mort Stern clapped his hand to his forehead and muttered, "Mein Gott in Himmel!"

I couldn't help myself, zinging the old man a bit. I said, "Funny, an avowed atheist refers to his God in Heaven."

"Just an old expression," he said. "You shocked it out of me."

"Good come back, you old *kvetcher*. Then you'll stop calling him a Jew?"

"*Ja*, Francis. You didn't have to confirm it. I still haf good ears."

"Besides, Mikey Simon doesn't even look Jewish," I said with a grin.

"Bah, vat's a Jew look like anyway?"

"Like you, Mort. Your picture should be in the dictionary next to the word *Jew*. No, next to the words, *Grumpy Old Yiddisher*."

"Bah, and yours should be next to *Beak-nosed Wop.*"

"Hey, my nose is smaller than yours," I protested.

"Bah! Hey, vant another egg cream?"

"No, Mort, I gotta get back to the church."

He grabbed my arm and said, "Francis, what you told me, a terrible thing to have happened. Do you vant me there ven you tell him?"

"Yes, Mort, his mother and I already discussed it. Four years from now, when he graduates. I'll be there. We'll get Rabbi Berman there, too. Mikey's whole family will be there."

"I'm not looking forward to dat revelation," he said.

"Four years, Mort."

"Mit any luck I'll be dead by then."

"And, if so, no doubt happy with the Good Lord in Heaven."

"Bah! Humbug, too."

And what would I say to Michael Simon four years from now? I had no idea, but I did know God had reunited us, put me into Mikey's life, for a good reason. I had to figure that out, but by the time I got back to the rectory, I had no idea what I would say to him.

THIRTEEN

Although I had come to terms with my participation in the murders of Andrew and Veronica Simon, with the blessing of Fathers McClanahan and Johansson, I could not shake a feeling of guilt. Every time I performed a baptism and the infant cried – and it seemed they all did – I thought of the sound of Michael Simon crying down the hall from where I stood near the bodies of his dead parents. And every time I heard *Little Darlin'* or *Bye, Bye, Love* on a passing radio, my mind flashed back to that night I got into Pete's convertible.

Since I could not obtain absolution from the church or yet from myself, I decided to soothe my conscience by taking an interest in Michael Simon and providing special attention to his education at Bishop Loughlin. I also contacted Elizabeth Simon and asked if they had established a college fund for him, and when she responded in the affirmative, I began regular donations to it. I said, "Betty, Michael has been dealt a lousy hand in life. Fortunately, he found new parents and a fine family to be raised in. A college education will give him a leg up in life when he goes out on his own."

"Thank you, Father," she had responded. "With his three sets of grandparents also contributing he should be able to afford to go to Harvard."

"Three sets?"

"Yes, my parents, Alan's parents, and Veronica's parents, Mr. and Mrs. Silber."

"How do you explain that situation to Michael?"

"Jerry and Sara Silber were introduced long ago as 'good friends of the family,'" she said.

"I see. Something else he'll find out on D-Day. I know it's necessary, and the right thing to do, but I must admit, Mrs. Simon, I am dreading it."

"So am I, Father. So is Alan. So are all the grandparents. And we also worry about my daughters, Mary Beth and Betty Ann, who will suddenly learn they are Michael's cousins, not his sisters. Another deception we perpetuated."

"A necessary deception," I said, thinking that was going to be one helluva day.

·   ·   ·

Two years later, Father Fusco had a severe heart attack and was forced to retire from his pastoral duties. I was surprised when the Bishop named me as Pastor. I guessed, correctly, the priesthood was shrinking at a faster pace now. But again I wondered why, reflecting back on my discussions with Father Tom Reynolds at Holy Family. And I began to quietly ask around. The things I found out were disturbing and truly shocking. Tom was right. The church had a problem – a big problem. How long could they keep it under wraps?

The next two years flew by and suddenly it was D-Day. Although the guests were limited to four at the graduation ceremony, my priestly attire and my alumnus status got me right in. And the fact the aging principal, Father McClanahan, spotted me and escorted me to my seat didn't hurt, either. The good Priest and I had remained in contact after my ordination, and I had put in a good word for Michael with him. I knew certain school charges and fees for sports and other activities mysteriously never showed up on his school bills.

Although I had kept in touch with Michael through the church and Mort's candy store, I was struck by his appearance as he strode across the stage smiling widely to receive his diploma, resplendent in his purple gown and cap with gold trim. The cap made him appear taller than his actual height, which was a shade under six feet, and he had filled out to a muscular, fit, athlete's body. He lettered in track and field and basketball on the Lions' teams, and the four colleges he had been accepted to all offered him a modest sports scholarship. A great future lay ahead of him, but a nagging dread began to ache in my stomach as we took photos and headed out to an early dinner at a nearby restaurant. And when dinner was over, we would go back to the Simon's house for cake and coffee where we would be joined by all the grandparents, Mort Stern, and Rabbi Marc Berman.

We were all assembled nervously around the large dining room table awaiting the arrival of our guest of honor. In its center sat a huge sheet cake with yellow icing and purple trim and lettering. It said, "Congratulations, Michael. Class of June, 1974. BLHS."

I looked around the table and noticed Michael's "sisters," both beautiful young ladies now. Mary Beth, age twenty, a college sophomore, closely resembled her father in looks, with brown hair and eyes. Betty Ann, age eighteen, was a secretary at a legal firm in Manhattan and a clone of her Irish mother, sporting blond hair and blue eyes.

My feeling of dread increased as Michael bounced into the room, out of his graduation attire, now dressed in a crisp button-down, light-blue shirt, and pressed khakis. His aquiline nose and bright-green eyes strongly reminded me of his birth mother from the pictures Betty had shown me, pictures Michael would soon get to see. We all applauded as Alan handed him a big knife to cut the cake. This was not a birthday, so there were no candles on it, and when he began to slice it, no one suggested he make a wish.

As Michael cut up the cake and Betty Ann passed the slices around, I wondered if he was curious why Rabbi Berman was here. Then I realized the Rabbi visited Mort's candy store probably as often as I did, and there had been several occasions where Marc and I were there together taking great joy in badgering the old non-believer. We would only stop when he said, "*Genug!* Enough. Vun more word from you two and you get no egg creams today!"

We dug into our slices of cake and sipped coffee when I suddenly realized, with four years of preparation, no one had mentioned who was going to initially break the news. I assumed it would be Alan, his "father," but as the dessert wound down he had not broached the topic. Rabbi Berman said, "Where are you going to college, Michael?"

He hesitated a bit and said, "I was happy to be accepted at four schools, and I first chose St. John's over the others, mainly because it was close to home and a Catholic university. As I was finishing my senior year, I came to the conclusion I didn't want to continue in that direction. After twelve years of strict Catholic education I felt I was living in a strait jacket. I changed my mind and decided on a state school, SUNY at New Paltz, where I could live away from home and get a break from the narrow views I had been exposed to."

I was impressed by Michael's insight and maturity and Mort Stern said, "Good decision, Mikey," grinning and glancing pointedly in my direction.

"But then I thought about the whole college idea, and decided I don't want to go right now. I want to take a year off and see what's out there in this big world."

Although his parents and grandparents seemed stunned by this revelation, I felt it was a perfect time to begin our discussion of Michael's true life story. I said, "Michael, I believe that's a good decision and apropos to what we have to tell you. Alan?"

Alan began fidgeting and stammering. "Uh, Mikey... er..."

"Tell me what, Dad?"

"Uh, Father Manzo, could you? Uh, it might be better..."

You son-of-a-bitch! roared through my brain and I stared hard at him, but he hung his head and refused to look at me.

"Father, what is going on?" Michael asked.

"Michael, there's no easy way to say this, but it's time you know who you are."

"What do you mean by that?"

"You are Michael Simon, biological son of Andrew and Veronica Simon, who were killed when you were an infant. Alan is your father's brother, and he and his wife, your Aunt Elizabeth, adopted you and raised you as their own child. Your sisters are actually your cousins."

The first reaction came from Mary Beth, who was always a bit of a potty mouth. She raised the bar on her level of profanity this time saying loudly, "What...the...fuck?"

Betty Ann followed with, "Holy Crap!"

Mary Beth looked all around the table and said, "And all of you here knew this all along?"

"Yes," Sara Silber said. "Jerry and I are not just friends, we are Michael's grandparents, his biological mother's parents."

We all sat silently as Michael took this devastating news in. He finally said, "How did they die?"

Alan, having regained his nerve said, "My brother and his wife were shot dead by an intruder. Your father was a young Nassau County Police Officer. You were six months old and were in a bedroom down the hall when the crime took place."

"Why didn't you tell me sooner?"

"Do you think that would have been a good idea?" he responded. "We didn't think so – all of us."

"You could have told me and Betty Ann," Mary Beth said.

"And how long could you have kept that from your brother?"

"He's not my brother though, is he?"

"Yes, I am," he said, "and you two are my parents. Thank you for taking me in, and raising me, and educating me. I love you both, and I love my sisters as well. You will always be my parents and my sisters."

Impressive for a seventeen-year old, I thought. I said, "Michael, take your time to wrap your head around this. Your father has a box of memorabilia from your parents and we're all available to answer your questions when you're ready."

"Thank you, Father. I have one question right now. Grandma Sara, am I Jewish?"

"Yes," she said. "Both your parents were Jewish, as is Alan."

He nodded, looked at Mort Stern, smiled and said, "You were right, you old survivor. You had me pegged all along."

Mort nodded and said, "Maybe being a Jew is not such a good thing, Mikey."

Rabbi Berman shot Mort a dirty look and said, "Michael, whenever you wish to discuss your Jewishness, I will be available. As will Father Manzo. We'll kick around this whole religious thing, and you can come to your own conclusions."

"I'd like to be part of *dat* discussion," Mort said, with a wicked grin on his face.

"That won't be necessary, Mort," Rabbi Berman said, ice dripping from his words. "Michael has been exposed to your views for years, and you have a store to attend to."

No doubt Mort Stern had more to say on the subject, but he just leaned back in his chair and said, "Bah!"

. . .

One week later, at a dinner to which I had been invited, Michael said to his parents, "I have decided to enlist in the Army for two years. Although the war in Vietnam is over, the draft isn't, and my number will come up shortly anyway."

"If you go to college full time," Elizabeth said, "you can get a deferment."

"I don't want to go to college now. Will you sign the approval?"

Alan and Betty looked at each other then over to me. Alan said, "Father Manzo?"

"I think it's a wonderful idea. See some of the world. Learn new ideas. Learn some new curse words. Get your head straight while you serve your country."

That's what I said, but what I was thinking was, *Yeah, Mikey, run away from your problems like I did. But that turned out to be a good thing, didn't it? At least so far it has.*

"Then we approve," Alan said, as a tear slipped down Betty's cheek.

"Thanks," he said. "Can I look at that box of memorabilia now?"

"It's in the attic," Alan said. "I'll go get it."

If Michael had uneasy feelings about what he was about to see, I assure you they were mild compared to the emotions that now raged through my mind and body. Visions of bloody, bullet-ridden bed clothes, gruesome photos of the murder scene, and gory autopsy photos passed in front of my eyes, and I took a deep breath. But all that evidence would not be in that box, but still be in police custody if they suspected a second perpetrator, or disposed of if the case had been officially closed, as I desperately hoped.

Alan returned in a few moments with a large cardboard box. Printed on top in black ink were two words, "MY BROTHER." I stifled a sob, realizing not only had Mikey lost his parents, but Alan had lost his only sibling, Betty lost her brother-in-law, the Silber's lost a daughter, and Alan's parents had lost a son.

This tragedy had no end.

"Go ahead, son," Alan said. "Open it."

Michael pulled back the brittle sealing tape and unfolded the flaps of the box. The first item he withdrew was a large white photo album. On its cover, in gold script were the words, "Our Wedding Day" followed underneath by "Veronica and Andrew Silber – November 6, 1955."

He passed his hand over the cover, wiped a tear away that had started down his left cheek, and said, "I'd like to take this box up to my room and go through it by myself. If I have any questions, and there will probably be many, we'll talk then."

We watched him gently cradle the box in his arms and head for his upstairs bedroom. I started to say goodbye but Alan stopped me and said, "Father Manzo, please stay awhile longer. I'd like you to be here to help me answer Michael's questions when he comes back down."

With a heavy heart and raging memories of that terrible night eighteen years ago, I reluctantly agreed.

FOURTEEN

An agonizing hour later, which seemed an eternity to me as my apprehension increased to near the bursting point, Michael came down to join us in the living room and said, "I carefully went through the box of my real parents' memorabilia, and when I finished I did have a lot more questions, the main ones being who really are these people? And what really happened to them on that night? Dad, were you close to my father, er, I mean your brother?"

Alan smiled and said, "I guess it's all right to call us both your dad, Michael, but if you want you can call me your step-dad, or your uncle. I won't mind."

"No, you'll always be my father. I cannot ever know the other one, but maybe you can tell me all about him, and my mom, too."

"To answer your question, I was very close to my brother who was two years younger than me. I was the best man at your parents' wedding as you probably saw in their photo album. I won't bore you with childhood stories right now, but I'll tell you as best I can what I believe you really want to know. Come sit on the sofa with me and Father Manzo."

He did, and Alan reached down on the seat cushion next to him and withdrew a book. He said, "This is a journal I kept back at the time to commemorate my brother and his wife. Here is how they met and got married, and here are the events of that terrible night from newspaper reports and my conversations with the investigating police officers and detectives. I pieced it all together and put it in the form of a story. Do you want me to read it?"

"Yes, Dad, I do," Michael said as my apprehension grew into outright fear.

Alan opened the journal and swallowed hard. "Here goes, Michael…"

.   .   .

Patrolman Andrew Simon had been with the Nassau County, NY Police Department for two years and was assigned to the Fifth Precinct, which bordered the NYPD's 105 Precinct, to its west. Nassau County, as most of the Boro of Queens, was considered a suburban bedroom community for the "City," which meant chiefly the Boro of Manhattan. Many of Nassau's inhabitants partook in the great, rushing, crushing, commute west each weekday morning by car, bus, and train and Andy Simon had been part of that daily exodus and return for two years prior to joining the NCPD.

Andy smiled as he drove sector car 506 to his assignment. He had the windows all the way down on this fine spring day and breathed in the fragrance of the newly-opened trees and flowers, occasionally poisoned with exhaust fumes spewing from the bumper-to-bumper, stop-and-go traffic heading westbound on Hempstead Turnpike. He cruised east at a steady thirty miles per hour. It was eight a.m. and he had been assigned by radio to cover the school crossing on Jackson Street in Franklin Square. Andy, not yet permanently assigned to a steady sector car post, was filling in this week for the regular assigned patrolman who was on vacation. This was his last day tour of five and, after his two days off, he would return to his foot post in Elmont on Thursday's four-to-twelve shift. School crossings were not usually a favorite assignment for an active officer who would be happier to be looking for bad guys, but they were part of the job when a school crossing guard was absent or on vacation. Since he knew SCG Lynn Markey had been on her post Friday, he figured she had called in sick today.

He pulled up on Jackson Street, got out of his vehicle, donned his white cotton gloves, and awaited the first batch of youngsters to show up at the intersection and cross to their elementary school. As they arrived, full of energy and smiles, a few asked him where Miss Markey was today.

Since he didn't know, he answered, "Probably has the day off. I'm sure she'll be back here tomorrow."

The last few kids he crossed at 8:55 were the final batch before he would return for the afternoon crossing at 2:30 p.m. And, unknown to him at the time, that return would change his life forever. To be exact, at 2:42 p.m. a large group of children accompanied by a young woman — their teacher, no doubt — crossed the street as he held up his white-gloved hands to stop the traffic. As she passed him she nodded and smiled, and Patrolman Andy Simon literally fell in love on the spot. Head over heels in love. Knee-knocking, light-headed, dry-throated love. The immediate heart-stopping love that happens only in the movies.

His short glimpse of her revealed a dark-haired, green-eyed beauty reminiscent of Elizabeth Taylor, one of his fantasy movie idols. Liz had those blue-violet eyes, but these green ones were no less entrancing. He followed the group over and assumed the teacher must be leaving for the day. He said, "Hello, ma'am. I'm Patrolman Simon, uh, filling in for Miss Markey today."

"Pleased to meet you, Officer. I hope there's nothing seriously wrong with Lynn?"

"Oh, no. I found out from the desk sergeant she had a stomach virus. She should be back tomorrow. Uh, but I won't, even if she isn't here. I go on my days off."

"I see," she said, starting to turn away.

"Uh, Miss…? What's your name?"

She looked at Andy as if he'd been a bit too bold, but smiled and said, "Veronica Silber."

"That's a lovely name," he said, extending his hand.

She hesitated, but still smiling, took it and shook hands with him. "It was a pleasure to meet you, Officer Simon, but I must be going."

"Uh, Andy," he said. "My name is Andy. Uh, Miss Silber, before you go can I ask you a question?"

Rolling her eyes a bit she said, "Okay."

"Will you marry me, Veronica Silber?"

She now looked deeply into this handsome young man's dark-brown eyes and her legs quivered. She realized they were still clasping hands. She said, "Perhaps I will, Andy Simon. When can I meet your folks?"

Andy was flabbergasted, but ecstatic. He couldn't speak for a few seconds, and it seemed Miss Silber was enjoying the state of shock she had put him into. He said, "Uh, maybe we should go on a few dates first?"

"Absolutely," she said. "When?"

"Tomorrow night. I know you're working, so we will do an early dinner and a movie. You'll be home by ten."

"Sounds great," she said. "Pick me up at five-thirty."

"See you then," he said, heading back to his patrol car.

"Uh, Andy?" she called out as he strode away drinking in her lilac-scented perfume.

He turned and said, "Yes?"

"Perhaps you might want to jot down my address and phone number?"

"Oh, my God," he said laughing. "What a jerk. See what love does to a guy?"

She wrote the information down on a small notepad she fished out of her purse and handed it to him. Love, indeed! Either Andy Simon was the biggest con man with the phoniest line she ever had put to her, or he was the real thing, wearing his heart on his sleeve, right beneath his bright gold and orange police patch.

.   .   .

Veronica shortly found out Andy was definitely the real thing. On their third date he had asked, "Does Silber mean silver in German?"

"Yes, but I'm not German. I'm Jewish." She was curious to see how he reacted to that.

He said, "At the risk of dragging out an old cliché, I could say, 'Funny, you don't look Jewish,' but I won't."

"What would you say?"

"I would say you look like a movie star to me, and I don't care what religion is inside that body of yours."

Veronica, Ronnie as she was called, laughed and said, "Is Simon a German name?"

"I think some Simon's are, but some are Jewish, too."

"No! Don't tell me you're a fellow Jew?"

"That I am, my love."

With a serious deadpan look she said, "Funny, you don't look Jewish."

They both cracked up and that line became a favorite of theirs to start them giggling. Once, while watching the old black-and-white King Kong movie, Andy whispered, "Funny he doesn't look Jewish, but I think he's circumcised," causing Ronnie to burst out laughing and to draw hostile stares from the movie goers nearby.

Their whirlwind romance culminated in a traditional Jewish wedding in November of 1955, which was somewhat ironic since neither one had considered, nor cared, their new found lover was Jewish. The wedding had not been lavish, but was the best their sets of parents could afford. Andy's dad was a car salesman, and his mom worked as a bookkeeper in a small business. Ronnie's parents owned a dry cleaning business in Queens and put in long hours there. The newlyweds rented a small three-bedroom house in the quiet neighborhood of Cambria Heights in eastern Queens. The house had an option to buy, but they were unsure if they wanted to stay there or look for something in Nassau County. For now, it was ideal, their reverse commute being less than twenty minutes in each direction.

Their son, Michael, was born in January, 1957, and when he was six months old, they moved him from the bassinet in their bedroom to his own room down the hall. And after paying a lot of rent, but managing to save enough for the down payment, they bought the house and started to make it their own home.

■ ■ ■

June 15, 1957 was a Saturday night and unusually warm for this time of year. They had opened up all the windows to the night air and even left the solid-wood front door open with the screen door latched in place to maybe catch a cross breeze in their non-air conditioned house. Although they lived in a low crime, safe neighborhood, Andy knew burglars could, and would, strike anywhere, so he kept his fully-loaded, off-duty, five-shot, S & W revolver in the top drawer of his night stand. He and Ronnie had already discussed the necessity of relocating it to a safer location when little Mikey began crawling around.

A call came into the 105 Precinct at 1:05 on the morning of June 16 and the man said, "Listen, I think I heard gunshots from across the street. Maybe they were firecrackers, but I think the owner of the house is a cop. Maybe you could have the sector car check it out?"

"I will, sir," the desk sergeant said. "Give me the location, and your name and address, and I'll get someone over there right away."

The sector car was there in five minutes, and a backup one minute later, at the premises located at 119-04 on 230 Street. Two officers crept up the four brick front steps. They noticed the slit in the screen door leading into the house and motioned for the other two officers to move around to the back of the house. Before trying the door one of the officers shouted, "Police officers! Is anyone home?"

There was no answer and also no answer when, his finger wrapped in his handkerchief, the officer pushed the door bell hard, followed by several loud knocks. With flashlights in one hand and service revolvers in the other, they opened the screen door and entered the living room.

Searching for table lamps and light switches, Patrolman Bob Livoti once again shouted, "Police! Is anyone here?"

Patrolman Neil Brogan finally found a standing lamp and switched it on displaying an orderly, modestly furnished living room. He stopped moving and whispered, "Bob, do you hear that?"

Livoti stopped and listened. "Jesus, Neil, that's a baby crying."

They followed the sound and turned on the hall light switch, creeping toward the open doorway, entering the room, guns drawn. Livoti flicked on the light and Brogan went over to the crib. The instant the infant saw the man in the uniform he stopped crying, smiled, and lifted his tiny arms up toward him. Brogan remembered the dispatcher saying the resident of the home may be a police officer and figured that's who the baby thought he was seeing.

They retraced their steps to a partially closed door which was most likely the master bedroom. There was light coming from inside the room and Livoti knocked and said, "Police! Are you all safe in there?"

When they received no response they stepped to the sides of the doorway and Brogan reached out and gently pushed the door open. Revolver pointed straight ahead, he entered the room and stepped to one side. Livoti entered immediately after him and stepped to the other side.

They saw a scene before their eyes that would be seared into their memories forever.

"My God," Livoti whispered. "It's a massacre."

Brogan holstered his revolver and said, "Let's check for signs of life."

When they found no pulse and no breathing on the three bodies, Livoti, the senior officer said, "Notify the other sector to call the dicks and the desk sergeant and tell them what we have here. And let's not touch or disturb anything."

What had stunned the two veteran police officers was not the sight of three dead bodies, but the volume of blood soaked into the bed and the carpet. Most of the shots fired – how many at this point was anybody's guess – seemed to have caught an artery on all three. Livoti, now alone in the bedroom, saw two definite entrance wounds on the young female's nightgown, but couldn't see any on the young man slumped over half out of his side of the bed, his back facing him. Nor could he see any on the male body which was lying face down on the carpet at the foot of the bed. He most definitely noticed the two guns, one in the right hand of each dead male. The metallic smell of the congealing blood and the sharp odor of gunpowder filled the room and made him retch.

He shook his head as he tried to piece together what had happened, but couldn't keep his eyes and mind off the bright-red blood displayed on the queen-size bed. He was overwhelmed, but his head cleared when his partner returned and said, "The dicks and Crime Scene Unit are on the way."

The detectives from the 105 Squad arrived, followed by detectives from Queens Homicide, and the investigation into the deaths of Andrew Simon, Veronica Simon, and an as yet unidentified male white, began in earnest. All the stops were pulled out for a fellow cop, albeit one from another department, but whose precinct was literally right next door.

The initial assessment was that the Simon's had left their inside front door open, with a locked screen door, due to the excessive heat. The perpetrator spotted the open door and decided to commit "a crime of opportunity." He figured people were home and sleeping, but he would control them with the threat of his gun, and force them to give up their valuables. But apparently Andy Simon had heard something and came up shooting. Three dead, including the perpetrator, and a six-month old infant left all alone. *Our family tragedy.*

.   .   .

My emotions got the better of me when Alan finished the last page of the journal and closed its cover. I ran to the bathroom holding in a sob as Michael burst into tears and hugged Alan who was sobbing in short, convulsive gasps. Some priest I was, running away when I should provide comfort to the grieving, but to hear the events of that night repeated so matter-of-factly from another point of view was like re-living the murders all over again. I splashed some cold water on my face, composed myself as best I could, and came back into the living room. Andy and Michael were still embracing and, thankfully, the tears and sobs appeared to be winding down. Apparently satisfied with his newly discovered revelations, Michael said, "I have a lot to think about. I'm going to lie down for a while. Goodbye, Father Manzo. Thanks for being here. Love you, Dad."

I breathed a sigh of relief as I walked to my car. Alan's journal concluded there was only one killer, Pete Selewski. The case was closed. Or had the police not told him everything at the time, withholding certain blood and fingerprint evidence they had found pending further investigation? Were they still looking for me after eighteen years?

FIFTEEN

Michael Simon joined the United States Army as planned, and when he emerged, a strong young man of twenty years, he applied to take the examination for police officer in all the surrounding departments – the Nassau County Police as well as the Suffolk County Police, Port Authority Police, and the NYPD. While he awaited the test results and eventually passed them all, and went through the physical and psychological exams, he attended Queensborough Community College and got his Associate's Degree in Criminal Justice. Having already decided to take the first job offer from a police department that came his way, two weeks later his letter of acceptance to the ranks of the NYPD arrived.

A week before he was to be sworn in, I was again at the Simon household for afternoon coffee. Andy Simon said, "Michael, I have another box for you, a bigger box I saved for you just in case."

"Just in case of what, Dad?"

Andy smiled and said, "Just in case you decided to follow in your father's footsteps."

Michael ripped the box open and withdrew an assortment of leather goods and navy blue police uniforms. Andy said, "You can take off the Nassau Police shoulder patches and replace them with NYPD patches. I think you are about the same size as my brother was. A few bucks for tailoring and you save a few hundred bucks on your uniform bill."

"Thanks, Dad. I ...I don't know what to say...."

"Say you'll go try all this stuff on right now," I said, peering into the box. "What shoe size are you?"

"Ten and a half."

I withdrew a pair of polished black brogans and passed them over saying, "Looks like they might fit also. Maybe save you a few more bucks, Mikey."

Michael's mom had been with us this whole time, but had not uttered a word. It was obvious she had not wanted Michael to join the army and also obvious she was not thrilled with his choice of career. When Michael went upstairs to change into his dead father's uniform, Betty broke down in sobs. "This can't be happening, Andy. Please stop him from going ahead with it. For God's sake! Do you want to lose him, too?"

Andy grabbed Betty in a hug and said, "Father?"

"I'll speak with him," I said, now knowing no words I could say, or anyone else could say, would sway the decision of young Michael Simon. He had found his mission in life – to adopt his father's mission as his own – and he would not be deterred. And some day, in the not too distant future, Police Officer, or Detective, or Sergeant Michael Simon, would ask permission from the current commanding officer of Queens Homicide if he could review an old, cold case from many years ago. And when that permission was granted what would Michael Simon find in those musty folders? The existence of a never publicized second perpetrator? And if so, I knew what he would do, and I shuddered to think of his knock on my door.

Or maybe I would welcome it.

. . .

On Sunday, as we did every so often, Rabbi Marc Berman and I joined Mort Stern at his store for some spirited conversation. Mort closed early on Sundays, around six p.m. After he hung the CLOSED sign in the window and pulled the shades down, he would make three egg creams and we would talk, and argue, on a number of the world's problems – past, present and future. And tonight the topic of discussion first centered on Michael Simon and how well he had coped so far with his new identity, and his goal of becoming a police officer.

It didn't take long, no more than ten minutes, for us to conclude the newly-discovered Jew, with the Catholic upbringing, would do fine in his life to come, Mort Stern taking full credit for what he called teaching Mikey the facts of life, and not the religious fairy tales I and the church had preached to him. He added, "Now dat the poor boy is out of the army, Berman here will try to stuff his head wid his own brand of fairy tales."

That comment prompted our usual heated discussion, which always failed to sway Mort, and probably never would. When we all ran out of arguments, Mort said, "Listen you two, I need some advice."

"You're kidding us, right?" Marc said. "You never took a word of advice from me or Francis in your life."

"Bah. Be quiet and listen for a change. I vant to read you this newspaper story first. Then ve talk."

Mort reached into his back pocket and unfolded a small newspaper clipping. He said, "This vas in the *Times* two veeks ago." He adjusted his glasses, but hesitated. "You know, maybe you two should read it yourselves. I haf…uh, difficulty vid it."

Marc looked at me and raised his eyebrows as he took the clipping from Mort, whose hand, I noticed, was quivering. After Marc read it without comment, he handed it to me and here is what it said – *Hamburg, Germany* – "From his post as a teenage SS Private in a watchtower in the Auschwitz-Birkenau concentration camp, Bruno Dettler could hear the screams of Jews dying in the gas chamber. And Dettler later told investigators the carting of their dead bodies to the camp's crematoria was a daily sight. Twenty-nine years later Dettler, now forty-seven years of age, went on trial Tuesday on 3,782 counts of murder. Caught two months ago in his native city of Dresden, by the famed group of Nazi hunters, Dettler showed little expression, but appeared to be listening attentively as the prosecutors detailed the charges against him. 'The accused was no ardent worshipper of Nazi ideology,' they argued, 'but there is also no doubt he never actively challenged the persecutions of the Nazi regime.' Dettler's defense counsel argued 'he was drafted into the SS in December of 1944, as soon as he turned eighteen, and was assigned to the camp for a period of less than six weeks until it was liberated by the Soviet Army on January 27, 1945. They claim that had he challenged his superiors by demanding they stop the killings, he himself would have been shot and his body burned up with the others.' If Dettler is convicted he will spend the rest of his life in prison, as Germany has no death penalty."

When I finished reading the article I handed it back to Mort and he said, "Is Bruno Dettler guilty of murder, and if so, should he spend the rest of his life in jail?"

Rabbi Berman immediately answered, "Yes, and yes."

Mort nodded and said, "And you, Francis?"

"I'm not as certain as Marc, but he was a part of the apparatus – the great killing machine – after all."

"Yes, he vas, and, as they say here in America, payback is a bitch. And it is now the Jews' turn to exact retribution and vengeance, *nicht wahr*? Isn't that right?"

"You sound skeptical," Berman said stroking his salt-and-pepper beard, "and I'm wondering why, since you were a prisoner there yourself and suffered tremendously."

"Ya, for less than two years. The Nazis grabbed me at my house in Dresden in late 1943."

"Dresden?" I said. "Isn't that where this Dettler came from?"

"Ya, four houses down from me, on Apfel Street. Growing up he was friends mit my son, Benjy. My wife, Ruth, and I were friends with his parents, Kurt and Greta."

I figured Marc Berman was as stunned as I was at this revelation. He managed to speak first and said, "My God, Mort, I never knew you had a family over there."

"Sometimes their existence is like a dream to me. Ven they came for me, they took them, too. I never knew vat happened to them, but they took them someplace other than Auschwitz."

"Did you encounter Bruno when he came to the camp?" I asked.

"Oh, ya. I think he arrived there around December 20, and I first saw him – no, he spotted me first – on December 24, Christmas Eve."

"How did he react?" Marc asked.

"Shocked beyond vords. Finally, he said, 'Mr. Stern, I vill help you if I can, but I'm scared.'"

"I told him to be very careful vit consorting vit the prisoners. He vent away, but snuck back later vit a loaf of bread and other food for me.

Enough to share vit the others. He said they got extra rations for Christmas."

"When the Red Army arrived and liberated the camp, what became of Dettler?" I asked.

"Ve vent together back home to Dresden," Mort said.

"How did you manage that?" Marc asked. "I mean, he was in an SS uniform. Why wasn't he captured?"

"Bruno had tried to save me by continually providing me vit the food I needed to survive and continue to work. If I was strong enough to work, they vudn't burn me up. So I saved him. My friends in the tailor shop – ve Jews have always been good tailors, you know – made him a suit of civilian clothes. I told him ven the Russians came, all the Nazis vud flee, but he should come to me, and that's vat happened. I told him to keep his boots, they were brand new, and also his overcoat but with the insignia ripped off. I said if he vas questioned he should say he got the boots and coat off a dead soldier. I also told him to say his papers vere lost and he vas sixteen years old."

"So you got away and headed for home and you made it there safely?" I asked.

"Ya, but it vusn't easy. It vas vinter and ve had to walk across a lot of Poland vit hardly any food. Ve got there on February 20, and if you read *Slaughterhouse Five*, you know what ve found."

"A bombed-out destroyed city," Marc said. "Wiped out by a massive allied bombing attack and resulting firestorm on February 13, 1945."

"There vus nothing left but rubble. No opera house. No my house, or Bruno's house. No block ve lived on. No store I owned vit my partner, Izzy. Nothing."

"What happened to Bruno?" I asked.

"He stayed and helped rebuild the city. He vowed to try to find out what happened to Ruth and Benjy and to his own family, who it was assumed had been obliterated in the bombing. He failed on both counts, but became a successful businessman there. A vunderful boy. Him and my Benjy reminded me so much of Mikey. Maybe dat's vhy I took such a liking to him."

We sat in silence for a minute sipping our egg creams. Mort slammed his glass on the table – I was surprised it didn't shatter – and said, loudly,

"Now, I ask you vunce more. Is Bruno Dettler guilty of murder, and should he spend the rest of his life behind bars?"

The Rabbi didn't answer so fast this time. He took a deep breath, looked directly at Mort, and said, "Yes, and yes."

"And you, Father Manzo? Do you agree vit the vengeful Rabbi here?"

"No, I do not. Not at all."

"Because you're not a Jew, Francis –"

"No, but I am," shouted Mort. "And a terrible injustice is about to be committed on a righteous man who saved me from the gas chamber. And the sad part, Rabbi, is they all agree vit you."

"What do you mean?" he asked.

"Dat's the advice I vanted from you two. Should I travel to Hamburg and testify on behalf of Bruno Dettler?"

"Do you think you could convince them to change their accusations against him, based on your experience at Auschwitz and your life in Dresden before that?" I asked.

"No. I spoke with the defense attorneys and they said the mood was such in Germany that my story, while beneficial to Dettler, would not change anyone's mind, nor alter the course of his inevitable punishment."

"Then why even ask the question?" Marc said.

"Because unlike you two holy men I feel a responsibility to a fellow human being, a *goy* no less, a German no less, who became an SS soldier for five weeks against his will, and who was truly a *mensch*. A good human being."

"That's an unfair accusation, Mort," Marc said.

"No, it isn't," I said. "Mort's right. If it were me I would go testify, whether it was a wasted trip, or not."

Mort smiled and said, "Thank you, Francis. I'll buy my ticket tomorrow."

Marc shook his head and said, "You two are misguided sentimentalists and are missing the bigger picture."

"Vich is?" Mort asked.

"Bruno Dettler was a piece of the worst regime to ever exist on this planet. As everyone, from Hitler on down the chain of command, he must be brought to justice and pay the price, if only to convince the rest of the world no one will ever again get away with perpetrating another Holocaust."

I had to admit the good Rabbi had a valid argument, but there are always exceptions to all blanket suppositions. I did not respond, but Mort did, looking Marc right in the eye, and saying, "Bah! Humbug!"

Mort Stern flew to Hamburg, and provided his moving, emotional, first-hand testimony on behalf of the former SS soldier who saved his life. And, as predicted, it had no effect on the outcome. Throughout the following years Mort maintained a written correspondence with Bruno and would occasionally send him a parcel of food, or cookies, or candy bars. The package always contained the same note, written by Mort in German – *Vielen Dank, Bruno. Ich werde es nie vergessen.* "Thank you, Bruno. I will never forget."

And Bruno would always respond, "May the God of Abraham always protect you, my friend." It was in German and I badgered the old survivor to translate it for me although I could pick out a few words myself. Mort would smile and say, "Bruno is a *mensch.* I say no more," forcing me to take a trip to the local library to get it translated. Diplomatically, I also said no more.

SIXTEEN

Michael was sworn into the New York City Police Department on a mild spring morning in April, 1979 taking the oath to uphold the constitutions of the State of New York and the United States and to serve and protect us all. Six months later we all attended his graduation ceremony at Madison Square Garden where newly-minted Police Officer Michael Simon came in fourth in his class of over a thousand recruits. We all cheered wildly as Michael stepped smartly across the stage and shook hands with the mayor and the police commissioner, and I believe our group, which included Michael's entire family, Rabbi Berman, and Mort Stern, was the loudest bunch in the arena. The announcer said in a somber voice, "Police Officer Michael Simon, from the Police Academy to the Seven-Five Precinct in Brooklyn." We didn't cheer that assignment at all.

I could see the looks of consternation on his six grandparent's faces, and Betty grabbed her husband's arm to steady herself. It would not have surprised me if Michael had lobbied for the assignment himself, to one of the most violent and crime-ridden precincts for the newly crowned blue knight. No tree-lined streets in Forest Hills, Queens or the North Bronx for our Mikey. If he suited up, he wanted to play the game.

And play the game he did. Three years and hundreds of quality arrests later got him assigned to the plainclothes Anti-Crime Unit. And three years later, the coveted gold shield of a detective was bestowed upon him by the commissioner with an assignment to a busy upper Manhattan precinct detective squad.

While Michael was making his bones on the NYPD, I was making my own in the church. After two more assignments as Pastor in larger parishes, I was promoted to the rank of Monsignor and assigned to the Bishop of Brooklyn's staff. Whatever I had thought this assignment entailed was nowhere near what it was. The best word to describe the bulk of my duties was *fixer*. I was handed the problems of the Diocese and fixed them. I buried them, transferred them, disavowed them, plastered and painted over them, and lied about them, to our parishioners and to the press. And I did it all with a broad, toothy, Italian smile on my hypocritical face.

The Bishop had assured me what I had been assigned to do was truly "God's work" and necessary to protect Holy Mother Church from the heathens who were bent on destroying her. "We must take care of our problems internally, Francis. We cannot let outside forces intervene. We will root out the evil ones among us and cast them from the church ourselves."

We never did any such *casting out*, but merely moved our problems from one parish to another or from one Diocese to another. And the reason no action was taken against deviant priests was that they were protected by deviant bishops, and yes, even a deviant cardinal or two. I was sickened by what I had seen and been a part of, and was contemplating resigning from the priesthood, when the smiling Bishop called me into his office and in essence told me since I had been so good at my job in Brooklyn, the Cardinal of the New York Archdiocese had reached out for me to provide the same services to him in Manhattan.

This promotion I likened to a transfer from the position of *consigliere* for the Brooklyn mob to the same position for the Manhattan mob, and I vowed to not accept it and leave the church. And on the way back to my quarters from the Bishop's office, I had it – an epiphany – a first-class, bright vision accompanied with a booming voice in my brain. The words, spoken in a mocking, sneering tone said, *Run again, you coward. Run like you ran away from those three dying people years ago.* And the vision accompanying those words was of a squealing new-born baby desperately reaching his tiny hands out to me. Suddenly the baby stopped crying and said in a commanding voice, *Save me, Joey. Save yourself. Save the church. Only you can do it. You must do it.* I staggered over to an armchair and collapsed into it. I could now truly imagine what

Saul experienced on the road to Damascus, his epiphany, his burst of light with instant conversion to become a follower of Christ. The message to me was clear – *To atone for your actions and finally quiet that crying baby, you must expose the rottenness of the church.* And I vowed to do exactly that.

Before my transfer to the Archdiocese, I compiled a detailed list of all the transgressions and dispositions of the cases. It contained the priest's name, victim's name and address, parish, responding police officer's name (if any), detective investigating (if any), monetary settlement (if any) and all case numbers. They numbered in the hundreds, and I filed them under the categories of, "Consensual Sex," "Non-consensual sex," "Pedophilia – male," and "Pedophilia – female."

There were dozens of cases of consensual sex between priests and the laity – both hetero- and homosexual interactions, and the same with nuns and the laity. And several between priests and nuns. These cases came to our attention from one of the consenting partners deciding to "come clean" or from a tipoff by another priest, nun or parishioner who was aware of the behavior and wanted it stopped. And I was the one charged with stopping it.

I had called Mike and asked him to lunch and to accompany me back to my office for a chat. "I need your investigative expertise," I had said.

"You have a crime you want me to investigate?"

"No, I'll do the investigating. But I need tips on the interviewing process including signs of deception and statement taking – those sorts of things."

"When we meet it will be helpful to know exactly what type of …uh, bad behavior you will be targeting."

I hesitated a moment. "Sexual mis-behavior. Can we leave it at that for now?"

He chuckled and said, "See you Tuesday."

. . .

Thus began our weekly meetings which continued upon my transfer to Manhattan. One day as Mike was leaving he said, "Frank, can I ask a favor?"

"If I can do anything for you, I will. What is it?"

"I've been a detective for several years now and have applied for a transfer to homicide, but never seem to get it while others, who I believe are less qualified, do get it. I know you're close with the Cardinal and I know he's close with the police commissioner –"

"Change your name to Kelly."

"What?"

"What religion and ethnic background did you put on your police application?"

"I don't remember. Probably *None* for religion and *Jewish* for ethnicity. Why?"

"The New York City Police Department is run by Irish Catholics and they take care of their own first. After them, the pecking order is tied between Irish Protestants and Italian Catholics, followed by other Catholics, other Protestants, and then the Jews."

"Meaning I'm at the bottom of the barrel?"

"No. After the Jews come the blacks, Latinos, and Muslims, not necessarily in that order."

"That's a lousy picture you're painting, Frank. I guess I'm screwed."

"Maybe not. I have been waiting for an opportunity to test my influence. I have an important position, but more importantly I know where the bodies are buried, if you know what I mean. I'll get back to you soon."

"Thanks, Frank. Your intervention is most appreciated."

"You're welcome. Oh, how are Vivian and the kids?"

"Viv's great, and Maddy and Andy are growing like weeds."

"Say hello from me. Oh, don't forget our monthly Sunday get-together at Stern's.

"I'll be there. I *vudn't vant* to miss the old man breaking Marc's and your balls."

I laughed and said, "Bah. Humbug." As Mike got up to leave I said, "Mike, which homicide squad do you want if I can swing it?"

"Queens, the borough of my birth, and their office is close to home."

Queens Homicide. Were those the only reasons he wanted that assignment?

•   •   •

I had remained close to Mike, Marc Berman, and Mort Stern over the years, and valued highly their friendship and spirited discussions. The four of us could say anything to one another, including insults and profanity, but only when we four were present. Occasionally a wife or two, and a child or two, would join our get-togethers and we would act like model citizens. One Sunday afternoon a few years ago, twenty-five year old Mikey Simon brought an attractive young woman into the store. He introduced her as Vivian Saunders, his fiancée. Mort immediately said, "Vat's a good looking schicksa like you doing vit this ugly Jew?"

There was no doubt in my mind Mike had forewarned Vivian what to expect from us. He would have been a fool if he hadn't. Vivian, her hazel eyes flashing, feigned surprise. She put her hand up to her mouth, looked at Mike and said, "You're a Jew?"

"Yes, dear," he said.

"Funny, you don't look Jewish."

As the laughter began she turned to Mort and said, "But you definitely look like a Jew, you old *kvetcher*."

Mort burst into laughter and said, "You got me, young lady. I'm *likink* you already."

•   •   •

Vivian was a Lutheran, and in deference to his new wife, they were married in her church. By now Mike was as much a non-believer as Mort, although he used to say he was an agnostic – someone who couldn't know if there was, or was not, a God somewhere.

We all jumped on him for that, saying that was the perfect cop-out and we finally forced him into a decision, and he chose to side with Mort. He said, "I've had twelve years of brainwashing by the Catholics, including having to learn Latin. Then the Rabbi here tried to brainwash me into converting, getting mitzvahed, and learning Hebrew. No thanks, one institution is as bad as the other."

Mort jumped up and down with glee and said, "Mikey, I knew you vere the smartest guy here. About time you gave up the fairy tales."

Mike said, "By the way, Father Manzo and Rabbi Berman, I'd like you both to say a few words of blessing for Vivian and me at our wedding along with the minister."

"Vat?" Mort said.

Mike smiled and said, "Calm down, old man. I'm going to quote you here. 'It vudn't hoit, vud it?'"

"Bah." Mort said, waving his hand in my face.

. . .

Life moved on as it always does and the joys were mixed with the sorrows, as they always were. Three of Mike's grandparents had passed on. My dad, Vincenzo, had a heart attack and died in his early seventies. Fortunately, I had visited them in Florida twice a year and had seen him alive about a month before the attack. Momma Maria bore it well and looked as if she could live forever. Both of Mike's sisters, Mary Beth and Betty Ann were married and had careers. Andy and Betty were anxiously awaiting a grandchild, but their daughters, so far, had not shown any interest in procreating. Maybe Mikey and his lively new wife would come through for them. I had spoken to the Cardinal about Mike Simon and he smiled and said, "Let me see what I can do, Frank."

Two weeks later a Detective Division order came out transferring Mike to Queens Homicide. I knew it before he did and showed surprise when he bounded into the candy store that afternoon with his good news. After we all congratulated him he said, "You know, when I get there I'm going to read the case investigation on my parents murders."

"Why would you want to open old wounds?" Rabbi Berman asked.

"Curiosity, I guess, but maybe they overlooked something back then."

"Like vat?" Mort said. "Dey got the guy, right?"

"Yeah, they did, but I want to read it anyway."

I said nothing as a cold lump began to form in the middle of my stomach.

. . .

At our next monthly meeting a quiet Mike Simon sipped his egg cream and said, "I have some surprising news –"

"She's pregnant already?" Marc said.

"No, not yet, but we're trying. My news is about my parents' murder. It seems there was a second perpetrator involved."

"How can dat be?" Mort asked as the cold lump again made its presence known in my belly.

Mike took out some papers and said, "Evidently they didn't tell my step-dad everything at the time. I pieced this together from the hundreds of pages of reports in the file. They found an unknown blood type in the bedroom. It was A-negative and did not come from my parents or Selewski, the killer. They also found a partial unknown fingerprint on the bedroom wall. The CO of Queens Homicide and the lead investigator would have liked to wrap the case up fast in a tight package, but had to face the obvious fact that a second person was at the murder scene. But who was he and what was his degree of involvement?

"The forensic investigation had gone as far as it could go. The Automated Fingerprint Identification System was a dream of the future. DNA profiling was something out of a science fiction novel. Selewski's white convertible had been found parked around the corner on 119 Avenue. No fingerprints other than his were found in, or on, the vehicle. And no other items of evidence pointing to another person's presence in the vehicle were discovered.

"The deaths of my parents were investigated as thoroughly as humanly possible. The neighborhood was canvassed numerous times to the point that some of their neighbors exclaimed. 'You guys, again! I told you already what I know – nothing!' All of my dad's prior arrestees were investigated for a possible revenge motive resulting in another dead end. Selewski's friends, associates, relatives, and neighbors were interviewed – interrogated would be more appropriate – yielding nothing. All had alibis. Alibis were confirmed. The case was never closed, but gradually, as the years went by, it slipped into the back files of the bottom drawer in the office of Queens Homicide. Homicide Case Number Q-232-57 gradually became a cold case. And as the years passed by, it turned into an ice-cold case."

"And they never yet found any leads on this guy?" I asked, dreading the answer.

"No Frank, and based solely on that physical evidence we couldn't find him today either."

"Did they fingerprint Selewski's friends and associates?" Marc asked.

"They were going to, but the father of one of his friends was a criminal defense lawyer and advised them not to voluntarily get their fingerprints on record. He told the investigating detective he was fishing, and told Pete's buddies the cops would always have their prints on file and use them to frame them for a crime they did not commit."

"Vat a bastard," Mort said. "Lawyers. Bah!"

"What happens now?" I asked.

"The boss gave me permission to work on the case when I'm not busy on a current investigation."

"How can you possibly locate this guy now?" Marc asked.

"I don't know, but I'm going to try my damndest to find him and arrest his cowardly ass."

"For what, Mike? Wasn't Selewski the only shooter?"

"Yes, but that other guy is as guilty as Selewski just by being at the scene. It's called Felony Murder, and the charge will stick."

Not if he acted under duress, I almost blurted out.

"Exactly how will you proceed?" Marc asked.

"Re-interview all the witnesses who are still alive. Track down Selewski's associates and get their fingerprints and blood types –"

"How vill you get dat from them?"

"Ask politely, and do a record check on all Pete's known associates at the time. I bet a good percentage of them have been printed by now, and I bet a lot of blood types are also on the record."

"What if you ask politely and someone politely refuses to be fingerprinted and provide his blood type?" I asked.

"Zero in on him as the possible perp, but while I'm doing that I'll wait patiently for the science to catch up and help me out."

"What science, Mike?" Marc asked.

"AFIS. The development of a fully-automated fingerprint identification system is a few months away. And a new blood identification technique called DNA profiling. It's supposed to identify a suspect by this stuff called DNA. I think that means deoxynucleic acid or something like that, and it's present in every bodily cell. It's supposed to be as positive as a fingerprint in identifying a perp."

The stone in my gut grew noticeably bigger and colder and I envisioned Detective Mike Simon coming into the store one Sunday afternoon and saying, "I got him identified. His name is Giuseppe Mastronunzio, if you can believe that. Now all I have to do is find him."

And will I say? "Finding him will be easy, Mike. He's sitting right in front of you."

Or will I say nothing, and tremble in fear as I await my inevitable discovery?

.   .   .

The years passed by and my list grew to over a thousand names, but I was not yet in a powerful enough position to act upon it. I knew I needed the assistance of many bishops with similar problems who would have the courage to join my crusade someday, but the kindly, aging Cardinal I worked for wanted no part of exposing anyone during his tenure. "I'm getting old, Francis," he said, "and will retire when I reach the mandatory age. I sympathize with your cause, but let my successor handle it." Typical of the church and its leaders, always passing the buck, but I was determined the buck would not be passed by me. When the time was right I would confer with Mike Simon on how to proceed against these miscreants, preferably with a criminal arrest.

As I awaited that right time, and as I also awaited the dreaded knock on my door exposing me as a possible murderer, the Cardinal, who had recently come back from a visit to Rome, called me into his office and invited me to sit down. He poured us each an inch of fine scotch into two crystal glasses and handed one to me. He said, "I've just come back from a visit with His Holiness in Rome." He raised his glass and motioned for me to do the same. "To His Excellency, Francis Andrew Manzo, the new Bishop of Brooklyn."

I was flabbergasted. The present Bishop of Brooklyn had turned 75, the church's mandatory retirement age, a few months ago and the odds-on choice to be his successor was his current senior Auxiliary Bishop. My selection would come as big a surprise to all the auxiliary bishops in the Archdiocese as it had to me. I swallowed my scotch and said, "Thank you, Your Eminence. I will serve the church with honor, loyalty and dedication, but am somewhat mystified why I was chosen ahead of more senior qualified leaders in the church."

The Cardinal poured us some more scotch and smiled at me. "I put in a good word for you to the Pope himself." Then he leaned forward and stared into my eyes adding, "Oh, this appointment will keep you extremely busy. You may want to put those other matters we discussed on the back burner for a while, Francis – a long while."

I immediately got the message, but even if that message came not from Cardinal Callahan, but from His Holiness the Pope himself, I would not be dissuaded one iota from my mission. I would not be bought off with a promotion.

And, by giving me this promotion, I now had the power to pursue it full steam ahead.

PART FOUR

THE COLD CASE

(SUMMER 2000)

SEVENTEEN

I arrived at IAB's office at a leased facility in Rego Park, at 8:45 Wednesday morning. It was a foreboding, red-brick, two-story building, and the minions of Internal Affairs were its sole inhabitants. The single sign on the front door said, *City of New York, Administrative Offices.* Who the hell were they kidding? Every cop in the city knew this location, and no doubt more than one of them dreamed of attacking it with bombs dropped from a helicopter. My *invitation* said I was to report to a Deputy Inspector Elliott in Room 213. I walked up the stairs and found my delegate, Lieutenant Tony Rafferty, Irish eyes smiling in his smooth, round face, awaiting me. I gave him a rundown on the case and he said, "Sounds righteous to me, Mike, but they'll try to make something out of nothing. They always do."

"Let's go get this over with," I said, as I opened the office door and walked inside. We were greeted by a female secretary who did not ask us to sit but pressed an intercom button and said into her handset, "Inspector, your nine a.m. appointment is here," followed by a, "Yes, sir." She got up, opened the office door and said, "Go right in, please."

There were two men behind the desk in suits and ties and both stood up as we entered. The man in the middle of the desk extended his hand, smiled and said, "D.I. Ray Elliott, Lieutenant." I shook his outstretched hand and the other man extended his and said, "Captain Bill Presti."

They were starting off in friendly mode and so would I. "Mike Simon, Queens Homicide, sirs," although they already knew that. They offered me a chair in front of the desk and Tony Rafferty walked to a chair at the back of the office, his accustomed spot. He said, "I know my place, Inspector."

"You should. You've been here enough times. I should order up a fold-away bed."

This was jolly, everyone smiling and joking, but I knew it wouldn't last long. Ray Elliott was tall and lanky with the faded, splotchy complexion of a reformed alcoholic. His watery hazel eyes were not friendly eyes, despite the smile on his face. Captain Presti was a little on the portly side, but his dark brown eyes seemed more friendly than his boss's. His brown bald head was fringed with white hair, and I wondered how he got this tan so early in the year. Maybe he was one of those Mediterranean types who browned up in one day. Elliott said, "Please begin by relating the details of the case from its beginning up to the time the defendant was shot and killed by Detective Paul. Take your time and try to leave nothing out. Oh, I should tell you this whole interview is being recorded."

"On video?" I asked.

"No, just audio. Video is in next year's budget, though."

Sure it is. While cops ride around in patrol cars with 150,000 miles on them.

.   .   .

It took me twenty minutes to relate the story, and they let me do it without interruption. The questions began, exploring my personal relationship with Mort Stern and hammering me on my decision to not utilize ESB for the arrest of Rosario. A voice from behind me said, "Excuse me, Inspector. It's time for a break."

"Certainly, Lieutenant Rafferty. Ten minutes."

We walked to the men's room where I took a long drink from the water cooler. "What do you think, Tony?"

"I think you are handling it well, but there's no doubt where they are going. They think you ordered Paul, directly, or implied by the circumstances of the case, to pop Rosario and exact revenge for Stern's murder."

"Yeah, I know, but that's not true. Why would I bother getting an arrest warrant? I had probable cause to make a summary arrest without it."

"For a cover story, which is what they'll accuse you of." He looked at his watch and said, "Let's get back in there."

The questioning and re-telling went on until we broke for lunch. They did not play good-cop, bad-cop with me, knowing I was too savvy to fall for that and, so far, they had been respectful and non-accusatory. That all changed when we resumed at 1:15.

It soon became obvious they had discussed the morning's interview over lunch and had to change their tactics to try to break me down. Captain Presti, his face in a scowl now, got right to the point. "We believe you are a liar, Simon."

I said nothing. I had not been asked a question.

"He said you're a liar," Elliott shouted. "How do you respond to that?"

"I told the truth in every detail this morning, sir."

"Baloney," Presti said. "You killed Ismael Rosario to avenge the murder of your friend, Mort Stern, didn't you?"

"I killed no one," I reminded them.

"No, Detective Paul pulled the trigger – on your orders."

And on, and on, it went for the next two hours, and then they took their final shot – a desperation move. It was after the three o'clock break and when we came back into the room, only Captain Presti was present. He had a smug smile on his face and said, "Inspector Elliott will join us shortly."

Ten minutes later, Elliott strode in and took his seat behind his desk, shuffling some papers he had brought with him. Here it comes, I figured, the acting performance of the day. I wondered if it would be Oscar worthy. "Lieutenant Simon," he said, "we will give you one opportunity to change your story and come clean with the truth. We're listening."

"I have nothing to change, sir. As I said numerous times before, I told you the truth all the way, all day."

"Too bad," he said. "You should have taken advantage of our offer because…"

Here it comes. Which one will they say turned on me? One of the rookies – guaranteed.

"…Officer Ferrand told us during the planning of the arrest of Ismael Rosario you stated you wouldn't be upset if Rosario weren't taken alive. Do you dispute that statement?"

"I do. I never said anything like that, or implied anything like that."

"He further stated Detective Paul told him after he shot Rosario he did so to avenge the death of your friend, Stern, and did so on your orders. Paul's exact words, according to Ferrand were, 'We're not taking him out of here in cuffs, Simon told me. I got the message.'"

Was this asshole serious?

"What do you have to say to that, Simon?" he yelled.

"If that is true, I assume Detective Paul has been placed under arrest for murder, and you intend to also arrest me at this time. I suggest you read me my rights, and then I will call my lawyer. I will not say another word."

Presti and Elliott looked at each other. I extended my wrists out and said, "Snap the cuffs on me, and I'll soon be a millionaire."

I had called their bluff and they sat frozen in place. I stood up and said, "If I'm not under arrest, I'm leaving right now. This interview is over."

"You sit back down," spluttered Elliott.

I turned from him and said, "We're outta here, Tony. Come on, I'll buy you a cup of coffee."

As I walked toward the door Elliott screamed, "You be back here at nine a.m. tomorrow, Simon. That's a direct order."

I said nothing and walked out the door. In the hallway Rafferty said to me, "Great job, Mike. I liked the way you called their bluff, but they are going to be in some foul mood tomorrow."

"I'm not coming back here tomorrow, or any other day, concerning this matter. This IAB investigation is over."

"Mike, you heard Elliott give you a direct order. You don't show up you will be charged with insubordination."

"Orders can be countermanded, Tony."

"You got the juice to do that?"

"I'll find out soon. I'm going back to the office and make the necessary call."

"Your rabbi better be a big one, maybe a real rabbi like the head Hassidim in Boro Park."

I laughed and said, "Maybe a real rabbi voodn't hoit vunce in a vile, as old man Stern used to tell me."

.   .   .

Back in the office the four-to-twelve crew and the night supervisor, Sergeant Charlie Seich, were signing in. I called both the day and night crews to listen up and said, "I'm back from IAB on the Rosario investigation. As the others come back, send them to my office. After we confer, I'll come out and fill you all in on the status of the case. No questions for now."

They nodded as I walked into my office and closed the door. I picked up my phone and dialed a number familiar to me. No secretary would intervene on this direct line. "Hello," the voice said.

"Hello, Frank, it's your favorite homicide lieutenant."

"Mike, how the hell are you?"

"I need a favor."

"If I can. Does your favor concern how you guys, uh…*handled* the killer of our old friend, Mort?"

"Yes, it does," I said and proceeded to relate the IAB harassment, and how I wanted it over.

"You know, Mike, I remember our Sunday meetings with Mort Stern fondly. As we already discussed it was a tragic shame what happened to him. And I'm glad his killer had street justice served on him saving the city a trial."

"Tough words from the Bishop of Brooklyn," I said, "but remember, Rosario went for a gun. We didn't assassinate him."

"Either way, I'm glad he is no longer prowling the streets selling his deadly wares. Now are you telling me straight up the Rosario takedown was on the up and up and done strictly by the book?"

"One hundred percent kosher, Your Excellency."

"Okay, I'll get back to you shortly. Stay near the phone."

Twelve minutes later my phone rang and Frank said, "It's a done deal, Mike. You should be getting a call from IAB shortly canceling your appearance, and the appearances of all of your men."

"Thanks, Frank, I owe you big time for this."

"No, you don't, you owe me a big *lunch*. Now when the hell are you coming down to Brooklyn and paying off? We haven't met in awhile and I need to bounce something off you after we eat."

"As soon as I wrap up this investigation and go back to a normal routine which should be soon. I'll call you next week. I promise."

"I'll hold you to that," he said and disconnected the call.

.   .   .

When Tony Rafferty was kidding me about my r*abbi* he was using a long-standing reference in the police department that meant a *hook, or friend in high places.* And Frank was my hook – my rabbi – and he occupied a high place in the church hierarchy. I was extremely fortunate to have met him many years ago, and he had guided my career as I moved up the ranks. How influential was he now? When a decision had to be made on who the new CO of Queens Homicide was to be, I was one among five other equally qualified lieutenants. However, a call from Frank to the detective boro commanders in both Brooklyn *and* Queens sealed the deal and I got the position.

And that was a favor I hadn't asked him for, although I was going to do so. He had beat me to the punch and called me and said, "Mike, how would you like a transfer from Brooklyn Narcotics?"

"To where?" I had asked.

"Queens Homicide needs a CO with the retirement of Lieutenant Edwards. Want it?"

"Oh, yeah, Frank. It's a dream assignment."

"Consider it done."

And, three days later, it was done. Just like that.

My reverie was broken by the ringing of the phone on my desk. I picked up and a woman said, "This is Sergeant Berni from Queens Internal Affairs. Inspector Elliott asked me to notify you, and all the officers on your team, that your nine o'clock interviews scheduled for tomorrow are postponed until further notice."

Postponed until further notice? The bastard wouldn't use the word canceled. He wanted to put the fear of a possible future interview into all of us. I wasn't going to play along. "Thank you, Sergeant. I will inform my team as directed. I'll inform them their appearances have been *canceled*, and this witch hunt is now over."

"But—"

"Good-bye, Sergeant Berni," I said, slamming the phone down and grinning ear to ear.

Yes!

.   .   .

Tom Catalano and Don Nitzky arrived back in the office first, followed five minutes later by Jamison and Ferrand, their lips tight in faces drained of color, deathly white above their navy blue uniforms. Finally, Micena and Paul came in and closed my office door. Richie said, "The bastards want us back there tomorrow."

"No wonder," I said. "I mean you confessed to murdering Rosario under my direct orders."

"What? Is that what those bastards laid on you?"

"Wait'll you hear—"

"Hold on, John," I said. "We'll all relate our tales of lies and deceit at IAB, but first I want to make an announcement. Come out to the main squad room."

Every detective had their eyes fixed on me not knowing what I was going to say or what had happened to their fellow officers in the dreaded rooms of Internal Affairs. I got right to the point. "This internal investigation is over. The grand jury found no true bill, and I have been informed by IAB all further interviews on this matter have been canceled. Officers Ferrand and Jamison will report back here in civvies for the next two days, as will Detectives Catalano and Nitzky, and we all will wrap up the paperwork on the Rosario case under the supervision of Detectives Micena and Paul."

"You mean John and Richie will get back in the duty chart on Monday?" Sergeant Seich asked. "My guys think they milked this Rosario caper long enough."

There were a few chuckles and Richie, a long-time friend of Seich said, "With all due respect, *Sergeant*, go fuck yourself."

Everybody broke into laughter at this much-needed tension reliever. Even Ferrand and Jamison managed weak smiles. I said, "I want everyone to listen to what these guys went through over at IAB. It will be good knowledge for you on your next visit." None of the guys on the day tour made a move to leave, wanting to hear the details. "When you're all done, let me know, I have a few more words to say to wrap things up. You nine to five guys keep hanging around. I'll sign OT slips for you."

I went back into my office to mull things over. I had something important to get into motion and this Rosario case interrupted it. My phone rang and it was Sergeant Lenny Miller from ESB. He said, "Hey, Loot, we got word our appearances at IAB tomorrow were canceled. I guess it went well today?"

"It went well," I said. "It's all over. When they finished with us, I guess they figured it wouldn't be worthwhile to speak to anyone else."

"That's great news. Not having to go to IAB is like the doctor telling you it's not cancer after all."

"An apt comparison, Lenny. And, again, thanks for your work at the scene in getting us through that door."

"Anytime, Loot. When you need a zip-zip-zip, I'll be there."

EIGHTEEN

By 5:45 it appeared they were all talked out with the tales of terror from their day at *Gestapo Headquarters*. I stood in the middle of them and gave them a brief rundown of my experiences there. I said, "Now, as unbelievable as this is going to sound at this particular time, let me tell you some good things about the Internal Affairs Bureau."

I waited for the groans and comments to subside and said, "We belong to a department of more than 35,000 men and women. As in any large organization we have our share of misfits – wife beaters, druggies, alcoholics, thieves, and even an occasional murderer. You know this as well as I do. That's why we need Internal Affairs. To police ourselves, so someone else doesn't have to. They do a good job of taking down those misfits, and if they stopped there, I would be their biggest cheerleader. However, their tactics in riding roughshod over us for bullshit allegations has caused them to be distrusted and despised."

"Amen to that," Don Nitzky said. "Look what we all went through today."

"Let me give you an example that happened to a friend of mine, a beat cop, several years ago. IAB received information that a cop's wife was a drug addict and the cop was obtaining drugs for her from the hospital on his post. They staked him out for over six months and the allegations were proved untrue. The cop went into the hospital once, to assist in bringing multiple aided cases into the ER. It was bitter cold and he stayed for a cup of coffee. At the conclusion of their investigation the cop received a complaint for leaving his post and not notifying the desk sergeant."

"You mean for the cup of coffee?" Cindy asked.

"Yes. Ten days pay for that. The other violation they observed was one day the cop took fifteen extra minutes for meal, and was apparently not disciplined by the desk sergeant. At his interview, the sergeant explained the officer apologized and said the diner, a half mile from the call box, was busy and he had to wait a long time for his food. The sergeant said he verbally reprimanded the officer."

"But I bet that wasn't good enough for them," John Micena said.

"Correct. The sergeant should have recorded that reprimand in the training ledger and the fifteen minute difference in the time log. He did neither. Ten days pay on each charge."

"Those bastards," muttered Tom Catalano.

"And, finally, the precinct CO was given a letter of reprimand – a certain career killer – for failure to properly train his sergeant."

"Unbelievable," Artie Ferrand said. "How can the top brass allow them to do this to us?"

"IAB does things like this to justify their existence because there are not enough bad cops around to do so. And the one guy who can change their culture, our police commissioner, has not seen fit to do so."

"Why not?" Nitzky asked. "Haven't the unions complained?"

"All the time, and he has always turned a deaf ear. He was a boss in Internal Affairs for a few years himself, so maybe that explains it."

"When you get to be the commissioner you'll set them straight, right, sir?" Ferrand asked.

"Artie, the last thing in the world I want is that job. But maybe you or Cindy could aspire to that position and set things straight."

■　　■　　■

We finally put IAB behind us and the day tour was out the door by six o'clock. So was I. I was home by six-thirty and Vivian and I had a glass of wine before dinner in the den, and the kids joined us with their cans of cola. I rarely brought my work home with me, but this case was an exception. We all knew Mort Stern, and I would often bring Maddy and

Andy to his store for an egg cream or root beer float. Many times Vivian would join us. My fourteen-year old son said, "I don't understand why you had to go to a grand jury and Internal Affairs."

"Andy," I said, "it's routine and necessary. No one would want police shooting civilians - even though they were bad guys – without proper and legal justification, right?"

"Yeah, I guess so, but it seems the bad guys have more rights than the good guys."

"No," I said, although I secretly agreed with him.

"Dad," Maddy said, "Do you think Mr. Stern is in heaven now? I mean I know he didn't believe in God, but –"

"But he was a good man, right? My answer to your question is this – if there is a heaven, Mordechai Stern should certainly be there. Picture this - Mort Stern finds himself at the pearly gates seconds after his death. He tells St. Peter, 'I can't believe it! I vuz wrong! Let me apologize to the Big Guy, and I'll vip him up an egg cream.'"

After the chuckles died down I said, "If you want to continue this discussion, let's do it after dinner. I had a long day and I am one hungry guy."

And continue it we did, discussing life, death, God, Jesus, Heaven, Messiahs, Moses, resurrections, faith, science, reason, and belief. The kids had been exposed to a lot of conflicting ideas in their years. They had a father who was raised a Roman Catholic until he found out he was a Jew, and he had explored and partook in that faith for a while. Their mother was a Lutheran and they were brought up in that faith. They had one set of Jewish grandparents, they never knew, and one set of Christian grandparents. Also a Jewish grand uncle and an Irish Catholic grand aunt. And they were adored by all of them. Confusion, indeed.

One day Maddy had said, "Andy and I discussed all of this and came to the conclusion, for the time being, we'll continue going to the Lutheran church with mom." She smiled and added, "You could come with us once-in-a-while besides Christmas and Easter. We are a family, you know."

I smiled back and said, "I am a man of all religions, my dear children. I admire and respect them all."

And believe in not one of them.

. . .

The next two days would be wrap-up ones. I called Captain McHale in the 106 Precinct and told him I was sending Ferrand and Jamison back to him on the following Monday morning. He said, "Oh, thank you, Mike. Didn't you say three days?"

"Has it been longer, Captain?" I joked. "Time does fly by."

"How did they work out for you?"

"Real pros. I'm sending over letters of commendation for them for their part in this investigation. They got great experience including grand jury testimony and a grilling at Gestapo Headquarters."

"I bet they loved *that*," he said, "but it was good they got their feet wet."

I next called Lieutenant Simmons in the 106 Squad and told him Catalano and Nitzky would be returning Monday with letters of commendation. "Glad to have them back, Mike. And congrats on solving that case."

"Thanks, Bert. Hope those captain's bars come your way soon."

On Friday I got a visit from not one, not two, but *four* narcotics squad detectives – Isnardi, Geyer, Evans, and Monroe. Charlie Evans said, "We got some info for you and your team, but first I gotta ask how you did it?"

"Did what, Charlie?"

"Get our IAB appearances postponed. Me and Doug were supposed to go over there yesterday."

"They weren't postponed," I said. "They were canceled. This case is closed."

"Uh, huh," he said with a smile. "You must have some real Big Kahuna motherfucker in your corner, you white devil."

"Could be. Now tell me, bro, what has you gots for us?"

We all gathered in the main squad room and I said, "Stop slaving over those typewriters and listen up to our brothers from Narcotics."

George Geyer said, "When word of Rosario's death got around, a lot of tongues magically loosened up."

"I had two of my informants tell me about cases similar to Stern's," Doug Monroe said. "They said two junkies they knew had been strong-armed by Rosario to set up robberies like he did with Vinny DeGiglio."

"We did some follow-up and sure enough there was a stick-up where the proprietor was shot in the arm and his *hidden* cash box stolen," Evans said.

"And a back door burglary," Isnardi said, "where a well-hidden bag of cash disappeared with the wind."

"Any word on the distributor of HHC?" Micena asked.

"Oh, yeah," Monroe said. "Another informant came through on that, but we missed him."

"What do you mean?" Catalano asked.

"When we raided his place," Evans said, "it was empty. A crummy two-bedroom apartment over a hardware store. All we found were traces of heroin in the floorboard cracks and a handful of glassine envelopes."

"With the HHC logo stamped on them?" I asked.

"Yes, on four of them."

"Any way to follow up on that?" Nitzky asked.

"Not until that logo shows up on the streets again," Monroe said. "But at least they're outta there and probably outta Queens completely."

As they left, Charlie Evans said to me, "Hey, bro, it was great workin' with you again. Like the old days when we walked the beat in the Seven-Five. Hey, do you remember the time we beat the shit out of –?"

I put my hand up and said, "Stop, Charlie, I don't remember anything from those days."

He laughed and said, "Be thankful they didn't have all these cell phones and video cameras way back then. Your white ass would be in jail right now."

"And so would your black one, bro."

"H-m-m-m, you do make a point. Adios, MF."

.   .   .

Friday arrived and the team went to lunch together for the last time. I told them as soon as they finished up they could go home – after I read and signed their reports which, I reminded them, had to be complete and grammatically correct. Richie Paul, certainly not an English major, said, "Don't worry, Boss. I used a couple of semicolons."

"Probably in the middle of a word," said John Micena.

"Uh, Lieutenant," Officer Ferrand said, "Can I ask you a question?"

"Fire away, Artie."

"I don't understand how you let Detective Evans get away with the language he used. He was outright disrespectful."

I smiled and said, "No, Artie, he was not. We have a friendship and camaraderie that transcends rank here in the dicks. I assure you he would call me Lieutenant Simon if a higher ranking officer were present. This is not the uniform force, different rules apply here."

"You can fucking say that again," Cindy Jamison blurted out, and then turned beet red and put her hand up to her mouth as we all roared in laughter.

"Goddammit, Cindy," Richie Paul said. "You're going to make a helluva detective."

"Fucking A," Tom Catalano said.

I looked at this fine group of cops assembled together for no doubt the last time and felt a swell of pride in my profession and the people I worked with. They were a dedicated, class act indeed. The whole bunch.

When I got back to the office there was a FedEx package addressed to me sitting on my desk. I zipped it open and inside was a sealed plastic bag and a note from Robert Stern. It said, "Debbie and I wish to thank you once again for your outstanding work in solving my dad's murder. I know you will distribute these ashes on your parents' graves, as you mentioned. Some are already in his store, so it is not necessary to sweep the floor ever again. I also wanted to let you know I received a call about a month after my father's's murder from Bruno Dettler hoping I would help him contact Mort, as the phone number he had for him had been disconnected. I knew the story of their time together in Auschwitz, and Dettler told me he had recently been released from prison and wanted to visit Mort in America. When I told him of his death, Bruno responded in broken English he and Mort had wept bitter tears when they had reached Dresden so many years ago and saw the utter destruction of their beloved city. Then he said, 'But I have not wept since, even after my conviction, but I will weep hard now for mein friend und your father.' All my gratitude and affection, Robert Stern."

It was a good thing my office door was closed as I reached into my back pocket for my handkerchief and automatically checked my other pockets for my comb and penknife. They were there, as Mort Stern instructed me so long ago.

As I wiped a tear from my cheek, there was a knock on my door. It was Richie Paul with a batch of reports for me to read and approve. "Just a couple left, Mike," he said. "We'll be done before four."

Good, I thought, I had a place to stop before heading home.

NINETEEN

As I drove east on the Grand Central Parkway in Queens, heading toward Beth David Cemetery in Elmont to visit my parent's graves, the memory of the items in the box of memorabilia came back vividly. When I was alone in my bedroom, I opened their wedding album. My immediate reaction was, *My God, they look so young*. And indeed they were, just twenty-five years old. My mother was beautiful, and a glance in the mirror left no doubt that I was her son. And my father, standing stiff, but with a smile that said he was the luckiest guy in the world at that moment in time.

What a treasure trove of memories and information were in that cardboard box. Right beneath the album was a smaller one containing black and white photos of him and others in uniform. He had been in the Army during the Korean War, and he had won a few medals of valor. My mother's teaching diplomas and pictures of her second grade class were there, and a thick journal she had hand-written over the years. A cardboard folder with an eight-by-ten photo of my father in his police uniform was lying atop a plastic box which contained his tie clasp, whistle, memo books and silver police shield in a leather case. And at the bottom of the box was me, the newborn baby boy, smiling in numerous photos alone, with my parents, with my grandparents and with my adoptive parents. And everyone was so damned happy, unaware of the tragedy that was soon to envelop them.

In those hours I spent examining those memories, two things cemented themselves in my mind. The first confirmed my decision to enter the army, like my father had done. And the second confirmed my decision for my life's work when I came out of the service. I, Michael Simon, would become a police officer. And that's exactly what I did.

Beth David Cemetery was about a mile over the Queens border in Nassau County and was within the confines of the Fifth Precinct where my father had served over forty years ago. I had no trouble finding my parent's gravesite in the confusing, narrow lanes of crowded headstones. I had been there many times before, the first at age eighteen soon after the family decided to tell me who I was, and who they were. I parked and walked over and put a pebble, in the Jewish tradition, on top of each half of the double headstone. First, my mother – "Veronica L. Simon – January 4, 1932 – June 16, 1957 - Our cherished daughter." Then my father, "Andrew H. Simon – August 2, 1931 – June 16, 1957 – Our cherished son."

"Mom, Dad," I said aloud, "I have a gift for you. The ashes of a once devout Jew who became a non-believer. I am also a non-believer, but I also believe in every non-believer there remains a tiny bit of hope, not for himself, but for those whom he loves dearly. And I hope Mordechai Stern has entered eternal happiness with you two in heaven."

I prayed the Jewish prayers for the dead and also said the rosary. A visage of Mort flashed through my mind of him saying, *Do both. It vudn't hoit.* When I finished, I got up off my knees, wiped the dust from my trousers, and scattered Mort's ashes around the gravesite. Once again speaking aloud I said, "Mom, Dad, I have not forgotten. I have not forgotten the second person who helped murder you. I have not given up. I am getting closer, I can feel it. I promise you justice, and I promise you closure. Your son will not fail you."

.   .   .

I was at my small cape-cod home in Fresh Meadows before six o'clock and told Vivian of my visit to the cemetery and my promise to my parents. She said, "Are you now getting closer to finding the second guy?"

"The science has advanced, but I need fresh eyes and fresh insights to look at the whole thing. I'm too close to it. I've read the files so many times nothing sticks anymore. I know I was put in charge of Queens Homicide for a reason—"

"Put in charge by God, perhaps?" she said, nudging me in the ribs. "Or is Divine Providence more palatable? Or maybe *Mysterious Unknown Forces?*"

I laughed and said, "Okay, okay you holy-roller, you got me. As I was saying, my drive to solve – fully solve – the murders of my parents caused me to seek out that assignment. First as a detective there, and now as the CO. Thus far, I have failed. But Mort's death has put a new impetus in me to attack the investigation."

"And who will be your new eyes with fresh insights?"

"My top two guys, John Micena and Richie Paul."

"Do they know who you are, and what happened forty-three years ago?"

"Not all of it. Few people outside my immediate family know."

"I hope they crack it for you. I fear it has been cranking up in your brain to the point of obsession."

"You noticed? Well, you're right. I truly want to solve this mystery and put it behind me. I want to move on. I need closure on this once and for all."

"Then what?"

"Maybe an early retirement – I have my twenty in, you know – or study for the Captain's test. It depends."

"Depends on finding the second man?"

"Yes."

"And what will you do when you find him?"

I thought for a moment and said, "Depends."

"On what?"

"On him. On who he became. On his story. On a lot of things."

"Will you kill him, God forbid, or arrest him?"

"I can't answer that now. It all depends on him."

"And dinner depends on me getting back over to the stove. Hey, my husband, I love you."

"I love you, too, Vivian, and always will."

Vivian had put the question right to me and I couldn't answer it. I had to find him first, and one thing we had not said or considered was he could be dead, but I didn't think so. He was out there somewhere, always looking over his shoulder waiting for me to appear. Waiting and trembling in fear, I hoped, the murdering bastard.

. . .

Paul and Micena were working 4 x12 this Monday and I got back to the routine of running my squad in the absence of another all-consuming whodunit like we experienced with Stern's murder. After our morning coffee and get-together I opened up the file storage room and, using the step ladder, retrieved the heavy pronto file from the top shelf. I mean, I *tried* to remove it, before realizing I needed some help. I got Sergeant Megara from his office and we got it down and carried it into my office and placed it on a table. "Looking for an old case in there, Mike?" he asked.

"That is the case."

"You mean three feet of paper comprises one case?"

"Yeah, Harry. It started out forty-three years ago and has never been solved completely."

"Wow, that's what you call ice-cold. What are you doing with it now?"

"I'm going to spend some time going through it, and when Paul, Micena, and Charlie Seich get in this afternoon the five of us are going to have a discussion about it."

"I have a hundred questions, Mike, but you don't want to hear them now."

"Correct, Harry. That's why you're my deputy CO, you always can read my mind."

He laughed and said, "See you later."

I looked over selected portions of the file and made some notes on a legal pad. I wanted to hit the highpoints and possible solvability factors, before I assigned Paul and Micena to dive into this old pile of crushed trees.

. . .

Four o'clock rolled around and my two sergeants, with Richie Paul and John Micena, were with me in my office. I said, "Richie, John, I have a job for you."

They looked at each other, then over to the pronto file, and nodded. "That box represents a case that began many years ago, on June 16, 1957 to be exact. It is a legitimate cold case belonging to this squad. Ice-cold, as Harry said this morning. I believe it is *partially* solved. I believe a second perpetrator was involved, a young man, who would now be about sixty years old , give or take, if he is alive. I want you two to read the appropriate sections of the case – I marked them – to convince yourselves that a second perpetrator was indeed involved."

"What if they don't agree with that, Mike?" asked Charlie.

"I believe they will, but if they conclude otherwise, and can convince me of their conclusion, I will move this case from *Open – Unsolved* to *Closed*."

"Do you want us to read this whole thing?" Richie asked.

"No, only pertinent sections as necessary. For now I want you to read the initial investigation and initial follow-up. Then we will put our heads together and discuss it tomorrow."

"Boss, why now?" John Micena asked. "What's so important about a forty-year old case?"

"Let me give you a brief summary of the crime and where it stands now. That should answer your questions."

"It's personal, isn't it?" Paul asked.

"Oh, yeah. On June 16, 1957 at about one a.m. an intruder, or intruders, cut the screen door on a home in Cambria Heights and entered. The assumption was their intent was burglary, but no items seemed to be missing. In the master bedroom slept a young couple, both twenty-five years old. They had intentionally left the inside front door all the way open, as well as all the windows in their bedroom in the hopes of catching a cross breeze on this unusually hot night."

"No AC back then, I remember," Micena said.

"No, I wish there had been. A locked front door most likely would have saved their lives. The young man was a Nassau County Police Officer assigned to the Fifth Precinct which, as you know, borders our 105 Precinct. It appears the officer kept his off-duty revolver close by, and when the intruders entered the bedroom and flicked the lights on a shoot out occurred resulting in the death of the couple and one of the intruders. It appears the second intruder fled the scene in panic, empty handed."

"If there was a second guy," Micena said.

"I'm certain there was, but we'll discuss that more fully at a later time. When the responding uniformed officers from the 105 Precinct arrived they immediately heard a baby crying from a bedroom down the hall from the master bedroom. When the police officer looked down at the baby, he smiled up at him and reached out to him."

"Figuring it was his father, I guess," Richie said.

"Yes, that's what their report concluded, but I certainly have no memory of that moment, of smiling and reaching for my father."

There were a few seconds of silence as they stared at me trying to comprehend what they had heard. Micena was the first to speak. "Are you saying that baby was you?"

"Yes, that was me. And the dead couple in the bed in the master bedroom was my parents – Andrew and Veronica Simon."

"Holy shit," two or three of them said simultaneously.

"Indeed. And I want you, John, and you, Richie, to find the second perpetrator and identify him to me. Will you take this task on?"

"We'll take it on, Mike," Micena said. "If he's out there, we'll find him, and we'll collar him, and deliver him to you on a silver platter."

"No, John, identify him and tell me where he is, and I'll take it from there."

"Uh, Boss, remember what we went through on the Rosario case?" Richie asked. "If you pop this guy…"

"I didn't say I was going to kill him, although that could happen."

"What *are* you going to do with him?" John asked.

"As I told my wife the other night, it depends. It depends entirely on him."

"I'm not getting you," Seich said.

"It depends on who he is now, what kind of life he has led, what his level of involvement in the murders was, and his state of mind. I want justice, and I need closure. One way or another I will get it. If you find him for me."

"We'll find him, Mike" Richie Paul said "As soon as you get these two useless sergeants the hell out of this office we two first-grade detectives will scrape the frost off this ancient box and get started right now."

TWENTY

I felt bad about taking my two top detectives away from the regular duty chart, and I said to Harry and Charlie, "Listen, guys, this won't be a full-time assignment. Use them to catch routine cases, but don't give them a complicated whodunit for a while."

They would have none of it. Megara said, "Are you kidding, Boss? They will work your case full-time. And if they need assistance, Charlie and I will provide it personally."

Who could ask for anything better? Two loyal sergeants. Two sergeants who were more than co-workers. They were my friends. They would go to the wall for me, as I would for them.

Richie and John started reading the case file and began making notes on a legal pad. I left them in my office and went out to the squad room to see what was going on. The squad team – the two detectives assigned to catch cases in this tour – was out in the field on a possible murder/suicide and Sergeant Seich got ready to ride out with them.

Around 5:15 I went back into my office and neither detective looked up as they concentrated on the files. "I'm heading home," I said. "We'll talk tomorrow."

They mumbled a good-bye as I left the office.

■　　■　　■

Micena and Paul were in my office the next day at 3:45 p.m. with cups of coffee in their hands. "Whenever you're ready, Boss," Richie said.

"Fire away, guys."

"First," John said, "we both agree, as far as we have read, those detectives back then did a first-class, thorough investigation."

"I agree."

"To get to the point, we also believe, as they and you concluded, a second person was definitely involved."

"What convinced you?"

"Although the partial fingerprint could have come from anyone, the same cannot be said about the Type A negative blood stains. They were wet and fresh – not old and dried out. The lab was easily able to get the type."

"And you agree he panicked and ran?"

"Yes," John said. "Either he didn't think to take Selewski's car, or he was afraid to do so."

"Yeah," Richie said, "if he did take it the dicks would have known for certain a second person was involved when the car eventually turned up."

"They kept the existence of that second guy to themselves for a while," I said, "but when the interviews were over, and no second suspect showed up, they had to tip their hand."

"And ask for fingerprints – voluntarily – from Selewski's associates," Richie said.

"Which never happened," John said, "because the father of one of Pete's friends was a lawyer for the ACLU and convinced everyone not to cooperate with the big, bad cops."

"Is that about as far as you got?" I asked.

"Yes," John said.

"Good, I marked the files with a red card where I want you to begin tonight. The stuff in the middle can be ignored for now, more likely ignored forever."

"I guess you read through this mess a few times, huh?" Richie asked.

I nodded and said, "More than a few."

"Oh, Richie and I were wondering why this paper still existed. Aren't cases this old all on microfiche?"

"Yes, including this one, but I rescued it from the shredder and took it home years ago when I was a detective here. I brought it back here about a year ago, but never got around to look at it again. But something recently happened that may provide the break we need."

"What?" asked Richie.

"First, that Type A bloodstain has now been profiled for its DNA. As you know, the FBI established a nationwide DNA database called CODIS – the Combined DNA Index System. Our suspect's DNA profile has been put in there, but so far, no matches have been found."

"So if our guy gets popped for a serious crime we should get a hit?" Richie asked.

"Yes, but that's a long shot. The automated fingerprint system – AFIS – has been around much longer, over twenty years. And that's where we may find something."

"Do you want us to read that back section which contains those possibilities?" John asked.

"Yes, I have been working with a detective in the Latent Prints Section in the Lab in Manhattan. His name is Joe Brala, and I want you to sit down with him soon and see what he has to say."

"Can we assume this is all we got as far as physical evidence is concerned?" John asked.

"This is it," I said. "If we can't narrow the print base down sufficiently, this guy will never be caught."

"We'll do our best, Mike," John said.

I smiled and said, "You always do."

■　　■　　■

The next day I was surprised to see Richie and John in the office when I arrived at 8:30. "We switched to a day tour," John said. "We have an appointment with Brala at 11:00 a.m. over at the Lab. I hope he has something better than what his last report said."

"You mean the list of suspects has been narrowed down from millions to a mere 350,000?" I said with a grin.

"You may think that's funny, Mike, but that's a lot of people to scrutinize, even for a couple of crackerjacks like me and Richie."

"Go spend some time with Brala. We'll talk when you get back."

Micena and Paul were back a bit before three o'clock and seemed eager to discuss their day at the Lab with me. John said, "Detective Joe Brala is a bulldog. When he gets his teeth into a problem he doesn't ever want to let go."

"Sounds like you two. Continue."

"He took the list of 350,000, which by the way is increasing every day, and he emailed it over to our computer data center downtown. They are going to crosscheck those names with their blood types, although not all of them have a blood type listed."

"A sizable percentage does not," Richie said, "but the military records do. If our guy was in the service, we could narrow the list."

"The computer guys," John said, "will also try to narrow the list further by the age of the suspect by assuming he was 16-24 at the time of the crime, and they will manipulate the data by concentrating on those residing in Queens at that time."

"How long will this take," I asked.

"They figure at least a week because the machines can only do so much before manual effort becomes necessary."

"Take another day or two to finish reading the case, then go back into the duty chart until you hear back from Brala. But I'll tell Megara and Seich to assign you only routine cases during that time."

"Thanks, Boss," John said. "I'm beginning to get itchy now. I smell the bastard, although he's not yet in my vision."

.   .   .

On Monday of the following week, with Paul and Micena back on day tours, they informed me they had finished reading the files and had an idea that might be worth following up on. "Let's have it," I said.

"What do you do when you get out of high school?" John asked. "Don't answer, because I'll tell you. You go to work, to college, or into the service. Those are your options."

"Or you can laze around the house smoking dope and shooting pool and drinking at the corner bar," I said.

"True Mike, although the killer, Pete Selewski, did have a job even though he was a heroin addict."

"Here's where we are going," Richie said. "The only one of those three options where you get fingerprinted is in the service. And your blood gets typed also. John and I are going to compile a list of names of friends, associates, and co-workers of Selewski and get it over to Brala. He'll have the computer guys research the military's databases to find out who from among his cronies went into the service. Then they'll cross-check that info with what they're working on already when it's completed."

"Assuming our guy *did* go in," I said, "but those two other options comprise a much larger group of possibles."

"They do," John said, "but I have a hunch here. What did you do when you were eighteen years old and hit over the head with the news of who you were, and what happened to your mom and dad?"

"I mulled it over a couple of days and then enlisted in the army."

"You ran away from a horrible situation," Richie said. "We have a feeling our second suspect may have done likewise."

I thought this over for a few seconds and said, "You two may be onto something here. Keep me informed, as always."

■   ■   ■

The days dragged by, and another week passed as we awaited word from Brala. Finally, on a Wednesday afternoon, John and Richie came into my office and John said, "We're going over to the Lab first thing in the morning. Brala and the computer geeks finished their compilations. They need us to make sense of it, based on our knowledge of the case."

"Sounds like we may be getting somewhere," I said. "Are you going there directly from home?"

"Yes, and we'll call you right away if we find something valuable," Richie said.

Now that something positive seemed to be happening I wanted to jump in with my two guys, but I refrained from interfering. I had lived with this case for twenty years, and I could live with it a bit longer. John and Richie didn't need me looking over their shoulders and sticking my nose in. They were pros. If they needed my advice, or help, they'd ask for it. I said, "Maybe we'll get lucky."

When they hadn't called by lunchtime I got Sergeant Megara to join me for a couple of slices of pizza at *Angelo's* a couple of blocks away. He said, "I know you're preoccupied Mike, but rest assured the squad is running smoothly under my sure hand."

"I know Harry, and you have my thanks. We're hoping to catch a break soon."

"Tell me about it."

When I finished he said, "That does sound promising. Mike, have you ever thought about what you'd do if you found him?"

"Every day for the past twenty years."

"And?"

"It depends."

Harry thought for a moment and said, "I think I know what you mean. This guy could be the president for crying out loud."

"Or a senator, or governor. Or a cop."

At 2:20, back in my office, the phone finally rang and John Micena simply said, "We got a name, and we're on our way back."

"What is it?"

"Giuseppe Mastronunzio."

"That's a helluva name, John."

"You can say that again, Boss. Giuseppe enlisted in the Marines three weeks after the murders, from an address in Richmond Hill. We're going to stop there first and nose around awhile, if that's alright with you."

"Remember that was forty years ago."

"You'll wait for us?"

"I'll be here," I said and put the receiver down.

Giuseppe Mastronunzio, where are you now?

TWENTY-ONE

Richie and John were back in the office at 4:30 and John said, "You were right, Mike, forty years is a long time. Nobody at that house ever heard of anybody by that memorable name, and the other four doors we knocked on gave the same negative answers."

"What are your plans now?"

"Back out there tomorrow," Richie said. "First stop will be the A&P where Selewski worked, then the local high school to check the yearbooks."

"If you strike out with the yearbooks, check out Bishop Loughlin High School in Brooklyn. Mastronunzio is likely a Catholic, and that was the place we kids from Queens and Brooklyn would go to if we didn't attend our local public high school."

"You went there, Mike?"

"Yes."

"Do you have any other ideas or ways to go on this?" Richie asked.

"No, you're doing fine. Keep going and follow the leads wherever they take you."

"I'm hoping Giuseppe's sunning himself on a beach in Hawaii," John said.

"You wish," I said, "but tell me something. You called me and said, 'we got a name.' Now how the hell did those geeks in Manhattan pick him out? I must say I'm impressed."

"You and us, Mike," Richie said. "Those guys put a lot of effort into this for us. The military records search came up with 127 guys from

Queens who enlisted in the service during the period of one day after the murders to ninety days later."

"And," John said, "the other database spit out 188 names of men in the 17-24 year old age group living in Richmond Hill and within a five mile radius of it. We had to do a hand comparison, and the only name that appeared on both lists was Mastronunzio."

"We confirmed it by his fingerprints," Richie said. "The partial from the scene could have come from his left index finger, but as Brala reminded us, he couldn't testify in court to a positive match with six points of comparison."

"Did his military records have his blood type listed?"

"Yes it did," John said smiling.

"Are you going to tell me what it was, or just sit there with that shit-eating grin on your face?"

"Yes, Boss, I will tell you. A-fucking-negative."

"Terrific! This could be our guy. Let's say you find out tomorrow he did work with Selewski and went to high school nearby. How do you propose to locate him?"

"We're already working on it," John said. "The computer guys are searching the locations of all Giuseppe Mastronunzios in his current age group throughout the country."

"And, Mike," Richie said, "All these guys worked through their lunch hour on this so we sprung for sandwiches and sodas for them."

"Put the expense chit in right away. And tell them if they zero us in on the one and only Giuseppe we are interested in, I'll take them to Peter Lugers Steakhouse."

"Does that include us two?" John asked. "It would be an added incentive to know a thick, prime porterhouse awaited us."

"With pleasure," I said, as if these two needed a steak dinner to motivate them. They were on the hunt. The gleam was in their eyes. They couldn't wait to run Giuseppe to ground. I hoped I could control them when they did, before they chewed him to pieces.

"Good," Richie said. "I'm getting real optimistic now. I mean how many Giuseppe Mastronunzios can there be in this world? And in that age group?"

"You'd be surprised," I said. "I once was chasing down a guy named Stanislaus Warzejewski. There were seventeen with that name in Greenpoint alone."

"Did you ever catch him?"

"No, I got close, but he had beaten feet back to Poland, or the Ukraine."

"No doubt joining thousands of others with the same name," John said.

"Right, and I gave up the chase. It was only a bullshit burglary. Nobody hurt. Certainly not worth a trip overseas, which wouldn't have been approved anyway."

Richie reached across the desk and put his hand on my forearm. "Mike, me and John will never give up the chase on this guy. Never."

"I know you won't. Good luck tomorrow."

.　　　.　　　.

June 16, the forty-third anniversary of the death of my parents, had come and gone and my two detectives were now at a crossroads. They had ascertained Giuseppe had worked part-time at the Richmond Hill A&P during the same time as Peter Selewski. They also determined he had graduated from Bishop Loughlin High School, my alma mater, in 1957, three weeks before his Marine Corps enlistment. A thorough canvass of the neighborhood failed to turn up anyone who remembered him from that time. The A&P knew nothing of importance about him, except for his dates of employment there. The notation under his high school yearbook picture indicated he would attend college after graduation. No doubt the murder of my parents squashed those plans.

A visit to the Marine Corps facility in Garden City, Nassau County, resulted in some good information. The officer who accessed their historical personnel database informed my guys Corporal Joey "Nunzio" was a good marine and was made an offer to continue service in the Corps, which he refused. His MOS was in aviation mechanics, and he performed his repair and maintenance duties excellently. Unfortunately, there was no information on where he went when he left the Corps in 1960.

John and Richie figured that with his training, Nunzio, as we now called him for brevity's sake, could have hooked up as a mechanic at one of the airlines at JFK or LaGuardia. A record search of all the airlines maintaining a facility there at that time failed to turn up an employee with that name. They threw the search back to the computer section to expand it to airports nationwide. In a few days that search also came back negative.

A few days after that, the computer section came back again, this time with three Giuseppe Mastronunzio's between the ages of 60 and 65 living in the United States. In The Bronx, Phoenix, and San Francisco. With database research and a few phone calls it was readily determined none of the three could be our man. The one from the Bronx spoke broken English and had emigrated from Italy ten years ago. The one in Phoenix had been born in Chicago and school records confirmed his attendance there. He had been in college in Michigan at the time of the murders. And the one in San Francisco, now deceased, had been a fisherman all his life out there ,working in his father's business since he was thirteen years old, eventually owning it.

We sat around my office that afternoon evaluating our results, disappointment hanging heavy in the air. We needed the proverbial lucky break, or an inspiration, or a new direction. Halfway through our second cup of coffee, as we were browsing through our latest reports, Richie Paul pointed to a page and said, "Wait a minute!"

He grabbed for my phone, dialed a number, and hit the speaker phone button. When the phone was answered, Richie said, "Captain Ahearn, this is Detective Paul. I was out there at the base with my partner a couple weeks ago?"

"Yes, I remember. What can I help you with?"

"Once or twice you referred to Mastronunzio as 'Nunzio.' Did he change his name?"

"Not likely, but I bet his drill instructor may have. Let me explain…"

After Richie disconnected he said, "That's it. The bastard changed his name. He had to or we would have found him by now."

"To Nunzio?" John asked.

"Maybe. Maybe to Mastro. Maybe to something else."

"How the hell are we going to find that out?"

"Start with the civil court in Queens where he lived," I said.

"That's why he's the boss," Richie said. "We'll be there first thing in the morning."

And at 10:08 the next morning, John Micena called me and said, "Bingo, Mike, we got the son-of-a-bitch. We'll come right back after we copy some paperwork."

"Listen, while you're out there check at the two airports again under his new name. Who knows? He could still be working there. Maybe he's the chief mechanic at one of the airlines."

"You're some optimist, Boss. As you said, forty years is a long time. He could be retired by now, but we'll check it out. See you later."

"Oh, John," I said, "tell me, what new name did our suspect adopt?"

"Completely different. I guess to throw us off the scent. But he used some of the letters from his last name to make a shortened version of his new one."

"Nunzio?"

"No. Manzo. Our guy is now Francis Andrew Manzo."

I sucked in a deep breath and put a death grip on the telephone receiver. I felt the blood drain from my brain. My knees shook. Thankfully I was sitting down, for surely I would have fallen to the floor. And, fortunately, John and Richie were not in the room when John spoke that name, because one of them would have said, "Mike, what's the matter? You look like you saw a fucking ghost."

"Mike?" John said. "Are you there? Is something the matter?"

I regained my composure a bit and said, "No, no, I'm fine. We'll talk when you get back and plan our next moves."

Francis Andrew Manzo.
Father Manzo from St. Anthony's.
Frank, my longtime friend and NYPD Rabbi.
His Excellency, the Most Reverend Francis Andrew Manzo, Bishop of Brooklyn.

Impossible! It couldn't be him. I poured a cup of coffee, sat back, and thought about this startling revelation. And the more I thought, the more it made sense. He murdered my parents, and to somehow make amends, devoted his life to God, and became my life-long benefactor to mitigate his guilt. This was something right out of a Charles Dickens novel. My twenty year search was over. The second man had now been positively identified, and I knew exactly where he was. Now what the hell would I do about it?

PART FIVE

THE BISHOP OF BROOKLYN

(SUMMER 2000)

TWENTY-TWO

I shut my office door, reached into my bottom desk drawer, and retrieved a bottle of twelve-year-old scotch which I kept for special occasions. I was not much of a drinker, but I needed one now. I couldn't remember where the lo-ball glasses were, so I poured a double shot into my coffee mug, and slugged it down. I waited for its warmth to work its way through my system and, as if by magic, I calmed down and regained my senses.

I began to question myself. Suppose it wasn't him? Suppose there is another Francis Andrew Manzo out there? Or several? Certainly a heck of a lot more than his previous name. But deep down, I knew it was him. Father Francis Manzo of St. Anthony's parish had first taken an interest in me when I was about fourteen years old, for a reason I was to discover four years later when the truth was told to me.

He had taken me under his wing, and I know he contributed to my college fund set up by my step-parents, and he supported my decision to enter the army and postpone college. He had said, "Go in, Mike, and leave us behind for a while. You need to get your head together before you decide how to move forward," or something to that effect. I now know he himself had done the same years ago, and it seemed to have done well for him. "And when you come out, you can decide if you want to be a Catholic or explore your Jewish heritage," he had said.

When I came out I did explore my Jewishness with Rabbi Berman and with Mort Stern. I came to the conclusion Mort was correct. There was no

God, and both the Old and New Testaments were compilations of fairy tales.

All these memories and thoughts boiled through my brain, chasing around in there, searching for the truth. But facts are facts. *The Bishop of Brooklyn. It had to be him.*

. ∎ ∎

Richie and John were back before lunchtime. I said, "Tell me what you found out there, my two top detectives."

"You're not going to believe this, Boss," Richie said. "We found Manzo worked at TWA in LaGuardia Airport for two years as an aviation mechanic, and resigned on good terms to pursue another career."

"He joined the seminary," John said. "Manzo may be a Priest, of all things."

"Are you guys Catholic?" I asked.

"I am," John said. "Richie here is some kinda German Prot."

"Died in the wool Lutheran," Richie said.

"As is my wife," I said.

"Hey, Mike," John said, "You have all the bases covered – A Jew brought up Catholic, married to a Protestant."

I chuckled and said, "The comedian Bob Hope once commented he made sure he entertained groups of every known religion on earth, because he didn't want to get shut out of heaven on a technicality."

After the laughter subsided I said, "John, does Manzo's name sound familiar to you?"

"Vaguely, but I can't seem to place it."

"You're not an observant Catholic, are you?"

"Nah, Christmas and Easter. That's about it."

"Francis Andrew Manzo is not a Priest anymore, guys. He is the Bishop of Brooklyn, the head of the Diocese."

My two detectives looked at each other for a moment and both said simultaneously, "It can't be him."

"It's him," I said. "Without a doubt. It all fits. His middle name is my father's first name. We have known each other for thirty years. He has looked over my life and career for a long time."

"The Bishop of Brooklyn has been your hook all these years?" John asked.

"That he has."

"Holy shit," Richie said. "This is unbelievable."

"What do you want us to do now?" John asked.

"What I want you to do now is nothing. I'll take it from here."

"Uh, Boss, nothing crazy, right?" Richie said.

"No, I don't think it will come to that. I owe him a call for our regular lunch meeting. I'll wing it from there."

"That will be some lunch," John said. "I'd love to be a fly on the wall at that discussion."

"Mike, see if you can grab his water glass when you leave. We'll get his DNA and prints and know for certain if he's the guy."

"He's the guy, Richie, and I doubt those forensic exams will be necessary. I think he'll tell me everything I want to know."

"Why should he, Mike? He's had over forty years to come clean, and he hasn't done so."

"Good question, but I think he *wanted* to be discovered. By me. He was the one who put me in charge here. Maybe he had a good reason not to come forward. I'll be sure to ask him."

"Do you want all what we found out yesterday and today to be put on paper officially?" John asked.

"No, type it up and hand it to me when you're done. I'll tell Sergeants Seich and Megara you're both back in the duty chart effective tomorrow. If they ask, tell them the case has reached a dead end for now."

"But in case the Bishop is not the one —?"

"He's the one, John. Now hit the typewriters. Oh, by the way, thank you for a great job, a first-rate investigation. I'd put you in for a promotion, but you're already first graders."

"Peter Luger's would be a well-deserved treat," Richie said.

"Indeed it would," echoed John.

"You're on," I said, "and we'll take our wives. Right after I wrap up my visit with Francis Andrew Manzo, the good, or not so good, Bishop of Brooklyn."

·　　·　　·

I reached for the telephone, and then withdrew my hand. I had to think about this a bit. I went back in memory trying to remember the first time

I met Frank. It had to be in Mort's store when I was about thirteen. I also remember attending a couple of masses he presided over before being introduced to him by Mort. He seemed to like me, and when I was accepted to Bishop Loughlin High School, he told me of his attendance there, and we swapped stories about the staff and teachers, some of whom were still there from his time.

And, thinking of him, brought to mind Rabbi Berman who also popped into Stern's. And when the three of them got going arguing over religion, God, and philosophy, I soaked it all in and kept my mouth shut mainly because I had nothing to offer. One day, near closing time, both the Rabbi and the Priest were berating Mort over his denial of the existence of God. He went to the front door and locked it and said, "Let me tell you why."

I said, "Mr. Stern, should I leave?"

"Unless you got something important to do, Mikey, I vant you to hear vat I got to say. You should hear both sides, not just vat these two preach about."

Mordechai Stern told us of his life in Germany, and how good it was, and how accepted into society he and his fellow Jews were. But that changed after Germany lost the first world war and the Nazis rose to power. A scapegoat was needed to blame all their woes on — hyperinflation, lack of jobs, lack of money – you name it. And the German Jews, who thought themselves a class above the other European Jews, realized too late they, too, were a target of the new regime. Too late to escape. Too late to avoid being rounded up and sent to the concentration camps. He thrust his forearm out and pointed at the numbers tattooed on it – a sight I had noticed, but had been afraid to ask about. He said, "Number 192708 was put on my arm in 1944 at Auschwitz, which was the only camp that did it. And, let me tell you something, I was thrilled to have it. Those who didn't get the tattoo vent straight to the gas chambers. I vuz thirty-six and strong. The bastards needed me to work for them."

I sat in open-mouthed disbelief as he related the terror of Auschwitz. None of us said a word, and I figured Berman and Manzo already knew of this, but they didn't interrupt. Mort finished by saying, "What kind of God allows men to be tattooed like animals? What kind of God allows six million of his supposed chosen ones to be gassed and burned? If God made the Pharaoh to let my people go, why did he not make Hitler do the same? I'll tell you why. There is no God. The scriptures are a collection of fairy tales. And I'm afraid, Father Francis, your New Testament is a second collection of fairy tales."

Mort Stern made a powerful argument for the non-existence of God, and I wondered how the two clergymen were going to dispute him. Rabbi Berman said, "You once believed, but events caused you to lose your faith. Francis and I have strong faith and belief in God's existence despite our knowledge of the evils that exist in the world."

"Goot for you," he said, "though how any Jew can believe after vat happened to us is beyond belief. I vunder vat you two holy-rollers would think after a year in Auschwitz. I said my piece, now let's go home."

I had never forgotten that conversation, but I do remember one thing. Shortly after that, Mort never called me a Jew again, and I knew why when revelation day happened a few years later. Father Manzo and Rabbi Berman knew who I was at that time and didn't want Mort to press the issue and cause me to become too inquisitive.

Father Manzo's friendship continued and later, after two years at Queensborough Community College, he backed my decision to become a police officer. I have to assume, knowing what I had learned, he was constantly atoning for his guilt for my parents' death. It was now time to confront him and discover the extent of his involvement in the murders. If he was seeking forgiveness, I was seeking closure.

I dialed his private number and after we said hello he said, "Mike, I was about to call you. You promised to call me last week, remember?"

"I do, Frank, but things got hectic around here."

"Have they quieted down enough for us to get together?"

"Yes, but after lunch I need to speak with you privately in your office about something."

"That's interesting, Mike, because I was going to request the same of you. I have a situation that has me worried, and I wish to discuss with you at length."

We decided to meet for a short lunch then adjourn to his office in the cathedral for our discussions. Two days from now, on Wednesday, June 28. I began to mentally prepare for this confrontation while wondering what his situation was that he was so worried about. I'd find out soon enough. Perhaps he was ready to finally give it up.

TWENTY-THREE

We met at a local Asian restaurant, The Lotus Blossom, which was a two-block walk from the Bishop's office at St. James Cathedral. The smiling owner bowed and showed us to a corner booth in the rear. After we sat, and the waiter handed us menus, bowing to Francis again and saying, "Good afternoon, Your Excellency. It's wonderful to see you again."

"Come here often?" I asked as I looked around the beautifully decorated restaurant which emphasized a variety of pink and red lotus blossoms on ivory-colored and gold backgrounds.

"Yes, it's one of my favorite places. There's also a great Italian place and a Jewish deli with the best pastrami sandwich in all of Brooklyn."

I looked over the menu and said, "Frank, I'm not that hungry, and you look troubled about something. What do you suggest?"

"How about a cup of their excellent hot-and-sour soup and splitting an order of sesame chicken?"

"Sounds good," I said as the waiter set down a bowl of crispy noodles, a cup of duck sauce, and a pot of tea. The topic of discussion was the recent untimely death of our mutual friend, Mort Stern. We reminisced about our conversations and arguments with him. I told him of my sprinkling of his ashes on my parent's graves and of his son's decision to sell the store. He said, "God, I miss the old curmudgeon, and I miss his egg-creams, too."

"So do I, Frank. Best in New York, as we used to say."

We were finished eating in thirty minutes and I chose to walk with him back to the church, opting to leave my car parked near the restaurant. The weather had cooled down and it was a pleasant early summer day with bright blue skies and a gentle breeze. Even now, at midday, the temperature hovered in the mid-seventies. Beautiful. I should get out more. Yeah, sure.

We settled into leather chairs and Frank had his secretary bring coffee in and told him, "Please don't disturb us for anyone, Brian."

With a twinkle in his eyes Brian said, "And if Pope John Paul calls to offer you a red hat what should I tell him?"

"Tell him I don't want to be a Cardinal. I am happy being the Bishop of Brooklyn."

Then his smile faded and he added, "For as long as it lasts."

What did he mean by that?

Brian shut the door and Bishop Manzo smiled at me and said, "I believe I know why you are here, Michael."

"Oh?"

"You want to return to the church you abandoned so many years ago. You have found Jesus again and wish to make a full confession to me, and Him, and seal the deal."

"No, Frank," I said, drawing in a breath and steeling my nerves, "that's not why I'm here. Not for you to hear my confession, but for me to hear yours – *Giuseppe*."

If I had thought he would grasp his chest in shock, I was mistaken. He merely nodded, smiled, and said, "Ah, Michael, it's about time you solved the case. I was wondering when you would, and now that moment has finally arrived."

"You were expecting this weren't you? It was why you pushed for me to get Queens Homicide, right?"

"Correct."

"Why didn't you tell me yourself, and tell me a long time ago?"

"Cowardice, Mike. I was afraid of being arrested, embarrassed, and thrown in jail, despite my innocence."

"Innocence? You took part in a murder. *Two* murders. My parents, remember?"

"I have remembered every day of my life, Mike. Will you hear me out?"

"That's what I came for Bishop. Closure. I need to know what happened. I'm listening."

"Thank you, and when I finish if you want to slap the cuffs on me, I won't object. I will also give you DNA and fingerprint samples and a recorded confession to you and the district attorney. But before I begin, can you tell me how you finally tracked me down?"

"Basically your blood type, A-negative, from the drops you left at the scene. A partial fingerprint you left there also. And when we discovered your name change, it all fell into place."

"Where did you find my fingerprint?"

"On the light switch plate in the bedroom. It was just a partial and not enough points of comparison for a conviction in court."

"Did you find any of my prints in Selewski's car? I was worried about the door handle on my side."

"No, only his prints were found, and some unidentifiable smears on the passenger's door handle."

"I figured you might have located my last living relative – my remaining brother."

"No, we failed in our search for relatives. Your parents were listed on your Marine Corps history, but we discovered they were now both deceased."

"As is my one brother, and the living brother changed his name to Mastro a long time ago."

"I can see why," I said.

"So did the civil court judge who approved my name change."

"Before you begin, I am curious as to how you became a Priest. I assume you didn't tell them everything?"

"On the contrary, Mike. I wouldn't enter the priesthood on a bed of lies and deception. I told them everything and they concluded I was innocent of sin."

"And innocent of a crime as well?"

"Yes."

"Tell me how you, and they, arrived at that decision, please. See if you can convince me also, *Giuseppe*."

.   .   .

The Most Reverend Bishop of Brooklyn spoke clearly and softly as he related the events of that dreadful night in Cambria Heights so long ago. I kept my silence until he finished with the part where it was all over and he ran away. I said, "Who fired the first shot?"

"I believe your dad and Pete fired at each other simultaneously. One shot each."

"And then?"

"Everything went super fast. Pete swung the gun and shot your mother as she was rising up, I think at the instant when your father's second bullet hit him. Pete started to stagger and shot at your father again, then one more at your mother. That's when your father's third or fourth shot caught me in my upper left arm. Damn! I should have grabbed for Pete's gun –"

"How badly were you hurt?"

"It was basically a burn, maybe an eighth of an inch deep at its center. I was afraid to seek medical attention."

"What did the Marine Corps doctor ask about it when you went in, when was it? Three weeks later?"

"He didn't notice it, because I had a tattoo put on over the entire wound before I signed in."

"I imagine that hurt?"

"Like hell, Mike."

"What kind of tattoo?"

"What else? The Marine Corps Globe and Anchor."

"With the words Death before Dishonor and Semper Fidelis surrounding it?"

"Yes."

"The shooting was all over in a matter of seconds and you panicked and ran out the front door?"

"Yes, like a yellow, cowardly chicken."

"Did you first check the three bodies for signs of life before you ran?"

"No, my ears were ringing, and as I thought about it, I heard a baby crying."

"Me."

"Yes, which drove my panic level sky high, and I ran for the hills."

"All the way back to Richmond Hill?"

"All the way, jogging, walking, and scared to death."

"Tell me why you didn't turn yourself in if you thought you were innocent?"

Frank went through his whole line of reasoning explaining the circumstances of duress and how, even if true, it would never have been believed by a jury. I mulled over the circumstances of the crime and had to conclude he was correct in his reasoning. I would never have believed this seventeen year-old punk who was obviously concocting an alibi to save his no good ass from the electric chair. I said, "I understand, and I agree with your conclusion. But technically, you can still be arrested for felony murder."

"Yes, and I will raise the duress defense at trial and hope the jury would believe a former Marine and a man who dedicated his life to the service of the Lord."

"You were afraid to come forward to me, yet you knew I would pursue the case as it was now directly under my jurisdiction. I'm a bit confused."

"As I said, I and Father Johansson were convinced I had committed no crime, nor any sin. But I have carried that night around with me every day, and whenever I hear a baby cry…"

"There's something you want to clear your conscience once and for all, and you can't get it in the confessional, and you can't get it from yourself, correct?"

"Yes."

"The only person who could give me the closure I needed all my life was you, the guy who got away, and you now gave it to me. And the only person who can give you absolution for your burden of guilt is me, isn't it?"

"Yes, Michael. Only you."

I looked at this dedicated man, tears beginning to drip from his eyes, and I knew exactly what I had to do. I rose up in front of him, and drawing upon my high school Latin, I raised my hand and said, "*Ego te absolvo*, Francis." Using my hand to make the sign of the cross, I added, "*In Nomine Patris, et Fillii, et Spiritus Sancti. Amen.* I absolve you, Francis. In the name of the Father, the Son, and the Holy Spirit. Amen."

The Bishop of Brooklyn convulsed in sobs and buried his head in his hands. I walked closer and patted him on the shoulder. I said, "Giuseppe, it's all over. For both of us. Closure and absolution. Finally."

After several minutes he regained his composure clasped his hands around mine and said, "Thank you, Michael. Thank you."

I smiled and said, "And thank you, Frank. You're too good a person to go to jail."

"I'm impressed by your Latin, but you forgot to add something to the absolution litany."

"It's been a long time. What did I forget?"

"*Vade et amplius iam noli peccare.*"

"Go and sin no more?"

"Yes."

"That wasn't called for here. I mean how can you sin no more, when you didn't sin in the first place?"

"Thank you, again, Michael. Would you agree we might need something a bit stronger than coffee right about now?"

"I would definitely agree."

"I have some excellent brandy," he said, buzzing for Brian.

When the secretary came in he said, "The Pope did not call Your Excellency, but the Cardinal Archbishop did. He would like to speak with you at your earliest convenience."

"Thank you, Brian. Would you set us up with the good brandy and glasses?"

"Certainly," he said, walking over to the sideboard. He returned and poured us a small amount and began to walk back to the sideboard.

"Brian, please leave the bottle here."

Brian raised his eyebrows and placed the bottle on the Bishop's desk and left the room without saying a word.

"Good man," I said. "Very discrete, I presume."

"Yes, and most trustworthy. He knows how to keep a confidence."

He raised his glass to me and said, "To closure and absolution."

We drained our glasses and I said, "You mentioned you were worried about something, Frank. What seems to be troubling you? Something besides the matter we finally resolved?"

"Yes, and it is as serious as, and much more complicated than, our troubles. And I believe that call Brian received from the Archbishop is an ominous one. I believe a decision may have been reached about me from Rome, and he is the messenger."

"Frank, what in God's name are you talking about?"

"I believe the clan of the highest-ranking Cardinals in Rome, the Princes of the Church closest to the Pope, has decided to eliminate me."

"Eliminate you? As in fire you, or whatever the church does to remove you from office?"

"No, Michael, I mean *murder* me."

TWENTY-FOUR

I stared at the Bishop, shocked by his words. I filled our glasses and took a large sip from mine. I said, "Murder you? Are you sure you're not overreacting to some perceived comment or threat?"

"Maybe I am, but you can decide that after you hear my story, and it's a long one."

I glanced at my watch and said, "I have a suggestion. I'll call my squad and tell them I'm not returning today, and you'd better return that call to your boss. Then we'll hash it all out."

"Good idea. You may want to take notes."

"I will, but it may be a better idea if we record the whole story."

"That is a good idea, Mike. We should get it down on the record. I'll get Brian to set it up."

I went outside his office to make my call leaving him the privacy he needed to call the Cardinal. Brian showed me to his desk and said, "Please use my phone, Lieutenant."

"Thanks, Brian. The Bishop is calling the Cardinal and then we're going to resume our conversation, and he is going to ask you to set up a tape recorder for us."

"I'll get on that right away. Thanks for the heads up."

I got my deputy on the phone and asked, "How are things going, Harry?"

"Fine Mike, things are quiet. Oh, and thanks for giving me Richie and John back. Summer vacations are coming up, and I'm glad they're back in the duty chart."

"Yeah, there may be a problem with that. I'll know more soon. I'm not returning to the office today. The Bishop may have a problem of his own brewing. He's going to tell me about it soon."

"That shouldn't affect us, right? I mean he's in Brooklyn North."

"True, but I'm his favorite son, and if he wants us involved…"

"He picks up the phone and pulls the string."

"Correct. Uh, is Micena or Paul around?"

"Both just came back from lunch. Which one do you want to speak with?'

"John."

I heard him shout, "Boss is on line two for you, Micena."

Two seconds later he picked up and asked "Is it all over?"

"Yes, it is."

"Did you shoot him?"

"No."

"Did you arrest him?"

"No."

"Did he confess?"

"Yes he did. I'll fill you, Richie, and the sergeants in tomorrow."

"Uh, we can't close the case, though. I mean the second perp has been identified, but is not in custody."

"We'll figure something out – tomorrow."

"Got it, Mike. See you in the morning."

When I returned to the Bishop's office, Brian had finished setting up the recorder. He said, "It has a one-hour capacity. If you need more, Your Excellency, buzz me and I'll bring another cassette in."

"Thanks, Brian," he said.

I noticed Francis was a bit pale in the face and he sunk heavily into his chair when Brian left the office. "Bad news?" I asked.

"I have been summoned to Rome. I leave in two days."

"Couldn't that be a good thing?"

"I doubt it, Mike. I have been pushing an agenda – a cause – if you will, and I believe it is not being well received."

"Is this related to the situation you wanted to talk about?"

"Yes."

"Is the Cardinal going with you?"

"No, he has already been there a few months ago on my behalf, and on the behalf of the other Bishops who are aligned with me. He reported our concerns to the Vatican brass."

"The Pope?"

"No, to a group of five Cardinals who are the real powers in the church. They control everything over there, and they decide what gets brought to the Pope. If they say he doesn't have to hear it, it doesn't get heard."

"Similar to the hierarchy in the NYPD," I said, smiling.

"The comparison of our organizations is remarkably similar. They are highly dysfunctional, centralized structures, and in both, the supreme decision-making power lies with one man – the Pope, or the Police Commissioner."

"Do you think this powerful clan of Cardinals has reached a decision on your agenda?"

"I believe so, and I also believe I will be told to stand down and retreat from my proposals. And I believe they will threaten me with dire consequences if I don't relent."

Jokingly I said, "Do you think they'll whack you right there in the Vatican? Maybe slip you into one of the buried Pope's caskets?"

"This isn't fucking funny, Mike," he said, but he burst out laughing anyway.

"*Fucking* funny? You shock me, Bishop."

"I bet," he said. "Blame it on the Corps. Thankfully, profanity is my sole vice. Unless you count heresy, which is what the clan of Cardinals in Rome will conclude."

"You've got me interested in this unfolding mystery. Maybe we should turn on the tape recorder, and as they say, begin from the beginning, my son."

He nodded and flicked the recorder's switch on.

.   .   .

"When I was a young Priest I was warned I would be hit on by some attractive, young parishioners looking to bed me for a night, or longer."

"Naturally. You were a good-looking stud back in those days. I guess it was to be expected."

"No, Mike, that's the point. It *shouldn't* be expected. What kind of Catholics were these young women to engage in this behavior?"

"Normal, healthy, red-blooded gals, I presume."

"Yes, and we priests are *abnormal* by virtue of our vow of celibacy, but are also healthy, red-blooded males. And as such we also have a strong desire to get laid."

"But you remained chaste?"

"Yes, I was true to my Marine Corps vows and to the vows I took with the church."

"And there was also that self-inflicted punishment brought on by the events of the night of June 16, 1957, correct?"

"Correct. I fended off those amorous advances, and what made it more difficult as the years went by, was that I sometimes wondered if I was the only one in the whole damn Diocese who remained loyal to the faith."

"No kidding?"

"Oh, yes, Mike. I saw it first hand. Priests and nuns included. And when I was promoted to Monsignor and assigned as an aide to the former Cardinal in Manhattan, my job was to investigate, and cover up, the sexual misdeeds of our priests."

"And there were that many?"

"Dozens. Every month. Priests caught with prostitutes, with girlfriends. Priests caught with nuns. Nuns caught with men. I was shocked by the number of them involved in these acts."

"Not to mention those afraid to engage with others, but with *themselves*, eh, Frank?"

"I can only imagine. As time went by and I got to know more members of other religions – rabbis and pastors – I came to the conclusion they were right, and we were wrong. Point one on my agenda was to convince the church to finally allow priests to marry, have children, and have housing provided nearby to their church."

"A parsonage?"

"Yes, or a vicarage, it can be called. And you know, Mike, it used to be that way for a thousand years."

"I remember that from some religion course in Loughlin. Why did they change the rules?"

"Money. The church wanted to retain all the property that would otherwise have been passed down to the priests' children."

"I believe there has been some talk about marriage for priests, already."

"Yes, but despite much local support on the priest and bishop levels, Rome has continued to turn a deaf ear. I would go one step further and *require* priests to be married, or married within two years of ordination, for them to become a Priest in the first place."

"Good idea, but I don't understand how you are so fearful over proposing and advocating it. I mean, you do believe they will kill you over this?"

"Mike, this is a minor part of my reform agenda. The next part, a situation of monstrous proportions, is what they are most worried about."

"Which is?"

"Pedophilia."

"Are you saying some priests are pedophiles?"

"No, not *some*, Mike. A *lot*. A huge amount. I know from bailing them out. I believe Holy Mother Church is a veritable powerful magnet drawing them in. They have to be dealt with. They have to be arrested and charged with these sickening crimes of depravity."

"I think I may have read about a case of a priest being investigated for sexual abuse of a boy. A few months ago, out on Long Island."

"Yes, they can't cover them all up, but they sure as hell try to."

"How?"

"Like in the police department. They transfer them. Make them someone else's problem."

"But don't the Bishops complain?"

"A few do, but those that don't are either afraid, or pedophiles themselves."

"Bishops?"

"Bishops, and rumor has it, two of our five Cardinals."

"That's hard to believe, Frank."

"When a cop who is a drunk gets promoted to sergeant, he's still a drunk, right?"

"I see your point. What is your solution to the problem?"

"Address it head on. Admit guilt and clean house. Institute a background check thorough enough to eliminate them getting ordained into the priesthood, which brings me back to my first point. Protestant clergy and Jewish clergy – married clergy – have extremely low rates of pedophilia."

"And Cardinal Callahan brought these ideas of yours to Rome a few months ago?"

"Yes, but I'm not alone in this. Seventeen other U.S. Bishops signed on to my agenda, including the Bishop of the Rockville Centre Diocese of Long Island."

"But you are the leader of the pack?"

"Yes, and to kill the pack you behead its leader."

"Do you have more details?"

"Plenty, but I need a cup of coffee first, and I think that tape is about to run out.

■   ■   ■

With the second tape turning I asked, "You said you had seventeen Bishops with you. How many Bishops are there in the States?"

"Two hundred and forty."

"You don't even have ten percent on board."

"No, and several of them have personally called me urging me and the others to stop our crusade. They feel if it gets out, the church will be destroyed. I countered by saying if it doesn't get out, and get put out there by *us*, they will be correct."

"Do you have any of this documented?"

He smiled and said, "Oh, yes, I have a list of all the violators here in my office safe, but the detailed records, which include every piece of information on each incident, are not kept here for obvious reasons, primarily if I am ordered to turn them over to the higher ups."

"Where are they being safeguarded?"

"You are not going to like this, Mike. They are being held by a member of your department who I trust as much as you."

"Why won't I like it?"

"Because my man inside the department is none other than Deputy Inspector Raymond Elliott of Internal Affairs."

"What? That son-of-a-bitch –"

"Hold on, Mike, let me explain. I first met Ray when he was a lieutenant here in the 84 precinct. We have a mutual friend, the Episcopal Bishop of Brooklyn, Harold Masters. I called him and the Boro Commander, to get Elliott off your back."

"I'm confused."

"Ray Elliott's presence in Internal Affairs is crucial to my cause. He hates it there, and wants out badly, but he plays the bad guy role perfectly. This impresses his bosses and allows him to remain in his position a while longer to help my cause."

"Exactly why, and how, is he critical to your cause?"

"He has unlimited access to all the records of the NYPD. As such, he has documented all the cases I made him aware of, and he found hundreds more on his own."

"What's your plan of action? What's your endgame?"

"It depends on the outcome of my meeting in Rome."

"And if, as you suspect, they turn a deaf ear to you, and the problem, what do you do?"

"I'll tell them I'm going to explode the story to the media and demand the appropriate police departments investigate and arrest all the miscreants."

"You do have a death wish, don't you? Maybe my joke will become a reality – *The Bishop of Brooklyn was killed in a horrible motor vehicle accident right outside the Vatican walls.* Or maybe – *Beloved Bishop of Brooklyn found drowned in the Tiber River.*"

"Mike –"

"No, listen to me. If they stonewall you and threaten you to cease and desist, here's what you do. You smile, bow, kiss their rings and say, 'Yes, Your Eminence, I will obey' and then get your holy ass back here forthwith. We don't want to lose a man who is without sin, right?"

"That's good advice, but I think the Bishop of Rockville Centre would step up to lead our efforts in the case of my untimely death and follow through as I had planned."

"Are you certain? Will he and the other Bishops say to themselves, 'Fuck this, I got the message?'"

He sighed and said, "I've been around long enough to know I can't predict future human behavior. And maybe the Vatican will see it my way after all."

"Good. Go to Rome. When you come back we'll plan this out together depending on their reaction. I'll be thinking about it while you're gone."

TWENTY-FIVE

The next morning, Richie Paul and John Micena joined me in my office and I filled them in on my meeting with the Bishop and, as expected, they peppered me with questions. John said, "He went for it immediately?"

"Yes, as I told you he would."

"Yeah," Richie said, "forty years of guilt is a heavy cross to bear."

"And you bought his story completely?"

"One hundred percent, John. I knew he told me the absolute truth."

"And you absolved him of his guilt?" Richie asked. "That took a lot of guts, and a real Christian belief in forgiveness."

"It was the right thing to do," I said not reminding him I was no longer a believing Christian, but a Jew who did not adhere to that faith either. But that would have invited questions I was not prepared to answer, or deal with, right now. *Coward,* flashed through my mind.

"Can we now close this case once and for all?" John asked.

"Technically," Richie said, "the second man is still out there undetected and not under arrest."

"I was thinking of saying a Giuseppe Mastronunzio was found dead in Italy," I said, "or something like that, but there are too many loopholes fabricating something like that."

"How about we write it up that the guy was identified, but all efforts to locate him met with negative results?"

"I like that, John," I said. "We'll make that the final report on the case and microfilm it. But we'll still have to classify it as a cold-case, unsolved."

"Okay," Richie said, "but we did type up the reports you asked on the real identity of Nunzio. They are on your desk."

"I'll shred them," I said. "And after you add that last report to the file, we'll shred the whole damn thing."

"That may take a long time," John said. "Probably burn the damn shredder up."

"A little at a time," I said. "A couple of inches a day."

"Will do, Mike. Oh, you told Sergeant Megara you might have something new for us? A situation involving the Bishop?"

"Could be," I said, "but not right now. It could end up being nothing. I'll let you know if something develops."

"Okay," John said. "Come on, Richie, let's wrap this one up and start shredding."

"Thanks once again guys. Pick out a date for dinner at Peter Luger's."

"Ten-four," Richie said. "My mouth is watering already."

.　　■　　■

When Charlie Seich arrived at four o'clock I called him and Harry into my office. I said, "I wish to inform you, my two loyal sergeants, Paul and Micena are now back working for you full time."

"Nothing came from the Bishop's situation?"

"No, not yet, but if it does, I want to include you two and Richie and John to plan our response. I need all your brain power and experience if this problem blows up."

"That serious?" Charlie asked.

"Yeah, but let's not jump the gun. Maybe it will all go away."

"That other case, uh, *your* case, is all concluded?" Harry asked.

"Yes, here's what happened…"

When I finished and they were shaking their heads in disbelief that the Bishop of Brooklyn was indeed Giuseppe Mastronunzio I said, "I know I don't have to say this, but the resolution of that investigation is between us and Micena and Paul. It is to be held in the strictest confidence and never spoken about to anyone else. Although, I owe the explanation to my wife, as you can imagine."

"Got it, Mike," Harry said. "Vivian's not a gabber if I remember rightly."

"Not on important things, just like us," I said, "but on unimportant things, she can chatter away with the best of them."

"Just like us," Charlie said with a chuckle.

.　.　.

The day after Frank returned from Rome he called me and when I picked up the phone I said, "At least you're alive. How did it go?"

"Good," he said. "They were cordial and appeared genuinely interested in the problem. Evidently, the Cardinal did a good job of setting it up for me."

"How much did you tell them?"

"Not all of it. I documented a dozen or so cases, but when I mentioned hundreds of more cases in our Archdiocese alone, there was definite disbelief."

"You took my advice, though?"

"Yes, I kissed all their rings, and they said they would contact me in the future through Cardinal Callahan, with their advice on how we should proceed."

"Any idea when that will be?"

"No. Should we do anything now?"

"No, but I have some ideas in case things go sour."

"Such as?"

"Target hardening. Hidden CCTV cameras and microphones in your office there, and your office in the co-cathedral. Private security bodyguards. CCTV cameras on all entrances at both cathedrals. Things like that."

"Jesus, Mike, I hope it doesn't come to that."

"Frank, if you blow this up in the media, that's the least amount of protection you will need. But let's hope for the best. Let's hope the powers that be in Rome see the light and see the error of their ways and allow the church to come clean."

"What do you think the chances are of that happening, Mike?"

"Unfortunately, slim to none, I believe."

"Me, too, but I'm keeping my fingers crossed."

"Fingers crossed? You heathen! Shouldn't you be praying to Jesus instead?"

"Every day, Mike. Every day."

.　　.　　.

Vivian was relieved the mystery of the second man at the murder scene was finally solved. She said, "That burden of not knowing who it was all these years took a tremendous toll on you. And the fact the man was known to us all these years as a friend and Priest, and is now the Bishop of Brooklyn is unbelievable. Maybe it's an omen, Mike."

"An omen? How so?"

"To come back to your church, or my church, or a Jewish temple. It doesn't matter, but you need to restore your faith in a supreme being."

I smiled and said, "I'll think about it, Viv," as a vision of Mort Stern's tattoo flashed through my mind. *There is no God, Mikey. Six million of us. Where was he?*

"Good," she said, "remember, God works his wonders in mysterious ways. Father Frank Manzo. Wow! Oh, by the way, I understand you are treating a few of us to an expensive steak dinner at Peter Luger's?"

"Who have you been gabbing with?"

"Barb, Richie's wife. We're looking for next weekend. I'll make the reservation."

"And I'll definitely pick up the tab."

"You bet your butt, you will."

.　　.　　.

Two weeks went by and the dinner at Peter Luger's was now but a delicious memory. The medium-rare porterhouse steak, the dark-red cabernet blend, the baked potatoes, the flaming dessert, all served professionally by grumpy, old, male white waiters who acted as if they were doing you a big favor by being seated at their table. Some things never change, and dammit, sometimes that's a good thing.

On the following Tuesday morning the Bishop called and he said, "I heard from Cardinal Callahan a few minutes ago."

"And?"

"He wants me to gather up all my documentation and notes on what I've discovered – the originals and any and all copies. I'm to deliver them to him in his Manhattan office ASAP, whereupon he will personally fly them to Rome for examination by his superiors."

"Whereupon they will be promptly shredded and burned," I said.

"Not according to the Cardinal, Mike. He said, 'They will bring them to Pope John Paul if the information is deemed accurate, and will be guided by his Holiness's decision.'"

"Wanna bet the Pope never gets a glance at them?"

"No, but I'm hopeful. I have to give them a chance."

"You're certainly not going to give them *all* the copies though, are you?"

"Not on your life, Mike. I may be hopeful, but I'm not fucking crazy."

"Spoken like a true Marine," I said. "Keep me in the loop. Oh, I have a suggestion. Make me a copy of all your records and let me keep it."

"May I ask why?"

"Insurance, Frank. Not that I don't trust Elliott, but we don't know how far the reach of the church powers go. Can they sway the police commissioner to jump in and destroy the files? Who else knows about all this? Maybe I'm paranoid, but right now the one person you should trust is me, and maybe Elliott. And keep your copy in your office safe. Let me know when I can come over to pick up my copy. I have some more suggestions for you."

"I'll call you soon."

■　　　■　　　■

Two days later I was in the Bishop's office, and with the door closed and locked, I went over all the files he had. I said, "This is a lot of paper, Frank. I can't believe these names of victims all came from the New York Archdiocese."

"They don't, Mike. This contains the victim's names sent to me by the other sixteen Bishops."

"Did you inform Cardinal Callahan of the names of those Bishops?"

"No, he didn't ask, and I didn't volunteer."

"But he knows there are others?"

"Yes."

"How about the Cardinals in Rome?"

"I told them of what I knew in the Archdiocese of New York. They don't yet know of any other Diocese's involvement."

"When is Callahan coming back?"

"I don't know. A few days, I think."

"It's going to be important for you to get a read from him when you next speak with him as to what happened on his visit. The reaction to the list, and what he feels will be their next course of action."

"You mean to interrogate him like you would if you had the chance?"

"Yeah, Frank, but you're probably as good at it as I am, if not better. All those confessions you heard? You knew who was bullshitting you and who was telling the truth."

"After a few years, I most certainly did."

"We'll hold off on the security measures for now. We'll decide what to implement after your talk with the Cardinal. Oh, does Brian have the combination for your safe?"

"Yes, and I trust him with my life. He has never betrayed any confidence in the five or six years he has been my secretary."

"What's in there besides your copy of the files?"

"Important diocesan records and a lot of cash."

"I want you to change the combination to the safe right now, but do not inform Brian. Not that I don't trust him, but I don't trust someone higher up asking him to open your safe after the church bosses whack your holy ass."

Frank smiled and shook his head. He said, "Your paranoia knows no bounds."

"Paranoia saved *my* ass a few times, Bishop. You should start developing some yourself."

"I guess that will depend on my next conversation with the Cardinal, won't it?"

"I guess it will," I said, gathering up my copy of the list. "And call me with the new combination to your safe right after you change it."

TWENTY-SIX

A week later my phone rang and Bishop Manzo said, "I just got off the phone with Cardinal Callahan. I believe they're going to bury it, and they won't make the Pope aware of anything."

"I figured that. Give me the details."

"Cardinal Callahan was directed to obtain any other allegations of sexual abuse his other Bishops may have in their possession and forward them to Rome. He feels the other four American Cardinals will be likewise directed."

"Did Callahan come right out and say they were going to bury it?"

"No, but he did say he was glad he was hitting the mandatory retirement age of seventy-five in a few months, and this would become someone else's problem."

"That someone else could be you, Frank. A big promotion for your silence."

"Could be, if they don't whack me instead."

"Now who's paranoid," I said laughing. "But you have to take some action right away."

"Like what?"

"Call those other Bishops in your group and tell them to lay low. If they are surveyed by their Cardinals, they should divulge nothing for their own safety. Make it sound bad – and it is. I wouldn't say their lives are in danger, but their careers in the church would be severely damaged. You can come up with the right words."

"I'm beginning to be more than a little concerned, Mike."

"Good, now how long are you going to wait?"

"Wait?"

"Yeah, before you release the lists of violators and the allegations against them?"

"Right after Callahan retires and I brief his replacement of my plans."

"That's too long. How did the Cardinals in Rome leave it with Callahan?"

"They told him to stay silent until he hears from them."

"That will be never. I would give this no more than a month, Frank. We'll install the security devices and CCTV systems. After that you may have to push the issue."

"How?"

"Call Callahan and demand he gets an answer from Rome on what they are doing to address these serious allegations."

"John Callahan is a good man. Can't we wait until he's retired and out of the picture?"

"Frank, think about that. He *can't* be out of the picture. Never. Most of that shit happened on *his* watch. He can't pass it on to the new guy in the red hat."

I heard him sigh and he quietly said, "Okay, a month."

.   .   .

The month zipped by, and there was no call from Rome to Cardinal Callahan. When the Bishop put in the call to his Boss, I was sitting in the office and the speaker phone was enabled. "Good afternoon, Your Eminence," he said.

"Hello Francis, how are you?"

"I'm fine, and I hope you are, too."

"I've been in better health, but I'll be relieved of this office in a few more months. What can I do for you?"

"I was wondering if you had heard back from Rome on the material you delivered to them? Did they reach a decision?"

"No, I have not heard back, but may I offer you some advice?"

"Certainly, Your Eminence."

"You are in contention to succeed me here in the Archdiocese. This mission of yours will definitely ruin that opportunity. Give up this crusade. It's not good for you, or for me, or for the catholic church."

So he did get a call from Rome!

"But Your Eminence –"

"No buts, Francis. Take this message and listen to it closely. I can't protect you if you persist in this unholy quest."

While they were speaking I scribbled a few words on a sheet of paper and passed it over to Frank. He read them and said essentially what I had written. "Yes, Your Eminence, I will cease my efforts. As always, your wish is my command. Perhaps things will change in the future of their own accord."

"That's the spirit, Francis! Remember, these allegations are merely that – allegations. I'd bet ninety percent are untrue, maybe ninety-nine percent."

"Yes, Your Eminence. Thank you for your concern and your assistance."

"You're very welcome, *Cardinal* Manzo."

When we disconnected I said, "He got the call and he got the message. Now *you* have the message. Are you going to heed that message, *Cardinal*?"

"Fuck you, Mike. In our long acquaintance you know me a helluva lot better than that."

"There you go, jarhead, swearing again – but maybe the Cardinal is right."

"Wh-a-a-t?"

"Listen, if you get the powerful red hat maybe you can institute your own cleanup and reforms. If you leave it alone for now, you could postpone or prevent getting whacked – actually, or professionally."

"You obviously don't have a clue as to the real power of a Cardinal in the United States. It's what Rome allows. Much like the power of the chief of detectives is limited by what the police commissioner allows."

"They'd kill you as a Cardinal, too?"

"Kill me? I know I mused about it, but now that you say it out loud…"

"Yeah, and I'm starting to think if they are going to do it, they are going to do it soon. Maybe make that pre-emptive strike before you can go public with this."

"But they believe they have all the copies of the lists of allegations. There is nothing for them to fear or for me to release, right?"

"Give me a break, Frank. Do you believe this clan of powerful Cardinals got their positions because they are stupid? They *know* you kept a copy. And even if they believed you were too dumb to keep one, they can't take a chance. You may be a dead man walking soon, I'm afraid."

"Shit! What do I do now?"

I thought for a few moments and said, "Here's what I want you to do. Write a letter and send copies to the Brooklyn North Detective Boro Commander, the Brooklyn South Detective Boro Commander, the Queens Detective Boro Commander, and the Chief of Detectives over at One Police Plaza in Manhattan. Send them by certified mail, return receipt requested. When those receipts come back, give them to me. I also want a copy of your letter. Then put another copy of your letter and a photocopy of the mail receipts with the files in your safe. Oh, include the new combination to your safe on the chief of detectives' letter, but it doesn't matter if the files disappear. I have copies already."

"I'm not following your reasoning here."

"If something happens to you I want to know if the chief had gotten the word from the PC, or the Cardinal, to get the lists from your safe and squelch their disclosure."

"You do have a devious mind, Mike."

"Not devious. Focused would be a better word. Focused on preserving your life, and your mission."

"What should I put in the letters?"

"Say that you have information of wrongdoing in the church – allegations of pedophilia and sexual abuse committed by a huge number of priests in the Archdiocese and your Diocese – and that you trust the church hierarchy will address those allegations promptly. However, in case they decide to 'shoot the messenger' and you suffer an untimely demise, you wish your death be investigated by your good friend and able investigator, Lieutenant Michael Simon and his team from Queens Homicide."

"You are starting to scare me, Mike."

"Good, I hope I have, because I believe the threat is real. Limit your outdoor excursions until those letters are mailed and the receipts returned. I'll be curious to see who calls you, if any of them do. Who's your best friend of the four?"

"The Brooklyn North Detective Boro Commander, Deputy Chief Roger Hendriks. Oh, and the patrol boss, Assistant Chief Kevin Grogan, is a good friend, also."

"Let's stay with the detective commanders. Are you ready to write?"

"I'm not a great typist, Mike."

"You write it out longhand. We'll both edit, and I'll type them up."

.   .   .

Five days later, I breathed a slight sigh of relief. The mail receipts and a copy of the Bishop's letter, along with the files, were in my possession, safely stored at my home. All the four chiefs who had received the letter personally called Frank and expressed their concern and offered whatever assistance he might need. As per our plan, he said he had taken some precautionary measures and hoped those measures and the offered assistance from the NYPD would not be necessary. He said he had confidence the church leaders would address the problem in a short time.

But then Frank told me of his conversation with Chief of Detectives, Kevin O'Connor, which was a bit more probing. "He specifically asked me about you, Mike. He wanted to know if I had told you I was requesting you to lead the investigation if I happened to die a mysterious death."

"And what did you say?"

"I told him yes, as we discussed. He then asked me the extent of your knowledge of the sex abuse allegations, the locations of the lists, and verified with me my safe's new combination. And, also according to plan, I told him you had no knowledge of any of it."

"Good work Frank. Anything else?"

"Yes, the chief persisted. He wanted to know if you prodded me on why I thought I might get whacked. I told him you did, then added I told you I might be paranoid and not in any danger after all."

"Do you think the chief bought your explanation?"

"I believe so, Mike, and then he said, 'Bishop, what are you going to do if your superiors seem to be ignoring your information? How long are you prepared to wait before taking action?' I told O'Connor I haven't figured that out yet. He told me not to act rashly and to call him first before I did anything. I said I would, and thanked him for his concern."

"Be super careful until you make your decision. And, call *me* first, not O'Connor."

"Now I have some thinking, and some soul-searching, to do."

"Oh, you *did* record that conversation with O'Connor like I told you?"

"I did."

"Good. Stay alert, and when you are out and about, which I suggest you keep to a bare minimum, keep an eye out for any suspicious people on foot or in cars that may be tailing you. For all we know, Rome has already dispatched a couple of zips to take you out."

"Zips?"

"You don't know what a zip is?"

"No."

"Are you sure you're Italian?"

"Uh, Giuseppe Mastronunzio, remember?"

"Do you remember when mob boss Carmine Galante got blasted away while eating lunch in Joe and Mary's restaurant in Bushwick, here in your own Diocese of Brooklyn?"

"Vaguely, that was many years ago, wasn't it?"

"Twenty-one, to be exact. It happened in July, 1979."

"What about it? It seemed those mob guys were killing each other every day way back then."

"That they were. Now, do you recall who killed Galante?"

"Uh, no."

"Nobody does, because nobody got caught. Three zips imported from Palermo did it, and got clean away. Galante was set up by the other bosses and by his own men. His two armed bodyguards, sitting close by at the same table, were not shot and did not shoot back at the zips while they were whacking their boss right in front of them."

"A zip is a hired killer from Sicily?"

"Usually, although some come from the Italian mainland as well. The zip name comes from zipper, the rushing noise a zipper makes when being opened or closed. It refers to the fast speech of the Sicilian dialect which is difficult to follow, even by Italians."

"Are you making all this crap up just to scare me, Mike? And if not, where the hell did you learn all of this trivia?"

"It's not made up, and I learned right here on the streets of New York that I have worked on for twenty years. Unlike you, I don't hide in the sanctuary of the church."

"Ouch."

"Sorry, Frank. I was going to add that you should get out more often, but that would be terrible advice right now."

"Zips. Sent from Palermo by the cardinals in Rome. Sent to whack me. It is difficult to fathom they would go to such lengths."

"Why? They are protecting their fiefdom, their money, their power, and their control, like every despotic centralized regime has done throughout history."

The Bishop smiled and said, "I believe I detect the voice of Mort Stern in there somewhere. Did the old survivor teach you that while you were sweeping his floor? You didn't learn it at Bishop Loughlin."

I smiled back at him remembering those days in the candy store. I said, "He sure did, but now I want to impress upon you the need to call me immediately if you spot a tail."

"And what exactly am I looking for? What does your typical zip look like?"

"You may be smiling, Frank, but this isn't funny at all. And a zip is usually a young guy with typical Italian features."

"Just like me?"

Now it was my turn to smile. I said, "Yeah, Frank, but their hair is black, not gray, their noses aren't as large as yours, and they are much better-looking."

I left the Bishop's office hoping he had gotten the message. Obviously I had convinced myself, as I drove away with one eye on the rearview mirror.

TWENTY SEVEN

Furio Vazzo had flown from Palermo, Sicily to Newark, New Jersey with a passport and NY State driver's license issued under the name of Joseph Giordano, with a Brooklyn address. After landing, Furio proceeded to the Avis car rental counter, rented a mid-size sedan, and drove south on the Jersey Turnpike getting off at Exit Eight. A short drive from the exit took him to a Marriott Fairfield Inn where a room awaited him under his assumed name. About an hour after his arrival, he opened the door to a knock and Renzo Turano, who had arrived from the Philadelphia airport in his rental vehicle, walked in. The two friends embraced and enjoyed the beers Renzo had purchased from the market in the motel's lobby, as they awaited the arrival of their contact, the man who would lay out the details of their mission.

At a few minutes after eleven p.m. Gianni Trapani, who had arrived from Palermo at JFK airport in Queens, knocked on their door and was respectfully ushered inside where he was warmly greeted by his two hired zips. The three of them got right down to business, speaking in their native tongue. Trapani produced maps and photos of Bishop Manzo's residence at the cathedral and the streets of the neighborhood. He said, "The people who hired us feel it would be difficult to find someone easily compromised in the Bishop's inner-circle of friends. Time is of the essence, so the three of us will do a close surveillance of the cathedral and of the Bishop's comings and goings. If we feel we can break into his residence without triggering an alarm, we will kill him as he sleeps."

"Is there something he has which we must recover?" Vazzo asked.

"Yes, but that is a secondary consideration. If conditions are such that we can get in the Bishop's quarters and convince him to hand the item over, a printed list of names most likely kept in his safe, we should do so. But the goal is to kill him regardless of our success in retrieving that list. If we have to do it in broad daylight on the street, then that's what we will do. We leave for Brooklyn early tomorrow morning. Get a good night's sleep. We will meet in the lobby at seven a.m. I've reserved some rooms for us at the downtown Ramada in Brooklyn. We'll individually scout out the cathedral and the streets of the local neighborhood and meet back there at 3:00 p.m., check-in time. See you tomorrow."

After Trapani left for his room next door, Renzo Turano said, "Furio, what do you think about killing a Bishop?"

Furio chuckled, "We're getting twenty-five grand apiece for this hit with half up front. I'd kill the fucking Pope for that much."

"Me, too. We're already going to hell anyway. What's the devil going to do? Make the fire hotter?"

They got into their individual queen-size beds and were soon asleep dreaming of the girls and cars they would buy back home with their new fortunes.

∎　　∎　　∎

After five full days of surveillance, the three Sicilian imports discussed their observations and conclusions. One, it would not be possible to break into the cathedral and kill Manzo inside. There were CCTV cameras everywhere. The doors and door locks were sturdy and all the doors and windows were alarmed. There appeared to be no easy access to the roof. Two, the man who had visited the cathedral's door that led to the Bishop's quarters on three occasions was a cop. Renzo had twice tailed him back to his office in Queens and both times he parked in a spot reserved for Queens Homicide before entering the building. Three, that cop had walked with the Bishop to a restaurant called the Lotus Blossom for lunch one day. Four, after conveying all this information to his employer in Rome, Gianni Trapani was instructed to do the hit on the street at their first opportunity and, if possible, take out the detective, as well. And a few days later that opportunity arose.

As the Bishop and the cop exited the cathedral and walked the street toward an obvious lunchtime destination, Trapani called his two zips and said, "I'm assuming they are going to lunch. When we see where they go, we will plan to hit them when they exit the restaurant. I'll call you back in a few minutes."

Furio picked up his cell phone and Trapani gave him the name and location of Giacomo's restaurant as soon as he observed the two enter it. He said to Furio, "When they come out, hit the gas and drive your car over the curb and take them both out. Then jump out and run around the corner where Renzo will be waiting. I will be one block up from Renzo in case something goes wrong. Drive directly to our hotel. Flights are being arranged for later today. Any questions?"

"No," Furio said. "See you shortly."

.　.　.

For the next few days, Bishop Manzo did as I instructed. If he went out for lunch, he was accompanied by Brian or one of his four Auxiliary Bishops. Most of the days he had lunch sent in. When he bedded down for the night he made sure to engage all the electronic security systems. So far, so good, but the big question remained unanswered by him. When was he going to pull the trigger? And how? I picked up the phone and dialed his private number. When he answered, I put those questions to him. He said, "I've been thinking of nothing else, and I finally have a plan. I'm ready to pull the trigger, as you so aptly put it, but I want to run the scenario by you first."

"When?"

"Tomorrow. How about lunch at Giacomo's?"

"That's not the place we ate at a few weeks ago, which was pretty good."

"No, but I'm a Wop, you know. I need my fix of good pasta every so often. It's right around the corner from the Lotus Blossom."

"Sounds good. I'll meet you there at twelve-thirty."

"Get there early and scout the place out for possible assassins from Rome."

"Don't be a wiseass, my friend. Until those records are out in public view, you're probably not a target, but then again they might take that pre-emptive strike I always worry about."

"Maybe I'll get there before you, and check behind the toilet tank for a gun Rome had someone tape there. Who knows, they could have gotten to you, right?"

"Yeah, if the price was right. But the Corleone family offered a paltry hundred bucks for your untimely demise. I declined while awaiting a much higher offer."

He laughed and said, "See you tomorrow. Bring your appetite, I'm buying."

.　　.　　.

Unknown to the Bishop, I had brought my two sergeants and two top detectives in on the situation, and for a reason that had hit me like a bolt of lightning a few days ago. *If Frank was a target, couldn't I be also?*

I was a known friend of the Bishop. I had made several visits to the cathedral. Brian had noted that. I'm sure his four Auxiliary Bishops noted that. If any zips were tailing me or watching the cathedral, they would have noted that. And I was mentioned in the letters to the NYPD detective brass. The assumption had to be made that the Bishop had confided everything he knew in me, his trusted friend in the NYPD, even though he told Chief O'Connor otherwise. I took necessary precautions and prepared copies of everything for each of my four trusted co-workers and explained it all to them in detail. Sergeant Harry Megara was the first to speak. He said, "All I gotta say, Boss, is there's never a dull moment working with you. How do you get involved in all of this weird shit?"

"Just lucky, I guess."

"And you're meeting Manzo tomorrow to listen to his plans?" Richie Paul asked.

"Yes, we're having lunch at Giacomo's, and I don't know what he has in mind. There are several options open to him."

"Such as?" Harry asked.

"He can call the chief of detectives and give him possession of the list and request criminal investigation of the allegations. Or he could visit with the editor of the *New York Times* and have the paper expose the whole scandal and force the NYPD to take action, if the chief balks."

"Is there a chance he will take no action at all?" Charlie Seich asked.

"I presented him with that option, but told him that would not change his dangerous situation. If they are going to whack him they might do it soon, before he has a chance to release it. That's why I'm going to try to talk him out of calling Chief O'Connor."

"I'm not following you, Mike," John Micena said.

"He calls O'Connor. O'Connor calls the PC. The PC calls the Cardinal. The Cardinal calls Rome. Rome orders the hit." I was contemplating who would be the first to call me crazy, or a conspiracy nut, or a paranoid fool, but they merely nodded their heads until Harry said, "Yeah, it could happen that way."

"What if the *Times* or other media outlets want no part of this?" Charlie asked.

"I guess he'll cross that bridge when he comes to it," I said.

"Mike, are you coming back here right after your lunch?" Harry asked.

"I might stop at the Bishop's office first in case we have to make further plans. I'll be back after that."

"Call me right after you finish lunch and tell me what you decide."

"Worried about me, Harry?"

"Yeah, be careful, Mike. As you yourself thought, you could also be a target. Tomorrow they have a chance at both of you together. In a public place."

"I'll be on my toes, don't worry."

I saw Harry's eyes narrow and he said, "Wait, change of plans. John, Richie, I want you out there at Giacomo's tomorrow for surveillance and close protection. One of you inside and one outside on foot."

"Harry," I said, "that's not necessary."

Ignoring me he continued, "Start the stakeout at 11:30, I'll join you a few minutes later. Charlie, you run the squad."

"Harry, I —"

"Be quiet, Mike. I'm directing my detectives to an assignment, and I'm not asking your permission. Got it?"

I smiled and said, "Got it, *Sergeant.*"

.   .   .

I arrived at Giacomo's right on time and went inside not noticing any of my men, or any suspicious-looking zips for that matter, on the street as I did so. When I walked in, Bishop Manzo waved at me from a booth near the back of the restaurant. As I moved toward him I passed John Micena at a booth directly across from Frank's. He had a salad in front of him and a glass of red wine next to it. I slid in the booth across from Frank, and after we exchanged greetings, I said, "Let's order our lunch, and then we'll talk."

As the waiter brought us wine and salads, I noticed him place a huge bowl of pasta covered with red sauce in front of John Micena, whose face lit up in a big Italian smile. "What did you give that customer?" I asked the waiter, pointing to John.

"Rigatoni and our famous meatballs, sir."

"I'll have the same, but better make it a half portion."

"Baked manicotti, please," said the Bishop.

The waiter left and I said, "What's your plan?"

"I gave this careful thought including your option of doing nothing and opting for the promotion. I immediately ruled that out. These victims, children may I remind you, need justice. *Children*, Mike! I want these priests prosecuted to the fullest extent of the law. I want to see them taken out of their sanctuary closets in handcuffs and made to do the perp walk. This abuse has to end. The church must be cleansed so it can move on to a better future."

It was obvious to me he had chosen his course of action and nothing I could say would dissuade him. I said, "How are you going to go about it?"

"I'll call Chief O'Connor and arrange for him to take possession of the records and tell him of my strong desire to prosecute all of these deviants as soon as possible."

"I suggest you deliver them to him personally at his office in One Police Plaza and give him that message in person. I'll drive you over there when you're ready."

"Right after lunch I'll make the call to him, and try to get them to him this afternoon."

I didn't envy Chief O'Connor having an atomic bomb dropped on his desk. What would he do? If it were me, I'd run it down to the PC's office the minute the Bishop left and drop the bomb on *his* desk. And what would the Irish Catholic Police Commissioner, Sean Flanagan, do? Why he'd place a call to the Irish Catholic Archbishop of New York, John Cardinal Callahan, and ask for guidance. And then what would the Cardinal do?

"Your decision has been made, Frank. I'm relieved, and I'm hungry."

We ate our meals, but declined dessert, opting only for double espressos. Out of the corner of my eye I caught Micena sticking his fork into a big slice of tiramisu. Where the hell does he put it all? The check came and Frank grabbed it and slid his credit card into the leather folder. "Compliments of the Diocese," he said.

TWENTY-EIGHT

As we left Giacomo's, John was settling with the waiter, and as we walked south on Jay Street, I noticed Richie Paul across the street walking with us. It was a beautiful midsummer day, not too hot and little humidity, and a gentle westerly breeze blew the puffy clouds across a clear blue sky. I wondered what the reaction would be when the bomb hit. Would Frank and I be afraid to make this walk a week from now? Would –

"Mike!" Frank screamed and I felt a violent shove from him and the roar of a car engine whose front fender grazed my hip. I hit the cement hard and rolled into the wall of a building, hearing a thunderous crash next to me. After a minute, I managed to sit up, groggy, trying to clear my head when a pair of arms helped me up. "Mike! Mike! Are you okay?"

Those words were distant in my brain and I suddenly realized what had happened, and recognized my deputy through my foggy vision. "Harry! The Bishop!"

"It doesn't look good, Mike. We got an ambulance responding already. A civilian called immediately after the crash."

"What the hell happened?"

"A car jumped the curb and clipped him bad."

"An accident?"

"No way. As soon as the car stopped, the driver got out and ran like hell. Paul and Micena took off after him. Mike, we gotta get you checked out. You could have a concussion."

"My head is starting to clear up a bit, and –"

"Mike, what is it?" Harry yelled as I sat back down on the sidewalk and put my head in my hands. "Mike, are you okay!"

"Shit, Harry, I was supposed to watch out for him, but he saved *my* life. He must have caught a glimpse of that car bearing down on him before I did, and he shoved me out of the way. I should have taken that hit, not him."

"Mike, as we said before, you *both* could have been targets, and I'm betting you were."

I stopped a sob from emerging from my throat as a wave of hatred and determination washed over me. "Harry, I'm going to get these assassins one way or another. They will pay for this dearly."

"I'm with you on that. I hear the ambulance now."

"Help me up. Bring me to the Bishop."

Frank was lying on the sidewalk next to the car that had hit him. The front end of the car was crumpled into the façade of a brick building, its radiator hissing steam into the air. The Bishop's body was covered with a red and white checkered tablecloth from the restaurant. Two uniformed officers from the 84 Precinct stood by. I identified myself and asked the question I already knew the answer to. "Is he dead?"

"Yes, sir," one of them said. "I mean, he hasn't been officially pronounced by a doctor, but there's no doubt."

I chose not to uncover him. I wanted to remember him healthy and smiling as we ate our last meal together a few minutes ago.

The street was filling up with marked and unmarked vehicles from the nearby precinct. I stood by Frank's body until the ambulance crew picked him up, put him on the trundle, and wheeled him to their vehicle. I gave a half-hearted salute as they drove away. As I was wondering where Paul and Micena were, and if they caught the driver, a voice called out, "Mike, are you okay?"

I looked up as Deputy Chief Roger Hendriks strode towards me, a worried look on his face. I said, "I think so, Chief, but I'm going to get checked out at the hospital soon."

"Good idea. What the hell went down here?"

After I gave him the details I said, "As soon as I get done there I'll be back to take charge of the investigation."

"Take charge, Mike? I don't understand. This is Brooklyn, not Queens. Maybe you *have* received a concussion."

A little warning bell dinged in my non-concussed brain. I said, "The Bishop told me if anything happened to him – specifically an untimely, unplanned death – he wanted me to head up the investigation."

"I know you were friends, but –"

"We had lunch together, Chief. He told me he mentioned it to you. He said he sent you a letter with that request in it."

"Letter? Mike, I don't recall receiving any letter from Bishop Manzo. Are you positive he said that?"

The warning bell clanged much louder now. *You lying bastard, I got the return receipt and a recording of your telephone call to the Bishop after you got it.* I had to play this carefully. I said, "Maybe he said he was going to send you a letter, Chief. I could be mistaken. My head's a little fuzzy now."

"Maybe you'd better go to the hospital right away. And maybe this investigation will turn out to be an accident investigation handled by the patrol force. We have no indication this was an intentional act."

An accident? Unintentional? I played along and said, "You're probably right, Chief."

"We're thinking some kid took the car for a joyride and lost control. It checks out as a rental vehicle from Avis in Newark Airport. The dicks will follow-up on the guy who rented it, and if it was recently stolen from him."

Richie and John trotted up to us, sweaty and disheveled. "We lost him, Mike," Richie said. "He was booking like a fucking rabbit."

"Young kid?" Chief Hendriks asked.

Both Micena and Paul apparently did not know Hendriks as they looked quizzically at him. Before one of them had a chance to say, "Who the hell are you?" I said, "This is Chief Hendriks, guys, the boro commander."

"Oh," Micena said. "Not that young, Chief. I mean he looked more to be in his mid-to-late twenties, not some sixteen year-old joy rider."

"I see. Did you see where he went? Did he get in another vehicle or a motorcycle?"

"He may have been able to do that before we got around the corner," Richie said, "but he could have ducked down into the subway entrance at the end of the block. When we got down there, on the city-bound side, we didn't spot him on the platform."

"It was crowded," John said, "and a train was pulling out on the opposite platform. He could have been on that."

"Give that description to the 84 Squad detectives, and they'll take it from here."

John and Richie glanced at me and I shook my head slightly. They immediately got the message and John said, "Will do, Chief."

"Now, Mike, have someone take you to the hospital forthwith."

"Yes, sir. Sergeant Megara here will. John, Richie?"

"Yes, Boss?" they said.

"After you give your statements to the 84 Squad dicks, we'll all meet back at the office. I'm sure Harry and I will have to give statements to them also after I get checked out."

"Okay, Boss," John said. "Catch you later."

As Harry drove me to the hospital he said, "It's curious Chief Hendriks didn't ask you why you had your deputy CO and two of your dicks in Brooklyn while you were having lunch with the Bishop."

"I was wondering that myself, but we both know the answer to that, don't we?"

"Oh, yeah, Mike. The fix is already in. Hendriks passed that letter he got right to his boss, Chief O'Connor, and was told to dummy up about it."

"And they'll whitewash this as a tragic accident caused by a joy-riding teenager who lost control of his stolen car."

"And a million Catholics in the Diocese will mourn the death of their beloved Bishop."

"And the church will give him a grand farewell at St. Joseph's Cathedral to handle the huge crowd of shocked worshipers."

"And the Cardinal and all the Bishops will attend and put on their solemn faces."

"And all the high police brass will attend with similar phony solemn looks upon their hypocritical faces."

"What do we do now, Mike?"

"I'm not sure, Harry, but whatever it is it will be a big explosion. I owe that to Frank. I owe him my life. And I will repay him by taking up and leading the crusade against all of them. I guarantee it."

.   .   .

I was a lot longer in the emergency room of St. Vincent's than I expected, as they did a thorough exam of my entire body, which was now beginning to hurt in several places after my untimely contact with concrete and brick. A big bruise on my right hip. Scraped knuckles on my left hand. Abrasions on the right side of my face. A slightly sprained left ankle. The x-rays all showed no fractures, and the doctor's exam concluded I had no concussion. I smiled as he said, "The nurse will give you a couple of aspirin and that should be all you need, Lieutenant."

I was surprised he didn't add, "And call me in the morning," but concluded that omission was a good sign. Harry and I finally got out of there at four o'clock. As we got in the car I said, "I'm going to call Richie. I want to hear what they told the 84 Squad dicks."

"Like how they answered the question, 'Hey, what were all you Queens' Homicide guys doing down here anyway?'"

"Exactly," I said while dialing my cell phone.

"How did it go?" I asked when Richie picked up.

"It went well. We're pulling into the squad now."

"Did they ask what you, what all of us, were doing in Brooklyn?"

"That they did, Mike. We told them while you were having lunch with the Bishop we were chasing down a couple witnesses on a pending case."

"Good. Did you mention John was inside the restaurant filling his face on my dime?"

"No, it didn't come up at all," he said laughing. "Next caper, I want to be the inside guy."

"You got it. Listen, you and John pack up and go home. We'll talk tomorrow morning. Oh, what was your take on their investigation?"

"They seem to be taking it seriously, Mike. Even had a couple of Brooklyn North homicide guys brought in to get involved."

"I figured Chief Hendriks would have second thoughts. There's no way he can pawn this off on the uniform force. Not with a death involved. And that of the Bishop of Brooklyn, no less."

"So they pull out all the stops for the media, but it will go nowhere, right?"

"Right you are, Detective Paul."

"What now, Mike?"

"The five of us will hash it out tomorrow," I said.

. . .

The detectives from the 84 Squad and Brooklyn North homicide treated us cordially and professionally. Having been informed of my relationship with the Bishop they expressed their sincere condolences on his death before they got to their questions. And it didn't take long for Harry and I to figure out these guys had not been told to blow this investigation off at all. The chief was too savvy to do that. He figured, as time went by and the "juvenile joy rider" was never apprehended, the case would die on its own, as all old news does. And he also knew if the Bishop's death was an intentional hit masterminded by powers much higher up the ladder than he, it would never be solved.

I related my recollection of events, and one of the homicide dicks asked the question I would have asked, "Lieutenant, did you know if the Bishop had any enemies who might have reason to kill him? And if not, do *you* have any enemies that would resort to an attempt on your life?"

"Excellent question," I said. "No, I am unaware of any person or situation that would cause someone to target Bishop Manzo. As for me, after over twenty years of locking up assholes, who knows? But no threats have come my way lately, and no case comes to mind where I would become a target."

"Do you think the driver intentionally drove over the curb and onto the sidewalk to nail one, or both of you?"

"I can't say. I never saw the driver. I couldn't get a read on his expression. The chief thinks this might have been a terrible accident caused by a panicked, inexperienced driver. He may be right."

"It may turn out that way, sir, but we have been directed to look at every angle before we come to that conclusion."

"I know you will, guys, and I appreciate all your efforts."

We were done with their questions in another twenty minutes and on our way back to Queens. Harry said, "That was some performance. Do you think they bought it?"

"It doesn't matter. What matters is when they report back to Hendriks, that he buys it."

The events of the afternoon had been so hectic I hadn't had time to call my wife, although I knew that would not be an acceptable excuse. As I pulled into the driveway I realized I should have at least called her on the way home, before the six o'clock news broke on the TV. I turned off the ignition and dialed our home phone number. As expected, she said, "Wonderful of you to call now. What –?"

"Stop, Vivian. I love you. It was a bad day, but I'm alive. I'm in the driveway. Please pour me a double vodka over ice."

"Come on in and I'll get your drink ready. But I'm unsure if I'll hand it to you or throw it in your face. And isn't a double a bit strong for you?"

"I don't think my face would like that too much, and I need a double about now."

"Are you hurt badly? How stupid of me. Get that handsome face in here. It is still handsome, isn't it?"

"Beauty is in the eye of the beholder, thankfully."

I hobbled to the front door, my arms, legs, and torso starting to ache and tighten up a bit more. I might need something stronger than two lousy aspirin, after all. The vodka would be a start. The door opened, and if Vivian were going to chastise me further, she changed her mind when she glanced at my face. "Oh, Mike, come in. Sit down. Oh, you are hurt!"

I sat on the living room sofa and Vivian ran into the kitchen and came back with the vodka. I took a healthy sip and she said, "Be right back, I need one too."

She sat next to me and caressed my hair. "Tell me all about it. The TV said the Bishop is dead. How did it all happen?"

I told her everything – well, almost everything – of what transpired after the Bishop and I left Giacomo's Restaurant. Some things, as all cops learned, were better left unsaid.

"Then this was a tragic accident?"

"It seems so, pending further investigation. But who would want to deliberately run the Bishop over and kill him? He has a great reputation throughout the Diocese."

"Maybe the driver wanted to hit you, and missed."

"Same reasoning. I've put a lot of guys in jail over my years, but none that ever threatened to get me."

"That makes me feel better. How long are you going to take off?"

"Take off?"

"Yeah. From work. You have a line of duty injury, right?"

"A few bumps and bruises aren't going to keep me home. I'll be good as new in a couple of days. Besides, I have to write up a lot of reports on what happened and on my injuries."

"Can't that wait? Stay home with me."

I smiled and said, "As soon as I wrap this up, I'll take a few days off. Maybe we can get away somewhere – just the two of us."

"I like that. Want another vodka? You sloshed that one down awfully fast."

"Oh, yeah, and three or four Aleve, too."

TWENTY-NINE

By ten o'clock, with the regular morning business out of the way, we got down to it. After we all related our conversations and observations of yesterday's events, I said, "This guy who killed the Bishop and ran away was definitely a zip?"

"Oh, yeah," John said, "without a doubt."

"I agree," Richie said, "and I got a much closer look at the prick than my slow-assed partner here."

"Hey, I just had a big lunch. Gimme a break here."

"So I noticed," I said. "What is that feast going to cost the NYPD?"

"Don't worry, Mike, I took care of the tab with my own money."

"That I don't believe," Sergeant Seich said.

"The waiter asked me if I was a cop and when I told him yeah, he cut the bill in half. It still was a heavy hit."

"I guess the zip is already back in Rome, or Palermo, by now," Harry Megara said.

"And," Richie said, "he's either a dead zip, if he was expendable, or a happy zip with a big wad of Euros in his pocket."

"Wonder what he would have told us if you guys collared him?" I asked.

"*Non Capisco*," John said. "And after claiming he doesn't understand, he'll say whatever is Italian for, 'I want my lawyer.'"

"Do we all agree this case will never be solved and eventually go away?"

"I think we do, Mike," Harry said. "What now?"

"Chief O'Connor's letter from the Bishop contained the new combination to his safe. If the chief is a righteous guy, he would be at Manzo's office right now getting those records."

"And taking them to the nearest shredder," John said.

"Or doing as Manzo asked – conducting an investigation and locking up a lot of misfit priests."

"Who wants to bet on that scenario?" Seich asked.

There were no takers and John said, "So what do we do now?"

"We have the lists. We could start arresting them ourselves."

"Are you kidding? Homicide Squad dicks suddenly locking up sex abusers? The brass will throttle you and stop that dead in its tracks."

"What are your ideas, guys?"

"Go to the papers, Mike," Charlie said. "The *Times* will eat this up. If they publish the allegations the department will have to act."

"What if the publisher is in bed with the Cardinal and the department's top brass?" Harry asked.

"I doubt that," Richie said, "but you never know. I have a much better idea."

"Please," I said. "Let us hear it."

"Sue them."

"You mean hire a money-hungry firm of Jew lawyers, uh, no offense Boss, and take them to the cleaners?" John asked.

I laughed and said, "I like the idea of civil action, but a firm of *Jew lawyers* might not be a great idea. They'd be targeted as Christ-killers all over again if they took on the Roman Catholic Church."

"Howie Stein!" Charlie shouted.

"What about him?" I asked knowing, as we all knew, who he meant.

"After he left the DA's office years ago he joined a white-shoe law firm. I've been there. Howie's my personal lawyer."

"What the hell do you need a lawyer for, Sarge?" Richie asked.

"Estate planning, that's what. He made out our wills, but when I told him I wanted to leave you something he told me there was no way to bequeath my common sense to you, no matter how bad you needed it."

"Very funny," Richie said.

"What about Howie?" I asked. "How does he figure in this?"

"There are five partners. Howie is the only Jew. They have an Italian, an Irishman, and the firm's founders, two WASPS, German and English heritage, I believe. And their main practice centers on medical malpractice and personal injury. This would be right up their alley."

"I'm starting to like this," I said. "Hit the church hard in the pocketbook, but I also want the abusers exposed. No secret deals. No non-disclosure agreements."

"Do you want me to give Howie a call?"

"Not yet. I want to think this over some more. And I want to see what Chief O'Connor is going to do. We have to give him a chance. I'm going to give the Bishop's secretary a call now. I'll put him on speaker."

A dejected voice answered the phone on the third ring, "Bishop's office," he said. "Brian speaking."

"Brian, it's Lieutenant Mike Simon. How are you holding up?"

"Not well, sir. And you? How are you feeling? Were you hurt badly?"

"Some bumps and bruises, but I'm hurting a lot more inside for my friend."

"We all are. I can't believe it."

"I won't keep you long. I know you're busy making preparations for the funeral. I wanted to know if you checked his office for any notes he might have left."

"For you?"

"Not necessarily for me. For anyone. He said after lunch he wanted me to come back to his office. Said he had something to show me."

"I noticed nothing other than routine church business on his desk, Lieutenant."

"Maybe in his safe?"

"You know, I couldn't get into the safe this morning. I have to assume the Bishop changed the combination and didn't have the opportunity to tell me."

"I guess you'll have to call a locksmith."

"I thought about that, but decided to wait for the designation of the new Bishop for that. There was a lot of cash in there, I realized. I didn't want any suspicions directed my way. I'm sure you understand."

"I certainly do, Brian. Good decision. Any idea who the new Bishop will be?"

"Not a clue. For now the senior Auxiliary Bishop of the Diocese will most likely run things."

"Who is that?"

"Bishop Kenneth Stachurski."

"If he gets the job, and with a Polish Pope on the throne, the residents of Greenpoint will be ecstatic."

"Yes, they will, until they find out he's half Irish."

I couldn't think of a way to tell him to notify me if or when Chief O'Connor or his designee showed up to gain access to the safe. The best I could come up with was, "Brian, you must have observed Bishop Manzo was apparently concerned about something recently?"

"Yes, and I asked him about it, but he said it was minor, and nothing for either of us to worry about. Wait, you don't think —?"

"That the accident was not an accident? No, Brian, not at all. But if anything suspicious, or unusual, occurs in the near future, please call me right away."

"I'm not sure what you're looking for."

"Neither am I. Probably nothing will crop up. I'm a suspicious old cop. Forget it."

"Oh, okay. Uh, I have to go now."

"I understand, Brian. I'll see you at the funeral."

I hoped I planted a seed in his mind. I hoped he wouldn't *forget it*.

． ． ．

Another thing the NYPD and the Catholic Church have in common is they do funerals well. Some might say over the top. But when a cop gets killed in the line of duty, or a bishop gets killed in a tragic *accident*, all the stops are pulled out. And the Bishop of Brooklyn, His Most Reverend Excellency, Francis Andrew Manzo, was no exception. His two-day wake, with his body lying in state at the much larger co-cathedral of St. Joseph on Pacific Street, and his funeral mass, topped every one I had experienced over the years. And I had, sadly, seen too many.

The department had hundreds of uniformed officers stationed up and down Pacific Street and on the surrounding streets. The intersections were blocked off several blocks away. Only bonafide residents were allowed around the wooden barricades. I'd bet the top police brass and high religious officials had some sort of reserved parking nearby, but I, a mere lieutenant, would not even attempt to drive my NYPD sedan anywhere near the vicinity.

Vivian and I walked to the elevated subway line on Jamaica Avenue from our home in the Woodhaven section of Queens and changed at Broadway Junction for the A train. It was the first day of the wake, and I had taken the day off. When we got off the train at the Clinton-Washington Station and walked up the stairs to the fresh air, I was immediately reminded of the last walk I took with Frank on that fateful day not long ago. Same gentle breeze. Same deep blue sky. As we walked south on Washington Street, Vivian said, "What a gorgeous day. No one should be lying in a casket on a day such as this."

As we turned onto Pacific Street we were amazed, but not surprised, by the length of the line of mourners quietly standing in subdued silence. We joined the queue and it took us a full hour to reach the entrance doors to the Cathedral. Twenty minutes later we were at the open casket. The Bishop's body was resplendent in his clerical garments, all gold and cream-colored. His Bishop's miter was set atop his head, and his golden scepter was tucked under his crossed hands. A strand of golden rosary beads was intertwined among his fingers with his ring of office prominently displayed.

As I looked down upon his peaceful countenance I stumbled from the range of emotions that suddenly ran through me. Sadness that he was no longer with us. Rage at the manner of his death. Higher rage at those responsible for that vicious attack. Amazement at how an unfortunate teenager – Giuseppe Mastronunzio – sought atonement and absolution for a crime not of his making, became a model Marine, and a truthful servant of the church. I couldn't stem the silent flow of tears. Vivian grasped my elbow and said, "Mike, we have to move on. People behind us are giving us evil looks."

"Okay," I said, reaching for my handkerchief to wipe my eyes. *My handkerchief!* Now Mort Stern's visage floated through my brain, and I let out a loud sob.

"Mike!" she whispered. "Get it together, for Pete's sake! People are staring. Let's find a pew. You need to sit down for a few minutes."

"They're all full. I don't see a vacant spot."

A hand grabbed my arm and a voice said, "This way, Lieutenant."

I looked up and saw Brian with a concerned look on his face. He said, "Are you feeling okay?"

"No, Brian. I am not feeling well at all."

"I understand. Here, come this way."

He guided us to the first two pews at the front of the church and lifted a purple velvet rope motioning us to slide in. I genuflected and made the sign of the cross, automatically and unconsciously, and slid in after Vivian. Brian re-attached the rope and sat next to me. He had a quizzical look on his face. "Uh," he whispered, "I thought you were Jewish?"

"I am."

"But you made the sign of the cross."

"Oh, did I? Pure habit. I was raised in the church, you know. Went to Bishop Loughlin High School, a few blocks from here. Same as Frank. Uh, same as Bishop Manzo."

"I didn't know that," he said, looking at me a bit differently. "Are you going to attend the funeral?"

"Yes."

He reached into his coat pocket and withdrew a white card and a pen from his shirt pocket. He said, "Will your, uh, companion be also attending?"

"Oh, Brian, I'm sorry. This is my wife, Vivian."

"Pleased to meet you," she said. "Yes, I will accompany my husband."

He wrote something on the card and handed it to me. He said, "This will get you a good seat on Wednesday. Not the front rows, but not the rear ones either."

"Thank you. Oh, did you ever get that safe open?"

"Yes! The Cardinal himself came to the Cathedral and gave the combination to Bishop Stachurski, who, as I expected, will be in charge until a permanent bishop is named."

"The Cardinal, of course," I said. "He would be the logical one to have that combination. Bishop Manzo would certainly have given it to him."

"Yes, he would have, Lieutenant."

"But, Brian, why would he not have given that combination to you?"

"Um, you know, Lieutenant, I don't know."

I had to tread carefully here. "Maybe there was something in there the Bishop only wanted the Cardinal to see, or take possession of. I'm sure he trusted you fully."

"H-m-m-m, now that you mentioned it, when the Cardinal left the office he did have a package under his arm."

"Probably important Diocese matters Bishop Manzo wanted to trust with His Eminence."

"Yes, probably. Oh, please excuse me, Lieutenant, I have other business to attend to. Pleasure to meet you, Mrs. Simon. I'll see you Wednesday."

After Brian left, we bowed our heads in silence and Vivian whispered, "What was that all about?"

"I'll tell you later," I whispered back, as I hypocritically recited the *Our Father*. But it was for the soul of the Bishop, a true believer. It was for *him*. There is no God, but *he* believed there was. And then I thought about the Cardinal's visit to Bishop Manzo's office. *The chief of detectives took his letter with the combination to the police commissioner. The PC called the Cardinal and gave him the numbers, whereupon the PC shredded the letter. The Cardinal retrieved the documents from the Bishop's safe. Everyone breathed a sigh of relief. The crimes remained hidden. Rome was off the hook. Not so fast, you murdering bastards and cowardly accomplices, I'm coming after all of you. Soon.*

THIRTY

"So our wonderful chief of detectives took the smoking bomb and passed it up the chain of command, the fucking coward," Richie Paul said.

"And the PC threw it immediately to the Cardinal who retrieved what he thinks is the single remaining copy of the damning documents," Harry said.

"He also got the copies of the return receipts from the four letters Manzo sent to the brass," John said. "Which worries me."

"Why?" Charlie Seich asked.

"He'll know the originals are out there someplace else, and he'll conclude the only person who could have them in his possession is our favorite lieutenant here."

"Whereupon," Richie said, "another zip may be on his way to finish the job on our dear boss once and for all."

I smiled and said, "I'm not the least bit worried. Your favorite lieutenant is not as dumb as you think."

"Please tell us why," Harry said.

"The copies of the receipts were not ordinary copies. They were specially made by a detective in the Document Analysis section of our lab on the same green cardboard stock. They look and feel exactly like the originals."

"And you have the actual originals and copies of the letters safely tucked away somewhere," Charlie said. "Don't you?"

"I do, to be utilized at an appropriate time in the future."

"When do we want to call Howie Stein?"

"Sometime after the funeral tomorrow," I said. "I'd like to give it maybe a week, to see if anything happens with the church or the department."

"Guaranteed, nothing will," Charlie said. "They have tied up all the damning documents in a sturdy box and buried it forever."

"You're no doubt right, but I want to wait a bit. I want to see if the brass is going to make a move against me, or against Ray Elliott."

"The inspector from Internal Affairs? The guy that was Manzo's guy inside?" John asked.

"Yes. He accessed the department's records and passed the information on to the Bishop, as I told you before. My question is, are they on to him?"

"And if they are, did he give it up?"

"Right, Harry, but more importantly did he give me up?"

"Are you going to the funeral tomorrow, Boss?" Charlie asked.

"Yes, Vivian and I have been given seats in the church by the former Bishop's secretary."

"Do you think we all should go too?" Harry asked.

"No, not unless you want to stand in rank formation, in the forecasted rainstorm, and listen to a two-hour funeral mass on a loudspeaker."

"No thanks," Richie said. "I stood in formation for dead cops enough in my life. Besides, I didn't, I guess none of us didn't, know him at all."

"Good decision," I said.

.   .   .

The predicted rain was coming down hard as Vivian and I unfurled our umbrellas as we left the subway station. Pacific Street was lined with uniformed cops assigned there by the patrol commander. Hundreds of priests were in the ranks in front of them. They all stood at attention as the mourners entered the cathedral. A Marine Corps Honor Guard lined the steps of the church on both sides at rigid attention, eyes directly forward.

Not one of the Marines, priests or cops was dressed in rain gear. That was forbidden by protocol. I remembered the tail end of that old saying…

And happy are the dead that the rain falls on. However, the dead don't get wet, do they? But these hundreds of men and women certainly do. And, as I knew from personal experience, the uniforms would absorb the rain and get heavier and heavier, and your body would get chillier and chillier. The morning coffee would make your bladder scream for release as you shivered in the wetness and cold. And you were forbidden to break ranks, which didn't matter anyway because there were no bathrooms or porta-potties in sight. So you pissed your pants, and no one noticed, or cared, because they were pissing themselves. And the warmth running down your legs felt good for the minute it lasted.

Finally, when the ordeal was over, you were bussed back to your command where you peeled off your uniform, bagged it up, got into your civvies and went home shivering and cold. And you hoped the dry cleaners could work their magic and restore your duds to some semblance of its former condition – all at your expense, of course.

We passed into the cathedral and an usher took my invitation and escorted us down the center aisle, stopping at the tenth pew and pointing to the four empty seats at its end. We slid in and my eyes took in the spectacle of the pomp and circumstance of a Bishop's funeral. The first eight rows were filled with the clergy of every religion practiced in Brooklyn. The majority were Roman Catholics, but also what appeared to be Protestant hierarchy from all the major denominations. I assumed Frank's close friend, the Episcopal Bishop, was there among them. I saw imams and orthodox rabbis with their beards and side curls. And there was Rabbi Berman, and Brian, probably the only non-clergyman in the group.

The ninth row, right in front of us, was filled with high ranking brass of the NYPD and FDNY. The police and fire commissioners and their chiefs of department sat stoically. I spotted Kevin O'Connor, the chief of detectives, and the chief of patrol and several men in suits and ties who I assumed were deputy commissioners and other detective brass.

I glanced down my row which was filled with lesser chiefs and police brass from other departments. I recognized most of the Brooklyn and Queens boro commanders, uniformed and detective. And then the one missing one, Deputy Chief Roger Hendriks, and I assumed his wife, slid into the remaining two seats of our pew, next to me and Vivian. Although I didn't desire to do so, I nodded to him out of respect for his rank and he nodded back, but there was a questioning look in his eyes. He was no doubt thinking how a lieutenant such as I deigned to occupy the same row with the likes of him and his fellow chiefs.

The pomp and circumstance began and the smell of incense fragrantly filled the air. The casket, now closed, was blessed by the Cardinal who proceeded to say the mass. His voice was shaky throughout, and I was not surprised he did not give the homily or eulogy. Those tasks, performed with respect, and a bit of humor, were well carried out by the Bishop of the Rockville Centre Diocese and the Episcopal Bishop of Long Island. Several others, the Chief Rabbi of the Lubavitch orthodox sect, the Chief Imam of the Brooklyn Arab community and Auxiliary Bishop Stachurski, also spoke highly and kindly of their relationship with Bishop Manzo. All, thankfully and mercifully, were brief in their remarks.

Finally, the mass was over and the casket began to roll down the aisle toward the open doors of the waiting hearse. We followed out in turn after the pews in front of us emptied out. I caught a glimpse of Ray Elliott as we passed by his row near the back of the church. I gave him a smile and a nod, but he did not meet my eyes, and abruptly turned away. Not a good sign. Had he thrown me under the bus?

As we reached the steps and started to walk down them, I realized the rain had stopped. The clouds broke and a burst of sunshine momentarily swept over the Bishop's casket as it was being pushed into the hearse. Vivian poked me in the side and said, "A sign from God perhaps, as he welcomes his faithful servant into Heaven?"

"An abrupt change in the weather." I said.

"Heathen."

"No one knows if there is a heaven, Viv, but if there is, I hope the good Bishop is already there and arguing over egg creams with Mort Stern."

"That's better. I'll make you a believer once again."

"Don't bet on that, dear. Let's go home."

.   .   .

The next day everything returned to its normal routine in Queens Homicide after I recapped the funeral service and the reception I had received.

"Elliott didn't even look you in the eye?" Harry asked.

"No, he didn't want to engage with me at all."

"I don't like that, and I don't like the cold reception you got from the boro commander."

"They know all their bases are covered," I said, "but they also know the Bishop and I were close. They remember him calling them to push my career. Now that he's gone, they can do what they want to me."

"You mean transfer you?" Richie asked. "On what grounds? We have the best closure rate of all the boro homicide squads."

"They will do what they want, when they want," I said. "And they don't have to give me a reason if they do."

"When do you want to move ahead with the law firm?" Charlie asked.

"Since you're a client, why don't you make the call to Howie? Set it up for you and me to meet on Wednesday or Thursday next week."

"What do I tell him when he asks why we want to meet?"

"Tell him we're bringing in, oh, maybe fifty million dollars for him, in one neat pile that will barely fit on his oversized desk."

"That should get his attention," John said.

Charlie made the call and we were given an appointment on Thursday morning, September 28, at ten a.m. with Howie saying, "What the fuck? Are you jerking my chain, or what?"

We all laughed at our memories of the street-wise former prosecutor and I said, "Charlie, how did that tough Jew end up as a partner in that white-shoe law firm anyway?"

"They needed him to head up a new criminal division at the firm. It seemed many of their clients needed the expertise of a good defense attorney. They figured instead of referring them out, they'd keep it in house. Make more money that way, I figure."

"Listen, guys, I'm taking tomorrow off and next Monday. I need a four-day weekend. And Vivian needs it more."

"Going away?" Richie asked.

"I thought of the Catskills. Should be great weather this time of year in the mountains. I'll call her now, and she can search for a place for us. She's good at that."

"Why don't you blow outta here after lunch?" Harry asked.

I looked at my trusted deputy CO and said, "Thanks, Harry, I believe I will."

·   ·   ·

Vivian was ecstatic at the idea of a mountain getaway and got right on to her laptop to search out vacancies. In less than an hour she was back with lodge accommodations near the upstate town of Kerhonkson. "It's a second-floor, one-bedroom unit, and we can eat our meals at the lodge's restaurant if we go for the inclusive package."

"Do it," I said. "We'll relax on rocking chairs on the porch and take long walks in the woods."

"This is unlike you, Mike, to want to leave the gritty streets of the city. What's going on? Did the Bishop's death affect you more than your stoic face is showing? And the day of the wake you had a mysterious conversation with that Brian and you said you'd tell me about it later. What was all that about? It's later, isn't it?"

"Hold up, Viv. You sound like a vicious interrogator from Internal Affairs. Give me a break."

"Give me some information."

"How about tomorrow when we're in the seclusion of the Catskills? I'll give you the information you want, all of it. All the treachery and sordidness of what has been going on."

"Oh, dear, maybe I was too pushy. Maybe I –"

"No, I want you to know. You have to know. I am about to plunge into new territory and take up a crusade begun by Bishop Manzo, and I need your support."

"You know I've always supported you. Whatever you have to do, go do it, and you can count on me to be in your corner and have your back. Always."

I grabbed her close and kissed her firmly on her lips.

"Wow, what gives?"

"You may never want to kiss me again after I tell you what I'm going to do."

"Nonsense, let's have a glass of wine."

THIRTY-ONE

We got up to the lodge early Friday afternoon, and after checking in, we took a stroll around the grounds and surrounding area sucking in the mild, late summer air. After over an hour in the great outdoors we went into the bar and had a cocktail. I said, "How about we grab another drink and go sit out on the verandah where I will tell you my tale of woe."

"Good idea," she said as we headed inside the lodge.

Vivian asked for a pricey, chilled, oaky chardonnay which I had never heard of until we started dating. I opted for a Jack Daniels and soda. We spoke in generalities about our kids, their college plans, the house, and then she said, "How about you, Mike? What are your plans?"

"What do you mean?"

"I was looking at all the brass at the funeral. Some of those guys wearing eagles and stars didn't look much older than you. Some looked younger. Tell me again, why you won't take the captain's test?"

"I have a great position where I am the boss. I have a take home vehicle and I make captain's money already which my position calls for. I work mostly days with weekends off, except when we get a real whodunit. And I love digging my teeth into a real mystery homicide. Does that explain it?"

"I guess so, but unless you become a captain you can't become an inspector or a chief, right?"

"Right, if one wanted to be one of those ranks."

"And you don't?"

"No, and I have dozens of reasons why not, the chief one being I don't want to be involved in the political power plays and intrigue that goes along with those positions. I came on the job to be a cop – to do police work – not to be a politician."

"I'm not sure I fully understand that."

"Let's adjourn to our rocking chairs. Perhaps you'll have a much better understanding of why I despise the higher ranks when I finish my story."

After we settled in, our chairs facing some awesome mountain scenery, she said, "I'm ready for your tale of intrigue, darling."

"I won't repeat what you already know about Manzo, and who he was, and our meeting of revelation. He told me some stuff – horrible stuff of what was going on in the church – and backed it up with documentation. And when the church rebuffed his pleas to face their problems and clean up their act, they killed him."

"Wh-a-a-t?"

"And they almost killed me. And maybe they'll try again if that was their intent, especially after I expose them for what they are."

"You expose them?"

"I promised Bishop Manzo I would not let his mission die with him. I intend to keep that promise."

"Even if it puts you in danger of death?"

"Yes, now listen to the whole story, and then tell me your thoughts."

A half hour later, when I had finished with all of it, she said, "I believe I want another glass of wine."

After I returned to the porch with her drink, two were enough for me, Vivian took a sip, looked me in the eye and said, "Tell me exactly why *you* are doing this mission?"

"What do you mean? I told you –"

"You told me you promised the Bishop you would not let his mission die with him, and you would fulfill it."

"Right."

"I ask again, why?"

"Vivian, I'm not following you here."

"Who is he to you that you should take up this cause? Maybe get yourself killed in the process? Why do you owe him anything? After all, he participated in a burglary that got your parents killed, didn't he? And *you* forgave *him?* You *absolved* him? What in the world did he ever do for you?"

I know my wife, and this rapid fire line of questions had a meaning, and an end game, and an answer that would come as soon as I responded. I said, "I guess he gave me some humanity, and an example of what a truly decent human being is."

"Not bad, Mike, but you should have said, he was a truly decent *God-loving* human being. And by giving him the gift of absolution, a gift only you could have given him, he gave you his gift to you right then and there. He gave you back your *soul.*"

I normally would have countered with my standard atheistic retort, *I have no soul, my dear,* but I hesitated, looked at her for a moment, and reflected on the events that brought me and Frank together and how our lives had meshed and intertwined. I said, "Maybe he did."

"Maybe it wasn't destiny that brought Bishop Manzo into your life, honey. Maybe it was God. Now, before you get in a huff, I said God. I didn't say religion. You don't need to be a Jew who belongs to a synagogue, or a Catholic who belongs to a parish, or a Lutheran who goes to the local church, for you to believe in God. Look out there, Mike. Look at the mountains, and the trees, and the blue sky. God created them. The One who all our religions believe in. The one and only Supreme Being, a part of whom is inside all of us, even cynical you. And if you deny His existence, you are saying all of this – life, the earth, the stars, the whole shebang – it's all here because of some freak accident. I don't think so. Our existence has a reason and a purpose."

I learned a long time ago you cannot win an argument with a true believer. They had blind faith in God's existence. I didn't, although at times I wish I had. I needed proof, and it never manifested itself. I said, "I hope He exists, Viv, and I hope Frank Manzo has a prominent place with Him in Heaven. I truly do."

"I know you do, dear, and with your newly restored soul you will fight the fight for Bishop Manzo and slay the dragons of evil."

"Wasn't it St. George who slew the dragon way back when?"

"Wise guy! For someone who trivializes religion, you seem to know a lot about it."

"Drummed into me at an early age, back when I was a true believer."

"I guess you were, weren't you?"

"Yeah, all the way. Truly believed in God, Jesus, Mary, and the Holy Ghost – all of it."

"What changed your mind?"

"The death of my parents and the irrefutable logic of the Old Survivor, Mort Stern."

She nodded and said, "Now think about this a minute, Mike. If your parents hadn't been killed, Giuseppe Mastronunzio would not have been at the scene. He may not have joined the Marines, or maybe he would have, and made it a career. Or maybe he would have gone to college. But I seriously doubt he would have entered the priesthood to eventually become the Bishop of Brooklyn. And you would have been raised in the Jewish faith and would not have become a policeman because the reason to do so, the death of your father, would not have existed. You would not have met Mort Stern either. Your destiny would not have been fulfilled."

"My destiny? You mean the exposure of the deviants in the Catholic Church and the fulfillment of Bishop Manzo's quest is my preordained destiny?"

"Exactly."

"So my destiny was already determined by some mysterious set of circumstances?"

"Or by God," she said with a big smile.

I smiled back and said, "How about we eat a light supper and hit the sack early?"

"Sounds good. We can get an early start and get out and about in nature all day"

. . .

After a sumptuous breakfast buffet, surprising myself at how much I gulped down, I said, "I guess I didn't eat enough for dinner last night."

"Neither did I," she said. "I'm going back for some more French toast. It's the best I've had in ages."

We finished up and headed out on an easy – so it said – two-mile trail which looped back to the rear part of the lodge. "You look relaxed," I said.

"I am. Being out here in God's country puts me at ease and I'm thinking maybe you are not in danger at all."

"Oh? Tell me why."

"You've been too close to this. Assuming the facts are as you related them last night –"

"Just the facts, ma'am," I said mockingly.

"The police top brass is not in any danger from you because they passed the smoking bomb to the Cardinal. Rome believes all the copies of the lists have been accounted for. Case closed."

"You don't understand the paranoid personalities of the brass. If they even *think* I may have held a copy back, I'm a liability to them."

"How? Why? They passed the lists on and destroyed the letters, and what they believe are the *original* return receipts. What exactly is their exposure?"

I thought it over. Vivian certainly had a valid point. I said, "I may be safe from the brass, but what about the church? Maybe the Cardinals in Rome are not convinced. As one of my guys said, 'A zip could be on his way right now to finish the job.'"

"On what basis? Cardinal Callahan had to have assured Rome all copies were now accounted for. He wants out. He wants to retire to wherever cardinals retire to. Did you see him at the funeral mass? He's old and shaky. He couldn't even preach the homily."

"You are starting to make some sense, my dear, but –"

"But nothing. And you have forgotten one other possibility."

"Which is?"

"Maybe the clan of Cardinals will study the documents, make the Pope aware of it, and clean house on their own."

I smiled, looked up, and began to sniff the air – loudly.

"What the hell are you doing?"

"Sniffing the air for the telltale signs of burning marijuana. For there is no doubt you are definitely smoking dope."

She laughed at that and said, "It *is* a possibility, isn't it?"

"And it's also a possibility a Hollywood producer will knock on my door tomorrow and offer to make me a star."

"You're handsome enough, my dear, but maybe not *smart* enough, because when you get that list out in public, you will be bulletproof. Isn't that what you told Bishop Manzo?"

"Yes, it was."

"So there."

"So there?"

"Go for it. Take up the sword for the murdered Bishop of Brooklyn. Bring those deviant bastards to justice. Make the Church of Rome pay through the nose. Lead the charge for those hundreds of abused children who have had no one in their corner. Be their champion. Turn over the rocks those slimy priests have been hiding under. I'll be at your side – and your back – all the way, Lancelot."

I was speechless. Who was this woman I was married to all these years? Wow!

"What do you have to say now, Michael?"

I grabbed her in a bear hug and held her tightly. There was nothing to say. *Wow!*

PART SIX

THE AVENGER

(FALL 2000)

THIRTY-TWO

On Tuesday morning, I was refreshed and juiced up by the support of Vivian, and my cause was now clear in my mind. Harry came into my office and said, "Don't you look happy. I guess there was some good hanky-panky going on over your long weekend?"

"Yes there was, my good man. My wife is a wonderful woman."

"Uh, you told her the works?"

"All of it, and she's behind me one-hundred percent."

"Good for her, and good for you. I bet you can't wait for Thursday."

"You said it, Harry. Now fill me in on the homicide numbers of the past few days. Business must go on, you know."

There were no real whodunits in my absence, so after Harry left I focused on my upcoming meeting with Howie Stein. What would his reaction be? Would they accept the case? What would the results be? What –?

"Mike!"

I was startled out of my reverie and snapped my head up to see Harry standing in my doorway, white-faced and distraught. "What is it, Harry? Jeez, you look like you've seen Frankenstein."

He reached out his hand to me which clutched a bunch of papers. "Mike, these orders just came over the machine."

I grabbed them and said, "Tell me."

"You've been transferred, Mike. To the 50 Squad in the goddamn Bronx. And it's effective next Monday."

I took the papers from Harry and scanned down the list of promotions and transfers to my name. Son-of-a-bitch! They didn't wait long to stick it to me. "Sit down, Harry, let me see what else is on these pages."

Promotion orders start with the highest rank and work their way down the ladder. There were a handful of promotions to the chief level, none above two stars. Then came the inspectors, and I didn't have far down the list to spot, "Elliott, Raymond, from Deputy Inspector to Inspector." I jumped to the transfer list and saw, "Elliott, Raymond, Inspector. From Internal Affairs, to the Office of Chief of Personnel."

"Look at this, Harry. The bastard sold us out. He buried his lists of deviants and got rewarded with a cushy job at One Police Plaza."

"He got rewarded, and you got screwed, Mike."

I scanned further and saw what happened with my transfer. My friend, Lieutenant Bert Simmons, got promoted to captain and was transferred to the 113 Precinct as the executive officer. "They could have put me in his spot at the 106 Squad, but no, they transferred the lieutenant from the 50 Squad there and sent me to the Bronx to replace him."

"Coulda been worse, I guess," Harry said. "They could have sent you to Staten Island."

"They wanted me out of Queens and Brooklyn, that's obvious."

"What are you going to do about it?"

"I don't believe there is anything I can do. My rabbi, the only hook I ever had on this job, is now dead and buried. And, figuratively speaking, so am I."

"Hey, Mike, I didn't look to see who is taking over here."

I scanned the next page of transfers and finally spotted it. I said, "Here it is, Harry. McAuley, John. Lieutenant. From the 25 Squad to Queens Homicide, designated commanding officer."

"Do you know him?"

"No, I don't."

"I guess Charlie and I will find out. At least we weren't transferred, too."

"Not yet. They'll leave that up to McAuley. If he wants his own sergeants, you two will be history."

·　　·　　·

That night the same question that was put to me by Harry Megara, *What are you going to do about it?* was repeated by Vivian, and my answer was the same. She said, "What about the captain's test now?"

"Same answer for the same reasons as before. I'll go to the Bronx and run the squad. Same pay, but less pressure and a longer commute. Then I'll decide my future."

"Maybe retire and look for a position in the real world?"

"Maybe, but I'll give it some time and a lot of thought. In the meantime, we are preparing for our meeting with Howie Stein."

"What's the name of his firm again?"

"*Schroeder, Harwood.* That's how it's referred to in the industry. The full name is *Schroeder, Harwood, Curran, Marino, and Stein.*"

She chuckled and said, "A real equal opportunity employer. Are any of those partners female?"

"I don't know, but I doubt it."

"How do you think they'll react to this information?"

"I have no idea, but I hope they jump on it with all their resources."

·　　·　　·

We arrived at the building on Madison Avenue which housed their law offices, six floors worth, the *top* six floors, of the thirty-two story edifice. Charlie and I took the elevator to the top floor and the receptionist at the desk opposite the elevators gave us a million-dollar smile and said, "Are you the gentlemen here to see Mr. Stein?"

"We are," I said.

"I'll buzz him."

Charlie whispered to me, "Jeez she looks like she stepped out of Vogue magazine."

And when we went inside we were greeted by an equally attractive woman who opened Howie's door, which had a gold nameplate with his name and title engraved on it, and showed us in. Howie jumped up to greet us, and my jaw dropped when I saw him.

"What's the matter, Mike? Didn't recognize me?"

"Yeah, something like that. You look great, uh –"

"Prosperous?"

"Yeah, that's it. The secretaries here look like Vogue models and you look like you stepped out of GQ."

"Yeah, no more rumpled hundred-dollar, off-the-rack suits I used to wear at the DA's office for me anymore."

"What's that freaking outfit worth?" Charlie asked.

"H-m-m-m, let me think. The suit was two grand, the shirt a hundred and a half, the tie a hundred, and the shoes five hundred."

"Don't tell me what you paid for your socks, Howie," I said. "Probably more than my whole outfit."

"Yeah, I noticed. You look like a real schleppy Jew. If you had a rumpled raincoat on you'd look like fucking *Columbo*, for Christ's sake."

"Wasn't he Italian?"

"Yeah, his character. The actor who played him, Peter Falk, was one of us."

"You know, Howie, I noticed you no longer have grease under your fingernails, like you used to."

"Because, Charlie, I no longer have to change my own oil and filter in my driveway anymore. The once a week manicure, by the way, costs more than *your* whole outfit."

We traded a few more insults and then got down to business. Howie eyed the stack of documents and said, "Tell me what this is all about."

We did. He listened intently and flipped through the lists occasionally as we spoke. We left nothing out and when I finished talking Howie said, "Your story alone, up to where you discovered who Bishop Manzo was, could make a blockbuster movie. But what he gave you here will blow the roof off St. Peter's Basilica in Rome."

"I hope so," I said.

"Doesn't that bother you being raised in the Catholic faith? Something, by the way, which I never knew before now."

"Not one bit. Will you take the case?"

"Do you know the monetary potential here?"

"I'm not concerned with that, Howie. I want these bastards exposed and made to pay for their abuses. Either criminally or civilly. Preferably both."

We hashed it out some more and Howie said, "Can you two hang around for lunch?"

"I assume you have an expense account?" Charlie said.

"Of course I do. This ain't a civil service job, you know."

"How come you don't have a corner office, though? Mike, maybe we should have brought this to a more prestigious partner."

"Yeah," I said. "Usually they hide the Jew in the corner, but not in this case."

"You guys enjoy playing Abbott and Costello? There are only *four* corners on the floor, you jerks. And they are occupied by my *four* partners who are senior to me and have been here much longer."

"Yeah, all right," Charlie said. "I guess we'll buy that story. But this better be an expensive lunch."

"Oh, it will be," Howie said, patting the stack of files.

He picked up the phone and buzzed his secretary. "Madeline," he said, "I want you to contact all four partners and set up a meeting with me ASAP, preferably this afternoon. It's important enough for them to shuffle their schedules, and it is important enough to stay beyond five o'clock, regardless of their social schedules."

He listened for a few moments and I guessed she was asking what she should tell them was so damn important. He said, "Tell them Jason and the Argonauts paid me a visit and dumped the Golden Fleece on my desk."

"That should tweak their interest," Charlie said.

"Can you leave this copy with me?" Howie asked.

"You got it," I said.

"Good, let's have lunch and then you guys can get back to Queens. After we're able to evaluate this pile, I'll get back to you with our decision."

"I hope it's positive," I said.

Howie smiled and said, "So do I, Mike. Don't you see the dollar signs flashing in my eyes already?"

.   .   .

We ate, I should say *dined,* at a private club Howie and his partners belonged to. After we ordered drinks, we let Howie take over and order the food. We noticed he threw in a few words of French while speaking with the waiter. French! From Howie Stein! Whatever we ate, and I couldn't be specific about the three courses, was delicious, and our plush surroundings added to the experience.

We left the club a little before two and as we approached our car I said, "I feel guilty. I don't think I'll mention this to Vivian."

"Yeah, Mike, I agree, but I *will* mention it to our three compadres when we get back. Get their jealous bones in an uproar."

"I'm not saying a word, Charlie, except we're hoping for a good decision from Howie."

THIRTY-THREE

At ten o'clock the next morning, my last day as CO of Queens Homicide, my phone rang and Howie Stein said, "Mike, can you shoot over here right away?"

"Have you reached a decision?"

"Yes, and we need your advice on the process."

"You're going with it?"

"With all we have. I'll give you the details when you get here."

A half hour later I was ushered into a corner office of the senior managing partner, Frederick Schroeder. Howie was there and introduced me to the others. All were perfectly groomed and expensively dressed, no doubt to impress prospective clients – *rich* clients. Schroeder spoke first and said, "You have given us a monumental task, and we have decided to take it on. We employ a large number of associates, but will have to hire many more. We will also have to hire dozens of investigators to do the field work, and Mr. Stein has suggested retaining you temporarily to make recommendations for the chief investigator's position, and maybe three or four supervisory positions. Howie?"

"After we hire the chief investigator he will hire the rest with your input. I trust your judgment to find us a top man."

"How long will that job last?"

"At least five years," answered Schroder.

"Your retainer will be $10, 000," Howie said. "Is that a sufficient amount?"

"No, it is not," I said, and I could see the surprised looks in the eyes of the partners. "I don't want the $10,000 – I want the *job*."

"But Mike, you're the CO of Queens Homicide, how –?"

"Today's my last day there. I'm being transferred to the Bronx on Monday, no doubt due to my part in this investigation. My guys are throwing me a farewell party tonight."

"Mike, go out and have the secretary get you a cup of coffee."

"Will do," I said, getting up and heading for the door.

Ten minutes later, as I was draining the last drop of coffee from my cup, the office door opened and Howie said, "Come on in."

I sat down and Howie said, "You got the position. When can you start?"

"Monday," I said. "When I leave here, I'll go right down to headquarters, file my retirement papers, and go on immediate terminal leave. I'm not going to the Bronx."

"I'll bet your smug bosses will be shocked you're bailing on them."

"Relieved would be more like it," I said with a grin.

"Uh, Lieutenant?" Schroeder said. "Aren't you going to ask about your salary and benefits?"

"I'm sure you will compensate me fairly. Not that I'm pushing here but this is an important position, and it has to be done correctly with solid, dependable investigators under my control."

"We certainly realize that, and Mr. Stein has assured us you are supremely qualified for this task. We propose a starting salary of $150,000 with bonus performance percentages up to 50% of that. Four weeks vacation, a company car, and the executive package of health and retirement benefits. How does that sound?"

How does that sound? Was he kidding? I swallowed hard and said, "That sounds fine, Mr. Schroeder."

"Hey, Mike," Howie said, passing a piece of paper over to me. "Here's a check for ten grand that was supposed to be your retainer. Consider it now a signing bonus, and use it to buy some decent fucking clothes, will you?"

There were a few smiles, and I wondered how these reserved attorneys had adapted to Howie's salty street language.

"Oh, Mr. Simon?" Schroeder said.

"Yes, sir?"

"Have my secretary give you a blank company check. Use it to pay for your party tonight. And have a wonderful time."

I shook my head and said, "Thank you, Mr. Schroeder, but those detectives can drink a lot of alcohol. Are you sure about this?"

"I'm certain," he said. "Enjoy."

I then remembered something I had meant to tell Howie yesterday, and in my best Peter Falk interpretation I turned and said, "Oh, gentlemen, one more thing."

Howie immediately picked up on it and said, "What is it, *Columbo*?"

"The documents I gave you pertained to incidents within the Dioceses of New York and Brooklyn. I have an equal pile containing allegations from Long Island, New Jersey, and several other states. You can contract them out to appropriate law firms in those areas – for a piece of the action, I would think."

"Spoken like a true businessman," Mr. Curran said, the first words spoken by any partner other than Howie and Schroeder.

"Any other surprises?" Howie asked.

"Nope."

"Good, get outta here. We got some planning to do. Have a blast at your party, but show up here sober on Monday, and in appropriate business attire, I might add. My secretary will tell you where to shop, and you might want to take your wife with you."

Several wiseass remarks floated through my mind, but I could see the partners were anxious to get down to the business at hand, so I said, "Thank you for the opportunity, gentlemen. Good afternoon."

Twenty minutes later I was downtown at the Pension Bureau offices filling out the necessary paperwork to leave the job via service retirement. No one questioned my decision. No one offered any form of counseling. I was just another number in the vast quantity of numbers they processed every week. I left there at noon and would be officially on terminal leave beginning in ten days, for sixty-three days, based on my twenty-one years of service. I decided to take vacation days until the leave kicked in. As I told Howie, I wasn't going to the goddamn Bronx, not even for a day.

. . .

Vivian worked part-time at the Queensboro Public Library on Tuesdays and Thursdays and volunteered at Jamaica Hospital on Mondays and Wednesdays. Friday was her day off and she would be home cleaning, or out grocery shopping. When she didn't answer our home phone I dialed her cell and she picked up. "Hi Viv, where are you?"

"Heading home from the store. Why?"

"I'll meet you there for lunch. About one o'clock?"

"Sure, but you coming home for lunch is a real rarity. What gives?"

"I have some important news to tell you."

"What news?"

"When I get home," I said and disconnected the call.

Vivian had cold cuts and rye bread spread out on the kitchen counter and the smell of freshly brewed coffee wafted by my nose. I hugged and kissed her on the cheek and went over to the coffee machine. "You want a cup, too?"

"Yes, now tell me, Michael, what's your important news?"

"I'll tell you in the order it happened with this morning's telephone call and ending with a job offer."

When I finished, she said, "Uh, that's some job offer, but you already have a job."

"Not anymore. I accepted the position and shot downtown to the Pension Bureau and put my papers in."

"Just like that?"

"Just like that. I decided I'm not going to the Bronx. I'm going to lead the investigation to bring those miscreants to their judgment. I couldn't do that if I stayed on the job."

"What if the new position doesn't work out for some reason?"

"I have seventy-three days to decide if I want to go back on the job, but I don't see that happening."

"Anything else you want to tell me, as if this wasn't enough?"

I took the check out of my pocket and showed it to her. She opened her eyes wide and said, "Ten thousand dollars! For what?"

"You have to take me clothes shopping – tomorrow."

.   .   .

I was back in the office at 2:30 and asked Harry Megara to get Charlie, John, and Richie to join us. "How did it go over there with Howie?" Charlie asked.

"Spectacular. What's new here?"

"Our new boss called and asked to speak with you, but had to settle for me. This ain't gonna be good, Mike."

"Why?"

"Before he called, me and Charlie made some calls of our own. This McAuley is a real prick. He made his bones in Internal Affairs and they rewarded him with a detective squad. Now, a bigger reward with his transfer here, I presume."

"Other than his IAB background, what makes you think he's a prick?"

"One of our guys here has a buddy in the 28 Squad and he gave us the lowdown on him. Without going into details, suffice it to say they are going to have their own transfer party – without him."

"I'm sorry for all of you that he's coming here," I said. "How is the party shaping up?"

"Good," Charlie said. "I'm running it. Our usual party joint – The Triangle Hofbrau. A lot of guys have been calling, but I don't know if you want anyone outside the squad to attend."

"Like who?"

"Like everyone who worked the Mort Stern murder case with us. Catalano and Nitzky from the 106 Squad. And their boss, soon to be Captain Simmons."

"And," Richie said, "the guys from Narcotics – all four of them who assisted on the case."

"Get back to them and tell them they're all welcome. The Triangle can handle that increase easily."

"Uh, Boss," Charlie said. "You know, the host squad has to pick up the tab –"

"I know, and the more freebie outsiders, the bigger the hit. But this transfer party is special, and cost is no object." I reached into my pocket and withdrew the check with the law firm's imprint on it. "You see, I have been given a blank check to fill in at the end of the party with its total cost completely covered."

"Where the hell did you steal that?" John asked.

"Steal? Now, now, Detective Micena, this check was given to me by my new employer. And the reason this transfer party is special is it's also a retirement party. My retirement party. Fuck the department. I'm not going to the Bronx."

I didn't believe these four men could remain silent as long as they did as they processed the information. Richie spoke first and said, "You pulled the pin? Just like that?"

"Which were Vivian's words when I told her a couple of hours ago."

"And who is your new employer?" John asked.

"The same one who could be yours John, or yours Richie, or yours my loyal sergeants, if you join me walking out the door. Would you care to hear the details?"

When I finished giving them the lowdown of the opportunity that lay ahead of them, and answered all their questions, all four did not dismiss it out of hand saying they would certainly think about it. John asked, "When do you need a decision?"

"I'd say within two weeks, but the sooner the better."

They nodded, and as they left the office, I said, "Oh, if Inspector Elliott, or Chief Hendriks, or Chief O'Connor calls, looking to come to my party tell them to go fuck themselves. Tell them I said it."

"I'd be happy to say it myself," Harry said, "but they'll never call. They think they stuck it to you royally, and they'd be afraid to come anywhere near you – or us."

THIRTY- FOUR

The Triangle Hofbrau provided a spacious room for us, I estimated fifty people in all, and two bartenders worked an open bar set up at one end. The affair was for cops only, no spouses, and we had three female detectives in the squad, but I counted four gals, and I couldn't figure out who the extra female was. And whoever she was, she was one fine-looking young lady. In another twenty minutes, as the booze began to warm the insides and the inhibitions began to slide away, she would no doubt be the target of some unwanted advances. As I drew nearer, she did look familiar, and before I could place her, she stuck out her hand and said, "Cindy Jamison, Lieutenant. Remember me?"

"Cindy! As we sometimes say, you certainly look different out of uniform. Thanks for coming. Is your partner here? Artie, right?"

"Yes, he's down at the bar getting us drinks."

"I'm pleased you and Artie came, but how did you hear about it?"

"Detective Nitzky tracked us down. He figured we might want to be here since we worked so close with you and the squad on Mr. Stern's murder case."

"He was right, Cindy. We put together a great team to solve that one. I'm going to miss running those investigations."

"It was an exciting arrest experience for us. Oh, here's Artie."

We shook hands after he passed a cocktail to Cindy. What fine young officers with a great career ahead of them. Thinking back to my rookie days and looking at their young faces, I wished I could do it all over again myself. Well, almost.

Artie said, "I'm happy to be here for you, Lieutenant, but could I ask what happened?"

"Some boss had it in for me, and some other boss wanted a better position for one of his pets," I said, not the whole truth, but close enough for the occasion.

"That inspector from Internal Affairs?" Cindy asked. "You know, that was the part of the case I could have done without. It left a bitter taste in my mouth."

"Mine, too," Artie said.

"It could have been IAB, and it could have been a boro commander, but it doesn't matter because I have decided I'm not going to the Bronx."

"How could you not accept that transfer?" Cindy asked.

"By leaving the job. I'm retiring immediately."

"Wow," Artie said. "That had to be a big decision."

"It was, but I'll explain it when I make my remarks. Meanwhile, mum's the word. Just a handful of people here know about it."

"You got it, Loot," Cindy said. "Good luck with your future."

"Yes, sir," Artie said. "I wish you all the best."

After thanking them I mingled through the room happy to be with friends who I could trust implicitly, many of whom I would ask to work with me at *Schroeder, Harwood*. It was 6:30 and the restaurant's owner, the red-faced German-American, Herman Wedel, clapped his hands and shouted, "Okay, everyone, the buffet is open. Enjoy the fine food prepared for you in honor of Lieutenant Michael Simon."

Everyone applauded and cheered and lined up with their plates.

We ate the usual fare plus two trays of Herman's specialties – Wiener schnitzel and pot roast done sauerbraten style. Those serving bowls had to be refilled more than once. When it appeared everyone had a full belly, Sergeant Charlie Seich stepped up to the microphone and got everyone's attention. He said, "We all know why we're here. To honor a great guy, a great detective, and a great boss – Lieutenant Mike Simon."

I stood up and waved to everyone as they cheered. When they calmed down, Charlie continued, "The brass screwed my boss, and all of us in Queens Homicide, by transferring him without cause to a lesser command."

After the boos and hisses died down, he said, "But I assure you, Mike Simon will have the last word for those rats, and he will tell you about it himself shortly. But before I bring Mike up here, is there anyone who wants to say a few words? And I don't want anyone to come up, because I know you *all* can come up and share a Mike story, but we don't want that. That would cut into our drinking time too much. So save your words for Mike on a one-to-one basis later on. Now, without further ado –"

A voice from the room, loud and deep, said, "I want to say a few words."

We all looked to see Detective Charlie Evans standing up. Sergeant Seich rolled his eyes wondering what the foul-mouthed, racially insensitive, black narcotics cop was going to say. "Okay Charlie, come on up, but make it brief, okay?"

"From one Charlie to another Charlie, I will be brief."

He strode to the front of the room and got behind the small podium. He said, "One learns the true nature of a fellow cop when he walks a post and rides a car with him for three years in the East New York section of Brooklyn, the murder capital of the NYPD, the good old 75 Precinct. I would trust him with my life, and I hope he felt the same way about me. The NYPD is doing a great disservice to this fine man. I came up here vowing not to indulge in my usual profanity-laced rant, but I have to break that vow. Mike, ladies and gentlemen, the motherfuckers responsible for this travesty should be beaten and burned and have their balls – if those balls could be found – cut off with a rusty knife and stuffed down their motherfucking throats. That's all I gotta say."

The room erupted with cheers of "Right on!" "Fucking brass!" "Gutless bastards," and many other similar phrases. When the shouts died down, Charlie Seich said, "Well said, Charlie, well said. Now, come on up here Mike."

I rose and walked up to the podium. Everyone was cheering and applauding and, somewhat embarrassed, I sucked it all in. As the actress who won an Academy Award once said, "You like me! You really like me!" And that was exactly what I felt as I reached the front of the room. And goddamn it, it felt great. "Thank you all for coming and as Charlie Seich admonished, I will also be brief. No one in his right mind wants to keep an NYPD cop from the bar for any longer than necessary." After the laughter died down I said, "First, I thank you, Charlie Evans, for your kind words and the trust you have in me. I trusted you with my life back in Brooklyn and do so now. Second, I would like to thank the other Charlie in the room for putting this gig together on such short notice. Third, this is not merely a transfer party. It's a retirement party. My retirement party. I put my papers in today. I am not going to the Bronx. And to paraphrase Detective Charlie Evans, those motherfuckers who tried to stick it up my ass have failed to do so."

There was a few moments of silence as the audience absorbed what I had said. Then they erupted once more – a combination of cheers for me and jeers for the brass. "Now, let me wrap this up with my fourth, and last, comment to all you wonderful cops, detectives, and supervisors. I have accepted a position as the chief investigator for a prominent Manhattan law firm who will initiate a monumental series of lawsuits. I will need investigators – lots of them. Investigators like those in this room. If you have your time in, and want a good paying job that will last at least five years, let me know as we pass the rest of the evening here. But there is one drawback. You'll have to work for me."

Again, more laughter, and I said, "Oh, one more thing. My new employer likes me – and you guys – so much he has given me a blank check to pay for this party. So eat some more and drink as much as you want, provided you are not driving when you leave here, and see me if you're interested in a new career."

The evening wound down and I was approached by a lot of people interested in my job offer. Being savvy investigators they asked, "What's it all about, Mike? Who are they going after?"

I said, "Here's my card with my cell phone number on the back. We are going after an established, prominent, recognizable, venerable institution – The Roman Catholic Church. The church I was raised in, baptized in, and confirmed in, which has now abandoned its principles and turned a deaf ear and a blind eye to the rampant pedophilia now going on. If you're comfortable investigating them, call me."

THIRTY-FIVE

On Monday morning I was ushered into my new office by my secretary, Claire Rogers, another impeccably dressed woman, somewhere in her mid-thirties. She handed me a thick package of new employee forms and said, "Sorry, but the necessary paperwork must be done. If you have any questions or problems completing it, buzz me."

"Thank you, Ms. Rogers," I said. "Coming from the NYPD, believe me, I'm used to paperwork.

"Oh," she said, "I'm the secretary for three of the attorneys in our criminal division, and Marcy Goldner serves the other three. Either one of us will be available to you until you ramp up your staff. Then we'll hire one, or more, for your group."

"Sounds good, now let me get to work on these forms."

"Mr. Stein wants to see you in his office at 11:00 a.m. You should be finished with this pile by then. Maybe."

She closed my door on the way out. I took a moment to gaze out my window onto the buildings to the east, none of which blocked my view of the East River, the Queensboro Bridge to the north, and the Williamsburg Bridge to the south. Not bad. I was on the thirtieth floor, two down from where the partners resided, and my office was not a corner one. But I was now in the corporate world, one weekend away from the NYPD. Lieutenant Simon was now Mr. Simon, and Mr. Simon was a man with a mission. Rest easy, Frank, your untimely death – your murder – is about to be avenged. In spades.

A half hour later there was a light knock on my door and Claire opened it and entered bearing a silver tray with a carafe of coffee, cream pitcher, and a sugar bowl. "I figured you might need this about now," she said.

"You must be a mind reader, Ms. Rogers. Thank you, I do need a caffeine boost to finish this mound of paperwork."

As she left she said, "I hope you don't mind me coming into your office without buzzing you for permission. I won't do that if I see you are on the phone or have someone with you. Would that procedure meet with your approval?"

"That's fine, Ms. Rogers," I said, smiling at this new – to me – corporate protocol.

I completed the paperwork with ten minutes to spare and headed for the elevator to the top floor. When the doors opened I was greeted by the same secretary who I first met last week. She looked at me for a few seconds and then lit up with a big smile, "Mr. Simon! I didn't recognize you. Sharp suit, and I love that tie. I'll buzz Mr. Stein's secretary."

I smiled and said, "I even took a shower this morning rather than waiting till my usual once-a-week one on Saturdays."

She was startled and flustered and then, regaining her composure, she lit up and said, "I get it, Mr. Simon. You're putting me on, aren't you?"

"Yes, I am. No offense, I hope?"

"No, no, I'm not used to –"

"Cop humor. I'll try hard to suppress it. It may take some time."

She buzzed Howie's secretary and said, "Go right in, Mr. Simon."

I held out my hand and said, "I'm going to be in and out of here a lot. I'm Mike Simon."

She took my hand and said, "No, you're not. You are *Mister* Simon. And I am Ms. Darienzo. But you can call me Anne."

With another protocol lesson learned, I went through the open door into Howie's office. His huge desk was covered with files and his jacket was off. The sleeves of his shirt were rolled up and he was chewing on an unlit cigar. Without a glance up he said, "Sit down, Mike. Let's get to work."

"Uh, Mr. Stein," I said, causing him to look up. I raised my arms and did an about face. "Do I meet with your approval?"

"Not bad, for starters," he said. "Now as I said, *let's get to fucking work.*"

.　　.　　.

As we began to go over the individual cases I said, "Howie, these cases have sufficient information, I believe, to pursue a criminal and/or civil prosecution. However, there are certain details lacking, which do exist, but might be difficult to obtain."

"Enlighten me, please."

"Bishop Manzo, through the Episcopal Bishop of Brooklyn, had a high-ranking contact in the NYPD who researched each incident for all the information available concerning it. For example, take this case." I passed over the piece of paper and pointed out the bare bones data that was on it. "Basically we have the offender in this case, a Father Abruzzi, the victim, John Macy, and the allegation of forced touching on May 3, 1992. What's missing? The responding police officer. The police official who made the decision not to arrest Abruzzi. The parent's names and their responses. The disposition of the case, meaning how much did the church pay for silence in the matter? The church official who approved the payment. The check number. Abruzzi's other victims. The church's discipline, or lack thereof, of Abruzzi —"

"Wait, Mike, you're telling me all this information is available right now?"

"Yes, but I don't think the high police official, his name is Inspector Raymond Elliott, will provide it. No doubt he will probably deny its existence."

"And you're going to tell me why?"

I did, and when I finished, Howie sighed and said, "Call the prick right now on this phone. It's a recorded line. Let's see what he has to say."

I dialed headquarters and asked for Personnel. When the secretary picked up I asked to speak to Inspector Elliott.

"Who shall I say is calling, sir?"

"Mister Michael Simon. Until recently I was Lieutenant Michael Simon of Queens Homicide."

"Please hold, Mr. Simon," she said.

A long three minutes later she came back on the line and said, "I'm afraid the Inspector will not speak with you, sir. He does not recognize your name and requests that you do not attempt to contact him again by telephone, or any other means."

"Yes, ma'am," I said. "I got the message."

"Your buddy has pulled a Pontius Pilate on you, Mike. He has thoroughly washed his hands of this matter."

"I'm not so sure, Howie. The way he crafted his response had me reading between the lines. Let's give it a few days before I attempt to contact him again."

"Okay, let's get back to work. We'll sort this out and try to determine the investigative and legal staff required to do the job. Oh, by the way, although I'll be working on this case, I'm not heading the whole thing up."

"How come?"

"Primarily because I'm a Jew. The firm doesn't want my name out there, and we want to keep yours under wraps as well. I'm sure you understand the reasons."

"Who will be in charge?"

"It was a toss up between our two Catholic partners, Nick Marino and Ed Curran, and the nod went to Marino because of the Irish connection with the church and the NYPD."

"I understand, but ironically the first name we looked at was Father Abruzzi."

"Yeah, depravity knows no religious, racial, or ethnic bounds, does it?"

■   ■   ■

My hunch about Ray Elliott proved correct. As I was leaving my office on that Thursday afternoon a man in a business suit appeared at my side and said, "Hello, Mike. Let me walk with you to your car. I have a package for you." I glanced over and immediately recognized newly-promoted Deputy Inspector Bill Presti. I said nothing as he fell in behind me and followed me to the parking garage. When I reached my car on the third level I opened the doors and he slid into the front passenger's seat. "Sorry for the cloak and dagger crap, Mike, but we have to be careful on this."

"I understand, Inspector. Congratulations on your promotion, but I didn't see your name on the transfer order."

"I wish it was, but I gotta spend more time on *The Rock*. At least Ray got out."

"Inspector –"

"Call me Bill. Drive to the garage on 26 Street. My car is on the upper level. Not too many others near it. I got three large cardboard boxes for you from you know who."

I smiled and said, "I'm not wired, Bill."

"Sorry, Internal Affairs paranoia. Ray Elliott said to tell you, 'good hunting and good luck in your new career.' Let me say the same, too, Mike."

"Thanks, Bill, and pass on my thanks to Ray. I'm glad he came through on this. Gives me some much-needed faith in *some* of the NYPD ranking officers."

After we transferred the three heavy cardboard boxes into the trunk of my vehicle we shook hands and parted ways with Presti saying, "This is gonna be a big fucking deal, isn't it, Mike?"

"A bombshell. And when the shit hits the fan the high-ranking Cardinals in Rome and the high-ranking brass in the NYPD are going to be covered in it from their red hats and uniform caps to their soft slippers and shiny shoes."

I drove right back to my office building, parked illegally directly in front of it, and called our mailroom. I directed them to bring out a cart and load up the boxes. I left the mail room guy with my car and personally wheeled up the load to my office, unloaded it, re-locked the door, and headed home. No way was the evidence staying in my car or house, overnight. Maybe I was paranoid, but maybe Rome was still after my ass. Who knew? A zip or two could be on their way right now to finish the job.

•　　•　　•

With our new evidence in hand we laid out our general plan of action. Nick Marino had both a criminal and civil litigation background, and we hit it off immediately. He had five years with the NYPD, quitting after he finished law school whereupon he joined the prestigious Manhattan DA's office as a prosecutor of white-collar crime. He then went into private practice and eventually specialized in suing firms whose products had damaged their users. Dangerous chemicals, defective mechanisms, and shoddy building materials were among his specialties. He said, "I don't see much difference in these cases, Mike. We have a defective product, the hierarchy of the church, and we have damages due to their negligence. Rape, sexual abuse, forcible touching, and acts of sodomy committed on their trusting parishioners, who innocently had no expectations of being subject to these acts."

"Sounds good to me, Nick. How do you think we should proceed?"

"Let me ask you that question first. I know you're a man of action, as Howie told me, but we may want to begin cautiously."

"I agree. I believe we should, for now, bypass the NYPD and the media and lay some paper on the local hierarchy of the church, meaning the new bishop of Brooklyn and Cardinal Callahan. We build about a dozen solid cases first, and I need an investigative team to do that."

"Why not go to the NYPD right off the bat?"

"They were given that opportunity by Bishop Manzo and they took absolutely no action. The boro commanders and chief of detectives denied any knowledge of the cases and claimed Manzo never sent them a letter with his allegations. Why try again? And most grievously they alerted Callahan, who alerted Rome, and now we have a murdered Bishop, whose death remains unsolved by the way, and I want justice for him."

"I understand, Mike, but when we begin legal action, the media will pick up on it right away. They will question why we didn't go to the police with these *criminal* allegations. They will insinuate we are only in it for the money."

"That's *exactly* what will happen, Nick. And then you call a press conference and agree with the media one-hundred percent. You produce copies of the letters, and the original signed return receipts, and in your saddest tones say, 'Yes, you are right. We tried to do that, but we were ignored. And the letter to the chief of detectives had the combination to Bishop Manzo's safe where the lists of victims were kept.'"

Marino smiled and slapped his hand on the table. "I love it! Are you sure you're not a lawyer?"

"No way, but I do know how to go for the throat. Just like a good lawyer does."

"Terrific. Hire some people. Let's get rolling."

THIRTY-SIX

The sorting and compilation was completed by the firm's clerical staff a few days later. The final totals were staggering. There were over 4,000 reported incidents involving over 800 priests – and nuns – in the metropolitan New York area alone, to include New York City, Nassau and Suffolk counties on Long Island, and Westchester county north of the city. This was the area the firm decided they would handle directly. Cases outside it would be referred to other law firms after we got our feet wet and the procedures down pat.

Four thousand cases! I did some figuring on a piece of paper, and a couple hours later I came up with a tentative organizational chart with me at the top, four supervisors directly reporting to me, and eight investigators reporting to each supervisor. That was a lot of manpower, but these investigations had to be thorough, detailed, and professionally prepared to the legal standards of the firm. And we needed women – a lot of female investigators. And training in sex crimes investigations. And vehicles. And recording equipment. And surveillance equipment and...

I stopped and took a deep breath. Go easy, I told myself. Rome wasn't built in a day, and you're not going to destroy it in a day either.

When I put it all together I asked for a meeting with Howie and Nick to get their input. I said, "I'd like to start with a few cases in the Brooklyn Diocese."

"Of course you would, you vengeful bastard," Howie said

"And I'd like to begin with two supervisors and sixteen investigators. I figure a week of training, a week or two to get properly equipped, and then we'll give it a go."

"I like it, Mike," Nick said "but I think I know what's going to happen when our first lawsuits become public."

"And what is that, Nick?"

"Our phones will start ringing off the hook. *Abruzzi? He's the one who molested my child, too.*"

"Oh, yeah," Howie said. "Your files contain known victims who made a complaint against a specific priest for a specific incident. Who knows how many others he abused who didn't report it? Thousands?"

"Jesus," I said, "this may turn into a ten-year project."

Howie poked me in the ribs and said, "Job security, you dumb flatfoot. For you, your investigators, and my law firm."

.   .   .

Before I had a chance to begin the recruitment process, I checked the list of those who had already called during my first week of employment at *Schroeder, Harwood.* There were five names there, all of whom had attended my impromptu retirement party – Joan Yale, one of my homicide investigators, who I suddenly realized had been in the Sex Crimes Unit before she joined our squad, Dan Nitzky from the 106 Squad, Doug Monroe and Lou Isnardi from Queens Narcotics, and last, but not least, Johnny "The Jack" Micena.

I know I had told everyone they had about two weeks to decide. Those two weeks were not up, but I was anxious to get going. I picked up the phone and dialed Harry Megara. He screamed, "Mike, get me outta here. This guy is driving me crazy!"

"Why the hell do you think I'm calling? I want you as a team supervisor and I want Charlie, too. What are you waiting for?"

"It's a big decision, Mike."

"Get a hold of Charlie and come over to my house tonight after dinner. I'll lay it all out, and when I do you'll make the move as I did, and as fast as I did."

"See you later."

Harry and Charlie arrived on schedule at 8:00 p.m. and we went into the den where Vivian had set up four bottles of cordials. "I surmise it's not going well with Lieutenant McAuley?"

"I can see why the guys in the 28 Squad were happy to see him go," Charlie said. "He treats us like we are still in uniform. Would you believe I had to sign out on meal tonight to leave the office? And he holds you to one hour."

"How would he know how long you take for dinner?" I asked.

"He personally comes in on surprise visits," Harry said.

"And," Charlie said, "he transferred in a couple of guys, who we think are his personal rats, to spy on us."

"Not good at all," I said, "but I can offer you much better working conditions. Pour yourselves a drink, and prepare to visit the Pension Bureau tomorrow."

After I explained the particulars, Charlie Seich said, "Let me recap this deal to see if I have it right. We each supervise eight investigators – four teams of two. And for this we get $125,000 a year, a take-home car, full company benefits, and four-weeks vacation?"

"Correct, and a 50% bonus potential."

"And the position should last five years?" Harry asked.

"Yes, most likely longer."

"I need time to think this over," Charlie said. "Oh, wait. Time's up. I'm in."

"Harry?"

"I'm in, too, Mike."

"Terrific. Figure on starting next Monday. And during that time work on Richie Paul to come on board. Micena's already interested. Of these sixteen investigators, I want at least six females, and I want Spanish-speaking people, and African-Americans. These abusers were equal-opportunity predators."

"I have a few in mind," Harry said.

"Good. Talk to Joan Yale, she's expressed an interest. See if she can contact other sex crime investigators – from the Feds, the NYPD, the Nassau and Suffolk PD's, from all over the metro area –"

"Slow down, Mike. We'll get it done," Charlie said.

"Sorry, guys. I'm real itchy to get going. Oh, one more thing –"

"Yes, *Columbo*?" Harry said.

"Get some new suits and shirts and ties."

"Hey, Mike, what's wrong with what I'm wearing now?" Charlie asked.

I shook my head and said, "Fucking everything, Charlie."

∎   ∎   ∎

Two weeks after Harry and Charlie had joined us, and who both were now appropriately attired thanks to another check from Howie Stein, we had made substantial progress in our hiring process, with four positions left to fill. I had done my own research discovering Chief of Detectives Kevin O'Connor lived in St Edward's parish in the Fresh Meadows section of Queens. Over the past ten years, four priests had incidents detailed in our lists, but all four had been transferred to other parishes within the Diocese of Brooklyn. However, three other priests with similar transgressions had been transferred into St. Edwards. Talk about musical chairs. How about musical pedophiles?

I assigned the case to Team A where Harry Megara was in charge. All three victims, each in a different parish where the priests had previously worked, were white males between the ages of ten and twelve. The six victims of the four priests who were transferred out were a white female age thirteen, a black female age ten, two males with Hispanic last names, ages ten and eleven, and two white males ages twelve and thirteen.

Knowing we could not get all of them to agree to partake in a lawsuit, we chose several more incidents to follow up on. The two lawyers assigned to our team, Andy Forma and Sam Ehrenkranz, wanted to go with an initial batch of twenty-five to file on the first go round. My investigators hit the streets. Finally, the first step in this crusade had begun.

· · ·

Three weeks later the firm was ready to file. We had to interview thirty-seven victims to get the twenty-five to agree to sue the Diocese. The reports the team of investigators prepared had first to be reviewed by the team supervisor then signed off by me. If it passed my muster it went to one of the lawyers who reviewed it and, if all was in order, they called the victim and his parents in to sign the necessary legal permissions to proceed, and a fee contract for the firm's one-third cut.

On D-Day, November 15, the lawsuits were filed in State Supreme Court and the firm issued a press release to all its media outlets. They jumped at the story with all the major newspapers reporting it no further back than page four. It was one of the lead stories on all the local news channels at six o'clock, and several all-news cable channels ran with it. The firm also announced it would hold a news conference the following morning at 10:00 a.m. at its headquarters to answer questions and give out further information on future additional lawsuits. They also took out a full-page ad in four major newspapers naming the fourteen priests accused of committing the abuses, and asking anyone else who might have been similarly abused by any of them to contact the firm as "you may be entitled to a major compensation award."

We were on our way, and I couldn't wait for the fallout.

· · ·

"As the saying goes, *be careful what you wish for*," Vivian said as I finished relating the details of our first slew of lawsuits.

"What do you mean? You were fully on board with me on this, remember?"

"Yes, but now I realize a lot of lives are going to be affected – and ruined. This is a tragedy of huge proportions in the making."

"I see your concerns, but to sound like I'm on a soapbox, I feel justice must be served. Don't you?"

"I guess so," she said.

"Are you forgetting they murdered a Bishop and almost yours truly, to prevent these allegations from being exposed to the public eye?"

"No, but sometimes I wonder if Michael Simon is seeking justice or outright revenge."

"Both," I said.

"Remember, Mike, the Lord said revenge is –"

"Stop, Vivian. Please, no Bible quotes now. I am going to seek justice, if you will, against those who ordered the killing of Bishop Manzo, even if I have to go to Rome myself to hunt them down."

"All right," she said with a sigh. "But please be careful out there."

THIRTY-SEVEN

The sixteen investigators and two supervisors sat with me in our conference room as we watched the press conference on closed-circuit TV. The firm was represented by partner Nick Marino and the two lawyers who worked with us. Nick did not make an opening statement, opting to begin with questions, and the first one was what I was hoping for. "Mr. Marino," the reporter from the *Daily News* said, "It appears these allegations against those fourteen priests are criminal acts as well as civil ones. Why weren't they referred to the NYPD for investigation, and possible arrests, followed by prosecution?"

"An excellent question, Phil, and the answer is they were referred. *Twice*, as a matter of fact, and the NYPD chose not to act on them."

"Twice?" Phil followed up.

"Yes, on the original complaint the NYPD chose to let the Diocese handle it, and most recently they ignored the written pleas of the murdered Bishop of Brooklyn, Francis Manzo."

"Murdered? Did you say murdered?" shouted the entire media assemblage.

Marino held up his hand and frowned. "That's *exactly* what I said. And I place the blame for his death squarely on the shoulders of the NYPD hierarchy and the hierarchy of the Roman Catholic Church."

Nick waited for the shouting to die down before he spoke again. He held up the letters and said, "Before his death Bishop Manzo wrote these letters to the three detective boro commanders in his Diocese, as well as one to the chief of detectives, documenting the allegations of abuse and requesting they be investigated. I will provide copies for you at the conclusion of this press conference. All four police officials called the Bishop and promised their assistance. However, before that assistance was provided, the Bishop was killed by a hit-and-run driver who fled the scene on foot."

"And you think it was intentional murder, not an accident?" screamed out a reporter from CNN.

"Yes, I do. Brooklyn North investigated and covered it up, calling it an accident. And not one of the allegations contained in the letters was ever investigated. That was over two months ago. I suggest you ask them why. And, ladies and gentlemen, that is why the firm of *Schroeder, Harwood, Curran, Marino* and *Stein* is taking the action it began today. We will seek justice for these victims, even if the NYPD will not."

"How many more will you sue?" asked the reporter from the *Times.*

"Thousands," he said. "Now, that's all the time I have. As I said my staff will hand out copies of all the letters the late Bishop sent to the NYPD brass. Thank you all for attending."

We all applauded in our conference room as Nick Marino left the podium amidst the shouting and scurrying crowd.

"Great job," Charlie Seich said. "He stuck it to the NYPD real good."

"I couldn't have said it any better myself," I said. "I can't wait to see their reaction."

"They're all probably converging on the PC's office downtown right now to get their story straight," Harry said. "And I wonder what that story will be?"

"Nick Marino never mentioned we had the originals of the return receipts proving they did receive the letters," I said. "I wonder if they will deny, deny, deny."

"I know what I would do if I was one of those three boro commanders," Joan Yale said. "Play it straight and truthfully. I would admit I got the letter and immediately passed it directly to the chief of detectives."

"And if I was the chief of detectives," I said, "I would say I took the three letters plus the one I had received, and walked them down to the PC's office for further instruction."

"Do you think that's what happened, Mike?" Don Nitzky asked.

"I'd bet on it, and I'd bet the PC dumped it right on Cardinal Callahan to handle."

"Do you think they'll admit that at a news conference?" John Micena asked. "That they flagged it to the Cardinal and took no police action on sexual abuse allegations?"

"What else can they say?" I responded. "We didn't see any priests in handcuffs over the last two months, did we?"

. . .

Two days later, NYPD Police Commissioner Sean Flanagan stood behind a podium at One Police Plaza and said exactly that. He was flanked by his chief of detectives and the three boro commanders as he related the details of their actions, and then took questions. The key question first asked was, "Commissioner, you stated you passed on the combination number of Bishop Manzo's safe to Cardinal Callahan and he assured you he would handle the matter internally?"

"Yes," Flanagan answered, "and I assume he retrieved the lists from the safe himself, or had someone retrieve them for him."

"Did he give you a timetable for his proposed actions against these priests and what disciplinary actions he would take?" a second reporter asked.

"No, he did not."

"Did you ever call the Cardinal to push the issue?" the reporter persisted.

"No, but I was going to do so in a week, or so."

Everyone listening knew that was total baloney, and Flanagan began to fidget. He bent his head and someone whispered something in his ear. He said, "Ladies and gentlemen, I believe I have answered all your questions. I suggest you take your follow-up questions to Cardinal Callahan. If he decides the alleged violations are to be criminally investigated, the NYPD will take immediate action."

One last question was shouted out as the brass turned to leave, "If the Cardinal took the list from Bishop Manzo's safe, how did it end up in the hands of *Schroeder Harwood*?"

The PC turned back and said, "I have no idea. You will have to ask them yourself."

.   .   .

The media hordes now descended on the headquarters of the Archdiocese of New York and demanded the appearance of Cardinal Callahan to answer their questions. Callahan's press secretary, Monsignor Peter Kelly, said the aging Cardinal was feeling ill lately, but should be available in a few days to address the matter at hand. Charlie Seich said, "After he confers with Rome, he means. What do you think they'll do, Mike?"

"The cat's out of the bag. They can't cover this up any longer, but I don't know how they'll handle it."

"Maybe they'll send a couple of zips from Rome to take him out like they did with Manzo."

"You never know, Harry, but I doubt it. Especially when it's out there that Manzo was probably murdered."

So we waited and continued our hiring process. The lawyers wanted to file a hundred lawsuits in the next batch. Each suit named the individual priest, his parish and parish Pastor, the Diocese and the Bishop in charge, the head of the Archdiocese of New York, Cardinal Callahan, the Church of Rome, and the Pope himself. Talk about going after deep pockets, you couldn't go any deeper.

My goal was to bring my staff up to its full allocation of four teams. The next two would be headed by Richie Paul and John Micena. With Harry and Charlie it was like we were back in the squad again. I was supremely confident our job would get done professionally and expeditiously, but I wondered what the ultimate fallout would be as we proceeded with the lawsuits. Three days later I got my answer. Not to the ultimate fallout, but to the *immediate* fallout which was in the form of a tragedy, the Archbishop of the Archdiocese of New York, his Eminence John Cardinal Callahan was dead.

.   .   .

The announcement came as a press release from Monsignor Kelly simply stating John Cardinal Callahan passed away sometime during the previous night and was now with the Lord in heaven. You can imagine the uproar and questions this news caused in the New York metropolitan area. At our morning coffee John Micena said, "Rome sent the zips back to whack him, I bet."

"No way," Richie said. "He offed himself. He couldn't face the heat."

"Maybe it was a natural death," I said. "Frank told me he was sickly and couldn't wait to retire when he hit 75 years old."

"Is that my former homicide squad boss talking?" Charlie Seich said. "Have you forgotten all your police training and instincts already?"

"All right, all right," I said. "But it *could* be a natural."

The police department remained mum on the investigation into Callahan's death and referred all questions to the medical examiner's office. The ME stated there was no obvious cause of death, and the results of all the toxicology tests should be available in two to three weeks. "He wasn't obviously shot, or stabbed, or strangled, by some zip dispatched by Rome," I said.

"Like I said," Richie said. "He took the pipe."

.　.　.

It turned out we didn't have to wait two or three weeks to find out what happened to John Cardinal Callahan. He told us, told everyone, in writing, in his own hand, by means of a letter he sent prior to his death. The letter was addressed to his Holiness the Pope and began by apologizing, and asking the Pope's forgiveness, for committing the mortal sin of suicide. However, he added, "Your previous gift of twenty-year old single-malt scotch was generously used to wash down the sleeping pills."

He went on to take the responsibility for failing to act on the allegations in his Archdiocese because he was prevented from doing so by his superiors in Rome. And he named the names of the clan of five corrupt Cardinals based in Rome, and he also accused them of arranging the murder of his good friend, the Bishop of Brooklyn, Francis Andrew Manzo.

Copies of the letter were sent to a list of people named at the bottom to include the police commissioner, all the major media outlets, Salvatore Marino of *Schroeder, Harwood*, and one Michael Simon, also of *Schroeder, Harwood*. A box containing the lists of deviant priests he had obtained from Bishop Manzo's safe was sent along with the PC's letter. In his closing paragraph he directed his letter be read at all Sunday masses in all parishes of the Archdiocese for two successive weeks. Talk about a bombshell, this was a mighty explosion felt in all the Catholic churches in the metropolitan area and in all their parishioners.

And everyone was asking, *who the hell is this Michael Simon anyway?* I knew it wouldn't take the media long to find out, but my fears of being stalked by killers from Rome had probably been put to bed by Cardinal Callahan's revelations.

Unless they had already been dispatched before the letter, and the shit, hit the fan.

THIRTY-EIGHT

Vivian and I relaxed after dinner that evening and discussed the day's events. "What was your take on the Cardinal's letter?" she asked.

"He finally saw the light and got the old-time religion back in his soul. But I wonder if he would have fessed up if he hadn't been sick."

"I think he was sick and tired of the whole rotten mess, and wanted to do the right thing."

"Maybe, but we'll never know for sure."

"What do you think will happen now?"

"In what way?"

"The letter was addressed to the Pope. If those five Cardinals kept all these allegations from his eyes and ears, they can't any longer. He can't claim lack of knowledge anymore. He now knows. The whole world knows."

"From my several discussions of the church hierarchy with Frank, I think this Pope will do the right thing, and do it soon and decisively."

Two days later the funeral details for Cardinal Callahan were announced by the church, and reported on by both the print and electronic media. The mass would be on Tuesday at St. Patrick's Cathedral with burial immediately following at a cemetery in Westchester County. Unlike Bishop Manzo, the body would not lie in state prior to the mass. I picked up the phone and called Brian at the Bishop's Cathedral. When he answered, "Bishop's residence, Brian Starkey speaking," I realized it was the first time I had heard his last name. I said, "Hello, Brian, Mike Simon here."

"Lieutenant!" he cried. "So good to hear from you. I think of you often."

"I hope in a good way."

"Oh, yes. You have been instrumental in the beginning of forcing change upon my beloved church."

"That's what Bishop Manzo wanted, but has there been any real change yet?"

"Oh, yes, Lieu –"

I stopped him and said, "Call me Mike, Brian. I'm no longer on the force."

"For starters, Mike, his Holiness is going to appoint Auxiliary Bishop Stachurski as the permanent replacement for Bishop Manzo."

"Is that a good thing?"

"Most certainly. Bishop Stachurski was an acolyte, dear friend, and supporter of Bishop Manzo's crusade."

"That is a good sign. I'd like to meet with him someday."

"No problem, I can arrange that before he's officially installed. Oh, and his Holiness will shortly appoint a new Archbishop for the Archdiocese. He's one of the bishops from the Midwest who was one of Bishop Manzo's allies. I'd better not mention his name though, until it's official."

"I understand. I need a favor, Brian."

"If I can, sir."

"Can you get me and my wife a seat at Cardinal Callahan's funeral mass?"

"I certainly can. Maybe I shouldn't say this, but I hope you're not feeling guilty over his unfortunate death."

I thought that over a bit and said, "Maybe I am. Maybe he'd still be alive if I didn't utilize those records to try to obtain justice."

"Nonsense. Bishop Manzo pursued this with the Cardinal relentlessly, until he was ordered to back down. And they killed him anyway. I hold Cardinal Callahan partly, maybe mostly, responsible for his death. But his hands were tied, too. And, Mike, I forgive him for his weakness and his sins."

"You do?"

"Not officially, I have no priestly powers." He dropped his voice to a whisper and said, "Two days before his death, the Cardinal secretly came here to Brooklyn for Bishop Stachurski to hear his last confession."

"Do you think he told the Bishop what he planned to do?"

"I have no idea, and I'm not ever going to ask him."

"Yeah, the secrecy of the confessional. I guess that's still a good thing."

"The same as when you used to go in your younger years."

"Did Bishop Manzo confide in you about our *real* relationship? You must have been curious about my visits."

"I was, and he did. Remarkable story. And I'm glad you were able to resolve it before his untimely death. At least he died in peace after your forgiveness – your absolution."

"He told you that, too?"

"Yes he did. Mike, I may be out of line here, but someone who did what you did cannot be an atheist. Only someone who has a soul, and a living God within that soul, can do something like that. You think about that."

I was taken aback at the directness and forcefulness of Brian's words, and was at a loss trying to find words of response.

"Mike, are you there?"

"Uh, yes."

"I'm sorry for the lecture, Mike, but I wouldn't waste my words on someone not worth saving."

"I'm happy you believe this old, cynical, ex-cop is worth saving. But what are you saving me from?"

"Yourself, Michael. Yourself."

With that Brian disconnected, and those words, plus his words, *you think about that*, stayed with me for a while – a long while.

■   ■   ■

The funeral mass for Cardinal Callahan was a subdued affair, no doubt due to the manner of his death, with none of the pomp and circumstance we recently witnessed at Bishop Manzo's funeral. The police presence was the minimum required to maintain traffic and crowd control, if you could call a few hundred people on the sidewalks a crowd.

The Mass was co-officiated by Bishop Stachurski and the Bishop of the Rockville Center Diocese, and seeing those Bishops reminded me of Bishop Manzo telling me John Cardinal Callahan was a "good" man. What was good? What was evil? Can you be both? Can you do both? My deep philosophical musings were interrupted by a nudge in my ribs from my wife who whispered, "Stand up. It's over."

Our seats were near the rear of the cathedral, certainly nowhere near as prominent as those we had for Bishop Manzo, and I was able to observe those guests who now paraded by from all those pews in front of us. The highest ranking cops I saw were the two-star Manhattan patrol commanders and the one-star Manhattan detective commanders. No police commissioner. No deputy police commissioners. No chief of department. No three-star chiefs. They obviously wanted no part of this public ceremony whatsoever.

His Holiness did not wait long, naming the new Archbishop of the New York Archdiocese, and designating Bishop Stachurski the permanent Bishop of Brooklyn, three days after John Cardinal Callahan was laid to rest. And it didn't take long after that for Brian to call me and say, "Mike, the new Bishop of Brooklyn, his Excellency Kenneth Stachurski, would like to have a few words with you in his office here at the cathedral at your earliest convenience."

"Brian, you sound so formal, but I have to ask, is the new Bishop springing for lunch?"

If I thought I rattled him I was mistaken. He said, "Yes, Michael. Would take out from Maury's Kosher Deli be satisfactory?"

"Most satisfactory. Set the date and I will be there."

It seemed I couldn't shake attendance at the Catholic Church. Two funeral masses, now two promotion/installation masses, with all their attendant pomp and circumstance, loomed in the near future. Vivian remarked I hadn't lost a beat in following the mass as she struggled to mimic me in the proper sitting/standing/kneeling/beating the chest protocols. I said, "Twelve years of Catholic school takes their toll. I'm probably brainwashed forever. A zombie-like automaton mechanically performing the required rituals."

"Brainwashed? That's kind of harsh, isn't it, Mike?"

I smiled and said, "Ask another Catholic school boy or girl that question and see what they say."

"Are you attending both installation masses?"

"Yes, Brian is getting us both tickets, but I wonder why you want to sit through two more two plus hour ceremonies."

"I kind of like them, especially at St. Patrick's."

"Hey, are you getting sucked in here? Are they brainwashing you, too? Your Lutheran services are so much simpler, you know."

"Yes, but a change is rejuvenating once-in-a-while. Besides, Mike, I believe any house of worship is fine if you believe in the one true God."

"You are amazing, Vivian. I love you, and sometimes I wish I had your faith and never lost mine."

"Tell me why *you* are attending all these masses?"

"For one reason only. In memory of, and respect for, the late Bishop of Brooklyn, Frank Manzo. And when the next two are over, I hope to never attend another one."

"On another note, I'm wondering if you think you may be in any danger of retribution because your firm is pursuing all these lawsuits against the church and its hierarchy."

"Danger? From who? I don't think so. It's all out in the open now."

"Those five Cardinals named in Cardinal Callahan's letter, that's who. They no doubt hired those guys who tried to kill you as well as the Bishop. You could still be on their hit list, if only for revenge."

"Nonsense, Vivian, you're watching too many cop shows on TV."

"You be careful out there. Keep your eyes open, and check for tails while driving and walking."

I burst out laughing and said, "You sound like a sergeant giving a brand-new rookie instructions. Give me a break."

She laughed also, and said, "As Mort would say, 'It voodn't hoit.'"

"I promise, Vivian, I will be careful and observant."

"Good. Now you can go to the office."

Maybe Vivian had a point, and I knew John Micena and Richie Paul believed I could be a target, so I did become more observant of the people on the street and in the restaurants I ate in. I even went into my personal files on the Bishop's death investigation and dug out the composite photo the Brooklyn dicks had put out based on Richie and John's descriptions. I studied it carefully and slipped it into my inside jacket pocket.

．　　．　　．

The next day I was back in the office and things were humming along. Right before I was to leave for my lunch meeting with the new Bishop of Brooklyn, Brian called and said he had to postpone the lunch for a couple days and would Friday work for me. I asked if there was a problem and he said, "A lot of last minute preparations for the upcoming installation popped up."

I told him Friday would be fine and I hung up the phone just as John and Richie walked into my office. Richie said, "We need a favor, Boss."

"What is it?"

"You had a chance to get away with Vivian, and John and I would like to do likewise with our loving wives."

"Yeah, Mike," John said. "We, and they, need a break."

"You got it. I know things are going smoothly. I'll split up your work to Harry and Charlie. They won't mind."

"I bet," John said with a laugh. "See you next Monday?"

"Three days off and the weekend it is. Have a good relaxing time."

"Oh, we will," Richie said.

The work day ended and I had reviewed dozens more cases prepared by my investigative staff and passed them on to our two lawyers. At this rate of production we would have the hundred cases ready to file by early next week. Satisfied, I was walking along the avenue toward the parking garage when I spotted two young men coming toward me. One of them glanced at me then turned his face away toward his buddy and said something to him. They abruptly stepped off the curb into the street and dodged the cabs and cars as they ran over to the other side of the avenue. *What the hell?*

I reached into my jacket pocket and took out the composite photo of the suspect in Bishop Manzo's death. There was somewhat of a resemblance to the guy who looked at me, but not that definite. I dismissed the encounter and went home, but remembered Vivian's words of caution loud and clear.

THIRTY-NINE

Although I had dismissed my street encounter as a nothing incident, being by nature a distrustful, cynical cop, a bit of paranoia set in as I became super aware of my surroundings and the people in them. And damned if I didn't notice what appeared to be guys, and gals, tailing me on foot in Manhattan and in cars around my home. They were never close enough to get a license plate number, nor for a good physical description. I mentally slapped myself in the head and muttered, "It's all in your mind, stupid."

Friday came and I arrived promptly at the cathedral of St. James in Brooklyn at twelve noon. I was ushered into the new Bishop's office by a smiling Brian Starkey who said on the way in, "Lunch will be delivered by Maury's at 12:30, and I'll have it set up in the conference room."

As we approached the Bishop, who was seated behind his desk, he rose, smiled and extended his hand. He said, "Ken Stachurski, Mike. It's a true pleasure to finally meet you."

I was immediately struck by this man's presence and his humility in using his first name in his introduction. He stood tall and lean and his smiling, blue Irish eyes and ruddy complexion belied his Polish name, when I remembered Brian telling me he was only one half Polish. The Bishop motioned for me to sit down and he re-took his seat as Brian quietly left the room and shut the door. He said, "Mike, Brian said you had a special relationship with Bishop Manzo, but asked you tell me about it yourself. That is, if you don't mind."

"Not at all, Your Excellency –"

"Mike, when it's me and you alone, Ken is my name."

"Thank you, *Ken*," I said with a smile. "Here goes my tale of woe…"

When I finished, without interruption, the Bishop said, "That story would make a helluva fiction book, because nobody would believe it happened."

"As they say, Ken, truth is stranger than fiction."

"It's about time to head into the conference room for lunch, and I promise it will be an interesting one."

"Oh?"

"We have two other guests joining us, and they will have some revelations for us all."

"You have me hooked, Ken. What revelations —?"

He raised his hand to stop me and said, "All your questions will be answered, but before we leave my office I have a question for you."

"Shoot."

"Mike, you were born a Jew, raised a Catholic, and married a Lutheran. What religion do you practice now?"

"None."

"Do you believe in God?"

"No."

"I can certainly understand why, and I certainly won't attempt to change your mind."

"Thank you for that, Bishop. I'll relate your words to my loving wife. Maybe she'll take the hint."

The Bishop burst out laughing and said, "Also tell her this, Mike. God does not reside inside this cathedral, or in a Jewish Temple, or in her Lutheran church. He resides in no man-made building, and is not the property of any one religion. God resides inside *you*. You have to look in there to find him. Some people never do. You might be one of them, but I hope you are not. Enough lecturing, let's go eat some good Jewish food.

First Frank, then Vivian, then Brian, and now Stachurski. All trying to save my alleged soul. Bah!

· · ·

Brian was finishing up opening the bags of food and placing them on a sideboard as we walked in. Two men were at one end of the room conversing, and they turned toward us as we entered. I immediately recognized Deputy Chief Roger Hendricks and we shook hands. He said, "Good to see you, Mike."

"You, too, Chief."

"Call me Roger, even though you're not yet officially off the job. How many days left?"

"Seven. Terminal leave will be over on December 15."

"Ever think about coming back?"

"Are you kidding? To a command in the Bronx? No thank you, sir."

He laughed as did the Bishop and the other man who was dressed, as Stachurski, in simple, black clerical garb. I extended my hand to him and said, "Mike Simon."

"Walter Dietrich," he said, shaking my hand and saying, "Pleased to meet you, Mike. I heard a lot about you."

"Wait until you hear his life story," Bishop Stachurski said. "Oh, by the way, Walter here is the newly-designated Archbishop of the New York Archdiocese."

I know my mouth dropped open in shock and I was at a momentary loss for words. I re-took his hand and said, "Congratulations, Your Grace, although congratulations may be the wrong word. You are inheriting a huge mess here, as you are no doubt aware of."

"I am," he said, "and in the words that might have been uttered by my dear departed brother-in-Christ, Francis Manzo, 'Walter, this is a Class-A cluster-fuck you got here.'"

After the laughter died down, the Archbishop said, "Let's eat, and please, Mike, tell your story between bites. We have some serious issues to discuss this afternoon. As Michael Corleone so aptly put it in the *Godfather* movie, 'it is time to settle all our business.'"

We went to the sideboard and loaded our plates with the pastrami, corned beef, latkes, coleslaw, and pickles provided by Maury's Deli. I noticed not one of us went easy on the food, especially the potato latkes. When we were all settled in and the iced tea poured by Bishop Stachurski, Archbishop Dietrich raised his glass and said, "A toast to new beginnings, and to the burial of old deceptions."

We dug in and I told my story once again. I was starting to bore myself with its repetition, but Hendricks and Dietrich were obviously enthralled with it, stopping a few times with their sandwiches halfway to their open mouths. When I finished, the Archbishop said, "I'm going to love New York. I'm eating delicious Jewish deli food, surrounded by a Polish/Irish bishop, a Northern Irish Episcopal Deputy Chief, and a born Jew raised as a Catholic. Amazing! And me, a German/Hungarian/whatever else combo."

I added, "And I'm married to a Lutheran, don't forget."

"You have one redeeming trait at least," Chief Hendricks said.

There were smiles all around and Brian entered to clean up the lunch dishes. He said, "Shall I set out the brandy, Bishop?"

Dietrich, who was now obviously in charge, said, "By all means, Brian. And leave the bottle."

.   .   .

Archbishop Dietrich raised his glass and said, "A toast to new beginnings and to the end of the old ways. Here's what we will do, and this comes from the Pope himself. Going forward, any and all allegations of criminal behavior against a member of the church, be it priest, nun, or bishop, shall be referred immediately to the police department for investigation and arrest, if warranted. Whether it is sexual in nature, shoplifting, or jaywalking, there will be no more cover-ups and buy offs. Period. All cardinals, archbishops, bishops, and pastors will be so notified, in detail, by the Pope of this new policy. Now for what occurred in the past. Ken?"

Bishop Stachurski said, "We are taking up Bishop Manzo's cause and, with the cooperation of the NYPD, we will request and support the arrests of every miscreant on the lists he had prepared and which are now in your possession, Mike."

"The NYPD will go along with this?" I asked.

"Yes, Mike," Hendricks said. "This afternoon major changes will be announced in the department. Commissioner Flanagan will announce his retirement as will the chief of department. The new PC will be the current chief of patrol, Gennaro Isabella. Chief of Detectives, Kevin O'Connor, will also put in his papers."

"Do I see a deliberate attempt to break the perceived Irish Mafia connection between the church and the department?"

"You certainly do, Mike," Bishop Dietrich said. "And I hope the media and the general public see it as well."

"Who will be the new chief of department and chief of detectives?" I asked.

"Ben Goodman gets the four-star job, and yours truly will be the new detective boss."

"Congratulations, Roger," I said. "A Jew, and not a *real* Irishman. I like it."

"You were always a wiseass, Mike," Hendricks said, but he was smiling broadly. "However, in the future, I may insist on you addressing me as Chief."

"May I remind you, *Chief*, in the near future I will be permanently *Mister* Simon."

"Maybe you will, and maybe you won't," he said.

"What are you talking about?"

"Bishop?" Hendricks said.

"Mike, our old ways must be addressed now. The Pope and I want as many violators on the lists you possess, arrested and prosecuted for their transgressions. And I have been given a blank check from Rome to settle all pending lawsuits and future litigation fairly and justly to the victims."

"And I want you back on the job to implement those arrests," Hendricks said. "Remember, with the church willing to settle claims before a lawsuit is initiated, a lot of your present job will go away. May I go on?"

"Go ahead," I said, mulling over this information. I was not happy right now.

"I will form a special unit within the Detective Division headed up by Inspectors Elliott and Presti. Elliott will report directly to me, and you will report to him. You will run the field operations with your chosen investigators to make those arrests where the facts and statute of limitations allow. You may choose twenty-four investigators and two supervisors, similar to the way your current operation now runs at *Schroeder, Harwood*. Bring as many of them on board who are willing to return to the department before their terminal leave runs out."

There were a thousand questions racing through my mind. I swallowed a half glass of brandy and said, "I need a bathroom break."

"Not to throw up, I hope," Hendricks said.

"Who knows, Chief, but at least to throw some cold water on my face while I digest this information."

This train was moving a bit too fast here, and I didn't yet know if I should stay on or jump off.

FORTY

I didn't puke, but doused my face and head with cold water. I took the opportunity to release the tea and brandy I had consumed at lunch knowing I would need more when I went back. When I returned, the three others were standing around with their glasses of brandy in their hands. In Stachurski's other hand glowed a huge cigar. "Ah," he said, "our guest of honor has returned. Shall we continue?"

We took our seats and Hendricks said, "What do you say to my offer?"

"How do you know about my operation at *Schroeder, Harwood*?"

"Paul and Micena told me all about it. They gave me all the names of your new investigators. I must compliment you on your selections. Top quality people. Couldn't have picked better myself."

"Paul and Micena?"

"Yes, which brings me to the next topic – the zip who killed Bishop Manzo, and who tried to kill you, too."

"How do you now conclude that? *You* classified it as an accident, remember?"

"I conclude that because he confessed that fact to Detectives Paul and Micena yesterday afternoon –"

"Whoa, what the fuck? Uh, I mean –"

"First of all they are still detectives, and were willingly recruited by me, as were Sergeants Megara and Seich, when we discovered the suspect was en route to the states and probably sent back here to finish the job on you."

"How did you find him?"

"I had the case reopened – to be honest I never had it closed despite what the bottom line said – and detectives from Brooklyn North commands were assigned by me to try to track the perp down. When he flew back in we spotted him at the airport and set up surveillance and a tail. He led us to suspect number two at a motel in Jersey."

"How did you know he was coming in, and where, and –"

"Mike, detective work, pure and simple. Interpol contacts, Italian police contacts, informants here and abroad all had the composite photo. Standard stuff, or have you forgotten your police training already?"

I had to admit Hendricks impressed me with these collars. I said, "How many dicks did you have working this case?"

"Twenty, not counting your protection detail."

"Protection detail?"

"Come on, you must have spotted them near your house or in the vicinity of your office. Ten of my detectives and ten of your investigators from *Schroeder, Harwood* all supervised by Megara and Seich. One week, around-the-clock. You should give them a few days off soon."

"Like I gave Paul and Micena a few days off?"

"And they did a great job. The two zips, Furio Vazzo and Renzo Turano, were extremely cooperative since the second payment for the Manzo hit has not been forthcoming from the guy who hired them, but was to be paid after they hit you to complete their original mission."

"I'd like to talk to these two guys," I said.

"Negative," Hendricks said. "Richie Paul and Johnny the Jack Micena are doing just fine, if you know what I mean. The zips have since lawyered up, but seem willing to cut a deal and provide the name and probable location of their contact who hired them, who in turn was hired by one of those wayward cardinals in Rome."

"I'm shocked, Chief Hendricks, in this day and age, you would condone such brutal behavior from members of the NYPD," Bishop Stachurski said with a grin.

"Would you like to take a crack at their murdering heads with your golden staff?" the chief responded.

"I'd love to," he said, "but as a man of the cloth, I must decline."

"Ken," Archbishop Dietrich said, "when I think of Francis Manzo, I must admit I, too, would enjoy taking a few swings at them. Consider that my confession to you for thinking evil thoughts."

Hendricks said, "What's your decision, Mike?"

"I need some time, the weekend, at least. I have to bring Vivian into the loop."

"You got it. Oh, Vivian knows about some of this already."

"Huh?"

"We brought her in on the surveillance happening at your house. She told the kids, too. We didn't want them worried if they spotted our guys in the area."

"But you chose not to bring *me* in?"

"Nope, and you know why, don't you?"

"Yeah, I'd try to take control and run the operation, and you thought I'd screw it up."

"Right. Was I wrong?"

"Nah, I didn't know you knew me so well."

"I didn't, but I did my research. Which is why I want you back on the job – with me."

I nodded and said, "I'll call you Monday. Will Paul and Micena be back then?"

"They will. While you were in the bathroom I placed a call. It's all wrapped up tight. Vazzo will be charged for Bishop Manzo's murder and the attempted murder on you back in September. Turano will be similarly charged. Additional charges of conspiracy to murder you now, for the second time, will also be placed against both of them."

"That'll be a tough one to prove, Chief. I mean what's the overt act? They never got close to me. They never threatened me."

"You spotted them on the street Tuesday, right?"

"Those two were Vazzo and Turano?"

"Yes, and their plan was interrupted by your sudden appearance. But on Thursday, their plan went into action, and that's when we got them."

"Where?"

"Parked in a van near where you were parked in the garage. Each had a gun and a knife. One also had a taser. There was a large canvas bag in the van which you would have fit perfectly in. Paul and Micena made the collar with backup from my guys."

"And they went for it?"

"All the way, and they were promised a $10,000 bonus for your brutal demise."

"Ten grand? Shit, is that all I'm worth?"

"I would say that's a lot for an avowed atheist," Bishop Stachurski said.

"I agree, Ken," Archbishop Dietrich said. "And way too much for a Jew turned Catholic, married to a Lutheran, who now somehow claims he is an avowed atheist."

I smiled at the jabs from the two Bishops when Hendricks said, "But not near enough for a lieutenant in the detective division of the NYPD. That amount is incalculable."

If Hendricks' comment was meant to sway me, it was working. And I saw the two down-to-earth Bishops in a much different light than I perceived the rigid hierarchy in the church of my youth. I had a lot to think about, didn't I?

By the time we finished up it was after four o'clock, and we called it a day. Archbishop Dietrich handed an envelope to me containing a letter to my firm. He said, "This letter contains our proposal for settlements as we discussed today. Please deliver it to Mr. Marino."

"I will, Your Grace, and I will add my words of support to it."

"Thanks Mike. I know you have a big decision to make, so go home to your wife now."

"Thank you, too, but could I ask a favor of you two new bosses of the church?"

"Go ahead," Dietrich said.

"Tickets for me and Vivian to both your installation masses?"

"I'll tell Brian to arrange it," Stachurski said, "but why anyone would want to sit through not one, but *two*, long boring ceremonies is beyond my comprehension."

"Self-flagellation," I said. "Remember, I was raised a strict Catholic. I need punishment every so often whether I need it or not. But, boring or not, I believe you two are doing the right thing and I want to be there to be part of that future success."

"I would ask you to pray to God for our success," Bishop Dietrich said, "but I know that's out of the question."

Mort's words flashed through my mind. *You know, Mikey, it voodn't hoit.* "Maybe I can remember one or two," I said. "Maybe the *Pater Noster.*"

"Can you still pray the *Our Father* in Latin?" Stachurski asked.

"Do four years of Bishop Loughlin brain-washing ever go away?"

I took the letter and we said our good-byes. Chief Hendricks said, "Remember, call me Monday, one way or the other, but I need you on board."

I nodded and left the room.

.   .   .

"Hello, my dear," Vivian said as I entered our front door. "My, you're home early. Light traffic?"

"No, I had a meeting in Brooklyn and left from there. But I guess you already know that, since you know a lot of other things going on you chose to keep from me."

"Whatever are you talking about?"

"The protection detail?"

"Oh, that."

"Oh, *that?*"

"Chief Hendricks convinced me things would work much smoother if you were unaware of it."

"Did it take a lot to convince you?"

"Honestly, no. I know you, Mike, and you know yourself."

"The opinion of you all was I'd screw it up, or refuse it, or try to take it over? Something like that?"

"Exactly like that. All three possibilities came to mind. Now calm your pits and have a cocktail. You know we were right, so get over it."

I couldn't stay angry, because she, and the chief, were correct, but I was not about to admit it. I said, "I don't agree, but it doesn't matter. It's all over."

"Tell me all about it."

We got our drinks and sat in the den where I told her of the capture of the two hit men, and the house arrest of the five Cardinals in Rome. I told her of my lengthy afternoon meeting with the two new Bishops and concluded with Chief Hendricks' offer for me to come back on the job.

"Wow, you had quite an afternoon. What are you going to do?"

"I don't know. Any advice?"

"Let me think it over. I'll get us another drink. The six o'clock news is coming on. I want to see the announcements of the changes in the NYPD brass you told me about."

Hendricks' information was spot on and he was announced as the new chief of detectives. As his departmental photo flashed on the screen Vivian said, "You know, I spoke with him personally about the protection detail. He impressed me as truthful and as a man of integrity. Much like you. You could do worse than having him as a boss and a mentor."

"I'd be taking a big cut in pay."

"Since when did your salary become the most important thing in your life? You know what the most important thing is, and it's certainly not money, or status, or fancy expensive clothes."

"What is it then, oh oracle wife of mine?"

"Your mission. Bishop Manzo's mission which you took up upon his death. Bring the miscreants to justice, once and for all in the manner he wanted – arrest, prosecution, and public exposure. That's your mission now. Go fulfill it."

I smiled and reached over to kiss her and hug her tightly. "Thanks for setting me straight. I'll trade in my new suits for a suit of armor and a silver sword and prepare myself for battle."

"Maybe an NYPD lieutenant's shield and a rumpled *Columbo* raincoat would be better?"

FORTY-ONE

On Monday morning I met with Nick Marino, Howie Stein, and the two lawyers on my team, Andy Forma and Sam Ehrenkranz. I had told their secretaries it was of utmost importance they meet with me ASAP.

At 10:30 in a small conference room, Howie Stein said, "What the hell is so pressing, Mike? I had to postpone an important phone call."

I gently tossed the letter to him and said, "Read this. Maybe you should read it out loud."

He gave me a dirty look, but did as I asked. When he finished, Nick Marino said, "This is a whole new ballgame, isn't it?"

"And a much easier one for the firm," I said. "I mean a blank check, and settlements without lawsuits and court battles? What more could we ask for?"

"Good for us, but not too good for you and your staff of investigators. We won't need you going forward."

"Not all of us, but you'll still need a handful to take statements and get the facts on record. Probably eight, and a supervisor, should do it."

They all nodded their heads in agreement and Marino said, "And you'll be that supervisor?"

"No, I'm going back on the job. That's the second half of the equation. Let me explain."

"Unbelievable," Andy Forma said. "The church is indeed requesting these priests be arrested?"

"Yes, and the unholy alliance between the church and the department that condoned and allowed the cover-ups has been wiped out."

"The Irish Mafia is gone – for now," Howie Stein said.

"We can only live in the present," I said. "Let's take advantage of it while we can."

"I'll leave it to you to inform your staff of the changes," Marino said. "Sorry about the loss of jobs."

"I'm hoping to convince many of them to come back on the job and work with me on this. I need at least twenty."

"That's good news," Howie said. "I hope it works out for you and them."

"And thanks for doing a great job for the firm," Marino said. "For as long as it lasted, anyway."

Before I faced my troops, I had a call to make and when Chief Hendricks picked up I said, "Roger, did you happen to notice the suit I was wearing on Friday?"

"I did, Mike. Classy threads and no doubt very expensive as well."

"Correct. And if I wore that suit every day for ten years, it would still look better than that *shmata* you had on."

He laughed and said, "I guess your answer is no. You will stay in the corporate world of money, power, fine wines, and two-thousand dollar suits of clothes."

"On the contrary, Chief. My answer is yes. I would love to come back to work with you, but I have one condition."

"Which is?"

"You get a big bump in pay going from one-star to three-star rank, right?"

"That I do."

"My condition is you grab a few grand and accompany me to my tailor who will dress you properly. For Pete's sake, I can't come to work looking better than the goddamn chief of detectives, can I?"

"How about we have lunch tomorrow afternoon and then you take me shopping?"

"Deal. Come to my office around noon. I'll take you to the partners' club. We'll eat on the company's tab."

"Isn't that like taking graft? You know, a free lunch for cops is *verboten*."

"I'll buy. Does that make you feel better?"

"Yes, it does," he said knowing damn well I wasn't reaching into my pocket for one thin dime.

.　.　.

When I came to work that morning, I had deliberately walked through the bullpen area with a scowl on my face and said nothing to anyone, including my usual, "Good morning, everyone!" Now, after my meeting, I walked out of my office into the bullpen and said, in what I hoped was a stern, intimidating voice, "Paul! Micena! Megara! Seich! Get into my office – now!"

I didn't wait for a response, but turned on my heel and stormed away. They dejectedly filed in and stood there in front of my desk. I stared them with narrowed eyes and a scowl on my face for several seconds before I said, "Sit down, you traitors."

"Mike –"

"I don't want to hear it, Harry. You guys go behind my back and deal with that prick Hendricks? You think I can't protect myself and my family from these zips? You think I need you four to do that, and to collar these guys?"

None of them said a word or looked me in the eyes. "Let me tell you all something. Thank you, from the bottom of my shriveled heart. Thank you for looking out for me and my family. And thank you John and Richie for locking up those two zips before they could whack me and dump my stupid Jew ass in the Hudson River."

They sat in silence a few seconds longer until the meaning of my words sunk in. Then they broke out into smiles and laughter. "Son-of-a-bitch, Mike," Charlie said. "You had me going there for a while."

"Man, I thought for a minute you were going to fire us" John said.

"Not exactly," I said, "but something like that is going to happen. Listen up, questions after."

I ran through the whole scenario based on Friday's meeting and concluded with, "So I'm going back on the job to head up the arrest squad. I need twenty guys, starting with you four. What do you say?"

Charlie Seich, John Micena, and Richie Paul immediately said, "We're with you, Mike."

"And what say you, my faithful deputy?" I asked.

Harry said, "Mike, you said the firm can keep eight guys plus a supervisor, right?"

"Right."

"I want to be that supervisor. I got thirty-two years on the NYPD, and was seriously thinking of packing it in anyway before we got this gig. I don't want to go back. I like working here and will do so as long as it lasts."

I was taken aback by Harry's decision, but I could see it from his point of view, and immediately accepted it. I said, "I understand. I'd love to have you come along, but the decision is yours and yours alone. And I believe it's the right one."

"Thanks, Boss." He stood up and came over and hugged me. "It was a great run."

"That it was, but we'll still be seeing a lot of each other. I'm going to be the liaison between the department and the firm. You and I will be coordinating the arrests with the settlements. How about that?"

"Terrific, Mike. Terrific!"

"Now the five of us have to decide who stays here, and who comes with me. And, I'll tell you, it doesn't matter. We have thirty-two top-notch investigators. I could pick any twenty out of a hat and be satisfied."

"I agree," Harry said. "How do you want to go about it?"

"When they come back from the field this afternoon, we'll have a group meeting and throw it out there. It's basically their decision, not ours."

My group of investigators was truly surprised by this sudden turn of events after recently having made a major decision to leave the job. And now, after two months in their new position, they were being forced into another major decision. I said I needed an answer by Wednesday afternoon at the latest, no doubt adding to their anxiety.

Immediately a dozen hands shot up, and nine of them said they'd come with me. The other three opted to stay with Harry. That was a promising start. In the next hour four more made their decision and I now had twelve of my twenty.

When Wednesday afternoon came around, all decisions had been made. Harry had his eight, but I had only eighteen. Six of the oldest had opted to stay retired and seek employment elsewhere, or not seek it at all. Two opted to go back on the job, but not come with me. And that was a big disappointment because those two were Doug Monroe and Lou Isnardi formerly of Queens Narcotics. Both wanted to go back there explaining sex crime investigations were not their thing. Doug said, "To be honest, Mike, we were both thinking of quitting here before our terminal leave was up anyway."

"Don't tell me you miss my old partner, Charlie Evans?"

Doug smiled and said, "Yeah, that crazy nig… uh, I mean fellow African-American former partner of mine did make life interesting all right."

"And hilarious," Lou said. "I miss it – the laughs, the action. You know what I mean."

"Yeah, I know. You did a great job here even though it was tedious work. I'll miss you both."

.   .   .

On Friday afternoon all the paperwork had been completed by those scheduled to depart, and we all assembled in the bullpen for a farewell party and a farewell greeting from Nick Marino. He was joined by Howie Stein, Andy Forma, and Sam Ehrenkranz. Nick thanked everyone for a great job done and said, "This case has been and will be lucrative for the firm, so me and my partners would like to give you a small token of appreciation – a bonus if you will – for your work here. Mike will distribute these envelopes and then please enjoy your shrimp cocktails and real cocktails for the rest of the afternoon."

There were a lot of handshakes among the lawyers and the investigators and it took a good twenty minutes for the lawyers, drink in hand, to finally leave the room. I handed out the envelopes to each person

– those remaining as well as those leaving – and when Joan Yale peeked at her check she said, "Five grand! This sure isn't the NYPD."

The four supervisors – Harry, Charlie, John, and Richie – each received $10,000 and I got $25,000. The firm was making a lot of money and I was happy they decided to share it with their workers. Capitalism at its best, I figured. And as Joan just said, nothing like the NYPD.

The week was over. Chief Hendriks had three new suits and a free meal he thought I paid for. All retirement papers were retracted from the Pension Bureau and Monday would be a new beginning for all of us. I had a lot to be thankful for – my family, my friends and my co-workers,– but also for those whose hands I couldn't shake, whose faces I couldn't kiss, and whose bodies I couldn't hug. They were only in my memories, but I could still pay them a visit and offer my respect and my thanks.

.   .   .

I first stopped at the Immaculate Conception Pastoral Center in Douglaston, Queens, where all the former Bishops of the Diocese of Brooklyn were now interred. I located Frank's marker on the memorial wall behind which his body now lay. I knelt in his honor and in respect of his beliefs, made the sign of the cross, and prayed the *Our Father* once in English, and once in Latin.

When I finished I arose and said, "We got the guy who killed you, Frank. I am going to complete your mission as you foresaw it, and which you so bravely began. You have my solemn word on that, and you should rest in peace knowing your efforts were not in vain and that your revered Catholic Church will come away stronger as a result. Thousands of those abused will always remember you in their prayers, and thousands of others will not ever suffer the same fate.

"Although there is no God, I now say to you – God bless you, Giuseppe, the teenager who ran terrified into the night. God bless you, Joey, the Marine who loyally served his country. God bless you, Frank, the Priest, and my faithful benefactor. And God Bless you, Francis Andrew Manzo, the Bishop of Brooklyn. *Te absolvo,* my friend.

Once more, I made the sign of the cross and ran my fingers over his name that was etched in the granite wall. Then I got in my car and headed east to Nassau County.

.   .   .

My next and last stop was my parents' graves at Beth David Cemetery. I searched for Mort's ashes at the base of the double headstone, but the rain and wind had already scattered and dissolved them into the earth. I sat on a nearby bench in the cool autumn air and recited the Jewish prayers for the dead, *The Kaddish* and *The Eyl Malei Rahamin,* in respect for the beliefs of my parents, but also for the non-believing soul of Mordechai Stern. I had Rabbi Berman teach me those prayers in English. I refused to attempt to learn Hebrew. Latin was bad enough I had told him, much to his disapproval.

Although Mort vehemently denied the existence of God, he would occasionally make a reference to Him, but correct his mistake by either saying, "Bah!" or explaining it was a slip of the tongue based on his early days of growing up a devout Jew. When I pressed him on his *slips* he finally, grudgingly, conceded this one point. "Mikey," he said, "I believe there is no God, but I also believe I, and you, vil not know for soitin until ve die. Are you happy now?"

Just as Mort's words left my thoughts, a large golden-yellow butterfly passed in front of my eyes and settled on the metal arm of the bench farthest from me, about three feet away. I remember my step-mom telling me when you were thinking of a dead person who you once loved, their soul would pay you a visit in the form of a butterfly to say hello. I smiled and glanced around to make sure I was alone before I said aloud, "Is that you Mort, you old kvetcher, come to pay me a visit? Or is it you, Mom? Or you, Dad, come to visit your son? Or perhaps you are the soul of Bishop Frank Manzo come to lead me back to the Catholic faith?"

The butterfly turned to face me and unfurled its large wings as if to offer itself to me for inspection. I looked at its intricate black markings and said, "If there's a Star of David on there, I know it's Mom or Dad, not you, Mort, you non-believer. And if there's a cross on there, I know it's the soul of Frank Manzo."

There were no stars or crosses, of course, and as I got up to leave, the golden butterfly arose from its perch on the bench and flew slowly across my line of vision, not more than two inches from my face. And damned if one of its black markings – an inch-long, curved black line with a dozen thin black lines attached and perpendicular to it – didn't resemble a pocket comb. You're imagining things I muttered as the butterfly circled my head and landed on my right shoulder near my cheek. And then I realized I smelled of herbal shampoo and floral scented after-shave lotion. This butterfly was doing only what butterflies do. I brushed it gently off my shoulder, but it continued to follow me to my car which was parked on the nearby lane.

I dared not tell this story to my step-mom or to Vivian. I could hear them exclaim, "See, I told you so!" from those two true believers. But there is no God and butterflies are butterflies, not spirits visiting from an imaginary heaven. As I got into the car the butterfly flashed me the golden wing with the pocket comb marking on it and flew toward my parents' headstone where it alighted on the pebble I had placed on top of it. I looked at the beauty and serenity of my surroundings – the neatly-clipped green grass, the trees showing their autumn finery, the deep-blue sky, and one beautiful golden-yellow butterfly, now completely motionless. I started my car, put the lever in drive, and slowly pulled away.

A pocket comb!

Bah, humbug!

A butterfly is just a butterfly.

There is no God.

Well … maybe.

Also by Henry Hack

Harry Cassidy Novels

Cassidy's Corner
The Last Crusade
The Romen Society
Election Day

Danny Boyland Novels

Danny Boy
Cases Closed
Mommy, Mommy
Forever Young
The Marsh Mallows
The Group

Collection

Portraits in Blue

www.henryhack.com

ACKNOWLEDGMENTS

A big thank you to all my readers, especially those of you who kindly took the time and effort to post a favorable review of my previous work on Amazon and/or Goodreads. These reviews are important to assist potential readers to evaluate my books, and to encourage them to hit the "buy now" button. Yours have helped them to do so. My thanks also to my fellow author members of The St. James Writer's Roundtable for their support, inspiration, and advice.

My manuscript was typed onto the computer by my loyal, loving wife, Lorraine, who managed to decipher my long-hand scribbling. Editing with a sharp eye, Lorraine, provided quality insight and input, keeping me from straying off message. She and our dear friend and neighbor, Cheryl Ann Samuel, proofread the manuscript without complaint. Since I edit the work once more after Cheryl Ann and Lorraine have finished their tasks, any errors you may find are wholly mine.

With their permission, I used several real names for my police characters to acknowledge their friendship, loyalty, and assistance during my police and writing careers. My deepest thanks to – Bob Livoti, Neil Brogan, Richard Paul, Charlie Seich, Harry Megara, Bill Presti, and Ray Elliott. And to those no longer with us – John Micena, Artie Ferrand, Lou Isnardi, George Geyer, Joe Brala, Ken Stachurski, Lenny Miller, John McAuley, and Joan Yale – our good times together will always be remembered.

If you liked *Absolution*, a stand-alone novel, a visit to my website, www.henryhack.com, will acquaint you with my ten other published crime novels in two series. I hope you enjoy them all and continue to review them favorably.

ABOUT THE AUTHOR

Award-winning author, Henry Hack served twenty-two years in the Nassau County, NY Police Department rising to the rank of Inspector. He commanded the Scientific Investigation Bureau and was qualified as an expert witness in several forensic fields. He also commanded the Eighth Patrol Precinct in Levittown, NY. After leaving the police department, Henry served sixteen years as the Vice President of Security for a major cable TV company on Long Island. He now devotes his time to writing fiction and has published ten mystery/thriller novels in two series and a collection of stories. A lifelong New Yorker, Henry now resides in coastal North Carolina with his wife, Lorraine. Descriptions of his work can be found on his website, www.henryhack.com.

NOTE FROM THE AUTHOR

Word-of-mouth is crucial for any author to succeed. If you enjoyed *Absolution*, please leave a review online—anywhere you are able. Even if it's just a sentence or two. It would make all the difference and would be very much appreciated.

Thanks!
Henry Hack

We hope you enjoyed reading this title from:

BLACK ROSE
writing™

www.blackrosewriting.com

Subscribe to our mailing list – *The Rosevine* – and receive
FREE books, daily deals, and stay current with news about
upcoming releases and our hottest authors.
Scan the QR code below to sign up.

Already a subscriber? Please accept a sincere thank you for
being a fan of Black Rose Writing authors.

View other Black Rose Writing titles at
www.blackrosewriting.com/books and use promo code
PRINT to receive a **20% discount** when purchasing.

CPSIA information can be obtained
at www.ICGtesting.com
Printed in the USA
LVHW092012070821
694083LV00001B/3